Praise for *Reckoning Waves*

"*Reckoning Waves* is a gripping, emotional, and thou~~~~ our-
ney into love, loss, and ultimately redemp~~~~ res
not only his protagonist's struggle in th th-
er characters' journeys to find forgiven n,
hardest of all, realizing they may never b nd
it for themselves."

— Nicole Sobchack, award-winning writer and producer of
Please Tell Me I'm Adopted

"When you have what you want most—love, a passion for art, a home in
paradise—you think you've outrun your past. But without honesty, life is
fragile. *Reckoning Waves* tosses its protagonist right back into his guilt,
where he might lose everything. Foster writes with deep heart and keen
specificity."

— Sandra Scofield, American Book Award winning author of
Swim: Stories of the Sixties and *The Last Drafts*

"Equal parts thrilling and tender, *Reckoning Waves* is a triumphantly important novel about what we carry with us and how it might be possible
to seek redemption for our sins. Once again, Foster has written another
must-read."

— Robert James Russell, author of *Mesilla* and *Sea of Trees*

"In *Reckoning Waves*, Corey Flanagan's art imitates life and his life imitates
art. Foster deftly weaves together an artist's struggle to paint the perfect
scene with his struggle to navigate a reckoning with his past. In page-turn-
ing suspense, readers follow Corey's journey toward truth, both in his art
and in his life."

— Ronald C. Nelson, Executive Director, Long Beach Museum of Art

"*Reckoning Waves* picks right up where *Panic River* left off. Foster's effortless prose and creative suspense shine through yet again in this new work.
Readers will be swept up in a thrilling tale of new love, old friendships, and
the delicate bonds of family where each of those relationships is tested
in unexpected ways. *Reckoning Waves* summons readers deeper into the

resonant yet unique life of the novel's protagonist, Corey Flanagan. Foster delivers on the ultimate literary trifecta—compelling characters, a gripping plot, and drawing readers in to a captivating story."

– Catherine Dehdashti, author of *Roseheart* and
Our Daisy Sale Won't Last Forever (coming in 2022).

"Corey and Billy are wonderful characters. If I am reading fiction, I have realized that I need to be involved in the characters' lives from the start and I think you would be surprised at how few current writers can create human-enough characters for one to care about. And this goes for describing place and location, too. Whenever Corey leaves his house, I can picture him in his world. Fantastic read."

– Sue Zumberg, bookseller at Subtext Books

Midwest Book Review
Article excerpts:

"*Reckoning Waves* juxtaposes a story of retribution, redemption, and recovery with one of love and revenge."

" ... psychological depth ..."

" ... solidly intriguing and thought-provoking ... a vivid tale..."

"Readers won't anticipate the epilogue that concludes this story, or the forces that work both with and against Corey to help him create a different life."

Portland Book Review
5 of 5 stars
Article excerpts:

"... peak-level entertainment and engagement ... a spectacular and tasteful work of art..."

"Foster perfects the art of creating an addictive narrative ... just the right amount of suspense, camaraderie, romance, drama, and depth."

"... every seemingly insignificant event leads to a larger one that fits into the story effortlessly."

For Isaac and Jason

You deserve a love that wants you disheveled,
With everything and all the reasons that wake you
up in haste,
With everything and the demons that won't let you
sleep.

You deserve a love that makes you feel secure,
Able to take on the world when it walks behind you,
That feels your embraces are perfect for its skin.

You deserve a love that listens when you sing,
That supports you when you act like a fool,
That respects your freedom,

That accompanies you when you fly,
And isn't afraid to fall.

You deserve a love that takes away the lies,
And brings you illusion, coffee, and poetry.

—Frida Kahlo

Also by Elliott Foster

Panic River (Calumet Editions, 2019)

Retrieving Isaac & Jason (Calumet Editions, 2019)

Whispering Pines (Wise Ink Publishing, 2015)

RECKONING WAVES

ELLIOTT FOSTER

**CALUMET
EDITIONS**

Minneapolis, Minnesota

Part One: California

Chapter 1

Corey Flanagan was a free man and reveled in that freedom as he drove south along Pacific Coast Highway, radio blaring, headed for brunch at the Long Beach Museum of Art. . . . *A high of seventy-eight today for the beach cities, with temps in the lower eighties further inland. One hundred percent sunshine all day, folks! This is why we live here! Now, back to the music.* Turning his face to the sun, Corey felt his heart surge with contentment. He raised the volume of the music and felt pleased that he had for once lowered the canvas top of his Mini Cooper so that now the breeze flowed through his short-cropped, auburn hair. Boy, was that DJ right—this is why we live here.

At a stoplight, he paused to close his eyes and deeply inhale. He smelled the usual mixture of sea breeze and light smog, with an unexpected tang of Asian spice flowing from a Thai restaurant on the corner. Corey had become accustomed to the varying and unique fragrances of Southern California. All of them, together, calmed him in ways that aromas never quite did before.

He abruptly opened his eyes upon hearing the driver behind him honking her horn. He stepped on the gas and caught pace with the other southbound cars. The traffic in LA, as usual, was awful. Today, vehicles full of weekend beachgoers streamed south and west. The forecast beckoned throngs of Angelenos to descend upon miles of iconic beaches where they would drag coolers, lay towels in the sand, and watch sleek-looking surfers navigate the pounding waves. Corey looked forward to his own beach time later in the day when the crowds thinned, and he could stake a patch of sand for himself.

California's appeal to Corey was fierce. The reliable sunshine and subtle change in seasons were definitely a plus, but his enchantment was driven more by LA's laid-back vibe and diverse culture, as well as the anonymity of blending into a sea of over five million people. After living his entire life within a few miles of the upper Mississippi River, he felt born anew as he ate authentic Vietnamese pho, adored the showy purple flowers of Jacaranda trees, and smelled that briny seawater for hours on end as he sat along the Pacific Ocean's intoxicating shore. The expanse and awaiting discoveries of the LA basin seemed endless, dwarfing his prior life in the Midwest. Now, he had made Hermosa his home.

He pulled into a QuickMart on the Redondo-Torrance border and hopped out to fill the Mini's gas tank. Corey surveyed the cityscape before him as he stood next to the pump. He remembered thinking that Southern California was an endless chain of asphalt and low-rise buildings set amidst a paucity of green. Today he saw much more—terracotta and charcoal grey roof tiles adorning adjacent white and pink-stuccoed office buildings, one housing a small animal hospital and the other a psychic medium. Streams of cars unlike any he'd seen in the Midwest flowed past him—pricey Land Rovers and Lamborghinis, mixed in with California's newest automotive innovation, the Tesla Model X. And people of every race and shape walking in and out of those shops, showing off their taste. Corey tried to envision how he'd paint California, how he'd capture her uniqueness, her subtle beauty in one work of art. He quickly deemed that impossible to achieve in a single effort. Instead, he would be happily painting California for the rest of his life.

His gaze soon drifted down toward his flower-patterned Havianas. It was the middle of August, and he was wearing flip-flops. Why hadn't he moved to California years earlier? He glanced at the pump's digital display and calculated that his tank was half-full. He checked his watch and tapped his sandal against the back tire, willing the vehicle to fill up faster. The used Mini was his first major, impractical purchase—ever. Its mpg rating was low, but he didn't drive all that many miles in a week. And on days like this one, Corey figured it was the best investment he had ever made.

* * *

"Hey, over here." Corey's best friend, Billy Preston, had secured a prime table on the veranda outside the museum, with a clear view toward the ocean. "What took you so long?"

"Sorry. I got absorbed into my latest painting and lost track of time." Corey collapsed into the chair, exhaling audibly. "You're gonna like this one, Billy."

"Awesome, but next time let me know you're running late."

"I didn't think of that until I was in the car, and, well, I still don't have a cell phone."

"You might be the only person in LA without one."

Corey laughed, though mostly at himself. It was silly to think that he could hide from the world by not carrying around a trackable device. "In my defense, I would've been on time if it weren't for traffic."

"You need to lose that excuse if you're going to be a true Californian. The traffic's always bad. You build it into your commute."

"Sorry. Next time, I'll stop somewhere and call."

Corey took his first sip of coffee. Sunday morning brunch at the museum with Billy had become a routine. He stared for a moment at his life-long friend. Man, Billy had sure aged well, aside from a few sun-soaked wrinkles across his face. Billy still maintained a handsome shock of short blonde hair to compliment his blue eyes. Most days, Billy looked as carefree as the twenty-something surfers Corey hung out with in the ocean a few mornings each week. Today, though, Billy appeared as though he were carrying something heavy.

"So, what are you working on, man?" Billy asked.

"Landscapes. All landscapes."

"That's new. Last time I checked, you were painting portraits."

"You mean the last time you *listened*, that is. I've talked about my move toward panoramas a few times since moving here."

"Oops."

"Surely you remember me talking about Edward Hopper?"

"Nope. Wasn't listening then, either."

"Why do I waste my breath?"

"My innate charm?"

Corey laughed. "Yeah, I'm sure that's it. Anyway, I discovered Hopper in college but never appreciated his work until Nick and I spent a long weekend in New York several years ago. I lingered an entire morning in the Whitney while Nick attended a banking convention. The Whitney has most of Hopper's work."

"And he's into landscapes?"

"Wow, you catch on quick." Corey threw Billy a sarcastic look. "Yes, he's probably the more interesting of the American impressionists, a painter of the twentieth century."

"I'm aware. He painted that diner scene hanging at the Art Institute in Chicago."

"Yeah, it's called Nighthawks. Well, well. Look who knows something about art."

"No, just dumb luck—a combo of Humanities 101 and my folks taking us for a family trip to Chicago once."

Corey remembered Billy's family taking that trip to Chicago and how he had wanted to tag along as well. Billy's parents had invited Corey to join them, but Corey's father, Frank, said no. He didn't offer a coherent reason, other than that he needed Corey to help with an unspecified project around the house. Corey remembered waving goodbye to the Preston family as Billy's dad, Larry, backed their station wagon out of the driveway, then seeing Billy wave back as the car drove out of sight. He also remembered walking home and his mother saying that his father had left for a weekend alone to the family cabin, leaving Corey a long list of chores.

"Well, Nighthawks is certainly Hopper's most famous piece, but he segued from portraits to landscapes mid-life. He focused mainly on rural scenes and seascapes, and they're definitely an influence on my current work. Blackhead, in particular, is a Hopper painting that reminds me of the shoreline below Palos Verdes. I can't get enough of how the Santa Monica Bay bends from Redondo toward Malaga Cove, how the peninsula towers above those rocky cliffs before dropping sharply into the sea. I may have to paint it a thousand times 'til I get it right."

"I told you. The California coastline outshines those Wisconsin river bluffs by a mile. That's why I urged you to move here for years. I'm glad you finally did."

"Me too. And I have you to thank more than . . ."

"Okay, okay. We've been over this, remember? You made it here on your own. You made that happen. Dad and I may have helped with a few logistics, but you're here because of your determination, Corey."

He felt a lump forming at the base of his throat. He had only lived in California for three years, but it felt much longer; it felt like home. He rented a modest, one-bedroom cottage behind an ocean-front home in Hermosa Beach. He worked at a frame shop by day and occasionally waited tables at night for cash and tips at the touristy Pacific Café. He lived his life outdoors, on the beach as much as possible—biking, learning to surf and painting sunsets and landscapes upon a wooden easel he had found for a bargain at the sprawling Rose Bowl flea market in Pasadena.

"Corey Flanagan," Billy said quietly. "That name still takes some getting used to, I must admit."

"Would you have preferred my second choice, Fisherman-Extraordinaire?"

Billy smiled—not so much at the joke itself, but at the fact that Corey could make one. Corey was on a good path—happy again, like when they were kids.

"No, Flanagan is better. But don't get mad if I slip up and call you Fischer, though. Lifelong habits die hard."

It was one of the first things Corey did prior to embarking for California, with help from Billy's dad, Larry. The small-town Wisconsin lawyer navigated a few ethical shortcuts after learning Corey had left his original birth certificate and passport behind when he fled Minneapolis and after Nick refused to forward them. Without explanation, Corey begged Larry to leave an untraceable trail. Though Larry was a principled practitioner, this request was different. It came from his son's best friend, who Larry knew had already suffered enough—for a boy Larry considered one of his own.

Corey recalled that conversation clearly, including Larry's suggestion that he change his last name to Preston. *You spent enough time here as a kid to earn it. And I'd be honored to share my family's name with you, Corey. To me, you're just that—family.*

But Corey felt he needed a clean break from the past—all of it. He chose Flanagan without much thought, remembering the obscure sculptor, John Flanagan, who had studied at the Minneapolis College of Art and Design decades before Corey volunteered there on weekends, teaching art to at-risk youth. No doubt Flanagan still took getting used to, even for Corey, but he embraced his new legal name as a symbol of the monumental change he had made in virtually every aspect of his life—a different home, different vehicle, different job, different friends. The one constant was his mother back in Wisconsin and, of course, Billy.

"Say, speaking of my dad, there's something I need to tell you."

Corey noticed the serious look on Billy's face and heard it in his voice. The lump in his throat returned.

"Is he okay?"

"Dad was diagnosed with cancer last week—pancreatic, stage four."

Corey set his coffee cup down on the table.

"Oh, man. I'm so sorry."

Billy nodded his head but didn't speak.

"Was he having issues?"

"Not really. Just the aches and pains of growing old, he said. The doctor told him otherwise."

"Is it treatable?" Corey felt instantly warm, with sweat forming atop his brow.

"They're certainly going to try. Dad downplayed the gravity of it when we spoke on the phone. Mom gave a more sober outlook after Dad left the room."

"Fuck. What can we do? What can I do?"

"I don't know. Give him a call or send him a note? He would like that coming from you, Corey."

"Of course. As soon as I get home. Do you think I should try to visit him? Mom keeps asking me to come home and see her anyway."

"Not yet. He's going to the Mayo Clinic in Rochester for tests and to begin chemotherapy. We'll know more about his prognosis after that. I booked a long weekend trip to see him in two weeks."

"Billy, I'm not sure what to say. Is there anything I can do for you?"

"You're here, man, listening to me. I'll probably need more of that going forward. You know what it's like to lose a father, right?"

"You haven't lost him, Billy. At least not yet anyway."

"I know. My mind goes to the worst possible outcome, I guess."

"Perfectly natural."

Corey stayed quiet, hoping Billy would say more. When it came to matters of the heart, Billy normally used humor to deflect. But he kept quiet, staring at the sea. Corey ate the last bite of his breakfast then threw his napkin atop the empty plate.

"Come on, let's walk."

They each dropped twenty bucks on the table and set out along Ocean Drive. At Corey's prompting, Billy talked at length about the latest drama from his construction business. He had started working job sites soon after arriving in California twenty years earlier when he followed a girl west after college. With a small loan from his father and some informal training as a carpenter, he landed a job with a construction company building tract homes in booming Orange County. After a few years, with the market of the mid-2000s still red hot, he branched out on his own and soon had a non-stop flood of contracts based upon his reputation for quality work and honesty. Experienced and armed with a degree in business, Billy built a solid company for himself and a pair of employees.

Preston Construction was a success by any measure, but not without its costs. Fifteen-hour workdays six days per week for ten years, followed by the housing crash of '07, took a toll on his marriage. It ended before they had even discussed the idea of having kids, and that much was a relief to Billy. Since then, there had been a series of minor relationships, and he had been mostly happy. Corey always admired that—how Billy was a self-made, self-assured man. Whether due to innate optimism or the blessings of a supportive family, and even during the worst days during his divorce, Billy could find the silver lining in every situation.

As usual, Corey mainly talked about art and his newfound passion for eating an organic diet. Like an excited college freshman newly emancipated from the family home, he also spoke with spirited gestures about the routines of his life—biking on the Strand, creating imaginative meals with spices he had never heard of in the Midwest, and the simple pleasure of feeling a grit of sand between his toes or sipping an espresso at his easel while staring at the ocean.

Corey had sobered up after the failed suicide attempt in 2012 and had been celibate since the disastrous Thanksgiving night in 2013. He still felt no desire to drink and no inclination to visit the many gay clubs in nearby West Hollywood. About a year after arriving in California, he first entertained the idea of meeting someone, of dating again. But after his twenty-year relationship with Nick, Corey was clearly out of practice; he didn't know where to start. There was also his disastrous last hook-up with a trucker on that Thanksgiving night—a night that ended badly, to say the least. Corey had convinced himself that he was not the coupling kind and grew increasingly comfortable with the prospect of spending the rest of his days as a single man. With each new sunrise, Corey felt more confident, a bit more like Billy, except for those nights when he dreamed.

That was the story Corey more or less told Billy every Sunday when they met for brunch—until today.

"I need to tell you something, but I'm not quite sure how you'll react."

Billy stopped walking. He grabbed Corey's arm to halt him as well. Billy looked as if he had witnessed a miracle, his eyes wide and wearing a smile.

"I just had a moment of déjà vu."

"What?"

"Déjà vu. You said that exact phrase once before, remember?"

"Uh, no." Corey cocked his head and squinted.

"When you came out to me, back in college. How can you not remember?"

Corey strained to pull up this memory from the distant past. He soon recalled that long-ago Saturday morning at Bonnie's Cafe in Saint Paul when he approached Billy with caution after practicing what he would say. Back then, Corey hadn't admitted he was gay to anyone. He had barely confessed it to himself. The first person he dared to share it with was Billy. Here on the edge of the Pacific Ocean, that memory returned to Corey with ease, carrying with it a sense of relief.

"Sure, I remember. But what does that have to do with anything?"

"You started off this conversation the exact same way. I remember it word for word because you had me so damned worried. I thought you were on the verge of telling me you were dying or something . . ." Billy's voice trailed off, then resumed in a more somber tone. "Oh my God, man. I'm sorry. Did I totally just step in it? Are you okay?"

Corey pulled his friend into a bear hug, and his whole body shook as he laughed.

"Yeah, this is fucking hilarious, man." Billy spoke his muffled reply into Corey's shoulder. He then pulled back from the embrace, looked Corey in the eyes, and grabbed his shoulders with both hands. "Well, if you aren't dying, then what the hell's going on?"

Corey couldn't contain his smile.

"I think I met someone, Billy. His name is Miguel."

For the next half-hour, they walked along the oceanfront as Corey talked nonstop about the man who had come into Corey's workplace a few weeks earlier. He spared no details in the re-telling, right down to what each of them was wearing and the abundant aroma of Blue de Chanel that flowed across the frame shop's checkout counter as Miguel asked Corey out on a date. During a pause in Corey's story, Billy looked at his phone said it was time to go. He was scheduled to meet with a couple in Huntington Beach about a prospective home renovation. "What's on tap for the rest of your day?" Billy asked.

"My neighbor said I could borrow his paddleboard. I'm thinking about taking it out for a ride. I'll probably drown."

"You'll be fine. I hear it's easier than surfing, and you're pretty good at that."

"Yeah, I do love to surf. Who knew what I was missing all these years? When I'm out on the ocean waiting for a good wave as the sea washes over me, I feel at peace, Billy. There's nothing like it."

"I told you—for years. I still wish you would've stayed with me longer once you got here, though. I had plenty of room."

"Your condo in Huntington is awesome. But for me, Hermosa is home. It fits. The beach, the transient feel. It's just . . . home."

"Yep, you needed a place of your own. The Strand is great for a jog, too. What a perfect path for a life-long runner."

Corey thought back to his sunrise bike ride earlier that morning, all the way to the Strand's paved southern end in Torrance.

"Come to think of it, Billy, I haven't run since I got to California. Not once. Lots of biking—almost daily in fact—but not a single jog."

"Really?"

"Yeah. I think I only went running back in Minnesota because there was a lot to run from." Both Corey and Billy laughed. "But now I'm here and feel a sense of freedom I never really experienced before. So, I guess I just lost the need to run."

Chapter 2

Later that night, Corey dreamed.

He watched Nick drop the flashlight and fall to the damp, leaf-strewn ground. Nick clutched his buttocks, surely feeling the sting of the bullet that ripped through his skin and now lay deep into the muscle of his ass. From that position, Nick must have seen the wounded deer mere yards in front of where he lay, both now writhing in bewilderment and the terror of impending death.

"Corey! What the fuck?"

Despite an initial impulse to run, Corey instead walked closer to Nick, his partner of nearly twenty years. With each step, he felt the weight of what he had learned on this dark November afternoon: betrayal upon betrayal. Nick had confessed to his secret meeting with Corey's parents and the weekend in Miami with Evan, and then most shockingly, the revelation that Nick and Corey's marriage was nothing more than a lie. Corey reached the spot where Nick squirmed, looking pathetic and nothing like the handsome swimmer Corey fell in love with all those years ago.

"I'm bleeding. Call 911!"

Corey's right hand still tightly gripped the warm Colt Woodsman. His head hurt inside and out from the stress of their fateful argument and from being struck by Nick with a metal flashlight. Nick was shouting; Corey could see his mouth, so wide. Corey could sense Nick's profane yelling, but he could not hear the words. They evaporated into the cold autumn air.

Now what was he supposed to do?

Corey turned his attention toward the wounded buck on his right. The miserable creature cried out in pain as strongly as Nick, but Corey couldn't hear the deer's wailing. He considered the two injured creatures lying before him—both struggling for air and crying.

The guns that felled them both belonged to Corey's father.

What was he supposed to do now?

A voice in his head harkened back to Nick's earlier declaration—that they were morally obliged to pursue injured prey to the end, to put the mortally wounded out of its misery rather than let it suffer a slow and painful death. Corey turned his back to the deer and to Nick, then reached into his coat pocket for the extra bullets he had found in the cabin. He opened the cartridge of the Woodsman and refilled the chamber.

"Whoa, whoa. What are you doing?" Nick lay on his side, his hands clutching his ass and the flashlight flung several feet away, its light beam pointing toward the injured deer and barely illuminating Corey as he reloaded the gun.

Corey walked over to the buck and stood behind its head. He lowered the gun until it was inches from the deer. With tears streaming down his face, he pulled the trigger. A bullet pierced the buck's head. The wailing ceased once the sound of the gun's explosion filled the air. The deer shuddered for mere seconds, then stiffened and died. Corey wiped his eyes with the sleeve of his hunting jacket and strained to curb his rapid breath.

Then, something deep inside him took over.

He felt like he was watching his own clone acting on shared subconscious desires. He walked a few yards to his left. A tug of war raged inside him, between the man who suppressed every desire to fight back and the one seeking lifelong revenge. Corey walked toward Nick without hesitation until he stood directly above where Nick lay, squirming and blubbering in the dirt. At first, good Corey reached out a hand in supplication toward Nick, his lover of so many years. But then vengeful Corey took over. He cocked the lever of the Woodsman and put Nick out of his misery, mimicking what he had just done to the deer.

He awoke in a panic. Had he screamed? Perhaps, or was that part of the dream? He wasn't sure. But now he was wide awake, his heartbeat quick in his chest from the horror of the killings and his bedsheets soaked in sweat. He checked the alarm clock on the nightstand—2:30 a.m. He alighted from his bed and headed for the kitchen, filled a glass with cold tap water, holding it briefly against his forehead before gulping it down. He leaned against the sink, thinking.

What had he been dreaming? What was it all about?

He noticed his laptop in its usual spot on the counter, then walked around the peninsula and sat atop a stool. He opened the laptop and searched for his old name on Google: "Corey Fischer." Then he did the same on Yahoo and Bing. No hits. So, it was all a dream. No one was looking for him. Nick was alive. Or at least Corey had not killed him in the Wisconsin woods when he had the chance and the urge and the motive. Corey still didn't understand why Nick never pressed charges, and there was no opportunity to ask him directly. The two had not spoken again after that dramatic night in the woods. There were still so many questions Corey wanted to ask, yet he had no desire to see Nick, much less speak with him, ever again. There had been too many betrayals, too many lies. Corey wanted Nick out of his life completely. Thus far, the universe had granted his wish.

But why had Nick never reached out to him? If nothing else, Nick could have shoved all of Corey's failures directly into his face—his failures as an artist, as a lover, and as a son. Corey assumed that Nick had weighed the pros and cons, then decided to let Corey languish in his temporary new home in Wisconsin where he was once again living with Mommy. Corey had walked away from everything they jointly owned back in Minnesota, so in Nick's mind, he most likely figured that he had won and needed nothing from Corey ever again.

The dream-driven panic persisted, well after he remembered that he had not killed Nick. Corey knew why he was so uneasy; he was mixing memories. He typed in a new internet search: "southern Minnesota trucker slaying 2013." Within seconds the results appeared on his dimly lit screen, the only illumination in the dark apartment. There was nothing new posted about the incident. His heartbeat diminished. Corey ran this web search every few weeks, less often than when he had begun making those inquiries four years earlier. The last new article appeared roughly one year ago. In it, the Freeborn County Sheriff reported that the investigation into the death of Bennett Jackson was still ongoing but had entered a less active phase. Corey read it again.

No new leads have emerged in the past two months. The evidence collected to date includes a .22 caliber bullet from a Colt Woodsman handgun and DNA from the perpetrator. But there is no known witness, no recovered weapon, and no other identifying information about the assailant. There is no apparent motive, though we think the deceased was the victim of a sex crime. We are once again asking the public to come forward with any information about that Thanksgiving night in 2013, which might lead to further evidence or an apprehension for this crime.

DNA from the assailant.

When he read that disclosure three months after the killing, Corey scoured his memory to determine where he had left evidence of himself inside the truck. There had been no ejaculation, but he knew enough from watching TV crime dramas that he had likely left behind at least a hair follicle when his head hit the dash or a trace of sweat or other DNA on the trucker's body right before everything went haywire. Or perhaps his DNA wasn't inside the semi-truck at all. Corey had fallen hard onto the ground and had reopened a painful wound on his knee. Maybe a scab or a little blood had been left on the gravel?

He reached toward his knee, caressing the familiar scar and remembering how he took a nasty fall while running down a slight hill toward the Stone Arch Bridge in Minneapolis in 2013. That was the day a new wound opened up, exposing old, unhealed ones. On that day, he learned of his father's death, an occurrence that sparked a funeral and gave Corey an inheritance that included guns—the same guns that he would use to shoot two men and an eighteen-point buck all on the same damn day.

No other identifying information.

Corey thought about that night four years ago in southern Minnesota. He had stopped to fill up with gas on his flight from Barron County toward God knows where. Was he seen at the truck stop or remembered by the woman at the motel? Apparently not. No eyewitness, nothing other than some of his DNA and a bullet left behind at the scene, and nothing else identifying Corey or connecting him with Bennett Jackson's death.

He closed his laptop, folded his hands, and rested his forehead on his knuckles. Though there was relief in seeing no new reports, the guilt and shame remained. Corey closed his eyes and replayed in his mind everything he could remember about that awful night, scene after horrible scene. Four years on, his recollections were fuzzy. How did it all start again? What was it that led Corey to climb into the cab of a semi-truck? In the end, such details didn't matter. What mattered was that a man—a stranger to Corey—was dead. A man who had a name—Bennett Jackson—and a family: wife Cecelia and daughter Cristina. Corey could picture them even now; their images burned in his mind from his brief but shocking look at their photo on the truck's driver-side visor. Bennett Jackson—a man who never went home again to Arkansas. A man who was found dead inside a tractor-trailer at a remote Minnesota truck stop, a bullet having entered his throat and severed his left carotid artery. Bennett Jackson, husband and father of one, bled to death on a cold and lonely Thanksgiving evening while his killer fled south toward Iowa, trying to figure out what to do next.

Identifying information—none.

Corey lifted his head and rested his chin atop his folded hands.

"Corey Flanagan," he said out loud. He uttered a mocking snort, laughing at himself in retrospect for thinking that a change of his official last name might save him from getting caught. Corey remembered asking Larry Preston to help him legally alter his name from Fischer to Flanagan. Corey lied to Larry, explaining that he wanted a new name to celebrate the start of his new life. In his reasoning, Corey Fischer died out in the Barron County woods with that eighteen-point buck, and he was starting his life over as someone new. Thankfully, his mother didn't try to convince him to keep his birth name. Even Larry and Billy barely questioned Corey's motives. Instead, Larry drew up the paperwork free of charge, filed affidavits with the county, and within a few months, Corey began his new life with a brand-new last name.

He pushed back his chair from the counter, left the kitchen, and headed back to bed. Once under the covers with his head on the pillow, Corey scoured the dark bedroom, straining to discern the source of his once-again racing heartbeat. Usually, darkness soothed him as he lay hidden from what might be revealed in the light of day. Tonight was different, as if something lurked beneath his bed, waiting to grab him and pull him down to hell.

He reached over and turned on the nightstand lamp. He looked once again around the room, now dimly lit, but saw or sensed nothing amiss. Still, his anxieties were ascendant. In his prior life, Corey would have opened the drawer to the nightstand, grabbed a small translucent orange container, pried open the childproof lid, and popped an Ambien into the back of his throat. But he hadn't taken one of those in at least five years. Was it that long already? Mostly, the memory of his last-ever Ambien felt distant in time, yet now he could remember that 2012 night as if it were yesterday. If he focused long enough, he might well feel the despair again, the utter rejection and loneliness of that awful, awful night. His father's cruel words. His mother's inability to help. And Nick's flagrant betrayal in a Miami hotel room. Corey could even picture his former self swallowing that entire prescription full of sleeping pills and washing them down with a final swig of rye on a night where he consumed more alcohol than ever before.

Now, though, he had replaced sleep medication with a quest

to read an entire curriculum of classic novels, some of which he had read earlier in his life and others that had somehow eluded his past education. He grabbed a book from the nightstand and opened to Part Two of *Crime and Punishment*. It had taken Corey several nights just to reach the hundredth page of the daunting novel. It took him longer to get into this story than the rest because he couldn't bring himself to find empathy for the main character, Raskolnikov. Corey deemed the protagonist thus far to be a whiny, self-absorbed hypochondriac who overthought every detail of his messed-up life, including his senseless, impulsive murder of the old pawnbroker and her sister. Corey preferred either daring adventurers such as *The Count of Monte Cristo*'s Edmond Dantes or independent transformative types like *Pygmalion*'s Eliza Dolittle.

One aspect of the book's main character did hit Corey's gut like a familiar bullet—Raskolnikov's penchant for disturbing dreams and his inability to get a good night's sleep. Corey remembered underlining passages early in the novel where Raskolnikov awoke "bilious, irritable, and angry" after a troubled rest, yet "sleep had not fortified him." He laughed at the irony of reading a book whose protagonist shared similar reasons for insomnia when the whole point of reading was to tire himself into sleep. He continued for almost twenty pages before his eyelids drooped. He fell asleep with the novel's open pages resting atop the blanket covering his chest.

Chapter 3

Corey couldn't stop watching the clock above the store's entryway. His shifts at Framed By The Beach usually flew by. He loved working there. The friendly clientele, mostly driving into town from the Palos Verdes hills in shiny European cars, filled with chatter about their latest overseas acquisitions, challenged his patience on this afternoon. They usually afforded him a healthy budget to suggest the perfect matting and frame. He thrived on these interactions, but today he heard only half the story of Mrs. Graner's latest trip to Paris. She asked him why he was recommending an ornate gilded frame for her modernist Matisse.

"And why do you keep looking at the clock?" she said with amusement. "*Avez-vou un rendez-vous romantique?*"

The old woman's use of French snapped him back to attention. "*Mes excuses, Madame,*" he responded slowly, laughingly picking out the right words, "*en fait, je le fais.*"

She touched his arm with her bejeweled hand and said, "*Oh comme c'est beau.*" He found an appropriate matte and frame for her painting and listened to her prattle away about Paris, luckily in English, while he worked, feeling that her charming interest in his love life was a good omen for tonight's date with Miguel. He finished his shift then raced out the door at precisely 5:00 p.m.

This would be their fourth date. He had a *boyfriend*. He rolled the word through his mind with hesitancy. Back in college, he wasn't fully out of the closet. Instead of dates, he had flings, secretive dinners and casual sex—always at dim out-of-the-way places, and anonymity protected him. After that, there was Nick and no one else. Now, Corey lacked practice. This was only his second experience dating anyone publicly.

It was Miguel who noticed Corey walking down the street in Riviera Village two months earlier, heading back to work after a quick lunch. Miguel followed him from a distance then dropped into the frame shop to ask made-up questions about how to mat a piece of art supposedly resting in a closet back home. Corey was clueless about being checked out, but he certainly took notice of the handsome stranger. Miguel was slightly taller than Corey, with jet black hair parted on the left and an intriguing, dark complexion. He wore glasses that had disappeared from fashion years ago, but his broad smile and perfect white teeth caught Corey's attention. Miguel seemed to be in decent shape, probably not ripped or as buff as Corey, but nicely average with wide shoulders and a tapered waist.

Miguel looked nothing like Nick.

Corey finally suspected that the matting conversation was a ruse when Miguel invited him to experience *the best burrito this side of the border*. Corey quickly gleaned that Miguel might be interested in something more than picture frames. They met the following night at a taco stand along Pacific Coast Highway in Redondo Beach. Seated at an uncomfortable picnic table alongside the noisy road for almost two hours, Corey learned two things. Miguel was someone for whom he felt definite attraction, and this place had the best damn Mexican food he had tasted in his entire life. At home later that night, Corey's mind raced between extremes—from the anticipation of possible romance and even sex, to the anxiety of dating again after so many dormant years and the inevitability of having to reveal himself to someone new.

Their second date was to be something of Corey's choosing. Miguel insisted. Corey selected a visit to the Long Beach Museum of Art, located inside a pair of oceanfront buildings holding a major fine art collection. They perused the galleries and seaside for almost two hours, talking non-stop. Given their surroundings, the conversation veered heavily into Corey's own artistic talents, work history, and aspirations. He spoke about experimenting with drawings as a boy, then falling in love with painting before college. The captivated look on Miguel's handsome face spurred Corey on, confessing his eccentric inner capacity to look upon a scene or a person or a landscape and then render on the canvas perspectives that few if any others might see. At one point, Corey realized that he'd been blabbering on for several minutes, speaking to his passion for art in ways that he had only talked openly with one other person before—his erstwhile friend and only female lover, Carol. He remembered halting his monologue as his face grew warm, apologizing to Miguel for going so deeply into the self-consuming weeds about art. Miguel protested and encouraged Corey onward, so he did.

For his part, Miguel spoke about his work at a law firm in Santa Monica, where he had been a paralegal for the past twelve years. He loved working with the founding partner, a retired airline pilot turned lawyer who landed her closing arguments in court as if she were touching down on LAX's south runway at the helm of a three-hundred-ton jet. Miguel likened his investigative and trial prep work to solving puzzles, something he delighted in as a young boy. He also relished the intellectual interactions with the firm's lawyers, who made him feel that he was their equal and a pivotal part of the team, even though he didn't have "J.D." at the end of his name. Miguel said he often thought about taking night law school classes at Southwestern in central LA. He still might. After all, he was only thirty-two. Earning a lawyer's salary for the next three decades would certainly help pay off any law school debt.

Corey performed quick math in his head—their age difference totaled thirteen years. That meant when Corey graduated from Pepin High, Miguel was just entering kindergarten. He shuttered that calculation and its uncertain consequence, then continued listening as Miguel talked on.

He suppressed a gasp when Miguel revealed his HIV-positive status. Miguel spoke of it casually, as if he had nothing more serious than a bum knee. For a moment, Corey was speechless. How could someone share such intimate life details with a stranger? Didn't Miguel understand how vulnerable that made him? Then, after an awkward pause, Corey asked the least invasive questions he could muster. How did Miguel find out? Was he getting good treatment? What was his prognosis? Did he know from whom it was contracted?

Miguel's answers to these questions seemed genuine and straightforward. A positive HIV test was how he found out. Antiretroviral therapies rendered him undetectable, so the treatments were good. With consistent medication, HIV shouldn't in any way shorten or hamper his life. And yes, he got HIV from the man who sexually assaulted Miguel as a teen. Corey expressed empathy and support. Miguel was surprised that Corey hadn't yet met anyone known to be HIV positive. They chalked it up to Corey's relatively sheltered life in the Midwest and the fact that the majority of Corey's friends and coworkers had been straight. Despite an initial uneasy stomach, Corey's alarm at Miguel's revelation eased the more he heard Miguel speak so matter-of-factly about his diagnosis, about his reality. By the end of the date, Corey understood that Miguel's HIV status didn't define him; rather, it was merely a part of what made him whole.

The third date took Corey by surprise—a full day at the self-proclaimed *Happiest Place on Earth*. He had never visited Disneyland before. As a kid, Corey's parents never vacationed with him outside the Midwest. The idea at first made him wince. What would he and Miguel talk about for so many hours, and how would Corey avoid discussing his past? Was it possible to maintain a superficial conversation for an entire day?

On the morning of the trip to Anaheim, Corey went for an early walk along the beach and considered canceling the date altogether. He went back and forth, weighing the pros and cons, before finally deciding to go to the Magic Kingdom with Miguel. The date lasted ten hours, and Corey never once glanced at his watch. They toured most of the attractions and rode nearly every amusement—cruising on the Mark Twain steamboat, surviving Pirates of the Caribbean, and screaming at every stomach-churning drop of the Matterhorn which Miguel insisted they ride three times. Late in the afternoon, Corey declared this one of the happiest days of his life. Sunshine fell on them the entire time, with temperatures warm enough for T-shirts and shorts. Corey caught himself ogling Miguel's tattooed biceps several times.

Toward evening, they wandered past the arcade with its multiple opportunities to display athletic prowess—shooting basketballs into a narrow hoop, tossing rings onto soda bottles, and popping balloons with darts.

"Hey, come here." Miguel ran ahead.

"Where are you going?" The question, consumed by the crowd, never reached Miguel's ears. Corey struggled to catch up.

"I'm going to win you a giant stuffed animal. Which one would you like?"

"It's okay. There's no need."

"But I want to."

"That's sweet, but seriously let's move on."

"Nope. I'm going to win a prize for my date." Miguel walked up to the shooting gallery, reaching for the wallet in his back pocket.

Corey grabbed Miguel by the wrist and pulled him back from the arcade. "I don't want it. And we would end up carrying the damn thing around all day." Miguel paused, taken aback at the serious tone of Corey's voice and the matching look on his face. "Come on, let's go."

Miguel waved off the attendant and followed Corey toward Tomorrowland. After a few awkward minutes of silence, Miguel spoke.

"I didn't mean to upset you. I was trying to do something nice."

"I know, I know. And I appreciate it, I really do. I have a thing about guns, that's all. I'm sorry. I'd rather not talk about it." They walked through the bustling crowd without talking.

Miguel eventually broke the lull.

"Hey, how about some lunch? All this walking and riding has made me hungry."

"Sure, I could definitely eat something, too."

For the rest of the day, their conversation resumed its earlier, effortless flow, focusing on their jobs, favorite restaurants, sketches of their childhoods, and a deep mutual love for the sea. Miguel's lack of questioning about past boyfriends or sexual encounters left Corey surprised and relieved. He offered no details on his own. At one point, he caught himself before asking whether Miguel had ever been in a long-term relationship. That would have opened the door for a reciprocal question that Corey wasn't ready to answer, if he ever talked about it with Miguel at all. They departed the amusement park at dusk after watching the Main Street Parade. As they walked toward Miguel's truck, Corey cocked his head toward the entrance and beheld the sign that had greeted them on their way in. Now in the waning daylight—his stomach full of junk food and his heart full of hope—he thought to himself that this was indeed a happy day.

* * *

Corey biked home from the frame shop. For the first few blocks, he rode atop a bluff overlooking the ocean before descending onto the Redondo Beach Pier and peddling the rest of the way along the Strand. The beach was typical for a late Saturday afternoon—crowded with families holding toys and towels heading toward their cars and surfers rushing in the opposite direction to catch the perfect waves at high tide.

When he got home, Corey checked his watch. An hour and a half until Miguel would arrive. Plenty of time to get ready for the date. He made that happen with an hour to spare, leaving him time to drag his easel and canvas from the hall closet and resume work on his latest creation—a landscape of the Palos Verdes Peninsula at sunrise that cropped the view. You could buy a sunset painting or print in any gift shop up and down the coast. That was the view most popular with tourists, one they might see gazing west at the end of a perfect day, watching the Pacific swallow whole the burning sun.

Corey preferred a less ordinary perspective. Streaks of sunlight barely grazing the top of the shaded green hill, the dark and quiet ocean far below the cliffs. Before starting on this piece, he once again sought inspiration from Edward Hopper's seascape renderings, including *Groundswell* and the *Sea at Ogunquit*. While those works depicted scenes on the opposite coast, Corey admired Hopper's uniquely cropped views, defined lines, and saturated colors, combined with elusive employment of shadow and light to create moods reminiscent of *film noir*.

Corey didn't usually squeeze painting time in between commitments, but today's excitement to work on his art reflected his overall mood. Usually, he painted on the mornings when his shift at the frame shop started late or when he was off work for an entire day. He would rise early, grab a coffee and croissant at his favorite one-woman shop along PCH, and set up his easel at the corner of the Esplanade and Avenue G, waiting for the sky to become light. Corey embraced this solitude, interrupted only on occasion by fellow early risers walking dogs or the curiosity of a passing patrolman. "I'll never leave California," he declared to himself one morning. "Why didn't I escape here long ago?"

The doorbell buzzed. He awoke from the daydream and looked at his watch—seven o'clock, on the dot. Painting often conquered him, drawing him into a trance where his mind wandered great distances even as his hands moved across the canvas.

"Just a sec!" He yelled.

He debated whether to clean up and move everything back into the closet or leave the mess right where it was. This would be the first time Miguel visited Corey's apartment, and he wanted to make a flawless impression. The space wasn't large or fancy, but he had tried to make it comfortable and trendy. Billy had played a role, directing Corey to a furniture staging company in Costa Mesa where he scored a fantastic deal on a gently used designer sofa made of black leather, along with two petite, wing-back armchairs adorned with patterns of paisley on the front and a solid cream color on the sides and back. In addition, he found his own coffee table and small dining set on Craig's List from a guy selling his possessions and moving to Kauai.

Upon opening the front door, Corey saw nothing but a large bouquet of white roses.

"Aww, what a nice surprise. It's been a while since someone brought me flowers." He moved closer and inhaled deeply. "Oh, they smell divine. Now, who's behind this bouquet?" Corey forced the fragrant roses aside, revealing the handsome man he had hoped to see. He leaned forward, inches from Miguel, who was perched on the edge of the doorstep.

"As if you didn't know. I hope you were expecting only me."

"I was." He grabbed Miguel's free arm, pulling him into the apartment, then kissing him softly with a slightly opened mouth. He often thought about Miguel's full, dark lips and felt an instant shiver each of the handful of times he had kissed them.

"Come in, but you'll have to excuse the mess. I was painting and lost track of time."

"You call this a mess? I don't think the gay police would even give you a warning, much less a ticket."

Corey laughed. "Maybe not, but I wanted to make the place look nice. You're a well-put-together guy. I didn't want you to think I was a slob."

"So your apartment doesn't normally look this neat? It's all a front for your messy, true self?"

Corey winced before understanding the joke.

"Guilty as charged," he said. "I managed to pull myself together, all to impress a cute guy. It took me the entire day." They kissed again. "Make yourself at home while I wash these brushes and change my shirt. I'll only be a minute." Corey gathered his supplies and disappeared down the hall. Miguel glanced into the perfectly neat kitchen then walked to the center of the main room. His eyebrows rose at the sight of the furniture.

"High-end," he said under his breath. "Someone has good taste."

Then, he saw the painting.

Miguel was soon enthralled by the large triptych hanging near the front door. The first panel depicted a lion—a female with no mane. She sat atop a grassy plain with a single cub between her large front paws. The lion's long pink tongue rolled almost fully outside of her mouth, with its tip resting on the head of the cub. The eyes of both lions were closed. As Miguel took two steps closer, he noticed something he hadn't seen at first. The gold-colored trees standing tall every few feet to the lion's left were, in fact, not trees at all, but posts with a barely perceptible wire fence running between them. Then, Miguel squinted. In the dim evening light of the apartment, he could see the faint figure of a man in the upper right-hand corner of that first panel. The man wore an orange vest and a tall, dark hat and was mid-stride walking toward the lioness and her cub with a long black whip cusped in his hand.

In the second panel, there was a single, full-grown lion. This one was clearly a male, with a dark circular mane surrounding his face. The animal in this frame was on the run, one front paw and one in the rear touching the ground, the other two just a few inches above. Its massive head cocked backward, away from the direction in which it ran. The animal's eyes locked onto something outside of the triptych's second panel, a mystery to the observer.

Miguel stepped around the coffee table to look directly at the painting's final panel. There stood the male lion, its mane visible from behind. He assumed it was the same beast, though in this frame, the creature was facing away. The only parts of its body prominently depicted were the back of its head, its thick torso and its tail. A small pool of red lay underneath him, with drops of the same color falling from a gaping wound on the lion's right side. Ahead of him stood an open gate and a vividly painted scene of endless savannah beyond. Miguel stared at this final panel, mesmerized as if the lion would move forward at any moment to escape his fenced-in pen.

Miguel turned around upon hearing Corey return to the room. He smiled and pointed to the triptych over his shoulder.

"So . . . this?"

"Yeah, that." Corey paused, unsure what to say.

"Yours?"

"My magnum opus. Finished it just last month."

"Wow, there's a lot in there. I mean, it's fantastic, of course. Thought-provoking. Every inch of it made me wonder about the story behind the scene, if there is one. Is it fantasy? Or maybe allegorical?"

Corey paused once more, looking straight into Miguel's eyes, wondering what explanation he could devise on the spot. Corey knew that he would need one someday if he intended others to see it, maybe even buy it. At this moment, though, he couldn't think of what to say.

Miguel filled the awkward void, saying, "Well, I know that you're a vegetarian, so I'm guessing this has something to do with protecting wildlife?"

"Not exactly," Corey answered.

"But you're an animal lover. Perhaps it represents a beloved pet, or even several that you had as a kid?"

Corey looked at the canvas for a few moments, then back into Miguel's dark brown eyes.

"Actually, it's autobiographical."

Miguel cocked his head with a look of mild confusion.

Corey answered the question Miguel didn't ask.

"This painting is the story of my life."

Chapter 4

Miguel pulled the gear into drive and sped away from the apartment with Corey in the front passenger seat. Corey still had no clue where they were going. All Miguel told him was to eat before they left, but to save room for dessert. They headed east, away from the ocean, then turned north as Miguel navigated his late-model Toyota Tacoma toward the Santa Monica Mountains. Corey figured they were going to Griffith Park Observatory, one of his favorite non-beach destinations. He had been up there a half-dozen times since moving to California, mesmerized by the 180-degree view of the vast LA basin. But at the intersection of Fairfax and Wilshire, Miguel abruptly turned right then pulled into a metered parking spot one block later.

"We're here."

Corey pointed across the street. "LACMA? I thought the museum closed at seven." While Corey had visited most major art destinations in Southern California, the Los Angeles County Museum of Art had yet to be checked off his list.

"It did close. But we're not going inside."

They alighted from the truck then waited for traffic to clear before Miguel took hold of Corey's hand, and they crossed the busy street. Corey looked through the metal fence to see a pond of gurgling black liquid and smelled a distinctive petroleum odor. The La Brea Tar Pits were directly adjacent to the museum. As they approached the entrance to LACMA, the sun was setting, and Corey saw where Miguel was headed. Scores of old-fashioned streetlamps blanketed the front plaza, most of them at least ten feet tall.

"I read about this. It's called Urban Lights."

"That's right. When you mentioned you hadn't yet been here, I thought this would be a great place to take an artist on a date."

"It's perfect, Miguel."

They walked closer to the collection of lights, all two hundred and two cast-iron lamps standing in near-perfect formation, like an army of tall, shining soldiers.

"I'm glad," Miguel said. "I came here once with my sister and thought it was cool."

"The creator's name was Chris Burden, a true visionary. He began collecting these streetlamps back in 2000, I think, when he first bought one at the Rose Bowl Flea Market."

"One of your favorite places to shop, right?"

"Good memory." Corey squeezed Miguel's hand. "All these lights once stood on a street somewhere here in Los Angeles back in the 1920s or 30s. Bringing them all together like this is visually stunning."

"I'm glad you like my date idea."

Corey smiled wide. "I love it, Miguel. Very romantic."

"I'm no artist, but I do like to read. Nonfiction, mostly, and occasionally a good mystery."

"I wasn't much of a reader after college, sadly. I got too caught up in TV. I am making my way back through a few classics, though."

"Yeah?"

"Yes. I don't have a television in my apartment."

"I noticed. What are you reading now?"

"*Crime and Punishment.*"

"Ah, Dostoevsky. I liked *Brothers Karamazov* better, but *Crime and Punishment* certainly has some mystery and suspense—the cat and mouse game between a savvy prosecutor and the tormented young killer as told from his point of view."

"Well, well. Look who's a living Wikipedia on classic Russian literature. I like learning these surprising nuggets about you."

"I'm trying my best to impress you, remember?"

They walked among the lamps, along with several others there for the same experience. Corey and Miguel observed the sixteen different styles of lampposts then snapped dozens of photos from every conceivable angle.

"This certainly is a calming, thought-provoking collection of public art."

Miguel nodded in agreement. "Are you aware that in his early days, Burden was known mostly for performance art, focusing on personal danger as artistic expression?"

"Indeed." Corey looked at Miguel with a curious grin. "I think someone did his homework in preparing for this date."

Miguel laughed. "I wanted to be able to talk intelligently about the exhibit, that's all." Corey laughed too before planting a soft kiss on Miguel's cheek. "Anyway, this guy was fascinating. He was obsessed with guns. He once filmed himself shooting his pistol at a 747 taking off from LAX."

"Hmmm. Amazing he didn't get arrested." Corey felt slight abdominal pain.

"Exactly. He also created a well-known performance piece in which his assistant shot Burden in the arm with a .22 rifle. But perhaps his most notorious stunt occurred on live TV when he held a knife to the throat of his interviewer, threatening to kill her if the studio stopped live transmission. It's simply unfathomable that she never pressed charges and that he escaped legal responsibility for such outrageous acts."

"The life of an artist, I guess. Hey, let's ask someone to take our picture."

Corey diverted Miguel toward a group of young women, one of whom happily agreed to snap a photo. Miguel thanked her, then ushered Corey back to the car and told him it was time for dessert. Miguel made a quick U-turn in the middle of Wilshire Boulevard, then headed west toward Beverly Hills. The Tacoma sailed fast through the heart of West LA until he turned into Westwood Village and parked on a street just south of UCLA. They walked a few blocks until they smelled the scent of fresh-baked goods wafting through the air and saw patrons lined up to order from the Diddy Riese cookie and ice cream shop.

"Trust me, these are the best damn cookies you'll ever taste. And they're only twenty-five cents apiece." Corey smiled at Miguel's boyish enthusiasm and was impressed with his thriftiness. They each ordered two cookies. Miguel ate his with milk while Corey formed an ice cream sandwich, the twin chocolate chunk cookies surrounding a large scoop of mint chip.

"Damn, you're right about these cookies. Mmmmm."

"Glad you like them."

"Thank you again, Miguel, for taking me to see Urban Lights. It was really thoughtful."

"You're welcome. But it's not over yet." Miguel cast Corey a playful look and a suggestive wink.

"Sounds good to me."

They walked through the winding streets of Westwood Village and into the adjacent campus of UCLA. Tonight, they spoke about their respective upbringings—Corey's in Wisconsin and Miguel's in Houston, Texas. Corey listened with rapt attention to Miguel talk about his family's traditional Catholic and Mexican home. Corey was surprised by how different Miguel's childhood experience was from his own, despite the similarity in religion. Corey found himself envious of the tight-knit, supportive and loving home environment that Miguel apparently had enjoyed.

"So, Flanagan? You grew up in an Irish-Catholic home? I've heard about families like that," Miguel said playfully.

"Not quite. My heritage is mostly German. Emotionally, my parents and grandparents definitely fit the mold."

"Huh. Flanagan sounded Irish to me. My bad."

Corey let the comment pass.

They continued talking about their childhoods—school, favorite games, sports and their shared adolescent awakening of feeling different from the other boys. Corey hesitantly described his first physical encounter with another guy—Enzo, the foreign exchange student from high school. But he decided to leave the story of his lone and embarrassing heterosexual romp with Carol for another day.

Soon they finished their desserts and walked back to Miguel's truck. They returned to Hermosa Beach, but Miguel drove past the turn toward Corey's apartment. Corey almost mentioned something about the missed turn but decided to stay quiet and see where Miguel would go next. He drove into Redondo Beach and then all the way to the end of Riviera Village at the very bottom of Santa Monica Bay. Miguel parked the truck along a bluff above the beach then summoned Corey outside. He grabbed a blanket and a flashlight from the back before descending the long concrete ramp toward the shore. They walked to the end of the paved walkway, then continued atop the damp sand into Malaga Cove.

Once they passed the final blue lifeguard post, Miguel steered Corey closer to the base of the cliffs. There, he found a secluded spot, barely illuminated by the crescent moon hanging above the misty sea. Miguel spread the blanket atop the sand, then sat down and patted the spot beside him. Corey accepted the invitation. Talking ceased, and soft kissing began, followed by more intensity with intertwined tongues. Miguel then pulled Corey's shirt over his head, folding it up and placing it on the blanket to form a small pillow. Corey mimicked Miguel's maneuver, and soon they both lay in the soft moonlight—shirtless, wanting more.

Corey felt suddenly anxious, but not because of Miguel having HIV. After first learning of Miguel's status, Corey researched it and even consulted with a nurse at the free clinic near his work. He educated himself to the point of understanding that the same prudent precautions he should take to avoid getting any sexually transmitted infection would be good enough to prevent acquiring HIV. And if Miguel were truly undetectable, as he mentioned, then Corey faced no risk at all. No, neither HIV nor any other STI was at the forefront of Corey's worried mind. Instead, it was the prospect of having sex at all. Despite years of encounters with other men and one woman, this would be his first physical experience with anyone since Nick and, well, the dead trucker. Given Corey's faithfulness to his commitment with Nick for the entirety of their decades-long bond, he faced the prospect of being sexual for the first time in many years with someone for whom he cared deeply. Rejecting that inner hesitation, he willed himself to live in the moment and let whatever might happen, happen.

It did.

After checking numerous times to ensure that no one approached them or watched from a distance, Corey and Miguel removed the remainder of their clothes. They lay together with a cool and gentle ocean breeze wafting across their bare skin. The mild intensity of their initial kissing belied the pent-up desires inside each of their hearts. Corey felt emotions and physical sensations that had lain dormant for far too long. He touched Miguel everywhere, and Miguel reciprocated. Jolts of pleasure pulsed at random through Corey's body wherever Miguel brushed a nipple or caressed the head of Corey's aching cock. He responded by grabbing Miguel even harder, practically pinching the skin on his muscular ass.

After a few minutes, Miguel pulled away and gasped for breath.

"Whoa, did an octopus crawl out of the sea and onto this blanket?"

Corey laughed at Miguel's playful teasing, then resumed touching every inch of Miguel's enticing body. Corey's hand reached up to stroke Miguel's tattooed neck, his thumb brushing across the coarse dark hair of Miguel's goatee. Instinctively, he rubbed that hair between his fingers. That spontaneous motion sent bursts of erotic intensity rippling through his body. Now, he wanted even more. Once again, he grabbed Miguel's facial hair and became aroused like never before.

"Pull it," Miguel demanded. "Harder."

Corey obeyed. He yanked that hair until Miguel's lips yet again locked with his own.

Once more, Miguel pulled back to catch his breath.

"True confession: I've never been a kisser. But damn, Corey, with you, I can't get enough."

Corey smiled, the warmth of Miguel's body protecting him from the increasingly chilly night air. He then climbed on top of Miguel, scanning the beach up and down once more. Nothing moved. Corey and Miguel then made love safely on the edge of the Pacific Ocean, calling out in their coupling, each struggling for breath. They lay satisfied atop the blanket, caressing each other's arms while staring up at the star-filled sky, the crescent moon now falling inch by inch into the increasingly dark sea.

Chapter 5

Two weeks later, Southern Californians enjoyed another spectacular fall day. Corey pedaled at a loping pace along the Strand, careful not to produce too much sweat as he rode toward an early morning coffee date in Malaga Cove. *Glistening* might be sexy, he thought, but body odor was not. After locking his bicycle onto the rack and entering the Mango Café, he saw Miguel seated at a table near the front. A full one hundred eighty-degree view of Santa Monica Bay lay before them. A steady stream of locals filled half of the tables in the quaint cafe nestled amongst the north-facing cliffs of Palos Verdes, far from the southland's well-trodden tourist paths.

"Good morning, handsome."

Miguel rose to embrace Corey. An elderly couple turned their heads toward the men and smiled.

"Great choice, Miguel. I never knew this place existed."

"It's my go-to café if I want to impress a guy."

Corey's initial reaction dissipated quickly upon seeing Miguel's wink and broad grin.

"Kidding. My sister and I have eaten here twice. But the only man I've sat here with is you."

Coffee arrived, followed by warm croissants and two bowls filled with yogurt, granola and fresh fruit.

"I took a chance and ordered for you."

"Perfect. It looks delish."

They had not seen each other for five days but had spoken by phone every night in between. Their conversation over breakfast flowed smoothly like today's nearby ocean currents, with no lull longer than the break between crashing waves. Corey ate hungrily. After Miguel swallowed the last chunk of his papaya, Corey reached across the table with his napkin and tenderly wiped a remnant of flaky croissant from Miguel's chin.

"You ready?" Miguel laid down enough cash for both meals and a tip then pulled his chair back from the table and stood up.

"Ready for what?"

"This date is just getting started, and we have to be at our next stop by ten."

"I'm intrigued to know where you're taking me."

"Maybe you should relax and go with it. Come on, have I steered you wrong yet?"

Corey shook his head no then smiled and put on a pair of sunglasses. Truth be told, he would rather sit here sipping coffee for the next hour and perhaps order another croissant. His weekdays were typically filled with plenty of physical exertion; he preferred to rest and recover on the weekends. Yet, he took a deep breath and stood up.

"All right, I'm game. Lead the way."

The bicycle ride around Malaga Cove and further out along the peninsula was stunning. Million-dollar homes clung to steep cliffs with the wide blue ocean stretching as far as Corey could see. The cooler early fall temps erased summertime's marine layer, enabling him to look back toward the bay and see clearly all the way to Malibu. Despite two years of living in Southern California, he had never ventured this far south from Hermosa on his bike. He vowed to make it one of his regular routes from now on.

Miguel led them onward. Corey followed happily behind. He concluded that Miguel was not a regular biker. The blue beach cruiser was functional but cheap, not something one might ride regularly on the road. Yet he dressed the part in a helmet, yellow Lycra top and tight black shorts. Corey figured Miguel must have purchased the outfit recently—likely to impress. That heart-warming thought, not to mention the constant view of Miguel's muscular bubble butt, motivated Corey to keep up.

Soon their view was nothing but the sea as they reached the westernmost tip of Palos Verdes. Corey couldn't believe how dramatically the landscape had changed since leaving the cafe. The western edge of Palos Verdes held deep chasms in her arid, rocky soil—remnants from past earth movements and a stark reminder of the massive tectonic plates buried miles below the surface on which they rode, capable of sudden shifts that could open more fissures and send millions of Angelenos into reactions of fright.

And then he saw it. As they rounded a corner on the curvy road, Catalina Island rose straight up out of the sea like the Loch Ness monster, its two large humps left behind by an ancient volcano. Corey longed to one day visit Catalina and see her famed buffalo herd, descendants of the fourteen animals introduced to the island in 1924 to film a movie.

The sound of Miguel's deep voice brought Corey's attention back toward the road.

"Okay, we're turning left up ahead. Watch for cars because they won't watch for you."

Miguel had wrenched his head backward so his words wouldn't get lost in the wind. Corey signaled his reply with a single thumbs-up. After crossing the busy road, they pedaled up a steep incline and parked their bikes along a stone wall. Cars filled less than half of the adjacent lot. They removed their helmets and wiped sweat from their brows. Corey and Miguel then took turns drawing long swallows of cool water from a drinking fountain nearby.

"Wayfarer's Chapel? What's the story of this place?" Corey noticed the art deco-lettered sign and paused to read the single verse of scripture etched into the wooden banner below: *Come to me, all you who are weary and carrying heavy burdens and I will give you rest. —Matthew 11:28.*

"We're going to church today. I hope that's okay. The service begins at ten."

Corey nodded his head slowly, up and down, then said, "Lead the way."

He followed Miguel up the stone steps.

"I haven't exactly attended a religious service in some time. I hope the priest doesn't single me out. They can sense those things."

Miguel laughed. "There's no priest. It's an ecumenical service, and there's no church council or membership. Just plenty of us sinners who show up at random. I think you'll be fine."

They sat in the second-to-last row at Corey's urging. He felt at ease sitting in a pew again under happy circumstances. The clergywoman gave a Zen-like sermon—light on theology, heavy on spirituality. *Something for everyone*, Corey thought to himself. This would never fly back in Wisconsin. He paid little attention to the rest of the service; instead, he looked around at the architectural wonder of the unique chapel. Glass surrounded them, creating a feeling that they were sitting outside. The plates of the transparent walls met with imperceptible adhesive between. Banyan trees, aloe plants and rocky terrain appeared close enough to touch. For a moment, Corey worried about earthquakes. How in the world could this place withstand a solid shaking?

Surprisingly, the architecture reminded him of a childhood trip to southwest Wisconsin where he and his parents spent a long summer weekend attending a Shakespeare festival in Spring Green, toured the eclectic House on the Rock, and marveled at Frank Lloyd Wright's masterpiece, Taliesen. Corey finished his 360-degree perusal of the chapel then tapped Miguel's shoulder, indicating he wanted to read the service program. Upon reading the back flap, it occurred to him why that decades-old family memory sprung into his mind. The Wayfarer's Chapel was designed by Lloyd Wright, the famous architect's son.

Maybe Lloyd was trying to outdo his old man, Corey mused, creating this stunning all-glass chapel overlooking the sea. Wouldn't people find it far more impressive than the distinctive but numerous Frank Lloyd Wright homes and buildings that dotted the landscape of the upper Midwest? Corey felt a small, involuntary shudder flow along his spine. These odd coincidences brought his mind back to another Frank from Wisconsin, too. He couldn't imagine following in his father's professional footsteps as Lloyd Wright had done. Selling insurance? Not in a million years. As Corey's mind segued through a series of thoughts on his childhood and his father, he felt remarkably calm—no hatred, no fears, only peace. Perhaps the mystical sermon flowing into one ear and out the other had left fragments of serenity on its way through his brain. Or maybe the healing effects of time and distance were finally taking hold.

Miguel looked at Corey and smiled. He reached for Corey's hand, turning his arm over gently and whispering in his ear, "It makes me happy to see you happy."

Corey flashed a wide grin and spoke in an equally soft voice, "I am."

"May I ask you something?"

"Yes, anything." Corey's low, calm utterance concealed the alarm inside.

Miguel looked down at the arm he was still holding.

"Who is your friend for life?"

Corey glanced at his tattoo as if he needed a reminder of the inked words on his forearm that Miguel had just translated.

"He was the most important person in my life. Still is."

"Oh."

Corey noticed a slight shift in Miguel's demeanor and felt a quiet pressure to say more. "Would you like to meet *mi amigo de por vida*?"

"Sure," Miguel replied. "I would like that very much."

They listened to the rest of the sermon then sang along with the hymn "Morning has Broken." As the final prayer concluded and before the postlude music began, Miguel leaned in close, grabbed Corey's hand, and whispered with a playful smile, "You know, a lot of famous people have been married in this chapel." He then gave Corey's palm a tender grip and looked him directly in the eyes. "And plenty of not-so-famous ones too."

* * *

"Wait a minute. He took you to church? On a date?" Billy laughed. "Man, you gays sure know how to party."

"Funny, Billy. No, it was sweet. And perfect. Really."

"If you say so." Billy took a long sip from his bottle of Red Stripe.

"I do, and you can ask him about it yourself, tonight. I invited him to join us for a drink."

Corey was torn about his impulsive offer to Miguel the day before. Caught up in the strange intersection of a happy childhood memory and the surprisingly meaningful present, the invitation to meet Billy flowed instinctively out of his mouth. He could still hear his own voice after Miguel had kissed him goodbye and walked toward his bicycle—*Why don't you come by the Seagull in Redondo Beach at seven tomorrow night for a drink? I'll introduce you to Billy, mi amigo de por vida.*

Billy grabbed Corey's shoulder, pulling him back into the present.

"Wow, things must be serious if you're exposing this guy to me. Did you fall and hit your head? Maybe it was a divine intervention up there in the Wayfarer's Chapel?"

"Can you be serious for one minute?"

Billy nodded his head yes while taking another swig of his beer through a smile.

"I don't know if Miguel is *the one* or if anyone can be that for me. But it feels like something special, something I haven't experienced before."

"So, you want me to grill him, see if he's solid and right for you?"

"Something like that. But I also feel like I need to give Miguel more of a glimpse into my life, though not too much yet. I'm taking it one slow step at a time. Besides, other than the frame shop and my art, you're the closest thing I've got to an interesting life that I can expose him to."

"That's certainly a nice compliment, Corey, but it is also pretty fucking sad."

With that, they laughed and ordered another round. By the time Miguel showed up, Billy was three beers in while Corey consumed his second club soda with lime.

"Miguel, over here." Corey waved him toward their high-top table overlooking the beach. "Miguel, this is Billy. Billy, Miguel."

"Pleased to meet you."

Miguel extended his right hand and looked surprised when Billy got up from his barstool and wrapped him up in a welcoming embrace.

"It's my pleasure, Miguel. I've heard a lot about you." Billy flashed a smile at Corey before returning to his seat and his drink.

"That's good . . . I think?" Miguel's voice trailed off as he turned to give Corey a quizzical look.

"All good," Corey replied before getting up to hug him tight. "Now, what would you like to drink?"

Their conversation flowed with a balance of harmless introductory questions and replies. Billy talked mostly about his construction business and a little of his dating life. Miguel spoke about his paralegal job and about being the first in his family to attend college. Corey wasn't asked a thing.

"Excuse me, I'll be right back. Bathroom's this way?" Miguel stood up and pointed toward the back of the bar.

"Yeah, take a left at the dartboard," Billy said. "You can't miss it."

Miguel was barely ten feet away when Billy turned to speak to Corey.

"Okay, it is crystal clear to me why you like him."

"Oh?"

"Yeah, he's the gay version of me." Corey laughed and shook his head. Billy was just getting warmed up. "I'm serious. The guy's not only sweet and charming, he's also pretty damn hot. I mean, I'm as straight as they come, but hell, even I would take him to bed."

"Jesus, Billy. Keep your voice down," Corey admonished him even as he smiled.

"Relax, he can't hear me. Besides, what if he did? Are you afraid he might choose me instead?"

"Yeah, right. So, you really think so? The sweet and handsome part, not that other."

"I do, Corey. He seems like a genuine guy—sincere. Those things are hard to fake, and I'm a pretty good judge of character. I approve, man. Now don't fuck this up."

Corey appreciated the balance of directness and good humor. He knew in Billy-speak that Miguel now had the Preston stamp of approval. Corey looked up to see Miguel approaching their table.

"Did I give you two enough time to talk about me while I was gone?"

Corey's blushing smile prevented him from a believable denial.

"You're fine, sit down."

"My friend Fischer here was telling me about your date yesterday. I've never been to Wayfarer's Chapel. Sounds neat."

Corey stared straight ahead, hoping Miguel didn't hear the name Billy uttered. He felt an immediate need to cut the conversation short and frantically began crafting possible excuses in his mind.

"It's one of my favorite spots, not just here in LA, but anywhere."

Billy nodded and sipped his beer. "I guess I'll have to make my way up there then."

"I think you should. It's really a unique place." Miguel noticed Corey's unusually long silence and that he was staring toward the door. Miguel looked back toward Billy. "So, who's Fischer?"

"What?" Billy cocked his head while averting his eyes from Miguel.

"You said Fischer was telling you about the chapel. You meant Corey, right?"

"I did?" Billy sobered up quickly, without a noticeable change in posture or tone of voice. "You sure?"

"I think so. Not a big deal, maybe I'm confused."

Corey chimed in with a forced chuckle and a soberness of his own. "Sometimes Billy calls me that. It's sort of a joke from high school. There was this kid we knew named Fischer who went on all these failed dates and, well, that's your poor attempt at humor, right man?"

Corey stared Billy dead in the eyes.

"Yeah," he said, playing along. "But it obviously fell flat." He turned and looked at Miguel. "That's not your fault. You never even knew that Fischer kid, so the joke made no sense. Sorry."

"No, no, not at all. This is actually useful information." Miguel flashed a wide grin and reached his arm to touch Corey's hand, squeezing it firmly. "I need more stories about this guy. Everything, no filter. He hasn't told me all that much about his past. Let's order another beer so you can give me all the dirt."

Chapter 6

A month later, Billy showed up at Corey's apartment on schedule. It was early Saturday morning, and the sun cast its first rays toward the ocean, adding sparkle to the waves atop the sea. By the time Billy arrived, Corey was out front waxing the surfboards, both his own and one he rented from Riptide down the street. After years of badgering, Billy had finally given in to Corey's insistence that Billy learn how to surf. Though he swam well, Billy hadn't spent much time in the ocean. He mostly gazed at it from the shore with his phone in one hand and a Red Stripe in the other. Corey, by comparison, loved his almost-daily dive into the Pacific. Since moving to Hermosa Beach, he had mastered surfing and boogie boarding. He was a water sign—Cancer—who always felt most at home near or in the water, whether the lakes and rivers of his youth in the Midwest or the much grander ocean, now mere blocks away.

Corey was already dressed in his short-style wet suit and handed a full-length one to Billy, who went inside the apartment to change. Having forgotten that Billy was new to cold ocean swimming, Corey neglected to share his secret method for putting on the latex fabric. It was critical to dampen the body with water or lotion first. Corey realized his error upon hearing Billy's foul language through the open window as he yelled about pulling the tight rubber suit over his very dry skin.

"It's tearing my fucking leg hair off! And I almost lost the boys pulling up the zipper! Why do we need to wear these tight-ass things anyway?"

Corey yelled back through the screened window about the cooler water temps now that October had arrived. Billy soon emerged from the apartment dressed neck to ankle in a black wet suit with blue trim. They grabbed surfboards and towels then headed down to the beach. Billy continued to complain about how the wetsuit constricted his crotch and made his skin itch from head to toe. Corey wondered for a moment why he even bothered. After dropping their towels onto the sand, Corey persuaded Billy to walk into the water. They stopped when the ocean depth hit their knees and wrapped the Velcro straps around their ankles, tethering themselves to their boards. Corey offered a quick lesson on the basics of getting up on a surfboard.

Billy feigned bravado, claiming he was a fast learner. Ultimately, he followed Corey's lead as they walked further into the ocean. A medium-sized wave passed through them before they laid down on their boards and began paddling into the surf. Billy successfully stayed on top of his board, navigating up and over the crest of two gentler waves. On Corey's cue, they turned themselves around to face the sand, frequently looking back toward the ocean, awaiting bigger swells.

A few decent waves came and went, with Corey providing a bevy of tips and taunts as Billy lay upon his board, his hands tightly gripping either side. Eventually, Corey spied a wave he couldn't resist. Billy assured him that he would stay put and watch while Corey latched onto an ideal opportunity to stand and ride. He did. The wave broke slowly from north to south, with the Hermosa Beach pier several yards to Corey's right. He paddled briskly toward shore ahead of the swell, his timing perfect as he hopped onto his feet. He stood with bent knees, the roar of the wave crashing toward him and pushing Corey's surfboard with increasing speed as he raced toward shore. He rode that wave for nearly twenty seconds before it petered out when the water's depth subsided to less than three feet. Corey fell purposely into the water, his board temporarily flying away from him, only to be yanked back by its tethered cord.

He shook water from his hair and wiped droplets from his face, stood up, grabbed his board, and looked westward to see Billy still lying on his board, holding on with one hand and waving like a fool at Corey with the other. It was obvious Billy wasn't watching what was behind him and couldn't see the giant wave approaching. Corey yelled a warning to duck and hold on, but Billy was too far away to hear it. When Corey waved his hands and pointed toward the oncoming swell, Billy merely waved back even harder. Then, consistent with his daredevil demeanor, he removed his other hand from the surfboard and mimicked Corey by waving both arms.

The wave hit Billy barely a second after he must have heard it and briefly looked back. It was too late for Corey to do anything to help. The crashing wave bowled over him, and Corey watched Billy disappear. Billy's board popped up from the frothing water momentarily, but there was no sign of Billy. Corey launched into the water and paddled frantically toward where Billy had gone under. He ducked beneath the same large wave that had just rolled through Billy. Corey popped back up and lifted his head toward the horizon. He saw Billy's board bobbing and Billy's hands flailing in the water ten yards away.

Corey swam hard through the water with his board beneath him until that seemed too burdensome. He ripped the Velcro strap loose and slid off the board. It drifted away from him as he began once more to swim. The waves continued cresting higher than before, the tide rising and the swells forming deeper and closer together. Corey paused to lift his head in the direction where he anticipated Billy would be. He still bobbed up and down in the same spot, though his arm movements suggested distress. Corey took a pair of deep breaths, then looked behind him at the sound of a distant voice. He saw a lifeguard yelling from the shore and pointing toward another guard, mounting a jet ski.

Corey turned back toward the open ocean and swam. Three yards shy of reaching Billy, he paused once again. He strained to recall the training from his youth. During the summer, he completed a guard certification course at the YMCA. Corey drew a large breath, spied Billy's exact location, then dove under the water. He closed the distance between them and quickly felt thrashing water. Corey moved close enough to feel the rubber on the waist of Billy's wetsuit, then popped up out of the water and grabbed Billy across the chest and from behind. Billy collapsed into Corey's arms, began coughing up swallowed seawater, and gagged. Corey began to swim concertedly toward the shore with his right arm, holding Billy tight in his grip with the left.

He heard the buzz of the approaching jet ski, but by that time, he had Billy within twenty yards of shore. The guard atop the jet ski yelled at him, asking if he could make it the rest of the way. Corey nodded his head and breathlessly uttered, "Yeah." The guard said that it would be more dangerous at this point to transfer Billy to the jet ski but that he would follow directly behind them toward shore. Corey swam on, with Billy held tightly in tow.

Soon, he felt sand brushing against his wetsuit. He had been looking toward Billy and the open ocean, but now he glanced eastward to see the welcome sight of land. He stopped flutter-kicking with his legs and turned Billy around, so he was now between Corey and the shore. Both sat for a time in the shallow water before finally rising to their feet. Corey saw a small crowd of onlookers who had gathered nearby. A lifeguard ran up to offer assistance, but Billy waved her off.

"About time you got us here." Billy turned toward Corey, both of them still breathing more heavily than normal. "Man, are you out of shape. You should've covered that distance in half the time."

Corey continued to catch his breath. "Yeah? Well, I was dragging two hundred pounds of bravado and hot air. Took a bit out of me."

He remained bent over. Billy surveyed the wider beach, then turned back toward Corey and took two steps in his direction.

"Seriously, man, thank you. Things got a little crazy out there when that wave hit. I didn't see it coming."

"I know. I should have warned you about rogue waves like that. My bad."

"No, no, no. Not bad. You did good, Corey. Real good. To be honest, I would have drowned if you hadn't come back for me. I'm a decent swimmer and all, but that wave came out of nowhere. Once I tumbled in and swallowed all that seawater, I was in real trouble."

"It can happen to anyone, Billy. It's why I never surf alone. You can't underestimate the power of the ocean, or it'll kick your ass and more."

"C'mon. Let's get back on land and out of these constricting suits. I need a drink."

"A drink? Thought you would've got plenty hydrated taking in all that saltwater."

The reference made Billy gag on the spot. "Thanks for the reminder, but no. That saltwater was disgusting. I need to wash that taste out of my mouth with an ice-cold beer."

Corey laughed. "Sounds good. Let's grab our towels, shed these suits and get a table over at Good Stuff."

Corey pointed to a beachside cafe on the other end of the sand from where they were emerging on shore. Once seated, they relived the saga of Billy's near-drowning and Corey's heroics. At one point, Corey noticed that Billy's normally light demeanor had changed.

"Wouldn't that have been the kicker?" Billy shook his head. "Me biting the dust before my old man."

"Thankfully, we won't find out."

"Yes, thanks to you."

Corey shrugged his shoulders and took a sip of iced tea.

"I was scared out there, Corey. For the first time in my life, I felt like I might die. It makes me think that this is how my father must feel right now—staring into the face of death."

Corey let Billy's words hang in the air a moment before speaking. "How is he, by the way?"

"Who knows? He says there's been no change, that there's still hope."

"That's great."

"No, that's Larry-speak. He's trying to keep our hopes up despite knowing the chances of surviving pancreatic cancer at this stage are slim to none." Billy took a deep draw from his beer. "And slim just walked out the door."

"I'm sorry, man. Wish I could do more."

"I think you've done enough just today, Corey. If things out there had gone differently," Billy said while pointing toward the ocean, "my father would've died of a broken heart instead of cancer."

"I don't doubt that. Your dad sure showed his love for you, for the whole family. Even as a kid, I could see that."

Billy smiled wanly but said nothing. He looked as though a flood of childhood memories rushed through his head.

"Remember your first Pinewood Derby?"

Billy's smile grew wider. "You mean with that piece of shit car I made out of balsa wood?"

"That's the one. You were so proud of it. I remember watching you make it. You wanted to do it all on your own. You wouldn't let me even so much as sand it."

"Hey, it was the Cub Scouts. We were supposed to carve and finish the damn things ourselves."

"Yeah. How'd that turn out for you, when we got to race day, and your underweight racer got creamed by everyone else?"

"Not so good, at first."

"Exactly. At first. And who saved the day for you?"

"Dad." Billy laughed. "Yet he was subtle about it. Or at least I didn't realize what he was doing at the time."

Corey shook his head and smiled at the memory as Billy recounted it.

"I remember Dad asking me, in his usual calm way, why I thought the other kids' cars accelerated on the downslope, but mine didn't. I told him that the other boys' cars looked heavier— that they all appeared to have weights glued to their front and back ends. Also, mine had too much clearance."

Corey laughed openly. "I remember that. What were you thinking? The race was on a track, not off-roading over boulders."

"I thought it was aerodynamic." Billy shrugged his shoulders. "Anyway, Dad kept asking me about the apparent difference in car weights, all the while jingling his pocketful of loose change loud enough for people in the next county to hear. *What could you possibly do to give your derby car more heft?* he asked. Then it dawned on me—duh. *Hey Dad, could I borrow four quarters? I could superglue them to the bottom of the car before the next race!*"

A tear fell from Billy's face as he re-told the story. Corey noticed but didn't know if it arose from laughter or from pain.

"He knew what he was doing the whole time, didn't he?"

"Oh, for sure. I'd even bet that he was the one who put that tube of superglue on the table right in front of us because I don't remember placing it there myself."

"He's a good man, Billy. Always has been, always will be."

"I know. That he is."

Corey reached over and gave Billy's shoulder a soft, affirming rub.

"Thank you, Corey."

"For what?"

"For reminding me what's important. Oh, and for saving my life." Billy looked at Corey and cast him a playful wink before grabbing his beer. "You did my parents a monumental favor today."

"You mean by saving their fourth favorite child?"

Billy almost choked on his Red Stripe while laughing. "Yeah, something like that." Corey nodded and swallowed the final drop of his virgin mojito. "Seriously, thank you. I'm going to tell my folks all about this next week when I'm home in Wisconsin. Don't be surprised if Mom sends back some baked goods for you."

"I'll happily accept."

Billy drained the last of his beer and set it down hard on the table.

"Let's go. I need to get back to Huntington Beach, and you've got painting to do, my friend."

"Agreed."

They laid cash on the table and left the cafe. They walked back to Corey's apartment, and Billy changed. When it came time for Billy to leave, they began to hug like normal, but then Billy unexpectedly held on. Corey felt Billy's shoulders quaking, so Corey tightened his grip. When he finally let go, Billy wiped his face with his shirt sleeve, then said goodbye and walked toward his truck.

Chapter 7

The next morning, Corey turned away from the kitchen counter once he heard Miguel stumble out of the bedroom, rubbing his eyes.

"Morning, sunshine."

"Good morning," Miguel said through a yawn. "How long you been up?"

"An hour. I slipped out of bed to make breakfast."

"Aww, that's sweet. You should have woken me up to help."

"And disrupt the look of bliss on your face? Not a chance. I even sat there for a few minutes watching you breathe."

They kissed for what felt to Corey like several happy seconds.

"Now, mister, you sit down right here with a cup of coffee. I need to run to the store. I made homemade biscuits but ran out of jam."

"I'm fine with butter, really."

"No. The biscuits are my mother's recipe, and she served them with raspberry preserves. They wouldn't taste the same without it."

Miguel sat at the sun-soaked kitchen counter and opened the Sunday *Los Angeles Times*.

"I'll be back in twenty minutes. Sit and relax, you hear me?"

"Okay, love. I'll be here waiting for you."

* * *

Carrying a small bag of groceries in one hand, Corey walked into the kitchen after a thirty-minute absence and reached around Miguel, who was seated on a stool, to set the jam atop the counter while enveloping Miguel in a hug from behind. Corey sensed tension in Miguel's body and a lack of reciprocation for the embrace. He walked around the peninsula to face Miguel, instantly noticing a rigid jaw and steely stare.

"What's wrong?"

"Corey Fischer?"

Corey didn't answer.

"The kid you and Billy teased in school. That's you, isn't it?"

"Miguel, I uh . . ." A stab of pain shot through his temples.

"What? Are you thinking up another falsehood on the spot?"

"No, love. It's . . . well . . . this is a bit overwhelming for me."

"That makes two of us, Corey. Or whatever your name is."

"My name is Corey. You've seen my driver's license."

"Yes, and it also says Flanagan, not Fischer, which is confusing."

Corey stood silent as Miguel spoke.

"And how about Nick Parker? Is that your ex-husband's real name, too?"

"Where did you hear that name?" Corey's voice trembled.

"When I answered the phone while you were out, and Nick introduced himself. I answered, thinking it was you calling from the store."

"He wasn't ever my husband. He . . ." Feeling nauseated, Corey swung away from Miguel toward the sink. Miguel had yet to move from his stool or relinquish the intensity of his stare. After a minute, Corey turned back to face Miguel. His shoulders shook up and down, then he dropped his face into his hands and screamed through closed lips. Still, Miguel didn't move.

Corey gathered his composure and looked up. He began to speak softly, slowly. He continued for the next several minutes without interruption as he told Miguel most of the important things he could remember about Nick. Then, he spoke of his dead father and told Miguel everything else, aside from the fact that Corey was a killer. When he figured that he had said enough, he grew quiet. While speaking, his gaze migrated down toward the floor. Now, he looked up once more at Miguel, meeting the eyes that had never taken their gaze off Corey, saying nothing. Corey figured he was being polite, as usual.

"That's everything." Corey paused, feeling a knot tightening in his stomach. "Everything I should have told you before, at least."

Miguel continued staring back at him and finally spoke. "Thank you. Those must have been painful memories to carry. I'm sorry for your suffering."

Corey wanted to reach out to touch Miguel, to be embraced in return. Miguel took a deep, audible breath then continued.

"But why didn't you explain these things before? I know they're difficult, but I've shared the important things about my life with you. I told you on our second date that I'm HIV positive. Do you think that was easy? Risk free?"

"No, of course not. I know that."

"I opened up about my deepest wounds, but you never shared a damn thing of importance about yourself. Why didn't you trust me?"

"I do trust you. But this is part of who I am—an intensely private person. I'm guarded."

"That may be the truest thing you've said, but you also lied to my face the other night in the bar with Billy. That's not the kind of relationship I thought we had, Corey. I felt we had something honest and special."

"We do. We are special. I love you, Miguel, honestly."

"I'm sure you think you love me. But you need to take a long hard look at how you show it, and how you don't. If you loved me, you would have been honest and upfront from minute one. But you weren't."

Neither said another word until Miguel rose from his chair seconds later.

"I'm going home. You seem calm now, and I hope you'll be fine."

"I am. Calm, that is. But I won't be fine if you leave like this—upset with me."

"Sorry, but I need time to process all that you unloaded and the things you kept hidden. Please don't call me until I call you."

It took every bit of Corey's remaining strength not to cry. He simply said, "Okay."

Miguel walked to the door, slipped on his flip-flops, and left the apartment without taking time to grab his toothbrush or overnight bag from the bedroom.

* * *

Corey awoke with a start, in a fog. Once Miguel had left, he had taken an extra-strength aspirin and laid down on the sofa. He resisted the temptation to run to a nearby bar. He wasn't certain how long he had been asleep. Corey noticed light outside the window, though he couldn't be sure if it was still the same day. His head wasn't fully clear when he realized the landline phone on the kitchen counter was ringing. He grabbed it violently from its cradle and said, "Miguel?"

"No, definitely not Miguel. Is that the guy with the accent I talked to earlier this morning? Here's a little tip. If you're going to let the gardener answer your phone, you need to scold him for not passing along the message that I called."

"This isn't a good time, Nick. How did you get my number?"

"You mean because Corey Flanagan isn't listed in the directory?" Nick's familiar, grating laugh echoed through the phone. "You can change your identity, Corey, but your social security number follows you until you die. I figured it out. So, who's this Miguel character?"

"None of your goddamn business. What do you want?"

"Okay, okay. I see I caught you on a bad day. Guess I'll make this quick. I'm trying to be a nice guy here."

"Yeah? How's that?"

"Hey now, the last time we spoke, you had a gun in your hand, and you tried to kill me. You left me at that fucking cabin, and my sister had to come all the way from Hudson to pick me up, yet I never pressed charges, Corey. Cut me a little slack here?"

"You're right. Thank you for that, but that was all long ago, and I'm not putting up with any bullshit."

"Good. So, as you may or may not know, I finally sold the condo. And market conditions being what they are, we ended up making a small profit in addition to the equity that built up over time."

"I didn't know. I don't monitor your movements anymore, Nick, and I've got no interest in your condo. Billy's dad explained it all in the letters. I assume you received Larry Preston's correspondence after I left?"

"Yeah, I got them. Not exactly a model of legal drafting or even proper English, but your message came across. You were leaving town and our relationship for good. You wanted no part in anything related to me—financially or otherwise."

"Well, then I guess you can read after all."

Nick laughed. "That's pretty good, Corey. I always knew you had a funny side. If only you would have let it show a bit more, maybe we might have had a chance."

Corey let the comment pass. "Why are you calling me? We have nothing to talk about."

"Actually, we do. The condo was titled in both of our names, if you remember. I'm not sure why since my salary paid the mortgage. At best, your contribution covered the pantry."

Corey laughed and resisted an urge to blurt expletives and hang up the phone. "Always the comic. Get to the point, Nick. What do you want?"

"Glad you still find my humor so charming. But watch your tone, Corey. Remember—I was extremely gracious in not pressing charges against you or asking to be reimbursed for my medical bills." Nick paused to let his comments sink in. "But fine, we'll do it your way. Straight business."

Corey continued to listen but leaned back to look out the front window, hoping to see Miguel returning to the apartment, knowing he would not.

"The closing is in two weeks. I need you to sign the purchase agreement and waive your right to proceeds from the sale. Technically, the title company sees you as a half-owner and won't close until your signatures are obtained."

Corey considered Nick's unexpected words. "So you want me to sign documents so you can sell the condo?"

"Yes, and you can do it all electronically. It'll take no more than a couple minutes. I simply need an e-mail address where the title company can send you the documents. They only discovered this minor detail last night. Idiots. Oh, and I'll need your address to send your remaining stuff once I move, or would you rather I throw your things in the trash?"

Corey ignored the last part, for now. "So, you want me to let you take all the profits from the sale, all of the equity that built up during the years we lived there?"

"Well, given market conditions, the real gains were realized these past four years after you left, once the housing market here in Minneapolis finally recovered from the crash."

"How much?"

"The gain? Oh, not that much really. Couple of thousand dollars, max."

"How much?"

"I just told you."

"No. How much are you going to pay me to sign those?"

"Hold on there, Mr. Tough Guy. You're in no position to play hardball with me. I'm the one who could still sue you for trying to kill me, remember."

"Actually, Nick, you can't. The statute of limitations in Wisconsin is three years, and that time ran out in 2016."

Nick stayed quiet before uttering "fucking lawyers" under his breath but loud enough for Corey to hear. He silently conceded the point and switched tactics instead. "Come on, Corey. I already explained this. The gain is mine. You were on the title as a convenience, a long-ago misplaced kindness. Besides, Larry's letter said you wanted no part of the condo or my money."

"Well, I've changed my mind. If you want this sale to proceed for your *convenience,* then you're going to have to pay me half the gain. I'll have Larry draw up the papers and contact you. Then, I'll come to Minneapolis for the closing and to look over whatever of my things you say I left behind. But there's no way I'm giving you my address. Goodbye."

Corey hung up the phone and turned the ringer off. His heartbeat raced. He needed a distraction, an escape, but was in no mood to paint. Instead, he changed into his wetsuit, waxed his surfboard, and headed toward the beach.

Chapter 8

Corey awoke around nine the next morning and, for a moment, wondered if the interactions with Miguel and Nick were nothing more than another nightmare. He sat up in bed, rubbed his eyes, and determined that yes, the conversation with Nick was real; so too was Miguel's swift departure in the wake of Corey's lies.

He felt sick to his stomach. His mid-day shift at the store was hours away. He desperately wanted to go back to sleep, to forget for a while at least the unexpected shit-storm that rained down on him the day before. No such luck. He considered picking up the novel at his bedside but didn't feel like dealing with Raskolnikov's troubles on top of his own. Corey lay there for twenty minutes before deciding to get up and paint. Rather than setting up his easel by the shore, he stayed home and painted indoors. He was in no mood to face friendly inquiries from passersby. He didn't want to talk to anyone other than Miguel, and that likelihood dimmed with each passing hour.

He pulled his kit from the closet. Today he favored a dark palette of reds, brown, and black. Painting from memory, he knew he couldn't get the colors just right, but that was okay because what he really wanted to paint was his feelings. The guilt and self-loathing from yesterday imitated his feelings from that awful Thanksgiving night from years before when he had killed his first deer, and then a human as well. Corey threw a splash of chestnut brown onto the canvas, then shaped the creamy oil paint with his broad brush. First, he produced a barely rectangular-shaped mass of brown paint on the middle of the canvas, then added four columns of the same color protruding stiffly outward from the blob. Next, he switched to black. With a slightly larger brush, Corey laid down the color of fertile dark soil across the canvas, surrounding the first shape. He considered adding streaks of off-white emanating from one corner of the canvas. But then he recalled the scene he was attempting to paint and remembered the cold darkness of that horrible night—and he left the darkness untouched.

His final color choice was blood red. In contrast to his wilder initial application of the brown and black paint, he now applied the crimson paint with a small-tipped brush. Then he strategically added droplets in a trail that started from one corner of the canvas, making them ever larger as he approached the brown shape with its four appendages. Next, he grabbed a larger brush and applied a thick pool of red below the brown mass. Finally, he used the thin-tipped brush to paint a name in the lower right-hand corner of the canvas—Corey Fischer—the person who created this horrible, horrible scene.

He put down his brush and sat back on the tall stool he had moved from the kitchen. Looking upon his latest creation, he felt disgusted. He got up and grabbed the canvas from the easel, smearing his hands with wet, dark paint. He walked toward the front door and went outside to the end of the back sidewalk where there was a rubbish container. He lifted its lid and shoved the painting inside. He returned to the apartment and took a shower. He wanted to wash the paint and so much more off his guilty hands. Corey scrubbed and scrubbed his hands until they were throbbing and red, the hot water stinging his skin. He dried himself off and uncharacteristically dropped his towel on the bathroom floor. Then, he crawled back into bed.

After falling fast asleep, Corey was soon yanked into a terrible nightmare, pulled from scenes long ago filed away into his subconscious about the aftermath of that awful night when he defensively answered pointed questions from the Barron County Sheriff who seemed hellbent on making Corey confess his crimes. He saw an officer in a dark brown uniform circling the table where Corey sat handcuffed. The man screamed questions that Corey couldn't understand. It was as if the officer were yelling in a foreign tongue. Corey felt himself calling out for help, but the officer either didn't hear him or was ignoring Corey's pleas. The officer continued his rant, something about his dead father, Frank, and then about guns and then accusing Corey of running away from the scene of a crime. The dream felt familiar, as if this had happened once or many times before, either in real life or in another imagined terror during the night. At first, the officer was Nick, but then he suddenly shape-shifted into someone younger and muscular, someone angrier even than Nick at his very worst. The chiding cadence of questions continued. Why had Corey shot Nick? Where was the gun? And why did he run from the woods, leaving Nick to die a slow and bloody death?

In the dream, Corey wanted to yell back that Nick was all right and that Nick himself was the aggressor. And although he couldn't form any words, somehow the officer anticipated and answered every defense or excuse Corey wanted to say. The man showed Corey a newspaper headline, declaring Corey to be a convicted liar. And below that line, there were photographs of those Corey had allegedly betrayed—Nick and Miguel and even himself. Finally, words emerged from Corey's dreaming lips.

"Larry. Help me, Larry."

But the officer shut Corey down. "Larry's not here. He can't save you. You are going to prison for the rest of your life."

Corey then heard a distinct ringing. The officer had suddenly disappeared, but that ringing persisted. He could no longer discern his surroundings but figured he must be in some sort of room, possibly even now in prison. His half-conscious, half-dreaming mind began to reason that perhaps the ringing was like those on television—a signal of iron-barred doors being shut tight, closing Corey's life for good.

But the ringing was real, and it awakened him. Corey saw his phone on the nightstand and realized it was producing the sound. He shook his head and then lifted the receiver. "Miguel?"

"Yes. You okay?"

"Yeah, I just . . . I'm glad you finally called."

"Corey, I need to talk to you if you have a minute. It's important."

"Yes, of course. Miguel, I've been doing a lot of thinking the past few days. I've thought of nothing else. And I want to say how truly sorry I am . . ."

Miguel interrupted. "I know, Corey. You said that before."

"But I mean it. I realize what a mistake I made in not trusting you, in not revealing myself with more honesty."

"Thank you, Corey. I appreciate you're going through a lot right now. But it's not why I called, not what I need to discuss."

"Okay," Corey answered slowly.

"My sister called this morning. It seems that my mother had some sort of spell or maybe even a stroke."

"Oh my God, Miguel. I'm so sorry."

"Thank you. Me too. I haven't talked to Mom yet, of course. My sister called 911, and they're at the hospital right now."

"In Houston?"

"Yeah, I can't even remember which one. The news really shook me. I barely heard what my sister had to say. I guess I'll get more information when I arrive in Houston."

"When are you going? Do you need a ride to the airport?"

"I'm at LAX right now, but thanks. My boss was incredibly sympathetic. She told me to take as much time as I need and not to worry about work for now."

"I can come with you if you want."

"That's kind, Corey, but I need to go by myself. Besides, the flight leaves in forty-five minutes."

"Okay, but I want to help if I can. What do you need?"

"I actually do need something from you, Corey."

"Anything. Ask away."

"I need you to give me some space, to let me handle this emergency with my family, alone."

Corey's heart sank. He felt like crying but stayed composed

for fear of stealing the moment from Miguel.

"I know there's a lot to be resolved between us, Corey. But I can't handle that right now. I need to focus on Mom."

"Of course."

"I also don't want to leave you with the impression that things between us will be fine. Those were some significant revelations you made that day in your apartment. I need to process them and figure out what's best for me going forward."

Now Corey did cry. But he held his hand over the mouthpiece so Miguel wouldn't hear.

"One last thing then, I need to get in the line for boarding. I'm not asking you to wait for me, Corey, because I can't promise where my head will be after thinking about us and then this whole new situation with my mom on top of it. I'm just not in a good place, and that's my responsibility, not yours."

"But...," Corey protested. Miguel interrupted him once more.

"I don't need our drama hanging over my head, at least not until I get to see Mom and figure out what's next. I'm sorry. I'm not trying to be an asshole. I need to take care of myself and my family right now, and I wanted to be upfront with you about that."

Corey waited a moment before answering. Miguel's abrupt honesty felt like knives in Corey's gut, but at least Miguel was transparent, a much fairer approach than Corey had given to him.

"Okay. I understand. I'll give you all the space you need. But please know I'll be here for you, no matter what. I love you and want to be a part of your life, but only when you're ready for that."

"Thank you."

"I'm not a praying person, at least not anymore. But I'll keep your mother and your entire family in my thoughts and send healing intentions toward her through the universe."

"I appreciate that."

Corey started to ask that Miguel let him know once he got to Houston safely but checked his impulse to pull Miguel back in when he clearly needed to walk away. "Well, good luck and have a safe flight. I love you."

"Thanks, Corey. I'll be in touch."

Corey returned the phone to its holder, then laid back upon his pillow in disbelief. This was not the conversation he had anticipated. He decided to make good on his impulsive promise to Miguel. He slid out of bed, rested his knees on the carpet, and placed his head against his folded hands. He prayed for Miguel's mother, for Miguel, for Billy, for everyone, and finally for himself; *dear god in heaven, I am such a mess.*

* * *

As Corey showered before work, he thought how the earlier nightmare had made him sticky with sweat and noticeable body odor. He wanted to wash away this day's ugly feelings, if not those from the entire past week. After the shower, he pulled on a pair of jeans and a polo top—not his favorite shirt, but good enough. That sentiment about clothing matched his mood getting ready for work.

As he gathered his keys and wallet from their spots in the entryway, he paused to look at the painting on the hallway wall. It was the artwork he had created while living with his mother back in Wisconsin at the end of 2013. The realistic painting depicted a wide river basin, with intermittent islands covered in large basswood trees whose leaves had fallen to the ground and into the river a month or two before. The focal point of the painting was a tiny green boat being steered from the back motor by an elderly man; a young girl in a quilted raincoat sat nervously at the bow. Corey had used varying shades of white, blue and gray to show that a rainstorm had descended upon the river valley, and additional strokes with these same colors and a touch of brown revealed a river filled with cresting waves threatening that same green boat.

Corey had looked upon this painting a hundred times since he painted it and took it with him to California. He had initially given it to his mother, but she insisted that he take it with him when he moved. *It's the first painting of your new life,* she had said. *It is terrific and marks a brand new beginning filled with endless possibilities. Keep this artwork with you and display it where you'll see it—often. It's a testament to your resilience, Corey, just as it depicts the resilience of the fisherman in getting his granddaughter safely to shore.*

This was hardly the message he felt like remembering right now. Resilient? No. Corey felt defeated—by his own characteristic penchant for shading the truth and protecting his heart, even to the point that he had pushed away the first person he truly, deeply loved with that same soft heart.

Yet, he continued to stare at the painting. Perhaps his mother was right. Did Corey have an inner strength—even resilience—of which he wasn't fully aware? Like the fisherman and his granddaughter fighting that potentially fatal storm, was it possible, amid everything seemingly going to shit, Corey might be all right in the end? That he and Miguel might eventually reconcile? That Corey himself might finally conquer his own demons, grow up, and love people with an open and honest heart?

Chapter 9

Corey checked his new cell phone for the fifteenth time in the past hour. It had been over a week since he last spoke with Miguel. It felt silly to keep checking for missed calls or texts, but Corey did it at least once every hour. He knew that Miguel had received the voice message, though, when Corey called to say he had finally purchased a cell phone. This morning a postcard arrived. On the front was a photo of the Johnson Space Center. On the back, simply *Congrats on the phone and welcome to the 21st Century. Mom's got a long road ahead. I need more time. —Miguel*

Corey had plenty of time to burn waiting in the arrival hall at LAX. His mother's flight was running twenty minutes late. He looked forward to Ginny's arrival with genuine happiness but also a twinge of anxiety. He and his mother had spoken nearly twice per week since he last saw her eleven months earlier when they spent Christmas together at his grandmother's house in Eau Claire. Corey had only flown in for the weekend and didn't have time to travel the additional distance to Ginny's home in Pepin. That's what he called it now—*Ginny's home*—rather than *his parents' house* or *the place where I grew up*. After fleeing to Pepin in the wake of 2013's intense madness, he lived with his mother for an entire year. In that time, Corey watched and helped as Ginny transformed the home into a place more suited to her own personal desires. She painted the bathroom pink. She bought more feminine-looking furniture for the living room, as well as a new double bed to replace the king-sized one she had shared for so long with Frank. She also donated Frank's insurance plaques and hunting trophies, then filled the family bookshelf with Lladro statuettes and her own dressed-up childhood dolls.

That breakthrough return to Pepin and the one-year respite in his childhood home had sparked the beginning of a new rapport between him and Ginny—one that made Corey feel they were getting to know one another again. Their phone conversations since he moved to California in January 2015 waxed and waned between the mundane—the weather and local Wisconsin gossip—and the more meaningful—their lives, their passions, their plans. The one topic they never talked about much was Frank. Corey always shared details of his new life when they spoke. Ginny mentioned the idea of taking a senior citizen bus trip to Nashville. He described his paintings and how he enjoyed working at the frame shop in Redondo. She told him how she had become closer to her own aging mother. He hesitantly described the emerging relationship with Miguel. Ginny broached the idea of finally agreeing to a neighboring widower's repeated request for a date. Two months ago, Corey invited her to visit California, now that he finally felt settled. Ginny accepted.

"Mom," he called out across the crowd as she came through the glass security doors outside baggage claim. "Over here."

Corey shook his head in wonder at how his mother could look so much younger during the last two visits than she had in the years leading up to and following Frank's death. She wore her white hair a bit longer now, and today it was pulled back into a flowing ponytail—the kind she was never allowed to wear around Frank. She headed straight for Corey, dropped her handbag to the floor, and enveloped him in a warm embrace. Then she pulled back and looked at him with a broad smile.

"I made it. Who would have thought I would ever visit California?"

"Yes, you've arrived in paradise. Seventy-five and sunny here in LA, a twenty-degree improvement from back home. I checked."

She kept hold of his arms. "You look fantastic, Corey. I think the California sunshine has been good for you."

"Thanks, Mom. I can't wait to show you around. I think you'll love it."

She pointed out her suitcases on the baggage carousel, and he placed them both on a cart.

"Geez, are you staying for two weeks or two years?"

"I know. It's a bit much. I didn't have a clue what to pack since I've never been here. I brought some of everything, just in case."

They enjoyed their first laugh of the day and hugged warmly once more.

"Come on, my car is this way."

She followed him toward the parking garage. Soon, they were heading south along the coast. He looked over with satisfaction, seeing his mother staring out the passenger window in apparent awe at the panoramic view.

"My goodness, is it ever beautiful. And you get to see this every day, the ocean?

"Yeah. It never gets old, that's for sure."

"I'll bet. It sure beats looking out across that old river back home."

"Maybe. But that has its own beauty, too."

"So, you miss it? You're ready to move back to Pepin?" Ginny flashed him a playful smile.

"I wouldn't go that far."

* * *

"Are you hungry?"

Ginny turned away from the suitcase, lifting out the last of her things to place them into the closet.

"Yeah, a little. I know it's only four o'clock, but my stomach thinks it's time for a meal."

"You did lose two hours with the time change, so your gut is right. For your body, it's dinnertime. I thought we might walk down the Strand to a nice little café I'm fond of."

"Should I change? On TV, everyone in California always looks so nicely dressed."

He laughed. "No, you look perfect, Mom."

"I still feel bad about taking your room and leaving you to sleep on the couch."

"I told you it's fine. I fall asleep out there half the time anyway. Come on, let's go. I thought we'd walk instead of drive, so you can smoke."

"Didn't I tell you? I gave that up as a New Year's resolution."

"No, you didn't, but that's great news."

"It's been ten months, and I haven't had a puff since."

"How'd you do it?"

"Strangely enough, it came out of my Al-Anon meetings. I heard a man saying how he realized that his smoking was really an escape from his wife's drinking problem. It struck me that maybe I was doing the same thing all those years. And now that Frank's gone, I wondered if maybe I didn't need cigarettes anymore. So, I quit cold turkey and haven't had much desire to smoke since."

"Wow. Congrats, Mom. I'm really proud of you."

Walking toward The Sea Captain, Corey pointed out several landmarks, including the pier and an ice cream parlor.

"I never imagined it like this. What a busy place and so many things to explore. I see why you like it."

"It does suit me better than I expected. Guess I should have listened to Billy years earlier when he bragged about living the good life."

"How is he, by the way?" Ginny's tone turned quickly somber. "I heard about Larry. It doesn't sound very good."

"Billy's fine, considering. He's back visiting his parents right now, though he met them in Rochester and didn't make it all the way to Pepin this time."

"I feel bad for them. I've brought over a couple meals and asked if there's anything I can do. But you know Larry. He said he was fine and asked what he could do for me instead. What a lovely man."

"Indeed. The best."

"Do you see Billy much?"

"Most Sundays. We do brunch. He's excited to see you. We're going to meet him at Nelson's the day after tomorrow when he's back from his trip. Nelson's has decent food, but the best part is the setting, on the tip of Palos Verdes with a spectacular view of Catalina Island."

"Sounds wonderful, Corey. But please don't go to any trouble on my account. I'm here to see you and not interfere with your routine. I've got plenty to keep me busy while you're at work or doing what you normally do."

"Mom, I am absolutely glad you're here, and I want to show you around. I've been looking forward to your visit. You're not going to be in my way at all. Just the opposite."

"Okay, but if you need time without me, don't give it a second thought."

"Will do."

"And I expect you'll also want some time to see Miguel? Don't worry about me. I'll be fine at your apartment all by myself. Or I can take a long walk."

He paused, looking down to the pavement as they continued toward dinner. "Yeah, about Miguel."

Ginny stopped walking and halted Corey with her hand. "Is something wrong?"

He looked into his mother's eyes. He had never spoken to her with any depth about a love interest before. Broaching that subject lightly over the telephone the past several months had seemed safe, at a distance. Speaking to Ginny here and now about Miguel brought more hesitation.

"I think it might be over between us. I screwed things up." As they stood facing each other with the crashing waves of the Pacific behind, Corey explained as Ginny listened without interruption. "And I haven't seen him since."

She stayed quiet for a minute longer as they resumed walking toward the cafe.

"Did he say he didn't want you to call him?"

"Yes, and I think his silence speaks volumes. If he wanted to talk with me, he would."

"Huh. Well, perhaps you both need time to figure things out."

"I guess. Or maybe this is my punishment for lying to him from the start."

"Corey, don't be so hard on yourself. Not that I condone lying, but it is only a venial sin."

"I appreciate that, Mom. But think about it. What if you found out the person you were dating for months had such a fucked-up past? That he had a different last name and identity for over thirty years? And that he lied about it when he had the chance to tell you the truth?" Corey sensed his mother's discomfort with his salty language. "Sorry about the f-bomb."

"Oh, I've heard worse."

He raised an eyebrow and looked into his mother's eyes. He found her attempt to relate to him endearing.

"But I'm not sure I'm the right person to give you advice on secrets and lies, Corey."

"Why not? You're the most honest person I know. Certainly, more so than me."

Corey remembered Ginny's emotional revelation in the wake of Frank's death—how Corey had been conceived via rape. But something about her demeanor in this moment unnerved him. Were there other unflattering things about his perfect mother that he didn't know?

"Don't put me on a pedestal, Corey. Falling off it can hurt."

"Mom, are you trying to tell me something?"

She stopped walking and turned to face him.

"Did you know that your father had an affair?"

Corey's eyes widened as long-forgotten memories rushed into his conscious mind, including the uncomfortable experience at the café in Barron County when it seemed like Frank and the waitress—Judy—were much too cozy with one another. "Um, I had suspicions."

"Yes, with a woman at the bank. She lived just south of town. I'm sure everyone in Pepin knew, but no one said a word. I only found out by accident when riding past her house with Shirley Cavanaugh one day. We were on our way to lunch across the river in Wabasha. I was staring out the window as Shirley drove along. Suddenly, there he was—standing next to our car in the woman's driveway. They were locked in a very friendly hug. Shirley was jabbering on about something. I kept turning my head to watch your father holding that woman as Shirley sped on down the road and eventually out of sight."

"Mom, I'm so sorry. Did you confront him?"

She uttered a small laugh. "Confront Frank Fischer? I know he's been gone for four years, Corey, but surely you remember how he was."

"Yeah, I do."

Ginny and Corey resumed walking before she said more. "But I did confront her."

"Oh?" Corey looked straight ahead as they continued walking, feeling too uncomfortable at the moment to even glance at his mother.

"Yeah, I did. At first, though, I drove past that woman's house probably twenty times in the following two weeks. I'm not sure what I was hoping to see—our car in the driveway or the woman walking out to the mailbox so I could get a better look at her face. Who knows? I finally did see her back her car out of the driveway and head toward town. I followed her and watched as she parked right in front of the bank."

"The bank where Dad worked?"

"Yes. I parked across the street and watched. Through the plate-glass window, I saw her walk inside and take a position behind one of the bank teller stations. She worked there. I pounded the steering wheel and screamed. I thought about going in after her, but it was a busy morning, and I wasn't sure who all was inside. I sat in the car thinking about what to do next. All the while, that woman was still inside. I decided to start my engine and drive away, but I didn't go directly home. Instead, I drove back to her house and parked in the driveway. She lived in a small house on the edge of town, on a wide lot with a neighbor on only one side. It looked as though no one else was around. I can't believe I'm telling you this, Corey, but I got out of the car and walked around to the back of the house to peek into the window."

He continued to listen, expecting that the story might get worse.

"Clearly, no one was home, but I couldn't gather much about her from what little I could see inside. So, I turned to walk toward my car. That's when I saw a pile of brick pavers behind her garage. I guess she was going to do some landscaping at some point, though it looked like those stones had been sitting for a while. Still feeling anger at the thought of that woman inside the bank with Frank, I grabbed one of those bricks and threw it at a window at the back of the house. Glass shattered loudly."

Questions flooded Corey's mind, but all he could whisper was one. "What the hell?"

Ginny didn't hear him but continued, "I looked around but saw no one. Her garage blocked any view toward the neighbor's house. I wiped brick dust off my hands and onto my pants, walked back to the front of the house, got into my car and drove home. I'm not proud to say it, but I didn't feel bad about what I had done, Corey. I did, however, confess my sin to Father Frisch the next morning. He gave me my penance and an absolution, said I shouldn't do again."

"Was that it?"

"No. Two days later, I recognized the woman in Johnson's Market. I followed her around, watching as she felt the grapefruit and selected two kinds of cheese."

"Did she catch you, watching her?" Corey felt stupid for asking such an inane question, but by now, the story's drama had gripped him.

"Not directly. But I think she figured out who I was. Perhaps she was trying to avoid making eye contact for fear of creating a scene. I overheard her talking with Paul Johnson, who was working check-out that day. He recognized her and offered a welcome to Pepin. Then he added something about how it must be hard being new in town, a single woman renting a house, and that he looked forward to seeing her in church again the following Sunday. After that, she left the store. I finished shopping, paid for my things and left the store as well. Instead of going straight home, though, I drove out to the woman's house once again. She was still unpacking grocery bags from her trunk when I arrived.

"I pulled into the driveway, got out of the car, and walked toward her. She squinted at me and nervously said hello. I replied by telling her my name and that I was the one who had thrown a brick through her window days before. Her face turned suddenly pale and expressionless. I couldn't tell if she was feeling guilty or afraid. Then she spoke. *That's a crime, you know. Maybe I should call the cops.* I told her to go right ahead because I'd much rather go to jail than to hell for being an adulterous whore."

Corey could not believe the words flowing from his mother's reverent lips.

"By that time, the woman clearly knew who I was, or at least dropped any pretense about what was going on. *Frank is the one who hit on me*, she said. *I'm single and didn't know he was married—at first.* At first? As if that were a defense? I stared at her for a long moment as she stood there, still holding grocery bags in each hand. For a fleeting moment, I considered hitting her but then realized how much more trouble I might get in. After all, I had you at home to think about, Corey. You were still in grade school. Instead, I stepped closer and said this. *You need to remember where you live—in a small, close-knit town. You can report me to the police if you want, but ultimately the town will take my side. We don't tolerate your kind of woman here in Pepin. I think it would be best if you found a different job and a different place to live.*"

Ginny didn't say more. Corey wondered whether this was the end of her story.

"So, the woman never reported you to the police?"

"No one ever questioned me about it. Some months later, I saw a moving van out in front of her rented house."

"And you and Dad never spoke about this?"

"No. I suspect she told him what I had done, but he probably didn't dare bring it up for fear that the entire situation might ruin his business reputation if word got out. Besides, what would have happened if I had confronted him? I had no college degree, no work history, no source of income of my own. What would I have done? Where would I have gone? Back to live with my mother? No, my choices were made long ago. *Til death do us part* is what I promised. And Lord knows, I kept my vow."

They walked the rest of the way to the café in silence. Over dinner, their conversation moved on. Ginny told Corey that the Barron County cabin finally sold. Although they had cleaned it out together and readied it for sale during the year Corey lived with her in Pepin, the market for cabin properties had tanked by the time Ginny finally got it listed. A *For Sale* sign sat in the yard for two years before a buyer came along with a full-price offer.

Finally, they seemed to have said everything. They sat quietly for a few minutes, finishing their respective meals and sipping lemon water. Corey eventually looked up and saw his mother looking at him.

"I'm proud of you, Corey."

"For what?"

"For what you've overcome and who you are."

"Am I finally your favorite child?" he asked.

"I'm serious. You've come so far, and all on your own. I'm ashamed that I wasn't a better mother to you when you needed me the most."

Solemnity overcame him. "You were there, Mom. I've told you that before."

"But I could have done more—to stand up for you against your father or to ask more questions about Nick. I could always tell in your voice when you were unhappy."

Tears welled up inside but did not fall. "Thank you. That means a lot."

The waitress' inquiry about dessert provided the opportunity to segue to lighter topics. Ginny smiled at the waitress and politely declined. The waitress left the check on their table.

"I don't think I'll be able to eat for two days."

"You may change your mind when we get to the ice cream parlor."

"How do you find all these nice places?"

"I don't know. I bike a lot, and I notice interesting places I want to try."

"It's more than I could handle, that's for sure."

"You would do just fine out here, Mom."

"You think so? Huh, maybe I could live in a place like this, too. But Los Angeles is enormous, with so many people. Do you ever feel overwhelmed?"

"Overwhelmed?"

"Yes, like it's too much and that you'll get lost?"

"Not at all. I don't worry about getting lost out here. In truth, I've never felt more found."

She smiled at him. "You're never moving back to Wisconsin, are you, Corey?"

He hesitated before answering, "No." He glanced down at the table, then back at his mother's eyes, searching for a reaction.

Ginny nodded. "Well then, I guess we'll have to make the most of these visits, won't we?"

"Yes, we definitely will."

They rose from their chairs, heading for the street to begin their leisurely walk back to Corey's apartment. As they exited the door of The Sea Captain, Ginny stopped on the sidewalk and reached out to touch Corey's arm.

"Would you visit me soon, Corey, in Pepin?"

He cast her a quizzical look. "Sure. In fact, I'm heading back to Minneapolis next week to close on the condo and finally get my stuff back from Nick." He gave her only the briefest of explanations about Nick's recent call. "Maybe I could extend my stay for a couple of days and drive down to see you."

"That's perfect. Yes, the timing would be just right."

"Is there something I should know or be concerned about, Mom?"

Ginny shook her head slightly before offering a feeble smile. "No, but there's something I need you to do and something I need you to see."

Part Two: Upper Midwest

Chapter 10

Corey stretched out his legs ahead of his main cabin seat and settled in for the three-hour ride. Amen that the middle spot between him and the passenger on the aisle was empty. He pulled out his copy of *Crime and Punishment* and picked up reading where he left off weeks earlier. He had made little progress of late. With all of the drama in his own life, Corey had felt little enthusiasm for spending his evenings reading about someone else's.

Yet, today he had captive time to make progress on this novel so he could move on to something more fun. Nearing the middle of the book, Corey's interest in the storyline increased, and he read on with quickened pace. A mysterious stranger suddenly appeared, Raskolnikov revisited the murder scene, and a wily prosecutor emerged with an uncanny ability to solve cases where the criminal's trail had seemingly run cold.

He was engrossed in the story as the hours flew by. Before he knew it, the 757 was descending through the Minneapolis sky, aiming for Lindbergh Field. Corey recognized the familiar chain of lakes looking out from the airplane window, though he couldn't see as far as the Stone Arch Bridge or his former condo above the falls. The scene outside from a few thousand feet looked simultaneously familiar and foreign as the plane steadily descended.

Corey had not alerted anyone in Minneapolis of his impending arrival. There wasn't anyone left to tell. He had severed all ties upon fleeing the city like an escaped prisoner in the middle of the night, even his relationship with Carol. She had been his closest

Minneapolis friend and the only woman with whom he had ever been sexual. But Carol was married to Julian—Nick's best friend. The desire to cut ties with Nick overpowered any lingering fealty he felt toward maintaining a connection to Carol.

After the plane arrived at the gate, Corey grabbed his carry-on bag from the overhead bin and made his way out of the airplane and through the airport. He rode the light rail from there to downtown Minneapolis, clutching shut the wool-lined jacket he had borrowed from a coworker at the frame shop once he encountered the cool autumn air. Corey had discarded his own cold-weather gear along with so much else upon leaving the Midwest years ago. As he walked a few blocks to his hotel, the city streets felt simultaneously strange and familiar. He knew where he was going, yet some things were unfamiliar, such as Nicollet Mall, which now had a noticeable number of trees along with gleaming new bus stop shelters, public art and signposts that Corey didn't recall seeing before. He grabbed a sandwich from a deli along his route, then checked into the hotel and half-watched the local news before falling asleep. He awoke early the next morning to the sound of his buzzing cell phone.

"Good morning, Mr. Preston."

"Good morning, and for God's sake, will you please call me Larry?" The deep chuckle on the other end of the line signaled a good-humored demand. "You get in all right last night?"

"Yes, thanks. The flight was on time."

"Great. Billy and I just left Pepin and should be on time to pick you up at nine thirty. I thought we might grab breakfast before heading to the real estate office at eleven."

Corey expressed silent gratitude that Billy had flown in days earlier to visit Larry for the second time in one month. Corey had been reluctant to summon Larry to Minneapolis all alone, given the precarious nature of his health and the ninety-minute drive from Pepin. Billy's presence would be a comfort to Larry as much as it would be to Corey.

"Sounds good, Larry. See you then."

After ending the call, Corey glanced at his phone screen and figured he had time to kill before rising to meet the demands of the coming day. He showered quickly, then left the hotel and hopped on the Light Rail for a short ride to the university. He exited the train outside Coffman Union then went inside to find a cup of coffee. The morning chill hadn't bothered him as much as expected; rather, he felt invigorated. The cold against his cheeks gave him a sense of toughness and made him feel more alert. It was all so different from his usual, easy-going deportment back home in LA.

Coffee in hand, Corey walked past his old dormitory and then on toward the river, feeling his body grow warmer with each successive stride past historic buildings that held distant, fond memories. He paused in front of the Art Education Hall, flooded with recollections. He wondered what had happened to his study-mate, Sean Fisk. That guy sure had talent. Corey quickly searched for Sean's name on his phone's web browser, but nothing relevant came up. He paused again, walking down Fraternity Row in front of Phi Beta Upsilon, and thought of Carol. He wondered if she still rented his former studio in Northeast and if she still worked at the museum. He walked on, resigned to the fact that Carol was Nick's friend now, not his. Through the course of his relationship with Nick, Corey had simply and quickly grown apart from other college friends, too. He could see now, in hindsight, how possessive Nick had been in those early years of their relationship. Virtually all their time outside of work was spent as a couple, with friends from Nick's past, or with those acquaintances they made together. Corey had been cut off from his past friends, his past life. Perhaps that explained why it wasn't difficult for Corey to flee the Midwest and leave everything, everyone behind. Very little in his former life felt truly like his own.

* * *

Seated in a booth at the Uptown Diner, Larry previewed the upcoming meeting for Corey, repeating everything they had already gone over by phone the week before. Billy sat next to his father, ignoring the real estate conversation and scrolling on his phone.

"And remember, when signing the documents, use your legal last name, Flanagan."

"Okay."

"Who knows how the title agent will have it displayed. If it says Corey *Fischer*, sign it with Corey *Flanagan* instead. I brought along a copy of your certified name change that we did back in 2014. We can submit it along with the other papers if needed."

"Got it." Corey noticed the tremor in Larry's hands each time he lifted food to his mouth. And he looked as if he had aged a decade during the one year since Corey saw him last—the eyes sunken, his hair thinner, and his color pale.

"So, what else do I need to know?"

"That's it for paperwork—the legal stuff." Larry sipped his coffee, then paused. "How are you holding up inside? Are you ready to see Nick again after all this time?" Billy looked eager to hear the answer, too.

"I think so. I've done fine without him these past four years. Most days, nothing about him or my old life even comes to mind."

"Good. But be prepared. It's possible you might react once you see him or hear his voice. And neither of us knows what he might say. From all you've told me and that I've heard from Billy, Nick isn't exactly the kindest person around."

"That's for sure," Billy said.

Corey nodded his head yes. "I'm ready to see him, though. There's nothing he could say to upset me anymore, but I hear you, Larry. Thank you."

"Glad to help and glad to be here."

Corey reached across the table, resting his hand lightly atop Larry's.

"I'm glad you're here, too. I know I didn't need a lawyer present to sign the documents you pre-approved. I'm guessing your insistence on attending in person might have been prompted by your son."

Billy opened his palms upward in supplication. "Lawyer-son privilege, sorry. He can't answer that one, or we'd have to kill you."

Larry smiled and winked. "We may have had a conversation or two about it. But on the advice of my child, I've been instructed to say no more."

"You two are a comedic duo. The apple didn't fall far from the tree with that one," Corey said, pointing at Billy.

"In all seriousness," Larry said, "I wanted to be here for you. We both did."

"I'm not surprised. Not one bit." Then Corey added, "I know how lucky I am to have a friend like Billy, and how lucky we both are that he has a father like you."

"That's kind of you to say. But I was happy to make a detour toward Minneapolis before heading to my appointment at The Mayo Clinic."

They each returned attention to their breakfast plates. But Corey kept one eye fixed on Larry. He belatedly realized that this man sitting across from him had shown more kindness to him across Corey's entire life than his own father. And sacrifice, too. A memory popped into his brain. It was about one Saturday afternoon he had spent in the Preston's home, after quietly leaving his own house where his drunken father was yet again yelling at Corey's mom. Corey had fled to the Preston's as a personal refuge, knowing he would be welcomed there, offered milk and a snack, and not have to worry about facing Frank's rage. An hour after arriving, and in the middle of a competitive board game with Billy's siblings, the doorbell rang. Corey watched Larry walk toward the front door and spy through the window to see who was outside. Before opening the door, Larry asked Corey and Billy to please step into the kitchen for a few minutes and stay quiet. They did. Corey listened with a heightened heartbeat as Larry opened the front door and greeted Frank Fischer. Frank demanded to know whether Corey was inside. Larry calmly told him no. Frank's words were slurred, and he threatened to search the house to see if Larry was lying. Larry stayed composed but reaffirmed that he had not seen Corey all day, then offered to take a walk with Frank around the neighborhood to help him look for his lost son. Frank declined but demanded that Larry send Corey home immediately if Corey showed up at the Preston house later that day. Larry signaled agreement, then said goodbye to Frank and closed the door. As Larry passed by them in the kitchen on his way back to whatever he had been doing, he gripped Corey's shoulder then told both boys to have fun resuming their board game.

Now, that same man who guarded him as a boy was protecting Corey still. But for how much longer? "If I may ask, how is your treatment going?"

"I feel like a million bucks—but, a million bucks that've been through the wash."

Corey and Billy both smiled.

"The tumor hasn't shrunk much in response to chemo. It's still there and not likely to disappear. As I've told the family, I'll keep doing this as long as it works and doesn't make me intolerably sick. After that . . . well . . . we'll deal with that when it comes."

"I admire your spirit and strength, Mr. Preston. Larry."

"Thank you, Corey. You've got the same strength inside of you, too. I've seen it up close. And it obviously took all that strength to pull this guy out of the ocean," he said, pointing toward Billy. "Like I told you on the phone, I'm forever grateful for what you've done. But that aside, I'm proud of you, just like I'm proud of all my kids. I count you as one of them. Always will."

* * *

Nick was already seated when Corey and Larry arrived for the signing at eleven o'clock. Billy had decided to wait in the car. Nick rose from his chair to greet Corey, offering his hand across the table while saying it was nice to see him and to meet Larry as well.

"Maybe we can catch up after the closing?" Nick's tone was far friendlier and less sharp than when Corey last spoke to him on the phone.

"Sure."

Corey was glad Nick hadn't said more. He was afraid of awkward banter—or worse—that might embarrass him in front of Larry, the title officer and the young straight couple at the far end of the table. The couple then rose from their seats as well, introducing themselves to both Corey and Larry and repeatedly saying how excited they were to have submitted the winning bid for the condo.

The title officer led everyone through the painstaking steps of signing seemingly endless amounts of paper. Corey twice looked up to catch Nick staring at him across the table. The look seemed a mixture of curiosity and resignation. Corey was half-tempted to excuse himself and check his appearance in the restroom mirror. What was it that Nick found so intriguing? Had Corey's appearance changed all that much? Nick's sure hadn't; he looked just the same as the day Corey last saw him, minus the anger after Corey shot him in the ass.

The papers all signed, both Corey and Nick cast silent sighs of relief. The buyers, whom Corey pegged as budget-strapped millennials, hugged each other and then their agent before running off to commence their anticipated move-in.

"Geez, were we that giddy when we bought the condo?"

"Probably so. It was our first home purchase."

"First and only," Nick added. "We might've bought more if we had stayed together. I always saw us living in one of those pricey houses near Lake of the Isles."

"I didn't know that," Corey said before turning toward the listing agent. "Are we done here? Time to go?"

She nodded then led them all into the hall.

"So, you both have your checks. The only thing left is to vacate the condo by five." The agent thanked them and said her farewells, walking away with what Corey calculated to be a nice commission.

"Back when you called, you said you had things for me to look through at the condo?"

"Yeah. I can meet you guys there or give you a ride." Nick's voice was friendly, with no trace of the edginess Corey remembered. He didn't even seem upset any longer about Corey receiving half the proceeds from the sale.

Corey saw Larry glance at his watch. "Sure. Corey, we can drive you there."

Corey, too, noticed the time, calculating that if Larry and Billy left now, they could reach Rochester in time to enjoy a relaxing lunch prior to Larry's late afternoon chemo treatment.

"Actually, Larry, why don't you get going to Rochester. I'll grab my bag out of your car and ride with Nick over to the condo. When we're done, he can drop me off at the car rental shop." He turned to face Nick. "Is that okay?"

"Sure," Nick said. "But what's with the car rental?"

"I'm driving to Pepin to visit my mother. She's expecting me for dinner."

"Great, no problem."

"Okay," Larry said. "I guess I'll be going then. Hopefully, I'll see you again in Pepin before you head back home to California."

"You will. I promise."

They walked down the hall away from Nick. Corey hugged Larry and thanked him for all he had done. Then he watched Larry step into the elevator and strained his neck to catch one last glimpse before the doors shut. He walked back toward the title company's office door.

"Okay, let's go."

Nick led the way down the staircase and toward his car. Their awkward silence finally broke once seated inside, waiting for the car's heater to kick in.

"Nice vehicle. Traded in the Jeep?"

"Yes, time for some life changes, I guess. Like you but a couple years late."

"Good for you. New car, new house. Where are you moving to, by the way?" This was the most invasive question Corey had even considered asking when anticipating this trip. He had no intention of inquiring about Nick's love life or if he even had one. Not that it might make Corey jealous. Rather, he simply no longer cared.

"Not far, I'm staying in Northeast."

"It's a nice neighborhood—everything you really need. Is it a house or another condo?"

"A house."

Corey noticed the brevity of Nick's replies. He detected something—not so much hostility as reticence. This was not the Nick whose bravado in their recent phone conversation had made Corey angry in the wake of his rift with Miguel. Was Nick playing a game, waiting to attack? Or perhaps Corey's act of standing firm, of demanding his equal share of the condo proceeds, had finally humbled Nick into being less of a jerk? Nick turned to face him.

"Look, Corey. To be honest, I'm moving in with Evan—into his house just off Central Avenue. I wasn't sure if you could handle hearing it, but that's what's going on."

Corey's eyebrows lifted. He felt a slight twinge in his gut. Searing memories rushed back to him—Evan exiting the hallway of their condo building, and his voice in the background of a Miami hotel room. Yet Corey's voice now remained calm.

"Evan? The guy you allegedly didn't fuck in Miami? Huh. I thought he was married to a woman?"

"Yeah, that." Nick blushed as he turned to look out the car's front window and away from Corey. "They got divorced a few months ago. I guess she didn't approve when he told her that he's gay. Who would have thought?"

Nick offered a shrug and a laugh. Corey looked at him, and his initially cramping stomach quickly relaxed. Then, he laughed too.

Ten minutes later, Nick pulled into the garage of their old building one last time. They exited the car and ascended in the elevator to the top floor. As they walked to the end of the hall and stopped at their former home's front door, Corey pointed toward the neighboring condo.

"Have you told Mrs. Randall you're moving? I'll bet she had a thousand questions about that."

Nick had been leading the way but stopped abruptly and turned around.

"No, I didn't. I'm sorry to say that Mrs. Randall died earlier this year. I would've told you, but . . ."

"Oh, I'm sorry to hear that."

"Yeah, she's definitely missed around here. The place has been eerily quiet ever since she passed."

Corey smiled as a flood of memories of his interactions with his former neighbor flowed through his mind. "She was certainly a character."

"That she was. I went to her funeral. It was small, seeing as she had no children or other relatives in this area."

The news slightly depressed what had until now seemed like a light-hearted mood. They stood at the threshold for an excruciating minute, neither of them saying a word or moving to open the door. Though normally an accurate reader of non-verbal cues, Corey couldn't discern Nick's intentions once they entered the near-empty condo. Would this be an opportunity for revenge, to punish Corey behind closed doors for shooting Nick in the ass? Or might Nick suggest that they make their final day in the condo as memorable as the first when they christened their new home by having sex on the balcony after dark?

Corey steeled himself for whatever might come next, even to the point of imagining how he might thwart any unwelcome or violent advance. He would aim to keep their conversation brief and light, to peruse whatever of his belongings Nick had saved, and then get the hell out of town as fast as possible. Nick slid the key into the lock and opened the door. Corey followed him inside and stopped to catch his breath. The space was virtually empty, nothing more than a few boxes and brown paper-wrapped prints stacked and leaning against the white walls. It looked eerily familiar, like the day he and Nick first moved in. Back then, he felt excitement at taking such a grown-up step. Now, he wanted nothing more than to move on.

"Your stuff is in the bedroom. There's not much—just a box of personal items and a stack of books on the shelf. Once Larry told me you didn't want any of the furniture, it made things easier."

Corey walked into the master bedroom alone while Nick busied himself in the kitchen, packing some remaining dishware. The bedroom looked much bigger now in the absence of the dresser and king-sized bed. Even the adjoining walk-in closet appeared bare. He kneeled to open a box in the middle of the bedroom floor to see what might be inside. Corey had no expectations. He had taken everything he wanted four years ago. Staring at him from inside the box was a framed photo of him and Nick, the same one he threw across the room into a shattered chaos of glass on that terrible night in 2012. Nick must have reframed it, but Corey couldn't recall if that was done before or after he left the condo in 2013 for good. Regardless, there they stood in that picture, looking youthful and happy—getting married outdoors along the North Shore outside of Thunder Bay, or at least thinking that's what they were doing at the time. Beneath that photo were several more, and Corey began to regard them when he heard Nick walk into the bedroom behind him. He decided to peruse the remainder of the box's contents later when he was alone.

"Lots of good memories in here, right?"

Corey sensed Nick's playful effort, but the humor creeped him out.

"And now you're making new ones with that Hispanic guy, huh? How's that going, by the way?"

"Look, Nick. I appreciate your interest, but I'd rather not discuss our respective relationships, okay?"

"Sounds like I ventured into a dicey subject, but fine by me."

Corey quickly changed the subject. "So, I looked through the books but didn't see anything I want. Maybe we can dump them into one of those little free libraries on the way to the car rental?"

"Sure thing. And the box?"

"I'll take that with me. I need some tape to close it shut, though."

"I've got some in the kitchen, let me grab it. What about the print?"

"The print?"

"In the closet, the one I gave you for your birthday?"

Corey hadn't looked fully inside the closet door. At first glance, he assumed it was bare. He stood up and walked in, then saw *The Wounded Deer* leaning unwrapped against the wall.

"I took it down after you left. I never really cared for the damn thing anyway. It's been sitting in here ever since, and Evan doesn't want it hanging in our house."

Corey had completely forgotten about this print. He stood for several long, silent moments staring at Kahlo's autobiographical work. He now understood its magnetic appeal to his younger self. There, in a windowless closet, he summoned memories of events to match each piercing arrow goring the deer, along with feelings to echo the wounded look on the deer's face.

"Well? What do you want to do with it?"

Corey contemplated the print, the moment and the memories a bit longer. He could feel Nick's discomfort with silence as they stood together in the small, closeted space.

"If you have more of that brown paper, let's wrap it up. I would like to keep it. I can drop it off at UPS on my way out of town."

* * *

At the car rental shop thirty minutes later, Nick pulled his vehicle into a customer parking spot and stepped out to assist Corey with his things. After setting the moving box and one overnight bag onto the nearby curb, Nick turned to offer his goodbyes.

"Well, this is it," he said awkwardly.

"Yeah, I guess so." Corey felt no need to say more. Much more could be said, but none of it felt necessary any longer.

"Oh, I almost forgot. I meant to give something to you at the closing." Nick ran back to the driver's side door and returned with a large manila envelope. "Just some papers you left in the safe. Not sure if you need them anymore or not."

Corey took the envelope and stuffed it into his bag. "Thanks, Nick. Good luck." He put forth his hand for Nick to shake but got pulled into a surprising hug instead.

"Good luck to you, Corey. I really mean it—good luck." Nick kissed him on the cheek then released his embrace, walking toward his car without looking back. Corey stepped onto the curb in no rush to pick up his stuff. He watched Nick get into the car and thought he noticed an unfamiliar look of sadness, perhaps even a tear on Nick's face before the car's engine ignited and Nick backed up, then drove away.

Once he signed the necessary paperwork and was seated inside the rented Nissan Maxima, Corey started the engine and waited for the car to warm up. He reached over to the passenger seat, grabbed the manila envelope and looked inside. He immediately noticed his original birth certificate and passport, both issued in the name of Corey Francis Fischer. He searched for something more personal from Nick, a card perhaps, but there was nothing inside the envelope other than random papers from his former life—the lease to his art studio, and a health care directive listing Nick as Corey's legal next of kin, the decision-maker should Corey be unable to act for himself. For no good reason, he read through the document word for word, wondering if he had read it this closely back when he and Nick signed the documents after moving in together all those years ago. What power he had unwittingly handed over. It struck him at this moment how easy it had been to make major life decisions, and concessions, when he felt so deeply in love.

Corey glanced down the road in the direction Nick's car had gone. He turned once again toward the pile of papers on his lap. Then, he quietly tore the health care directive in half, instantly severing its legal impact. He removed his birth certificate and old passport from the envelope then stuffed the torn directive back inside. He got out of the car, walked toward the front door of the rental agency, and threw the envelope into the trash. Then he returned to his car, sat down in the driver's seat, and knew it was time to leave.

Chapter 11

Corey drove the Maxima across the St. Croix River Bridge, delivering himself into Wisconsin for the first time in almost a year. He planned to exit at River Falls then catch scenic Highway 35 and follow it south toward Pepin along the Mississippi River. It was only 1:30 p.m., and he had promised Ginny he would be home in time for supper at six. There was plenty of time to keep that vow. As he drove through Hudson, however, Corey remembered his discussion with Ginny back in California about the family cabin in Barron County, the same cabin where he had collected his father's inheritance—the guns that Corey used to wound one man and to kill another. In a way, he was relieved that the place had finally sold. After being in the family for half a century, the cabin would soon belong to a stranger. Corey felt no remorse about that transition, but something tugged inside him about the cabin itself, that place of unresolved woes, including that nagging concern about the eighteen-point buck Corey shot then left to die deep in the woods a few yards away from Nick. Corey never did hear what happened to the deer, though it was obviously near death when he ran out of the woods and drove away from Barron County. There was one person who could answer that one—Nick. Corey wrestled with the idea of calling him to find out.

He soon reached for his phone then typed *Barron Wisconsin* into his GPS app. It was an hour's drive from his current location. He quickly calculated that he could steer the car toward Barron, drive past the old cabin and still make it to Pepin with time to spare. If he drove fast, there would be time to step out onto the lawn and look around. It was possible Ginny had left the front door key behind for the new owners, in its hidden spot stuck between the metal plates of a hinge in the kitchen casement window. He drove past the River Falls exit and sped onward toward Barron County.

As he drove, Corey's thoughts turned to Miguel—1,200 miles away in Texas. Aside from sporadic text exchanges, it had been two weeks since they spoke. Corey felt grateful to have at least this much contact. Miguel had provided medical updates about his mother but little about how he was holding up. For his part, Corey wrote texts about Ginny's recent visit to California and how she wished she could have met Miguel. Corey also mentioned the trip to Minnesota for the condo closing, as well as his plan to indulge Ginny's request that he drive to Pepin for a few extra days because there was something she wanted him to see. The digital conversation was cordial and honest, but the playfulness and affection from their in-person dialogues had gone dormant. Corey discerned warmth and caring still present in their texts, and he hoped he wasn't just naively reading that into Miguel's written words. He yearned to hear Miguel's voice, with its deep tone and slight Spanish accent, so that Corey might hear clues of a still-present affection.

What the hell, I'm gonna call him, Corey said to himself, then connected his earbuds to his phone and touched Miguel's number.

"Hi there, stranger."

"Miguel, hi. I wasn't sure if you'd pick up. Is this a good time?"

"Actually, yes. They just wheeled Mom upstairs for some tests, so I'm heading to the cafeteria to grab a bite and then to my sister's house for a shower."

"Good. How's your mom doing?"

"Thanks for asking. She's been stable the past few days, but the doc's worried about another stroke. I can't remember exactly what I texted you, but they determined she had a series of small strokes leading up to the big one. They're not exactly sure what's causing it because she didn't have a history of high blood pressure, obesity, or anything like that. Today they'll perform a few more tests."

Corey listened intently while still watching the road ahead as he drove.

"Anyway, I'm babbling. How are you, handsome?"

Relieved, Corey smiled and exhaled audibly.

"I'm doing really well, thanks. The closing on the condo went smoothly, and I walked away with a nice, fat check. Now, I'm on my way through Wisconsin."

"Glad to hear it, Corey. How was it—interacting with Nick?"

A wide spectrum of thoughts and emotions raced through Corey's mind. Old Corey surfaced first, urging on a reply of deflection and half-truths. But emerging Corey followed quickly behind, coaxing an answer of raw honesty. Heeding the latter, Corey told Miguel everything he felt and remembered, including being struck dumb at Nick's news about Evan, unease while standing in the bedroom they once shared, and empowerment upon shredding the health care directive in half. Corey spoke uninterrupted for several minutes, occasionally hearing an affirming *oh* or *hmmm* from Miguel on the other end of the line.

"Wow, you've had quite a day. Thanks for sharing all of that. I appreciate your forthrightness, Corey."

The unfiltered monologue surprised him, too. He paused to let Miguel say more.

"I know we haven't spoken about *us* since our blowup. And if it's okay with you, I still need more time."

"Of course, no pressure. But I do like hearing your voice."

"And I like hearing yours, Corey. To be honest, this conversation was nice. You sound different in a way—less hesitant. I know I'm dealing with a lot down here and will be for a while yet, but let's have more phone calls like this and just see what happens. Okay?"

"I'd like that very much."

"Great. Well, I should let you focus on the road and get myself something to eat. Text me when you arrive in Pepin, so I know you got there all right."

"I will. Take care, Miguel. Get some rest. And give my best to your mother, even though she doesn't know who I am."

"Oh, she knows who you are. I'll tell you more about that in our next call. Drive safe, Corey. I'm really glad you called."

* * *

Corey neared the cabin along County Road V. He looked forward to a break from driving. He had forgotten that Wisconsin deer hunting season was a week away and now worried about hitting one as he drove seventy miles per hour on the winding country roads. During his childhood, Corey's father had told him more than once how deer sensed the oncoming hunt—spooked by an innate feeling that something bad was afoot. It made them jumpy, Frank had said, scaring the deer into darting toward the road unexpectedly and causing accidents. Thankfully, Corey hadn't yet seen one.

He pulled into the driveway, parked on the lawn and walked toward the cabin. He checked the window hinge, but the key was no longer there. He checked the one on the other side just in case, but it too was empty. He was surprised that his mother would have removed it. But then again, anything could have happened to that key in the years since Corey was last here. He opened the screen door and tried turning the main door's handle, only to find it locked. Short of breaking a window, Corey knew he wouldn't be going inside.

He peered into the cabin through a gap in the curtain covering the door's window. He remembered Ginny saying she had sold it fully furnished. *Even that forty-year-old sofa*, she had said, before they both laughed at its ugliness. Corey noticed the braided great room rug, the Lazy-Boy recliner, and the fifties-era dining table and chairs. Everything else looked sparse, as it did on his last visit, but with the framed family photos and his artwork now missing, leaving faded imprints where they used to hang on the walls. Corey smirked upon seeing the unlit neon beer sign, the one with the busty beer-toting woman. Frank had purchased the sign at the Foxtails Lounge. Corey wondered if that old metal shed of a building was still around, if men still gathered there during hunting season to drink cheap booze and catcall the lady dancers. It was also the closest place around to get a bite to eat, and Corey hadn't eaten since this morning with Billy and Larry.

He checked his watch. Three o'clock. There was still a little time before he would need to turn south toward Pepin and the Foxtails Lounge wasn't too far out of the way. The only other option was the old café on the way toward Barron where he'd had nothing but unpleasant memories—of his father flirting with that waitress Judy who always called Corey "Hon" and then eating there with Nick, who mocked Corey for eating rabbit food, a salad, in the middle of meat-eating hunting country. Corey got back into the car and let it idle while he took one last look at the cabin, remembering other unhappy snippets of what happened during his numerous trips to this cabin and the surrounding area. He instantly lost his desire to see inside the old family cabin. Instead, he revved up the car and headed onto County V. Within ten minutes, after a series of turns he had forgotten existed, he pulled into the gravel parking lot. Several lit neon signs around the door indicated that they were open, but only two other vehicles, both pick-ups, reminded him that it was the week before deer opener, and he felt relief that he would have the place more or less to himself.

He turned off the car but hesitated to go inside, flashes of remembered derision causing discomfort. Corey's bladder made the decision for him. He should have peed in the cabin's backyard. He alighted from the Maxima and headed for the door. Once inside, the Foxtails Lounge felt instantly familiar. None of the decor had changed, though it smelled a bit less like smoke. He wondered whether the owners finally complied with the law or if he just hit a time when no one was lighting up. A jukebox played country-western music, and two men chatted together at right angles in one corner of the bar. The tables were covered with upside-down metal chairs, so the only place for Corey to sit was at the bar. He chose a spot at the corner opposite the other men.

"Hi there, stranger. I don't remember seeing you in here before." The twenty-something barmaid wiped her hands on a rag as she approached him, then tossed it into a basket next to the kitchen door. She was bubbly, friendly and short with flowing blonde hair—no makeup.

"Hi. Yes, I'm passing through and needed a quick refreshment."

"Refreshment? Most people ask for a shot or a beer." She laughed. "You're not from around here, are you?"

"Used to be. I'm visiting from California now. In fact, I was in here once." Corey sensed a faint recognition as if he had seen this young woman someplace before.

"California? I've never been that far west. Closest I ever got was Colorado with my ex-boyfriend."

"Well, you should try to visit if you can. I moved to LA four years ago and haven't regretted it."

"Will do. So, Mr. Hollywood, what'll it be? Beer? Something stronger to take the chill off?"

"No, thanks. I don't really drink. Give me a diet of whatever."

"Coming right up."

Corey stood up and removed his coat, then set it on the barstool to his right. He walked over to the men's room, stopping to peer down the hallway toward the back where years earlier he learned that men would visit *the booths* to receive paid-for perks from the temporary, seasonal female *staff*. He entered the bathroom and relieved himself. After returning to his barstool, Corey found a soda waiting for him, the glass sitting atop a white napkin with the imprinted Foxtails logo. He perused the laminated menu resting atop the bar and saw that his only real option would be a reheated slice of cheese pizza. One thing about this bar had expectedly gone unchanged—every other item on the menu contained meat. Soon, the barmaid returned to check on him.

"You doing all right over here, hon?"

"Yes, all good, thanks. I'll take two slices of cheese pizza if you have them. Will it take long to cook?"

"Let me check." He watched her walk through the swinging door to the kitchen before returning with a wide grin.

"It'll be ready in less than ten minutes."

"Great, thanks." Corey looked directly into the young woman's eyes. She looked familiar. But she obviously wasn't working here on his prior and only visit when he was seventeen years old, and Frank was purportedly *initiating him into manhood*. That was twenty-five years ago, and she would have been a mere baby if she were even born at all.

"Good. So, what are you doing in this area anyway? You're a long way from Cali. By the way, my name's Samantha—Sam, for short."

"Corey. Nice to meet you." He reached across the bar and shook her hand. "I'm on my way from Minneapolis to see my mother for a couple of days before flying home."

"Well, then you're a good son. I see my mom nearly every day. She lives one town over. We're pretty close."

"Hmmm," Corey said through closed lips. "Say, did you ever live or work in Minneapolis? For some reason, you look familiar."

"No, but I've been there a few times. My ex and I used to shop at the Mall of America."

"Yeah, I avoided that place at all costs. Too crowded. I'm an introvert." Corey laughed, then took a drink of his soda and set it back atop the bar. "You still look familiar, though. You didn't happen to visit the Harbor View Café in Pepin a few years ago, did you? I worked there as a waiter for one summer season."

"No, I haven't heard of that place and never been to Pepin." Samantha bit her lip and hesitated before adding, "but my birth father used to live there, apparently."

"Is that right? What's his name?"

Corey noticed that she bit her lip yet again.

"To be honest, I don't know. I never met him. His name's not even on my birth certificate. Believe me, I checked."

Corey cocked his head and squinted. "Not sure I understand. So, how do you know he's from Pepin?"

"It's one of the few pieces of information about him that my mom revealed."

"Sorry about that." Corey didn't say more. He felt awkward talking so personally with someone he had just met.

"No worries. Mom says he did send her money to help raise me over the years, though. What a guy. Anyway, I should say that he *was* from Pepin, not *is*. According to Mom, he died somewhere up here a few years ago. She told me after the fact and still wouldn't tell me his name. Apparently, he had another family down in Pepin. Once I heard that I lost all interest in learning anything more about him."

Corey gripped the soda glass with one hand, steadying himself by holding onto the underside of the bar with the other.

"I'm sorry, I said way too much. I see I'm making you uncomfortable. Can I get you another?"

Corey looked at her with confusion.

"Soda?" Samantha pointed to Corey's near-empty glass. "Can I get you another Diet Coke?"

He didn't answer because he never even heard her question. "What's your mother's name?"

"My mom's name? Judy. Why?"

Corey felt an instant punch to his gut. He remembered Judy from the café when he ate there as a young man, with Frank.

"Uh, I don't know," he lied. "I'm guessing she was from Pepin also, and maybe I knew her."

"No, Mom has lived up here her entire life. Her parents—my grandparents—live in Chippewa Falls. She's a waitress and sometimes tends bar. Runs in the family, I guess."

Corey felt warm. He began to perspire in his armpits and across his forehead.

"So, a refill?"

"Actually, I'll have a vodka tonic. Make it a double—top shelf."

"Whoa. For someone who doesn't drink, that's a mighty strong choice."

Corey uttered a nervous laugh. "Guess I needed a slow start before jumping into the good stuff."

"All right, Mr. Hollywood. Coming up."

Samantha began making Corey's drink. As she reached for the Belvedere, he couldn't take his eyes off her. Is that why she looked so familiar because they shared half of the same genes? What the fuck? His heart rate was high, and he struggled to think about what to do next. Should he say something? Should he call his mother? Neither seemed like a good idea, but he wasn't sure if he would even know what a good idea under these circumstances might be.

"Here you go, hon." Corey's stomach dropped yet again, hearing Samantha call him *hon*. He instantly remembered how Judy had called him that at Slippery Sam's diner all those years ago.

"You feeling all right? You don't look as good as when you came in."

"I'm fine. Still adjusting to the cold. I'm not used to it anymore."

"Okay. You hang tight while I go check on these other fellas."

Samantha walked away, first refilling two beer glasses at the other end of the bar, then standing at the sink and washing used glassware. Corey slammed his drink in two swallows, then beckoned Samantha with his hand.

"I'll have another, please."

"A double? You sure about that?"

He nodded yes with absolutely no assurance.

"Suit yourself. Coming up. But you might want to wait until you put some food in your stomach to take the edge off all that booze, especially if you're driving to see your momma like you said."

"Thanks, I'll be fine. Just the drink, please."

She walked back across the bar and into the kitchen, then returned a minute later with the cheese pizza and Corey's second double vodka of the day—his first drinks since that fateful night in 2012 when he almost lost his life.

"Enjoy."

Once again, she walked away, but this time down a side hallway and out of sight. Corey slammed this vodka in one continuous gulp. He then set the empty glass on the bar, took two twenty-dollar bills from his pocket, and threw it down before pulling on his coat and walking out the door. The slices of hot pizza remained on a plate atop the bar. Corey marched urgently toward the rental car, got in and fired up the engine. He abruptly backed up, turned the car toward the exit of the parking lot and sped away from the Foxtails Lounge faster than a spooked deer.

Samantha was his half-sister. He was sure of it without needing proof.

He checked the clock on the car radio. It was now a little past four. Shit. He must've been in that bar for forty minutes. There's no way he could make it to Pepin by six. And now, it was getting dark. The damn clocks were set back only a week before, making it lighter when folks left for work at seven, but casting a darkness across the land when they headed home at five. To make matters worse, he had forgotten to grab the pizza and didn't know where he could stop next for something fast to eat.

Corey sped the car up to seventy-five. It was above the limit on these county roads for certain, but there was little to no traffic, and he felt the need to make up time. He reached into his coat pocket and pulled out his cell phone. He alternated glances between the road ahead and the device in his hand. He scrolled down in search of Ginny's number, then jerked the car back into his lane when he looked up to find himself veering left. He sent the call then held the phone to his ear. After three rings, she answered.

"Fisher residence."

"Mom? It's me, Corey."

"Hi there. Are you on your way from Minneapolis?"

"Yes. Well, sort of. Anyway, I took a little detour and lost track of time. I won't be there by six as promised. Is it okay if we eat a little late?"

"Of course. I'll turn the oven down a few degrees, so dinner won't dry out."

"Great. I'll be there as soon as I can."

"Take your time, honey. No sense driving too fast or getting into an accident. My homemade meatloaf isn't worth all that."

Ginny laughed. For Corey, it failed to register. His mind was back at the Foxtails Lounge. The image of Samantha's face was almost the only thing he could see, occluding the road ahead.

"Corey, is everything all right? You sound a bit anxious."

This time he heard what his mother said, prompting him to reply. "Yes. I'm, uh, just sorry about arriving late."

"Really, it's no trouble. Take your time."

"Mom?" Corey's voice began to quiver.

"Yes, dear?"

Just then, a large deer sprang from the ditch and onto the road in front of Corey's car. He gasped, then swerved. The phone flew out of his hand. The Maxima went sailing off the side of the road into an embankment, landing up against the solid trunk of an oak.

"Corey?"

Silence.

"Corey? Corey!"

The line went dead.

Chapter 12

Flashing red and blue lights woke Corey from his blackout. He saw movement in the rear-view mirror, someone approaching the passenger side of the car. There was no light inside the vehicle until a flashlight illuminated him. He looked around to gain his bearings, noticing a large tree smashed up alongside his drivers' side door and a steep embankment leading up to a road on his right. The car's engine was quiet. An airbag in front of him had deployed and now lay deflated. A policeman rapped on the passenger side window. Corey reached to his left and found the button to lower the window. It clicked but didn't work. He heard a muffled voice outside the car say, "Turn the key to see if there's any power." He did. There was. Corey once again hit the down button, and the passenger side window descended into the door.

"Are you all right, sir?"

Corey looked down at his body still strapped into the seat, then stared at his face in the mirror. He could barely recognize his own visage. He turned toward the officer.

"Yeah, I think so."

"Looks like you might've hit your head." The officer pointed.

Corey looked again in the rear-view mirror. The officer shone the light directly onto Corey. In the mirror, he saw a splash of red above his left temple. Corey reached up and felt a warm, sticky liquid. He brought his hand in front of his face and determined it was thickened blood.

"I think you stopped bleeding," the man said through the window. "Looks like it's coagulating."

Corey looked for a tissue or something to clean blood off his hand. Nothing. So, he reached down and wiped it on the carpeted floorboard.

"Okay, I'm coming around to your side of the vehicle. Don't move until I can help you out."

"Thank you, officer."

Barron County Sheriff Todd Coles walked through the frost-covered grass, surveying the path of the Maxima as he rounded the car. It was clear that the vehicle had swerved off the road across oncoming traffic and landed in the embankment, stopping when it hit the tree. Skid marks on top of the road indicated that the driver had initially slammed on the brakes, then lost control and driven into the ditch. A dent on the Maxima's side indicated that the car had slowed significantly before hitting the tree, though still fast enough for the airbag to deploy when it came to a sudden stop.

Corey hit the unlock button then watched as the sheriff opened the driver's side door. It stopped after a few inches, stuck. Corey started to get up. From this angle, he couldn't yet see the officer's face.

"Hold on. Let's see how you're doing before you start to move. I can radio for an ambulance if needed."

"I don't think that'll be necessary, officer."

"Well, you did hit your head, sir."

Corey grimaced. Suddenly, he began feeling a strong ache on the left side of his head.

"Okay, let's get you out of there. Unbuckle your seat belt and slide across to the passenger side door. I'll meet you over there."

Corey did as he was told. Sheriff Coles walked around the totaled vehicle and wrenched open the door. That is when Corey saw the man's faintly familiar face.

"Come out, slowly."

"Wait. My phone." Corey felt around the seat, then on the floorboard. He eventually felt the cold metal phone near his feet. He touched the screen. Instantly several banners lit up, reflecting a slew of missed calls and voicemail messages from his mother's landline, plus one each from cell phones belonging to Billy and Larry.

"Come on out," Coles said sternly. "But first, grab the keys from the ignition and hand them to me."

Corey climbed out slowly, fighting gravity from the angle at which the car had landed in the ditch. The sheriff held out a hand, and Corey reluctantly grabbed it.

"I've got you." With assistance from the officer, Corey stepped into the long, damp grass.

"You're lucky to be in one piece, mister."

"Yes, I can see that now." Corey surveyed the damaged rental.

"You feel all right, sir? You seem a little unsteady."

Corey sensed himself rocking while standing in place, unsure if it was nerves from the accident or the effects of slamming down his first two alcoholic drinks in more than five years.

"I think I'll be fine."

Corey looked the sheriff in the eye, then noticed the squint on the officer's face. At the same time, a flash of recognition hit Corey's brain. He had met Sheriff Coles once before.

"Sir, I have to ask—have you been drinking this afternoon?"

Corey closed his lips and held his hand to his mouth. He uttered through his fingers, "Just one."

"Huh. I'll need to see your license and registration."

Corey reached for the wallet in his back pocket and pulled out his California ID. He then turned back toward the car to search the glove box for whatever documentation might lay inside. Facing away from the officer, he said, "It's a rental, but I'll see what I can find."

"That's all right, never mind. They'll have to tow this vehicle anyway. I'll get the VIN number later."

Corey turned to face the sheriff and began chewing on his fingernail as the officer studied Corey's driver's license for a seemingly long time.

"You're from California?"

"Yes, sir. Hermosa Beach."

"You sure are a long way from home, Corey Flanagan. What brings you to Barron County?"

Corey noticed yet another change in the officer's demeanor, one that conveyed an uncomfortable recognition.

"I, uh, was visiting an old friend, but now I'm headed to see my mother." He was intentionally vague, hoping the sheriff wouldn't remember him.

"An old friend, you say? Who's that?"

"Well, not so much an old friend as an old familiar place I used to visit."

"So, a friend or a place. Which one is it exactly?"

"A place, sorry. I guess the accident's got me a little flustered."

"I'll bet you're flustered, and not just from the accident. You sure you're feeling all right? You're looking a little peaked and sweaty. We had better get you into town and checked out at the ER."

"No, no, I'll be fine. Definitely."

"Well, you're going to need a ride somewhere because you are not driving that vehicle anyplace," the sheriff said, pointing toward the wrecked Nissan.

Corey stayed silent, contemplating his winnowing options.

"I'll tell you what, Corey Flanagan. You come with me in the squad car, and we'll take a ride into town. We'll have the doctors look you over and have you submit to a blood alcohol test."

"But I'm not drunk, officer. I'm fine, really."

"I'm sure you are. But having driven a car into the ditch and with breath smelling like alcohol, it's standard procedure."

"Listen, there was a deer in the road. I swerved to miss it and unfortunately lost control. That's all."

"I'm not so sure that's all, Mister Flanagan. Or is it Fischer?"

Corey froze.

"I remember you, Corey. Did you think I would forget someone who shot his male lover here in my county and got away with it?"

Corey remained standing, speechless.

"We're going by the book on this one. I'll take you back to the station after the ER visit, so we can sort it all out. And when we get there, you can call one of your people down in Pepin. One way or another, either tonight or tomorrow morning after posting bail, they'll need to come pick you up."

Sheriff Coles motioned for Corey to walk toward the squad car. He obliged then abruptly halted.

"My stuff! It's in the trunk of the rental."

"Don't worry. I'll get it." Sheriff Coles put his hand on Corey's shoulder, urging him toward the vehicle. He opened the door to the back seat of the squad car, and Corey slipped inside. He watched from there as Sheriff Coles walked back down the embankment to retrieve Corey's belongings, both the packed items from the trunk and the now-scattered personal items up front. He deposited them into the trunk of the squad car and slammed the compartment shut, making the entire vehicle shudder.

Sheriff Coles got into the driver's seat and closed the door. He programmed something into the dashboard computer, glancing back at Corey over his shoulder as if to see if Corey were reading what Coles had written.

"Buckle up, California boy. You're going for a ride."

Corey looked out the back window as the sheriff's car pulled away from the gravel shoulder. He surveyed the damage to his rental car, thankful that he seemed to be relatively okay but worried sick about having to call the rental place and then his insurance agent, too. The ride lasted ten minutes but felt like thirty. He fondled his phone and re-checked the long list of unanswered calls and messages. He was tempted to listen to the voice mails but didn't want to raise suspicions from Sheriff Coles, who repeatedly glanced at Corey through the rear-view mirror. They arrived at the hospital and parked in a specially marked space adjacent to the emergency room door. After entering the hospital, Sheriff Coles stood uncomfortably close to Corey as the receptionist took down key information. Then, they sat next to each other in the lobby while waiting for a nurse to call Corey's name.

"May I make a phone call? I'm allowed one, right?"

The sheriff laughed. "Call whoever you want. You're not under arrest, at least not yet."

Corey didn't see the humor in Sheriff Coles' reply and didn't share in the laughter. Instead, he pulled out his cell phone and dialed Ginny's number.

"Corey, oh my God. Are you all right?"

"Yes. Well, not exactly. I had a minor accident." From the corner of his eye, Corey could see the sheriff raise his eyebrows and smirk.

"An accident? Are you hurt?"

"No, Mom. I'm fine, but the rental car is a mess."

"Where are you? What happened?"

"I swerved to avoid hitting a deer. I'm in Barron County near our old cabin."

Silence filled the other end of the call for several seconds, a pause during which Corey could visualize his mother taking in the news before she spoke. "Thank God you're okay. What can I do to help?"

"It looks like I'm going to need a ride." Corey saw Sheriff Coles begin to say something but then close his lips without uttering a word.

"Of course. I'll leave right away."

"Thank you, Mom. I'm at the hospital." Once more, Corey looked at Sheriff Coles, his eyes imploring the sheriff to confirm or contradict that they would still be here at the hospital when Ginny arrived, rather than at the station or in the county jail. Sheriff Coles stayed silent, not looking up from his own phone. "I'll text you the address. And please take your time."

Corey took a deep breath, then made two more calls—one to the rental car company's toll-free number and then to his own insurance company. The second of those two calls felt like *déjà vu,* for Corey found himself repeating the exact same story and answering many of the exact same questions. He was relieved at the kindness in the voices of the people at the other end of each call. Neither expressed judgment; both conveyed empathy for all that Corey had apparently been through. Between the two companies, Corey was assured that the car would be towed and all appropriate adjustments made. He turned down both representatives' offers of a replacement car; he would be much happier and safer riding with his mother from here on out.

No more than a minute after ending that last call, a nurse summoned Corey to an exam room. Sheriff Coles followed him inside. The nurse ran every standard test—blood pressure, heart rate, body temperature—and then asked Corey to change into a hospital gown for a full-body exam. As she went to leave the room so Corey could change, Sheriff Coles indicated that he would stay, then instructed the nurse to also return with a BAC test kit. Unless Corey objected, the sheriff would need the nursing staff to administer a blood alcohol test.

"Standard procedure," he said with a wink.

The nurse and the sheriff both looked at Corey for confirmation. He looked back at them like a deer in headlights.

"Of course, you're free to refuse, but that will be used as evidence if we charge you with a DUI."

Corey looked to the nurse for help, but she stood expressionless at the threshold holding open the door.

"Sure, I guess. I mean, I did have one drink. But I know I was sober enough to drive."

"Good choice," the sheriff replied as the ER nurse left the room and the door banged shut.

* * *

An hour later, Corey and the sheriff walked out of the ER exam room. Corey had a fresh bandage on his temple and carried a small bottle of prescription-strength ibuprofen.

"Thank you, officer. I can wait for my mother alone in the lobby."

"Oh, but I have a few questions for you, Corey. You didn't think we were done just yet, did you?"

Corey frowned and shook his head no.

"Good. My office has a designated room right over here past the entrance to the ER." Todd pointed toward a door marked *Barron County Sheriff – Official Personnel Only.* "We'll have our chat in there. You want some coffee?"

"Tea, if they have it."

"Of course, you want tea and not coffee. You prefer herbal, right? How could I forget from our last time together?"

Corey threw Coles a quizzical look. The sheriff laughed.

"You're the only person I've ever interrogated who asked for hot tea while in the hot seat. I thought that was the damnedest thing." More laughter. "You go on in. I'll be right back with your tea."

Corey walked toward the designated door, turned the knob and was surprised to find it unlocked. He hoped it would be as easy to exit that room later as it was to enter. Inside stood a plain metal table with two matching chairs, one on each side. A one-way mirror filled the wall on the far end of the room. He also recognized his cardboard box sitting in one corner and wondered when or how Coles had managed to bring it inside. Corey wheeled his roller bag over to the chair, letting it rest against the back wall. He decided to stand until the sheriff returned. The idea of sitting down made him feel guilty as if he had done something wrong.

He remembered that feeling well—guilty, and that he had indeed done something wrong. It certainly described his previous interrogation with Sheriff Coles. At least that session occurred in the somewhat comfortable confines of the Pepin police station, with Larry Preston by his side. Corey remembered Sheriff Coles' aggression in that first interrogation and his thoroughness, too. He had covered every possible angle, including Corey's movements before, during and after the altercation with Nick in the woods.

Back then, Corey told the story as Larry had coached him, and mostly true to the facts. Coles spent painstaking minutes on the time leading up to Corey shooting Nick—their arguments, Nick whacking Corey on the head with the flashlight, and what went through his mind in the exact second he pulled the trigger. Throughout that interrogation, Corey's thoughts had involuntarily drifted to the truck stop in southern Minnesota later that same night—the second time Corey pulled the trigger to shoot someone, and that time with dire consequences. But Sheriff Coles' relentless questioning of the Barron County shooting at least forced Corey's mind back to the first shooting that day.

The door sprung open, and Corey jumped. Sheriff Coles entered the room and handed Corey a Styrofoam cup with a dangling tea bag and barely warm water. He walked to the far end of the table and dropped a pen and notepad on top of it. Corey looked at the clock on the wall, realizing that he had been alone with his thoughts in this sparsely furnished room for thirty minutes.

"Have a seat, Corey."

He did. Sheriff Coles did too.

"Most people around here say *thank you* when someone hands them a free drink."

"Sorry. Thank you very much."

"You a little nervous?"

"I guess. Still a little shook up from the accident, that's all. I didn't see the deer until it was too late."

"Yeah, about that deer. Buck or a doe?"

"I'm, uh, not sure."

"You don't know the difference? I thought you were a big-time hunter with your family cabin up here and all."

"Of course, I do. I just don't remember if the damn thing had antlers or not. It happened so fast."

"I see. Where were you coming from again?"

"The Foxtails Lounge. I stopped to get a bite to eat after visiting our old cabin."

"Your old cabin?"

"Yes, my mother sold it recently. I wanted to see it one last time."

"Huh. So, what did you eat?"

"Excuse me?"

"At the Foxtails? Not that they're known for fine cuisine."

"I didn't eat anything."

"You said you stopped there for a bite."

"I did, but after a couple beverages, I realized I was running late getting on the road to Pepin, so I skipped the food."

"Corey, this will go a lot smoother if you tell the truth the first time. All right?"

"Yes, of course. I guess I wasn't very precise."

"So, what did you have to drink over there—*precisely?*"

"I started with a Diet Coke." Corey paused and looked away from the sheriff. Did he really have a drink, after all these years? Yes, and he remembered why—the discovery that he has a half-sister, Sam. He looked up to see Sheriff Coles staring back at him with a raised eyebrow.

"Where did you go, Corey? You looked pretty deep in thought there for a minute."

"Oh, just trying to remember the sequence of events tonight, that's all."

"I see. So, a soda? Sounds very fancy-boyish. You sure that's all you had over there at the Foxtails?"

"No. If you'll let me finish. I said I started with a cola. The bartender, she offered me something stronger, it being happy hour and all."

"Who's she, Samantha?"

Corey again looked away, this time briefly toward the ceiling before once more locking stares with Todd Coles. "Yes, I think that was her name."

"Good. Depending on how your blood alcohol test results come back, I may pay Sam a visit to corroborate your story."

"That's fine."

"Oh, well, thanks for your permission." The sheriff made a few notes on the yellow pad in front of him. Corey awkwardly tried not to read it. Coles finally looked up with an inquisitive mien.

"Something else I remember about our prior interrogation, Corey." He paused for what Corey deemed an unnecessary dramatic effect. "That you don't drink, or at least you didn't back then."

"I don't, usually."

"So, only when you're out driving at dusk in unfamiliar places? Not a good strategy, my friend."

"Look, I had one drink. That's the honest to God truth. I'm sure both the bartender and the blood test will confirm it." Just as he said it, Corey remembered ordering then slamming the second drink. He wasn't about to change his story now, though.

"Okay, okay. Don't get all testy. This is standard procedure." Coles wrote a few more notes.

"Corey Flanagan. Tell me about that."

"You mean my last name?"

"Yes. And also, why you're living in California now."

"After the last time we met, I lived with my mother in Pepin for about a year. I wasn't going back to Minneapolis, given how badly things ended with Nick, not to mention the discovery that I was single and without much savings. My best friend Billy kept hounding me to move out to Southern California where he lives— to make a clean start. One day I decided, what the heck, and did."

"Your best friend Billy? Sounds cozy."

"It's not like that!"

"Geez, don't get bent out of shape. I'm just messing with you."

Sheriff Coles' look changed from playful to impatient. "And the name change? What was that about?"

"Again, I wanted a fresh start. And that included a symbolic break from being my father's son. The only thing about him I still carried was his last name. With some help from my lawyer, I got it changed."

The questioning endured for another thirty minutes. They went over every detail of the accident and the hours leading up to it. Sheriff Coles was as thorough as he was the last time. Suddenly there was a knock at the door. The sheriff yelled, "Come in."

The same nurse who had treated Corey earlier stuck her head inside. "Ginny Fischer is here. She said she's supposed to pick up Mr. Flanagan?" Corey felt hope rising within his gut. "And I have the BAC test results." The nurse waved a stapled set of white papers back and forth inside the door. Corey's hopes faded.

"Great. Give me the report and tell Mrs. Fischer to hang tight in the lobby."

The nurse handed Sheriff Coles the papers, cast a straight-faced glance at Corey, then walked out of the room and shut the door.

Sheriff Coles perused each page of the packet, seemingly reading every sentence, every word and every syllable with great care.

"Huh. Looks like lightning can strike twice, at least for you, Corey. You are one lucky son of a bitch."

"I'm sorry?"

"Your test results came back below the legal limit—barely. And I've got no witnesses to contradict your alleged deer in the headlights story—at least not yet. Guess that means you've been involved in two spectacular debacles here in Barron County and will walk away from both smelling like a rose."

Corey was tempted to take the sheriff's bait, to angrily reply that he walked away from both debacles with deep wounds—from the first one with a ruined life and from this one with a damaged rental car. Instead, he recalled Larry's advice from the prior interrogation—keep your feelings in check, and only answer the exact question posed, succinctly.

"Am I free to go?"

Sheriff Coles looked at Corey with seeming contempt.

"Yes, you're free to go. But call the rental car company and have them get that wreck of a vehicle out of the ditch on my county road."

"Already done, sir."

"Good."

Corey pushed back from his chair, stood up and grabbed his roller bag. He walked toward the door as the sheriff stayed seated at the table.

"And Corey—Flanagan or Fischer or whatever your name is."

Corey stopped and turned to look at Sheriff Coles.

"You've caused enough damage in this county, fancy boy. I think it's best if you head back to California and not visit us here in Barron anymore. I would sure hate for your string of good luck to run out on you up here." He paused to rub his head. "And I'm getting tired of interrogating you, to be frank. Might be better if you and I don't cross paths again."

"No problem, sheriff. The feeling's mutual."

Chapter 13

As Corey emerged from the interrogation room, Ginny stood up from her chair. She waited as Corey approached her, pulling his roller bag.

"What happened to your head?"

Corey felt the bandage. "I jammed it against the window when my car hit the tree. But it's only superficial. Otherwise, I'm good."

"Thank God you're all right."

Ginny appeared to look him up and down before pulling him into a tight hug. He felt instant relief, consciously breathing deeply for the first time in hours.

"Mom, thank you for coming all this way. I'm sorry to be such a burden."

She released him but held his shoulders and gave him a knowing look.

"Okay, okay," he said. "I know. That's what mothers do."

They smiled at one another, then Ginny let go of his shoulders and curled her right arm under his left. "Come on, let's go home."

"Hey! You forgot something." Corey froze upon hearing the sheriff's voice behind him. He turned around to see Coles holding Corey's cardboard box of personal belongings from the Minneapolis condo. Coles stood still, forcing Corey to leave the roller bag with his mother and walk back toward the interrogation room. He wondered how long Sheriff Coles had stood there, watching

Corey hug his mom. A shiver ascended Corey's spine upon seeing a creepy half-smile on the sheriff's face.

"You don't want to leave this behind and have to come back here, right? Remember what I said about not returning to Barron County?"

Sheriff Coles held out the heavy box as Corey approached, then pretended as if he were about to toss it. Corey gasped and started to reach out. Sheriff Coles laughed.

"What did you think, I was going to throw it? You're a funny one, Fischer."

Corey resisted a smart retort. Just get out of here, he thought.

"Thank you, sheriff. I appreciate you bringing this to me before we left it behind." He reached out for the box, stiffly.

"Sure thing." Sheriff Coles looked beyond Corey, toward Ginny. "That your mother?"

"Yes."

"Shouldn't you introduce us?"

Corey didn't think he should, but the sheriff walked right past him toward Ginny and extended his hand.

"Mrs. Fischer?"

Ginny tepidly shook hands with Sheriff Coles. "Yes. Ginny."

"Pleasure to meet you, Ginny. I'm Sheriff Todd Coles, the officer who responded at the scene and pulled your son from the wreck."

Corey walked toward his mother, still holding the cardboard box. He wanted to short-circuit this conversation, to get on the road toward Pepin as quickly as possible.

"Thank you very much, officer. I appreciate you taking my son here to get looked after."

"Oh, we more than looked after him, ma'am. The staff here stitched up and bandaged Corey's head. Then he and I had a little chat about the accident and the dangers of drinking and driving."

Corey looked to his mother for reaction, then saw it and closed his eyelids in shame.

"Are you charging him with something, officer?"

"Apparently not, or at least not yet. Looks like he got away with another one here in our county."

"I beg your pardon?" Corey detected defiance in Ginny's tone, something he had rarely heard before.

Sheriff Coles seemed taken aback. "I'm referring to the 2013 firearms incident where Corey shot Nicholas Parker at your family's cabin, and how we never arrested him for anything because Parker decided not to press charges, despite how hard I urged him to do so."

"Yes, I'm aware. What does that have to do with today, sir?" Ginny asked.

"Well, technically nothing, but . . ."

Ginny interrupted. "Good. I guess we'll be on our way then. Thank you, officer."

She grabbed the handle of Corey's roller bag and motioned with her head toward the door.

"Come on, Corey. Let's go home."

* * *

She drove just under the speed limit, heading south out of Barron County. Corey sat silently in the passenger seat, calculating how to begin the inevitable conversation. It was Ginny who broke the quiet.

"Well, he certainly is a charming man."

Corey wanted to laugh but couldn't summon the energy. "Indeed."

"I gather he's the same officer who questioned you last time?"

Last time. Corey winced at those words.

"Yes. The one and only Sheriff Todd Coles—keeper of law and order in the Wisconsin north woods." Corey shook his head and bit his lip.

Ginny shook hers too. "I certainly didn't appreciate his tone, but maybe it's best to stay out of that county, as he advised."

"Hmmm." Corey hoped she wouldn't ask more questions. He wanted to rid his mind of Todd Coles' image as fast as possible and never think of that man again.

"So why were you in Barron, Corey? I thought you planned on driving straight home from the Twin Cities."

He took a deep breath. How much should he share? How much of this shitty day should he keep to himself? He didn't answer. He looked out the passenger side window but mostly saw a dark landscape, the sun having set more than an hour before. Surely his mother would let him off the hook, give him time to respond. She was patient that way, always allowing him to answer tough questions when he was ready.

"I think you owe me an explanation." Ginny cast him a stern look before returning her gaze toward the road.

Corey looked over at his mom.

"Yes, that was the plan. And then I veered a little off course." He turned his eyes again to the landscape outside the window before continuing to speak, in part to answer Ginny's questions and in part to answer his own. "I don't have a great explanation, Mom. I was driving on 94 and saw the exit for Barron. I was ahead of schedule for arriving in Pepin. Something inside drew me toward the cabin." He gestured toward his chest. "I don't know. Maybe it had to do with seeing Nick again for the first time since leaving him for dead in the woods. I fled the cabin in such a panic two years ago, leaving behind an unfinished mess."

"I told you the cabin was sold, Corey. I went up there myself to gather the last of our family things. There was nothing left for you to do."

"I know, Mom, I know." He closed his eyes and felt pangs of guilt deep in his gut. Ginny had been forced to do the very tasks she had asked of him four years earlier, to get the Fischer family cabin ready for sale by retrieving the few framed pictures and Frank's remaining personal belongings.

Corey couldn't explain his compulsion to return to the scene of his first crime, so he didn't. "I drove to the cabin and walked around the property one last time. I tried to get inside, but the door was locked, and the key wasn't hidden in its usual place."

"I removed it last summer. The real estate agent asked me to give him all copies."

"Makes sense. Anyway, I peered through the back door curtains and saw that the interior had been stripped down to its impersonal core, ready for strangers." Corey uttered a half-laugh. "Weird. I never liked the damn place, never wanted to go there."

Ginny interrupted. "Yes, I recall. Clearly."

Corey looked away from the passing scenery toward his mother. She had changed since Frank's death, and not only in appearance. She was bolder now, neither as deferential nor silent as she had been for the past forty-plus years—for Corey's entire life. Then again, he recalled her story about throwing a brick into that woman's window. Though it made him a bit uncomfortable at this moment, he welcomed these changes, for Ginny's sake. Maybe for both of their sakes. He continued his explanation.

"Once I couldn't get inside, I left. As I drove away from the cabin, I realized I hadn't eaten anything since breakfast. I was hungry for something greasy."

Ginny laughed for the first time since arriving in Barron, just as Corey expected. "That was one of your father's sayings—made me laugh every time."

Corey laughed as well. It felt good to release a bit of the tension. "Yeah, me too."

For a few moments, there was no conversation, but thoughts swirled in Corey's mind. Surely, he should tell her the rest of the story. But the question was—how much? From the corner of his eye, he watched as the smile slowly left Ginny's face, then he continued talking.

"After leaving the cabin, I remembered a bar and grill Dad took me to years ago. I was only there once but remembered it was on the way toward home." That wasn't entirely true. "I pulled up and went in."

"What's the name of the place? I stopped at a nice café last summer when I drove up with Shirley Claussen to clean out the cabin. Maybe it was the same place?" Corey was certain it wasn't.

"Uh, I can't even remember the name now. The Cattails Pub or something like that. Anyway, I stopped for a bite and a drink." He paused to let that last detail sink in.

"What kind of drink, Corey?"

Though he fudged other details and had decided to hide the most important one, this answer he felt obliged to give—fully, honestly and with haste.

"I started with a soda, then eventually switched to something stronger."

"You were drinking? Oh Corey, is that why you crashed your car?"

"I had one." Corey paused to think, remembering his vow of honesty. "Well, two, actually."

"With all of the progress you made after your hospitalization in 2012? Why?"

The answer was on the tip of his tongue, but he couldn't summon the courage to say it out loud. "I guess seeing Nick again after all this time brought back a lot of hurtful memories and old triggers. It consumed me on the drive from Minneapolis, and I snapped."

"Did something unpleasant happen during the condo closing with Nick? Did he say something to get under your skin?"

"No, nothing like that. He was cordial, in fact—even a bit on the nice side."

"Then I don't understand why you became upset to the point of going to a bar and ordering a drink when you know damn well you shouldn't."

Corey's mouth dropped upon hearing his mother curse.

"Fine. I guess there was one thing." He paused, then continued. "Nick told me he's moving in with Evan. Remember him? The same asshole Nick was with in Miami the night of the big blowup between me and Dad in Pepin, the last night I ever saw or spoke to him again." If Ginny could swear in front of him now, then Corey wouldn't hold back either. "Evan's the guy Nick repeatedly denied having an affair with for years. *Evan's married to a woman* Nick would mockingly tell me in his fucked-up effort to gaslight me. Evan apparently divorced his wife earlier this year and made a miraculous conversion to couple with Nick. Now they're moving in together. How about that?"

Ginny stayed quiet for a moment, letting the explanation sink in.

"I know you went through a lot in your life and that your relationship with Nick had its issues, to say the least. But you're forty-two years old, Corey. At some point, you need to grow up and realize that despite whatever gets thrown at you, you control your own reactions. Not anyone else, just you."

"I know, I know."

"Do you still want Nick wielding that kind of power over you? Where one piece of news about someone from your past makes you throw away the progress you've made, the person you've become?"

"No, of course not. I know better than that. It's just . . ."

"Instead of dwelling on what you've lost, Corey, or how you've been hurt by someone who simply doesn't matter anymore, maybe you should put your energy into fighting to win back Miguel."

Corey gripped the side of his seat—tight. There's no way Ginny could have seen his gesture of tension and regret, though Corey's silence probably said just as much. Miguel. Corey had barely thought of him since their phone call earlier in the day. And who knows if focusing on Miguel would have done any good in the wake of the news sending Corey into today's downward spiral? Corey had a half-sister. Samantha. A woman who carried many of Corey's same genes. Yet he didn't even know her last name or her age or where she lived. He didn't know her dreams, her fears or about her childhood. He gripped the seat harder, in frustration over his own selfishness in racing out of the Foxtails Lounge. He had been driven by the sudden fear of what the discovery of a half-sister meant to him. But maybe Samantha's existence had nothing to do with him at all. Maybe Frank's failings were only about Frank. Corey and Samantha did have that in common at the very least—they both had a selfish father.

Ginny's voice broke the silence. "Corey, I'm sorry. I said too much. I was surprised and upset. I do understand how the news about Nick and Evan would be unsettling, confirming all you had suspected across the years."

Corey looked over at his mother and waited for her to glance at him before replying.

"Everything you said was fair, Mom. I do need to grow up and stop taking everything so personally as if the world and the bastards in it are out to get me. It's funny." Corey paused to utter a half-laugh. "You mentioned Miguel, and that's exactly what he's been telling me all along—to stop taking things so personally, to live in the present moment and simply be myself, to let the rest of the world be damned."

"That's not bad advice, honey. I could follow a bit of it myself."

"You don't need advice from anyone, Mom. From what I can tell, you're doing fine. You've changed quite a bit since Dad died— for the better."

"Oh?" Ginny sounded surprised.

"Yes. Or at least you've been showing a part of yourself that I hadn't seen before. You speak your mind, you travel and you have a quiet confidence that is more obvious every time we speak. That's not how I perceived you growing up, no offense. Either you changed, or you are finally letting your true self shine. Regardless, it's a good look on you, Mom. I could benefit by following your lead."

Ginny nodded. She glanced over at Corey then back toward the road ahead. They would arrive in Pepin within the hour. "Thank you. I'm proud of myself too. I'm not proud of everything I put up with in my past, but I'm more than okay with who I am now."

"Good. You should be."

They rode along quietly for a while. Corey stared out the window, watching as the landscape segued from coniferous north woods to small towns and farms marked by bright yard lights atop tall poles. His mind drifted toward his meditative calming place—art. He thought about the works in progress sitting on his easel back home in California. And he thought once more about

Edward Hopper. In particular, the small town depicted in *Early Sunday Morning* and the white farmhouse on a lonely country road in *Route 6 Eastham*. Though such works were painted out East, they could easily have been inspired by virtually the same landscape rolling past him as their car sped toward Pepin.

Corey secretly hoped to have a professional breakthrough someday. He might never attain Hopper's fame, but he could hope for attention. After all, Hopper struggled for years before being noticed. They had more in common, too. Hopper was allegedly introverted and quiet with a gentle sense of humor; his works displayed unpredictable settings and a suggestion of melancholy. One of Hopper's famous quotes summed up Corey's own philosophy about art, and life. When asked to describe himself and his personal life, Hopper said *the whole answer is there on the canvas.*

Ginny slowed the car to thirty-five as they entered the town of Stockholm, fewer than ten miles from home. Corey smiled, remembering all his trips here as a kid to view local artisans' works. For a few years, he had submitted his own paintings in the annual Stockholm Art Fair. He noticed a familiar building on the corner.

"You know what this reminds me of?"

"What's that, honey?"

"You see that store back there on the corner?"

Ginny looked into the rear-view mirror. "Which one, the gas station?"

"No, on the opposite corner."

"Sorry, I missed it. What about that store?"

"It used to be a candy and ice cream shop. We passed by it all the time when I was a kid. I begged Dad to stop every time, but he never did. After a while, I stopped asking."

"You know how your father was—always in a hurry to get wherever he was going."

"Hmmm, that's true." Corey remembered that car rides with Frank were often tense or uncomfortably quiet. The only conversations were prompted by Frank when he wanted to talk. Even then, the topics were limited to Frank's interests—hunting, football and his work at the bank.

"But you took me there once. It was that time Dad was off at his insurance conference somewhere. Dallas, I think. I remember it because for once, he flew for an out-of-town trip and left the car behind for us."

"I remember that week." Ginny stayed focused on the road ahead, but a wide grin enveloped her face. "We had fun together if I remember right."

"For sure. You gave me rides to and from school every day. That was unique."

"And we drove across the river one night to Red Wing. We ate at that Liberty House place. They always did have good food."

"They sure did. I remember stuffing myself on the pork ribs special."

"It was a splurge, something Frank would rarely do."

"And on the way home, we stopped at that sweet shop back there. You bought me a triple scoop, and I got to pick out three different favors. At the time, I thought I had never tasted anything so good in my whole life."

"I think it's okay to spoil your children, occasionally. Lord knows I had some making up to do for all the times Frank never did."

"Do you remember how upset Dad got when we weren't home to answer the phone until long past supper time?"

"Oh yes. I heard about that a few times over. I felt bad making up an untrue story."

"About us being hard at work out in the garden and not hearing the telephone ringing inside the house?"

Ginny laughed. "Yes. I think it was your idea, wasn't it? I didn't feel entirely right encouraging you to tell a fib. But to tell you the truth now, I have no regrets."

"Me neither. None."

In a few minutes, they would be pulling into the garage at 123 Pine Street. Corey was never so glad in his life to anticipate arriving there. He sent an anticipatory text to Miguel, letting him know that Pepin was on the horizon and that Corey would call him with an update tomorrow. Miguel's affirming reply included a red heart and a few words. *With Mom now. Procedure went well. Talk tomorrow. Can't wait!*

Ginny spoke just as Corey finished reading the text.

"Corey, is there anything else you need to tell me about today? Anything at all?"

He looked out the window, thinking about all that he had still not revealed. But he had been through too much drama and emotion today already. He didn't have the energy to explain the accident to Miguel or the discovery of Samantha to his mom. Both of those things could wait one more day without consequence. What Corey wanted right now were a hot bath and his mother's home cooking. He turned to look back at Ginny.

"No, Mom, not now. But I know you'll be there when I need to say more."

Chapter 14

"It sure looked bigger when I was a kid."

Corey's voice echoed against the four walls of his childhood bedroom and bounced on the hardwood floor now emptied of furniture and half-full of boxes. Ginny had sold the guest room furniture and packed up photographs and other memorabilia for sorting.

"It's still hard to believe you're moving. Guess I never pictured you living anywhere else."

"We were here a long time—almost forty years. Where did the time go? But I'm not listing until spring. That gives me time to sort through four decades worth of stuff."

Ginny led him to the basement, where most of their weekend work lay ahead. Frank owned so many tools, kept so many scraps of wood and hunting gear and who knows what else.

"I don't expect you'll want to keep anything from down here, though you're welcome to it. But I need your help figuring out what to throw, what to keep and what goes to charity."

"I wouldn't be anywhere else, Mom. Between us, we'll get through it in no time."

Ginny's smile caught him in the heart, and tears blurred his vision. She had begun planning to sell the house immediately after returning home from her recent visit to LA. It was on that trip when the idea first came to her. The house was paid for, and Frank's estate settled long ago. She had donated all Franks' clothes. Four years after his death, Ginny was flush with cash and low on purpose. Friends and neighbors who had been so comforting and generous in the months following the funeral had fallen away, one by one. Shock, pain and empathy subside. People get on with their lives. It was time Ginny did as well.

She had been making twice-weekly drives to Eau Claire to visit overnight with her aging mother, taking turns with her sisters, who lived nearby. When Ginny was invited to move in with her divorced sister three houses down from her mother, it felt like the right thing to do for the next stage of her life.

"Get a load of this collection of awls and woodworking tools."

"Yes, your father certainly had a talent for carving wood. He made all of the shelves we used to have upstairs, you know."

"Yes, he reminded me every time I refused to let him teach me the craft, father to son. These look like they can still be used. I'll place them in the pile for charity."

"Okay." Ginny moved on to another box.

"Mom, are you sure you're going to be able to live with your sister? I know you two are close, but won't you feel like you're living in her space?"

"To be honest, I am concerned about that. But I'll have my own bedroom and bath. I guess we'll see how it goes. If it doesn't work out, I'll buy or rent a place of my own."

"So, you'll give it a try. That's great, Mom."

"And how about you, Corey? Do you think you might be getting a roommate soon?"

"Subtle, Mom. Very nice."

"Well, are you?"

"Miguel and I haven't talked about it, but I suppose it's a possibility. That is if we reconcile first."

"That's good. I worry about you out there all alone."

"Right back at you, Mom. I've been worrying about you here all by yourself since Dad died."

"Oh, I'll be fine. Say, Corey, come here for a second, please. I want to check something out."

He obliged, setting down the rusted hand saw he had been contemplating, depositing it into the junk pile.

"Give me your hand."

He did, meeting her in front of the wood stove where she now stood. Ginny took his hand then pulled her son lightly down toward the floor. He suddenly realized what she was doing.

"I want to compare then versus now."

"Geez, I forgot all about that. Funny what leaves your mind and rarely returns." He let go of her hand, splaying his fingers outward then reaching for the indented handprint left by his six-year-old self in the cement at the base of the stove. "Yup, guess I've grown quite a bit since then."

"That's for sure. Now you're about the same size as your father's, maybe bigger."

Corey looked at Frank's print adjacent to his own. "I guess the Fischer men left their mark on this house, permanently. Why didn't we have you dip your hand in the cement back then too?"

"Oh, I was probably upstairs cooking while you guys installed the stove and poured the cement. Hopefully, I left my mark on this house in some other way."

"No doubt, Mom. You certainly did on me. All my best memories of this house are the times I spent alone with you."

They embraced tightly, with Ginny smiling wide and closing her eyes.

"Come on, Corey. That's enough work for one day. Let me buy you dinner downtown at the café. Then, tomorrow morning, it's time for me to show you what I asked you to come back to Wisconsin to see."

* * *

After returning from dinner, both Ginny and Corey declared themselves exhausted and ready to turn in. With his old bedroom now devoid of furniture, Corey descended the stairs to the basement where Ginny had made up the spare sofa bed, piling on blankets to supplement the warmth emanating from the wood stove nearby. Corey stripped to his T-shirt and shorts, brushed his teeth, then happily climbed under the covers. He thought about reading but instead pulled out his phone and dialed Miguel.

"Hey! I was just thinking about calling you."

"You were?"

"Yeah. I'm at my sister's house. We had some extended family members over for dinner. Some of them are still downstairs, but I said my goodnights and came up to bed. How about you?"

"Same."

"You sound tired. Did your mom's surprise wear you out?"

"No, she's saving that for tomorrow, apparently. I have no idea what it is."

"Nice."

"How's your mother doing?"

"Not sure, to be honest. The tests they ran yesterday came back abnormal, but they don't know why. Tomorrow they plan to sedate her and send a probe down her throat to take close-up pictures of her heart. They suspect that might be the source of the problem. I guess we'll know soon enough."

"Wow. That sounds serious. I'll say a prayer for her tonight."

"Thanks, Corey."

"Listen, Miguel. I need to tell you something, but I don't want to burden you and don't want you to worry. I'm fine. Everything will be fine."

"You're not a burden. I could probably use a distraction. What's going on?"

Once again, he risked telling Miguel the truth—all of it. He spoke about the detour to Barron County and getting into an accident that totaled his rental car, sending him to the hospital.

"I'm so sorry, handsome. I wish I could be there to help."

"Thank you. I'd like that, too. But you're where you need to be right now. And Miguel, there's something else."

"Oh?"

After taking a deep breath, Corey told Miguel about his decision to drink again after all these sober years. For a moment, Corey told only that detail and not the reasons leading to it. He wanted to take ownership of his choice. Yes, the discovery of his probable half-sister had triggered old coping patterns. But Ginny was right when she said on yesterday's long drive that Corey should have known better and could have chosen more wisely.

Then, he told Miguel about Sam.

"Wow, Corey. I don't know what to say. That's certainly a lot to deal with."

The conversation segued to Corey's plan for telling Ginny. Miguel provided some thoughts on a gentle approach, but he mostly listened as Corey worked through how he thought it best to break the news to his mom that her dead husband had fathered a child with another woman. On the one hand, at least the cheating would come to her as no surprise, given what she had revealed to Corey on her visit to California. But the idea of Frank having another child felt wholly different. In the end, Corey couldn't predict how Ginny would react.

"I admire you, Corey."

Miguel's declaration surprised him.

"In what way?"

"You've had a day like few others, or maybe like no one has had, yet you're showing more empathy for your mom than dwelling on your own needs or hurts. Between that shocking news and then the accident, you've been through a lot. Yes, you shouldn't have had those drinks, but thankfully you are all right. You'll be all right, Corey. I believe that."

Miguel's words made Corey feel understood and loved, even though Miguel hadn't uttered that word to Corey in weeks.

"Thank you. I don't deserve your kindness, but I appreciate it very much."

"You do deserve it, Corey. We all do."

Corey silently shook his head, yes.

"If I were there, I'd give you a long, tight hug. Instead, I'm sending it through the phone. Did it arrive? Can you feel it?"

Corey smiled. "Oh, yes. I can feel it. Thank you for listening, Miguel."

"Of course. You've listened to my worries and stress with Mom. That's what people in our situation should be doing for each other."

Corey felt tempted to ask what situation they were in but quickly decided it best to save that question for another day. Instead, what welled up inside him surprised Corey—a desire to tell Miguel even more. This was the second conversation with Miguel in which Corey had revealed painful secrets and corrected outright lies. In the first conversation back in Corey's apartment, after Miguel had intercepted the call from Nick, Corey spoke forthrightly about that earlier relationship and its disastrous end, as well as Corey's difficult history with Frank. Then tonight, Corey revealed another personal failure—falling off the wagon. He also shared his newly inflicted wounds—the accident and meeting Sam. In both conversations, Miguel had remained calm, only asking questions to clarify but seemingly not to judge. Although the first conversation led to their current though lessening estrangement, Corey understood that Miguel was someone he could trust with the worst skeletons in his closet, even a horrible one that Corey had never spoken about with anyone at all.

"Miguel, if you have another minute, I need to tell you something more."

"Sure, but I can't imagine your day could have held anything more challenging than what I've just heard."

Slowly, methodically, honestly and chronologically, Corey told Miguel every dreadful detail about the night that he briefly met Bennett Jackson. He spoke for ten minutes, pausing twice to check that Miguel was still on the other end of the line.

"I'm here."

Corey went on. Finally, he had told the full story, including the sickening realization that he had accidentally cut short another person's life. After that, his voice went quiet, and he waited for Miguel to respond.

"Why did you tell me this, Corey, rather than anyone else? And why now?"

Corey had no rehearsed answer; he had not planned on making this confession when their phone call began. Instead, he said aloud what came into his mind, trying his best not to filter his words through a strainer to catch those extra details that cast Corey in an even worse light. For the past few weeks, Corey explained that he had experienced the fear of losing Miguel for good, and that possibility was far more painful than the current wound on his head. Corey said that he wanted to have a future with Miguel, but only one that was based on truth. Though he knew this carried risk, he had learned from their recent encounter that the greater risk was to be exposed for lying about his failings. If he had any hope of reconciliation with the man he truly loved, this was the time to divulge the worst thing he'd ever done, the consequences to himself be damned.

An awkward silence filled the cell phone connection as Corey waited for Miguel to speak. He thanked Corey for this shocking honesty and expressed that he would need time and space to digest all that he had heard, to which Corey said, "Of course." Miguel then asked questions that revealed his innate empathy more than judgment. How was Corey coping with this burden, despite that he never had an intent to harm? What did Corey think was the right thing to do after all this time? And did Corey ever think about coming forward to tell his story, to provide Bennett's family with some possible semblance of closure, despite the reality that Bennett was as responsible for what happened as was Corey?

Miguel also encouraged Corey to find either a lawyer or a priest if he felt compelled to expiate his guilt. Confessing to Miguel was good, but perhaps Corey needed more, possibly even turning himself in. While Miguel promised never to betray his confidence, the greater concern to Miguel was Corey's long-term mental health. "I don't have any experience in this area, but I suspect this kind of life trauma and guilt tortures some people until it is either judged or absolved in the light of day."

Corey didn't disagree. Down deep, he knew Miguel was right. Unless and until he confronted and owned up to what he had done, there would be no peace, no respite from his frequent nightmares. Corey vowed to Miguel that he would approach Larry Preston tomorrow evening when Larry returned with Billy from his appointment at the Mayo. Surely Larry would prove as receptive a listener as Miguel, yet again. And hopefully provide wise advice on what Corey might do next.

After the phone call ended, Corey lay awake for hours. He tried to sleep but got no significant rest. His eyes never remained shut for more than an hour at a time. He replayed the conversation with Miguel in his mind, then focused on what he would say to Billy's father the next day, provided Larry was even strong enough to hear Corey out. He tried prayer; he began meditation. But nothing brought him peace. He stoked the fire in the wood stove into the wee hours of the morning, awaiting daylight to penetrate the basement windows and the sound of his mother's footsteps on the floors above his head.

* * *

Ginny asked Corey to drive as they left the house at ten the next morning. He needed no directions, and they soon arrived at Calvary Cemetery on a hill outside of town. The front gate was open. He steered the car off the pavement and onto the two-track gravel drive. He admired the ivy-covered steel canopy with the graveyard's name as they drove underneath. Towering hardwood trees fenced in the cemetery, the resilient oaks still casting a canopy of shade across much of it.

"You're going to have to remind me where the plot is. It all looks different from the day of his funeral. I don't remember where he's buried."

"Over there, near that walnut tree." She pointed straight through the front window. He pulled the car up to the tree, then turned off the engine and waited for his mother's lead in stepping outside.

He saw his parents' memorial stone as soon as he slammed the door shut. Steel-cut granite, a dark shade of gray. They walked over to it. There was a large cross etched into the middle of the monument, and the names of the Fischers on either side, above the dates of their births and deaths. For Ginny, of course, the latter was only a smooth, yet-to-be carved space.

"This is it. What do you think?"

"It's beautiful, Mom. You did a nice job."

"It wasn't much of my own doing. It's the exact tombstone your father picked out when he first made his will." She paused and took in the affirming nod of Corey's head. "Well, with one exception."

"Oh?"

"Your father wanted our names inscribed on the front and his offspring's name on the back."

Corey's face contorted. *His offspring?* Did Ginny know about Samantha? Surely not.

He asked, "So, Dad wanted his children listed on the back, but you decided to leave me off? That's fine." He was speaking the truth in his heart, hoping he had guessed right.

"No, you're on there. Look."

Corey moved with hesitant anticipation to the other side of the stone, where he instantly saw his name, then looked up at Ginny and cocked his head in confusion.

"Your father's will specifically instructed that it say *parents of Corey Francis Fischer*, but I thought it should say *parents of Corey Flanagan* instead."

He shook his head and immediately choked up. "You're amazing, Mom, you know that?"

"I'm not so sure. Maybe I'm simply trying to make things right."

"This is a terrible thing I'm about to say, standing above the man's grave and all, but he didn't deserve you. He really didn't."

It was Ginny's turn to be consumed with emotion, but she said nothing.

"And I'll be sure to honor your wishes when the time comes, Mom, if this is where you would like your remains to go, too."

"Oh, heavens no, Corey. I'm not going to be buried here. Not a chance."

"What? I'm confused. Isn't your name on the stone next to Dad's?" Corey walked back around to the other side of the headstone to see if he had missed something significant.

"Yes, my name's on there, and they'll etch something in that blank space someday, but I'm not going to be buried here. I settled all of that when I met with Larry Preston. He finished drafting my new will, and I signed it in front of two witnesses."

Corey looked at his mother with keen expectation. He had no idea what might come out of her mouth next.

"I want to be cremated, Corey, then sprinkled in the ocean out where you live. I'm convinced you're never moving back. I want my last earthly act to have my ashes scattered near you—if that's okay."

"Of course." He was too stunned to say more.

"I'm sure some people might think it's weird or disrespectful, but I couldn't care less. I gave the better part of my life to Frank Fischer. I want to spend the rest of your life near where you live, then eternity in the sunshine, floating out on the sea."

"I love it, Mom. Surprising for sure, but I love it."

"Let's go home, Corey. I can whip up a batch of pork chops in herb sauce in no time. It's my specialty, you know."

He began laughing even before Ginny playfully swatted him on the arm. "Yeah, so I've heard."

They walked back to the car, reminiscing over tales of Ginny's cooking across the years—both the successes and the flops. The most memorable ones were, of course, the flops. The incredible nachos she made one Superbowl Sunday that landed all over the living room carpet as she tripped trying to bring food over the kitchen threshold to Corey and Frank sitting in front of the TV. A pumpkin pie that everyone sunk their teeth into following the Thanksgiving meal, only to cringe one by one upon realizing that Ginny had forgotten one key ingredient—sugar. And both would forever remember her famous ginger snap cookies—the time Ginny accidentally grabbed and added cayenne instead of cinnamon from her alphabetically-organized spice rack.

"Those sure gave the term *burnt sugar cookies* a whole new meaning," Corey roared. "They stung on the way in and definitely on the way back out!"

They reached the car and got in. Ginny started the engine and drove out of the cemetery. They had run out of funny cooking memories for the moment and traveled for the first minute in silence. After passing by the Kwik Stop at the edge of town, marking re-entry into Pepin, Corey decided it was the right time to talk— to tell his mother what made him so upset deep in the woods of Barron County two days before.

"Mom, there's something I need to tell you."

"Oh?"

They traveled two blocks as Corey wrung his hands, Ginny patiently waiting for him to say more. She turned left off the main highway. They were only five blocks from home.

"It's about something I discovered in Barron County."

Ginny said nothing. Corey continued wringing his hands. Ginny turned the car right at Pine Street. They were three blocks from home.

"Remember how I told you I stopped for something to drink?"

"Yes."

"Well, there's a little more to it than that."

The car reached the corner of Pine and Pierce. The Fischer's home lay but one-half block ahead.

"You see . . ."

"Corey, wait. Look." Ginny kept her left hand on the steering wheel, the pointer finger on her right directing Corey's gaze to his childhood home. A pair of squad cars sat parked on either side of the driveway, and four uniformed officers were scattered along the house, peering into the windows or standing at the front and side doors.

"What in the world could they want?" Ginny asked.

Corey knew deep in his gut that it couldn't be good news. Ginny pulled into the driveway and used her remote button to open the garage door. She slowly steered the car inside, casting sideways glances at the officers who descended toward them, closing in. She turned off the engine then rolled down the driver's side window.

"Are we allowed to get out?"

Pepin County Sheriff George Stevens walked up to the passenger side window without answering Ginny. At six foot seven, George had to lean down to make eye contact with Corey through the window. He rapped on the glass and indicated with a circular motion of his hand that Corey should roll the window down, which he did.

"I'm going to need you to step out of the car, Corey." By moving his eyes and silent lips, Corey implored George Stevens with non-verbal cues for a sign of what was happening, but George didn't give up a single clue. "Come on out, Corey, Sheriff Coles drove down here from Barron. He needs to talk with you right away."

Corey unbuckled his seat belt, pulled the door lever open, and alighted from his mother's car. He noticed his phone still resting in the pocket of the passenger door but resisted reaching back to grab it. Something told him he was about to be separated from his phone regardless, and it would be safer in Ginny's care.

"George, for God's sake. What's going on?" Ginny demanded through the passenger window.

"Ginny, I think it's best for you to stay where you're at. This matter doesn't concern you. Well, at least not right now."

George gently grabbed Corey by the arm to assist him in rising from the car and helping shepherd him toward Sheriff Coles, who was standing on the cement driveway at the edge of the garage.

Ginny ignored George's instruction. She quickly unstrapped herself from the lap belt, opened the car door and hurried toward Corey's side. Barron County Deputy Ron Clifford intervened, placing his large body between Ginny and Corey.

"Ma'am, I'm going to need you to stay where you are. We need to talk to your son, and only him. Okay?"

"No, it's not okay."

"Ma'am, this is serious business. Your son is being arrested for murder, and you mustn't interfere."

Corey felt instantly faint, then collapsed. But for George Stevens catching him with his arms, Corey would have fallen completely to the ground.

"What? What are you talking about? He was cleared of all that business with Nick four years ago. No charges were filed. He was acting in self-defense, for God's sake."

Ginny turned her head away from the stoic Deputy Clifford, directing her plea instead toward George Stevens, a man whom she and the family had known for more than thirty years, a man who now held her one and only child.

"George, you were there. Tell them!"

"Ginny, it's not about that. Please, everything will be fine, eventually. We need to let these officers do their jobs."

Sheriff Coles walked briskly up to George Stevens and took physical custody of Corey before handing him over to Deputy Clifford. After letting go of Corey's arm, George immediately went to Ginny's side to try and calm her. Arresting one Fischer today was more than enough. Sheriff Coles took a pair of handcuffs from his belt and waited until Deputy Clifford turned Corey around, holding onto Corey's elbows which now hung behind him.

Coles quickly slapped the cuffs onto Corey's wrists, abruptly pushed them shut, then spun Corey back around. Coles wanted to look Corey directly in the eye, face-to-face, as he delivered the delicious series of words he had been dying to say for so long.

George Stevens wrapped his arm around Ginny's now-quivering shoulders. She let him and placed hers around his waist. Together, they listened to the unthinkable words that began to flow from the Barron County Sheriff's mouth.

"Corey Fischer?"

"Flanagan," he muttered.

"Doesn't matter. Corey Fischer or Flanagan or whatever your name is, you're under arrest for the murder of Bennett Jackson."

Sheriff Coles let the words sink in. Then he held up a flimsy piece of paper whose words Corey could not make out.

"These are extradition papers from Freeborn County, Minnesota. They've authorized me to place you under arrest and deliver you to the Freeborn County jail, where you will be turned over to authorities in that jurisdiction to be prosecuted for killing a man in cold blood."

Ginny looked at Corey. Corey couldn't look anywhere but down to the ground.

"I guess third time's the charm, eh fancy boy?"

Corey refused to look up, either at Sheriff Coles or to his mom.

"Looks like that blood test you took in my county two days ago triggered a hit on the federal unsolved crimes database. Can you imagine the luck?"

Corey refused to answer.

"Now, let me read you a little something from Miranda versus the USA. You might recognize it from some of those Hollywood movies they make out in California, where you live. Well, where you *used* to live. No need to thank me in advance. This one's on me, Corey. The pleasure is truly all mine."

"George, please do something," Ginny pleaded.

"Hold tight, Ginny. I called Larry Preston on the way over. He's already making arrangements to get legal representation for Corey by the time he arrives in Minnesota."

Ginny turned her attention back toward Corey, who was standing at the edge of the driveway, his hands cuffed behind his back and his chin sunken into his chest. She listened as the Barron County Sheriff gleefully read Corey his rights.

"You have the right to remain silent..."

Part Three: Minnesota

Chapter 15

Corey awoke in a jail cell the following morning, alone. He instinctively reached for his phone to check the morning headlines and for missed texts but soon remembered that he had left it in his mother's car back in Pepin. He looked around as if to confirm that his cold surroundings were not the imaginings of a nightmare. The deep gut-turning dread he had felt as soon as he saw the squad cars returned. A metal bed with no blanket, a toilet with no lid, and everything within plain view of a guard sitting mere yards away. The guard watched Corey intermittently through thick metal bars. They exchanged no words. It was seven o'clock, and Corey hadn't yet been offered breakfast. Food finally arrived at eight. The room-temperature eggs had flavor, at least. Corey didn't touch the greasy fried bacon and cut away half an inch from the white part of the eggs in the places where the bacon grease had oozed onto them. He then used the toilet in the corner of his jail cell, emptying his bowels in full view of anyone who wanted to watch through the metal bars, though thankfully only the guard had a sightline to where Corey sat with pants rolled down to his ankles, and the guard seemed not to care.

He washed his hands in the adjacent metal sink and then reluctantly wiped his hands on his jeans rather than ask the guard for a hand towel. Corey looked into the mirror above the sink. It wasn't a true glass mirror, of course, but rather a square of shiny metal screwed tightly into the concrete wall. There was enough reflection, though, for Corey to see that for the first time in his life, there was something emerging from the light brown hair atop his head. It was subtle but real and undeniably a series of faint, gray hairs. After another hour of sitting impatiently in his cell with nothing more to do but think, Corey saw the guard answer a ringing black phone attached to the wall, listen for mere seconds, then hang up and leave the area. He returned five minutes later and approached Corey's cell.

"You've got a visitor."

Corey craned his stiff neck and rubbed it with his right hand. He shook the left repeatedly, attempting to return flowing blood to the arm that had served as his only pillow as he lay on his bunk.

"Come to the door and turn around. I need to cuff you before you walk to the visiting room."

Corey did as instructed, feeling another jolt of pain in his already sore left wrist and its tingling needles. Once handcuffed, he stepped back from the iron door, watching as it opened with a loud clang. He walked through toward the guard, careful to do what he was told and make no sudden movements. Corey's only familiarity with a jailhouse setting came from seeing criminal dramas on TV. It reminded him of Todd Coles' mocking statement about *Hollywood* and Corey being a *fancy boy* from California.

He walked alongside the guard down a long hall, the guard's firm grip on Corey's left arm.

"In here." The guard pointed toward a door, then opened it. "Have a seat and wait for your visitor to come through that other door." The guard followed him inside.

"Can you remove these? Please?"

"Once your visitor arrives," the guard said brusquely. "And then only if she agrees first."

"She?" Corey asked out loud. "Is it my mother?" He wasn't expecting Ginny at this stage. He assumed she was still back in Pepin.

"How should I know? But if that is your mom, she sure has aged well. Hmmm, definitely MILF material."

Corey bit his tongue. No sense getting upset until he saw who it was. Soon enough, he heard a faint commotion outside the far door a few seconds before it opened. A tall, slender Asian-looking woman dressed in a blue pantsuit and white blouse walked into the room carrying a brown-patterned Louis Vuitton briefcase. The bag was the first thing Corey noticed. The second was her countenance. She had steel cold eyes and an unblemished, unwrinkled complexion. He figured she was roughly his age or slightly younger. He watched her intently as she removed her coat and approached him. She looked as though she could be an artist's model—hair like silk, exceedingly pretty and a gait that screamed of confidence and class. Her beauty reminded Corey of Vladimir Tretchikoff's timeless portraits of Asian women.

"Rebecca Sayres," she said, extending her right hand toward Corey. He lifted both cuffed hands to meet hers. "What the hell? Guard, take these things off, this instant." Her voice was more commanding than Corey had ever heard uttered by any woman before. He instantly liked her, no matter who she was.

"Yes, ma'am. But just so you know, it's standard procedure here in Freeborn County to keep inmates restrained until their public defender arrives and gives the okay . . ."

She cut the guard off before he finished speaking. "First of all, I'm aware of your so-called standard procedure, and I've already told you to uncuff him. Second, I'm not a goddamned public defender. I'm on the verge of becoming a partner at Thompson & Foster in Minneapolis. And third, I would like time alone with my client if you don't mind. Now, please leave the room and close the door behind you."

The guard did as he was told, cowering as if having received instructions from a Catholic school nun.

"I'm impressed already," Corey said while rubbing his unrestrained wrists.

"Don't be. This is my first murder case."

Corey's fawning ended as his chin dropped to his chest. "Excuse me?"

"Oh, I've handled several criminal defense matters before—rape, armed robbery, other major felonies. Just haven't defended against a charge of homicide."

"Then why are you here?"

"Larry sent me. You can thank him later."

"Larry Preston? He sent you to defend me?"

"That's right. I'm the first person he called."

Corey looked up at the ceiling and bit his lip as he tried to make sense of this news.

"Don't worry, you'll get the best defense anyone in this state can offer. And I plan to win, by which I mean complete exoneration or, at worst, minimal time in state prison."

"Minimal time?"

"Yes. Worst case—three years. Five tops."

"Whoa, whoa, whoa." Questions flooded Corey's mind. He didn't know where to begin.

"Is there a problem? You do intend to plead not guilty, right?"

"Yes, of course. Or, at least I think so. But we've only just met, and you don't know anything about my case, not to mention that this is your first time defending a murder, which is apparently what I'm being charged with."

"Let's see," Rebecca said while cocking her head and keeping her eyes fixed on Corey's. She pointed her finger directly at him. "Wrong, wrong, and well, I guess you're right on that last part."

Corey looked as though Rebecca were speaking Greek. "Come again?"

"Two out of your three statements were incorrect. We have met before, and I already know quite a bit about your case after spending half the night on the phone with Larry, and then Pepin County Sheriff George Stevens, who I must say was rather cooperative with your defense in talking with me. I didn't expect that." She barely paused before continuing. "As for me never defending a murder case, I'll give you that one. But don't worry. I have a major motivation in seeing you walk away from this with no jail time."

Corey felt dizzy with everything Rebecca had said and the speed with which she said it, but he focused on the last, most relevant part. "And that is?"

"I'm up for partner in a few months. I need a major feather in my cap to convince my misogynistic partners to let me into their club. It's funny. I think the managing partner only let me take this case because he thinks it's a sure loser—me, an Asian American woman defending a gay killer in a rural Minnesota courtroom. But I see it as a chance to make my definitive closing argument for partnership. If, or rather when I win this case, my invitation will be a done deal."

Corey sat in his chair, riven. On the one hand, he admired Rebecca's confidence and candor, not to mention the way she deftly and convincingly articulated her arguments. On the other hand, maybe she was delusional, and the senior partner at Thompson & Foster was right—Corey was going to spend the rest of his life locked up in the state prison at Stillwater.

Rebecca sat motionless, still staring at Corey as if waiting for him to make the next move.

"You said we met before? No offense, but I don't remember."

"In college, at a party. I was interested in your friend Billy, but he wouldn't give me the time of day. Had some other chick in his sights."

"Must've been Amanda."

"No, before her."

"I guess I don't remember."

"No matter. I ended up talking to you because Billy was ignoring us both. We spoke for about twenty minutes. You didn't seem interested in me or any girl at the party, as I recall. Now I know why."

Corey shook his head, indicating that the memory eluded him.

"No? Anyway, the girl Billy was after brushed him off, and he finally turned his attention back toward me. We went out a couple of times after that party. I liked him, but the timing wasn't right.

We kept in touch, though. Billy helped me get an internship with his dad after my first year of law school."

"With Larry? In Pepin?"

"Yes, I was there for one whole summer. Nice place, but I wouldn't want to live there."

"Hmmm. I understand."

"Anyway, enough small talk. I charge by the hour, and this extended intro just cost you $250."

Corey's stomach sank. "About that. I don't know what Larry told you, but I don't have much money. Not sure what you charge, but I doubt I can afford you."

"Well, he did mention that you just received a nice check after selling your former condo."

Corey had forgotten all about that transaction as well as the check he left behind in his suitcase back in Pepin. "Right, a measly thirty grand. I'll need some time in order to get the check deposited or endorsed over to you."

"No worries. That should cover about half of what you'll need for a full-blown defense if this goes to trial, but Larry assured me last night that the rest will be paid by someone else."

"Someone else?"

"Yes. Your mother."

Corey closed his eyes, thinking back to the horrible scene yesterday in Pepin when Ginny watched him being arrested for murder and then hauled away.

"She's agreed to post bail, too, if the judge allows it. Assuming they process bail efficiently, you should be out of here by this afternoon. The arraignment is at eleven."

"Then what?"

"Then, whether you're back in jail or out on bond, we wait for the prosecutor to schedule the preliminary hearing. Based on what I heard last night from George and Larry, it sounds like the state's case is weak. I'll need to get your side of the story, of course, but for now, all they seem to have for sure is DNA from your recent car accident matching something left at the crime scene."

Rebecca paused upon seeing the confused look on Corey's face. "You know, the crime scene? At the truck stop?"

He gave Rebecca a slight nod of his head.

"We'll get to your version of events in a minute. But as for the process from here, the prosecutor's going to need a hell of a lot more evidence than some flimsy DNA match to convict or even survive the prelim. I've already written a motion to suppress their collection of your blood at the hospital. I'm guessing the Barron County Sheriff didn't obtain your consent?"

"I don't think so, but I'm not exactly sure."

"No matter. I'll get that thrown out. And then we're going to ask for either a dismissal for lack of evidence or exercise your right to a speedy trial. I'm going to make sure they have little to no time for making their case. In the meantime, you and I work to build your defense—solidify your alibi, interview potential witnesses, and deal with evidence as it comes to light."

Corey remained conflicted. The gravity of where he was and why felt like a heavy chain around his neck. Yet, Rebecca's passionate confidence was some consolation. Amid his doom, this impressive woman was offering his only chance at freedom.

"But we're getting ahead of ourselves. First, I need to know what happened, and I mean every detail, no matter how insignificant or uncomfortable. Understand?"

"I think so."

"Good. Now start from the beginning and tell me everything."

Chapter 16

Corey sat in his cell after Rebecca left, feeling better but not by much. Everything was off his chest. He had once more spoken aloud about the events of that terrible Thanksgiving night in 2013 for the second time in three days. And although his plan to tell Larry never came to pass, he knew that Rebecca was here now to guide him in Larry's place. The fact that Larry mentored her as a young lawyer gave Corey additional comfort that he was in the best possible legal hands.

And something about Rebecca's affect made it easy for him to tell his story, neither shading the truth nor holding back. The effect on Corey was profound. It was one of the few times in his life he had been completely, nakedly honest with someone, telling every gory, guilty detail: shooting Nick in the woods and leaving him for dead, fleeing Barron County fearing for no one but himself; packing up a few belongings from his condo and art studio without concern for those he left behind; stopping for gas and getting turned on in the men's room by Bennett Jackson's inviting touch across his shoulders; climbing up into the cab of Bennett's truck and fucking a stranger without protection; seeing the photo of Bennett's wife and daughter and wanting to suddenly run away; the gun going off during the struggle inside the cab; and finally, Corey falling painfully to the gravel-covered ground—once again caring only about himself as he ran away from death for the second time in the same goddamned day.

Corey also recounted his drive south into Iowa. He had realized that he needed sleep and had chosen a nondescript, out-of-the-way motel. He told Rebecca about feeling better after he called his friend Carol from the lonely motel room and heard that Nick had survived the gunshot wound. That was enough to enable him to take a much-needed shower and to sleep soundly that night despite the fact he didn't know the fate of the second person he had shot that day.

He explained his terror and immediate nausea upon hearing the radio newsflash the next morning about the murder of a man at a southern Minnesota truck stop. He knew instantly that he had killed someone, but he had nevertheless driven home to Pepin and tearfully welcomed the loving embrace of his mother, an embrace that Bennett Jackson would never again enjoy—not from his wife, not from his daughter, not from anyone. Ever.

Corey recounted how he had an opportunity to tell Larry Preston everything the following morning and how he had the freedom to tell Larry every excruciating detail, protected by lawyer confidentiality. Yet, due to his own pride and inability to fully tell the truth, Corey told Larry the bare minimum about the events surrounding Nick. And nothing at all about the truck stop.

A coward. He knew that's what he was, and he told Rebecca as much. She had offered him no comfort. *I can't help your feelings, Corey. That's not my job. I'm your lawyer, not your priest. Just tell me what happened next.*

She was right. What he gave to Rebecca in that unadorned, windowless conference room was not a confession; instead, it was a simple recitation of what had happened. No right or wrong, no judgment. That might come soon enough from a jury of his peers, but it certainly didn't come from Miguel. And telling Rebecca what happened—every detail he could scrape from his memory—at least released him from the imprisonment of his guilt. Now, he was caught. Now, he would be held to account. Now he had told the truth, and a biblical verse from his youth crushed him like a collapsing tower—he had told the truth, but would that truth set him free?

"Flanagan!"

The guard's voice startled him. He abruptly stood up, as if back in catechism, being disciplined by Mother Superior.

"Yes?"

"You've got another visitor. Aren't you Mr. Popular today?"

Corey looked at his wrist but remembered that his watch had been confiscated when he first arrived at the Freeborn County jail. Judging by the time since Rebecca had left and he had returned to his cell, it seemed too early for the arraignment. Perhaps Rebecca had come back, needing to speak once more before the proceeding? After being cuffed, he walked alongside the guard once more down the long hallway and entered the same visiting room. This time, his visitor was already inside and stood up when Corey entered the room.

Ginny immediately embraced him, even before the guard could remove the handcuffs. She held him for an entire minute. Corey struggled to stretch his hands wide open and lightly hug or hold her in return. The restraints prevented even that. Finally, Ginny released him, and there were tears in her eyes, but not in his. Corey turned around to let the guard unshackle him, then flexed his wrists and turned back to face his mother. He pulled her into a deep, long hug.

"Are they feeding you?"

Corey uttered a nervous laugh. "Yeah. I think they're required to by law."

They talked for half an hour, but on Rebecca's advice, Corey couldn't answer any of Ginny's questions about why he was here. She expressed understanding and said she had rented a motel room. She promised to stay in Freeborn County as long as he needed.

"I also found your cell phone in my car before driving up here this morning. I was packing up for the trip and heard something buzzing near the passenger-side door. I don't mean to pry, but you had a missed text from Miguel."

"Thanks, Mom. Where's the phone now?"

"It's in my purse, which I had to check-in at the guard desk before coming to see you. Guess I'll hold onto it until you are out on bail."

Corey grimaced and began to speak. He wanted to apologize for causing her so much trouble. Ginny interrupted him before he could talk.

"Don't worry about anything right now other than following your lawyer's advice, all right?"

"All right."

"Good." She looked at her watch. "They said I had about five minutes, and I think my time's up. I'll see you soon at the court-house, honey. Good luck."

* * *

The guard escorted Corey from the building and directed him into a white county van with tinted windows. Then a sheriff's depu-ty drove the half-dozen blocks toward the courthouse. Corey was handcuffed the entire time.

As they approached, Corey noticed another van parked di-rectly in front of the historic building. A television news chan-nel's call letters were splashed across the side. The deputy pulled around back and parked in a designated spot behind the build-ing. Corey watched as the reporter, a cameraman and a few nosy locals followed the sheriff's van on foot to the back door of the courthouse. The van's engine halted.

"Looks like you've attracted some interest."

Corey didn't respond. He simply watched as the deputy alight-ed from the van and walked around to the side door from which Corey would momentarily emerge and face public humiliation.

The door slammed open.

"Okay, let's get on with this."

The deputy sounded as reluctant as Corey felt. He rocked for-ward, and the deputy took his arm to help him step down. Ques-tions flew at him the moment before his feet hit the pavement.

"Karen Long, KMPZ news. Corey Flanagan, right?"

He neither looked at her nor replied. The deputy stayed silent as well.

"Did you sexually assault Bennett Jackson before murdering him? Are the rumors true that it was a lovers' quarrel gone bad? And that it was the second man you shot the same day?"

Holy hell, Corey thought. He could feel his heart pounding in his chest. How did they know this much detail already? He hung his head to avoid looking into the camera or into the reporter's eyes.

"Corey, do you intend to plead guilty? Do you plan to put forward any defense?"

A loud voice from a distance jolted his attention toward the courthouse doors. He looked up to see Rebecca Sayres rushing toward him.

"That'll be enough. Leave him alone. Haven't you heard of innocent until proven guilty?"

Until? Every good feeling from Ginny's visit to the jailhouse evaporated as the gravity of what lay ahead inside this courtroom fell upon his head in an instant.

Rebecca pushed her way in between Corey and the reporter, flashing her middle finger at the cameraman and telling them both to fuck off.

"Cut. We can't use that clip now, thank you very much."

"Oh, you're welcome. Now get out of our way." Rebecca grabbed Corey by the arm then dragged him toward the courthouse door. The deputy got pulled along with them, his hand still firmly gripped around Corey's other arm. Rebecca opened the glass door and let Corey and the deputy squeeze in first. She flashed a mocking wave to the reporter who was still standing at the edge of the parking lot before pulling the door closed behind her and ducking inside.

* * *

"All rise! The District Court of Freeborn County is now in session. The honorable Lloyd Johnson presiding."

Now unshackled, Corey rose beside Rebecca and in sync with everyone in the fully packed courtroom. He looked into the gallery to see Ginny sitting behind him in the first row. Everyone else was a stranger. Everyone other than his defense lawyer was White. It was also the first time he caught a glimpse of the district attorney, who was sitting at the table to his right. Donald Knopf didn't at all look friendly and didn't at all match Corey's preconception of a county prosecutor. He was medium height with an unkempt blonde mustache, and he was rather overweight.

Then, his heart sank. Still staring at the menacing prosecutor whose return glare was as cold as the Wisconsin winters, Corey noticed a hand gesture from someone toward the back of the courtroom, in his direct line of sight past the DA. Nick. He gave a small wave; his elbow stuck tightly to his chest. Why was Nick at the arraignment? How did he even know about it in the first place? Surely no one on Corey's side would have told Nick about the arrest, but perhaps there had been a report on the Minneapolis evening news? Or worse yet, maybe Nick was cooperating with the district attorney. After all, he was sitting on that side of the courtroom—alone, without Evan.

"Please be seated." Judge Johnson's voice boomed throughout the courtroom. Corey looked up at the bench to see a seventy-something, serious-looking man who personified what Corey had always stereotyped as a judge—perfectly coiffed auburn hair, a red and blue tie peeking out from the top of a black robe, and a demeanor indicating that he wouldn't tolerate any shit.

"We certainly have a full house today. What do you make of that, Mr. Knopf?"

"Good morning, Your Honor. I believe there's a bit of community interest in our first case on the docket—the State versus Corey Flanagan."

"Hmmm. All right, let's get started then." The judge opened a manila folder and glanced through the first few pages. "This is the arraignment for Mister Flanagan, who stands accused of first-degree murder. What is the state thinking in terms of bail, Mr. Knopf?"

"We strongly believe that remand until trial is appropriate, Your Honor."

"Rebecca Sayres for the defendant, Your honor." Corey felt Rebecca abruptly rise from her seat beside him, in sync with her loud first impression. "I object. That position is outrageous and obscene."

"Now, wait just a minute miss . . ." The judge searched his notes.

"Sayres. *Ms.*Sayres, Your Honor. I represent Mr. Flanagan, and I think that . . ."

"You'll get your turn, Miss Sayres. We do things in an orderly fashion in my courtroom. I advise you to be seated and wait for the DA to say what he has to say."

"Yes, Your Honor." Rebecca took her seat then leaned over to whisper in Corey's ear, "I'm setting the tone for these guys that I am no pushover."

"Proceed, Mr. Knopf."

"Thank you, Judge." The DA didn't read a single note or consult his files. He seemed ready for this moment. He turned to look at the reporters, who were poised to take notes for what would be his biggest case ever—a conviction that would put Donald Knopf on the map and earn him precious points with the local chapter of the Federalist Society, possibly even a judicial appointment once a Republican recaptured the Governor's Mansion. Knopf stank of ambition. He was the kind of lawyer who dreamed of gaining a seat on the Minnesota Court of Appeals and maybe even the Minnesota Supreme Court. He also dressed the part in his charcoal Brooks Brothers suit. This case—convicting a homosexual killer—was his ticket to achieving that dream. Knopf cleared his throat, then continued.

"We are seeking remand for the accused due to the heinous nature of this crime. And," Knopf drew out the word for added effect, "the defendant has already exhibited a propensity for running away from other crimes."

"Oh?"

"Objection, Your Honor. My client has only been charged with one crime. The DA should stick to the facts of that."

"It's all relevant, Your Honor—to Mr. Flanagan's penchant to flee from responsibility for his actions and the very essence of our request for remand."

"I agree."

"Your Honor," Rebecca rose from her chair.

"I said that I agreed. Your objection is overruled. Now sit down." Judge Johnson's voice was monotone, but his glare could have wilted lettuce. "Proceed, Mr. Knopf."

"Thank you, Judge. As you noted, Mr. Flanagan is charged with first-degree murder for the killing of Bennett Jackson here in Freeborn County on 28 November two thousand and thirteen. The accused first sexually assaulted the deceased in the cab of Mr. Jackson's semi-truck, then shot him in cold blood and left him to die a slow and horrible death. Mr. Flanagan then fled the scene, eventually making his way to his mother's house in Pepin County, Wisconsin."

"Are you saying he didn't go home? That he was instantly on the run?"

"Yes, Your Honor. And there's more. One of the reasons the accused presumably did not return to his home after killing Bennett Jackson is that Mr. Flanagan had already shot another man that same day."

Gasps filled the courtroom, uttered by virtually everyone other than Ginny, Rebecca, Nick and Corey.

"Is that right? So, he was already fleeing one killing when he committed another?" Judge Johnson anticipated Rebecca's objection and held up his hand in her direction. "Stay seated, counselor. You'll get your chance to respond."

"In a manner of speaking, yes, Your Honor. Though he didn't kill the first man, he only shot him. That man is alive and well and seated here in the courtroom today, Judge." DA Knopf turned to face the gallery and pointed directly at Nick. "The man's name is Nicholas Parker. We subpoenaed him for appearance in court today in case you needed information about that first shooting."

"That seems like a lot of trouble for Mr. Parker, counselor. Why not just ask for judicial notice of that first criminal file?"

"There was no such file, Your Honor. That crime occurred in Wisconsin, and Mr. Parker never pressed charges. Apparently, it was a domestic squabble between lovers. Mr. Flanagan was neither arrested nor charged with any crime."

"I see." Judge Johnson wrote a few notes onto the pad atop his elevated desk. "I remember another gay rampage up there in Minneapolis a few years back. Cunanan was the name of the killer, I recall. Killed a man in the Twin Cities, and then a few more between here and Florida. My word, what is this world coming to?" The judge and Rebecca exchanged knowing glares, but no objection was raised. He turned his gaze back toward the DA. "Proceed, Mr. Knopf."

"To sum up, Your Honor, Mr. Flanagan began his Thanksgiving Day in 2013 by shooting his lover, then while fleeing that assault, he attacked and killed Mr. Bennett here in Freeborn County. He then fled that scene and our state as well, hiding out in Wisconsin. The accused subsequently changed his last name and moved to California in a further attempt to evade capture for this crime. And he owns a passport. We seek remand for this defendant, Judge, because he represents a significant risk for flight from our jurisdiction. Thank you."

"Miss Sayres?"

"Your Honor, remand in this situation would be highly unusual. My client stands accused of something for which, according to the DA's initial disclosure, there is no motive, no witness and no weapon."

"Is that true, counselor?"

DA Knopf rose. "We're working on that, Your Honor. The defendant's identity only came to light in the past few days when his DNA sample from an automobile accident was matched with samples of bodily fluids found at the scene of the crime."

"A sample which we move be excluded from evidence, Your Honor. My motion." Rebecca's voice trailed off as she left the microphone and walked over toward the bailiff, handing him a short collection of papers.

"I'll take a look at these after the hearing as to bail."

Rebecca handed a second stack of papers to the DA before returning to her table and the microphone. "Absent that DNA sample, Your Honor, the state has nothing connecting my client with anything. You also now have my second motion—to dismiss this case altogether."

"We haven't had time to review defendant's motion, Judge. And you can be sure that Mr. Flanagan's identity and connection to this crime were inevitable, despite his efforts to cover them up. Mark my words—Corey Flanagan was inside that truck when the crime occurred." Knopf paused for dramatic effect before adding, "And he for damn sure was inside Bennett Jackson too."

"Your Honor! That kind of talk is uncalled for and prejudicial to my client's ability to receive a fair trial in this county."

"Hold on, both of you. Mr. Knopf, please try to be a bit more politically correct." Judge Johnson wrapped those last two words in air quotes. "And you, Miss Sayres, I will not have you insinuate that the good people of this county, much less myself, have any potential bias. I can't tell from here where you came from, but if you're going to try a case in my courtroom, you'll show proper respect."

"I'm from Minneapolis, Judge." She ended her sentence but continued her stare.

The judge looked as though he expected or even hoped for a more hysterical retort, but Rebecca didn't say another word.

"Fine. Let's get back to the issue of bail. Do you have anything more to add, counselor?"

"Yes, Your Honor. Given the current weakness of the prosecution's case and the likely success of my motions, the defense believes that bail is appropriate in this case for several additional reasons. First, Mr. Flanagan has agreed to surrender his passport. Second, his mother, Virginia Fischer, has agreed to post bond in whatever amount Your Honor deems reasonable. I feel that ten thousand will suffice."

"Ten grand? For first-degree murder by a proven flight risk?"

"Sit down, Mr. Knopf. You'll have your chance in a minute."

"Anything else, Miss Sayres?"

"Yes, Your Honor. The defendant will also agree to stay with his mother at her home in western Wisconsin. It is only an hour and a half drive from this courthouse, and he'll be present for any and all proceedings."

"Mr. Knopf?"

"Thank you, Your Honor. The state continues to believe that remand is proper. In addition to the heinous nature of the crime and the defendant's track record for running from the law, the proposal to have Mr. Flanagan stay with his mother pending trial is untenable. She doesn't live in Minnesota. He would be staying outside of our jurisdiction. According to *Darby v. Minnesota*, that simply isn't allowed."

"He's right, Miss Sayres." Judge Johnson abruptly adopted a more conciliatory tone, aiming to display an appearance of impartiality. "I was leaning toward accepting your proposal, but your client has no current connection to the State of Minnesota. My hands are tied here unless you have something else to add?"

Rebecca looked at Corey, but he could tell her mind was elsewhere—deep in thought. He then noticed in her eyes a shift that seemed to signal whirring ideas. Her gaze moved back toward the bench as she stood.

"I need a minute to confer with my client, Your Honor."

"Fine, but we're not taking a recess. I've already got a long docket today. You have one minute, and the court will remain in session."

"Thank you, Judge." Instead of sitting back down, Rebecca walked into the gallery and straight toward Ginny. She leaned down and whispered into Ginny's ear for what felt to Corey like minutes, though it was less than fifteen seconds. He saw his mother look up at Rebecca once the whispering was over, then he saw Ginny nod her head yes. Rebecca pointed to the other side of the courtroom and then to her watch.

Corey couldn't imagine what was going on and became alarmed as he watched Ginny scoot through the seated gallery in a beeline toward Nick. More whispering—followed by hesitation, more whispering, and finally another nod of yes—this time from Nick. Ginny turned and flashed a thumbs-up to Rebecca.

DA Knopf rose to speak. "Your Honor, this is highly unusual for counsel to be fraternizing in the gallery while court is in session, including sending who knows what kind of message—or threat—to my witness."

Rebecca had returned to her microphone. "He's not the prosecution's witness, Judge. They subpoenaed him without interviewing him or knowing exactly what he might say."

"Approach the bench, both of you."

Judge Johnson covered the microphone with his left hand, then leaned toward the front of his mahogany-paneled bench as the two lawyers stood before him.

"What's going on here, Miss Sayres? I agree that your conduct is highly unusual. I've warned you once about maintaining proper conduct in my courtroom. The next time you'll be held in contempt."

Rebecca offered no apology. "Your Honor said that you were inclined toward accepting my proposal for Corey's mother to post bond, but that the only barrier was her residing in Wisconsin."

"I know what I said, counselor. What's your point?"

"My point is that Mrs. Fischer is still willing to post bond, in any amount, and Nick Parker has agreed that Corey may stay at his home in Minneapolis pending trial or dismissal of the case."

"The same Nick Parker whom the defendant shot?" The judge sounded incredulous.

"Allegedly shot, Your Honor. They were partners for almost twenty years. Mr. Parker is a bank vice president and a pillar of the Twin Cities community. As you've already said on the record and in front of all these reporters, Judge, your only hesitation was due to my client not having a fixed place to stay within the state. Mr. Parker has agreed to provide such a place, and together with Mrs. Fischer's bond, they will vouch for Mr. Flanagan's appearance in your courtroom."

Donald Knopf's face turned bright red.

"This is outrageous, Judge. For all we know, after five minutes living back together again, Flanagan will shoot Parker once more, and the blood will be on your hands."

Judge Johnson's right hand flinched as if he might have smacked the DA across the face.

"Watch yourself, Mr. Knopf. I have no hesitation holding both of you in contempt. You hear me?"

"Yes, Judge."

"Good." Judge Johnson wiped his brow with his free hand. "Jesus Christ, you two should've worked something out on your own instead of bringing this drama into my courtroom. With all these reporters in attendance, people will think this is some kind of kangaroo court. I won't have it."

"She's the one who cooked up this cockamamie idea of housing her client with one of the two men he shot that day."

"The law simply requires that the defendant remains in the state, just like you said, Judge, and thanks of course to Mr. Knopf's excellent case law research." Rebecca struggled to restrain her self-righteousness.

The judge sat back in the chair and shook his head back and forth. Knopf could see what was coming.

"Your Honor!"

"It was your overconfident ambition that brought Parker here in the first place, Donald. This one's on you." The two lawyers each started to speak, but the judge silenced them with a wave of his hand. "Back to your tables. I'm ready to make my ruling."

Corey could feel his heart beating out of his chest. He was completely confused and couldn't hear a word spoken at the judge's bench, though he strained hard to try. He wasn't even relieved to see Rebecca walk back toward him at the defense table wearing a thinly veiled but distinctly confident grin.

"What's going on?" Corey whispered to Rebecca.

"You're going home with Nick."

"What? No, never. I would rather go back to the jail."

"This is what you're going to do, Corey. I can't drive down here every day to build your defense together. It will be easier for both of us if you're staying in Minneapolis, near me."

"Then I'll stay *with* you."

"Not ethically possible. This is your only option. Accept it."

"But..."

"Be quiet. The judge is about to rule."

Judge Johnson had briefly conferred with the clerk off-mic, then turned his attention back toward the wider courtroom.

"In light of the arguments made by both counsel, I am setting bail for Corey Flanagan at one million dollars. He is ordered to surrender his passport, and he will remain in residence at the home of Nicholas Parker, only leaving the city of Minneapolis to travel here to Freeborn County with his lawyer, Miss Sayres."

Rebecca rose. "Thank you, Your Honor. The defense has one more motion for the court's consideration."

Judge Johnson widened his eyes and slightly shook his head, trying to maintain his composure for the vulturous reporters scattered in his courtroom.

"And that is?"

"It's an alternative motion, Judge. If you deny defendant's motion to dismiss the case for improper gathering of DNA evidence, then we move for a speedy trial, per my client's constitutional rights."

At this point, Judge Johnson wanted nothing more than to get rid of this case for good. The prospect of a high-profile and salacious case with the media constantly in attendance was anathema to him. This close to retirement, he didn't need anything to detract from his perfect reputation for fair and proper justice, acquired over the course of his thirty mundane years on the bench.

"Mr. Knopf?"

DA Knopf considered his own motives. The investigators had yet to uncover the murder weapon, locate a single witness or construct a viable motive. But this was Freeborn County, and its people had been thirsting for justice for this heinous crime for four long years. Even with the paucity of evidence, he banked on the fact that a properly picked jury would convict a homosexual killer with minimal deliberation.

"No objection, Your Honor."

"Good, something we all finally agree on." The judge conferred with the clerk sitting to his left for several minutes, each of them looking at calendars. He returned to his microphone. "Trial for Corey Flanagan on the charge of murder in the first degree will commence on Monday, February 5, 2018. A preliminary hearing for the prosecution to present its findings will first be held in two weeks' time, on Monday the fourth of December 2017. The clerk will enter these dates and the details of my ruling as to bail into the record. Defendant will remain in the custody of the Freeborn County sheriff pending the posting of a bond. Thank you, everyone. The court will now take a short recess before returning to today's docket at one-thirty."

"All rise!"

Chapter 17

The ride to Minneapolis felt surreal. Corey didn't anticipate a return to his former city this soon, if ever. And he never imagined going back there to stay with Nick. His mind raced as he stared out the passenger seat window. This whole damn trip had been nothing but disasters. He should never have left California.

California. He longed for it now like never before. He longed to be back out west. He longed to be standing at his easel, perched above the Strand at sunrise, painting the vast blue sea that stretched toward the far horizon. At this moment, as Corey sat in the passenger seat of his lawyer's Volvo, California felt like a distant mirage—a place of freedom and warmth and light, a place where he started his life anew with very little money yet with everything he needed to be happy. The scene outside the car window flew past in stark contrast to that mirage. The thick, overcast November sky cast a dull light on the barren, harvested farmland adjacent to the freeway, mirroring Corey's mood if not his reality. His heartbeat ascended, reflecting a panic from all that entrapped him—the prospect of having to live for two weeks with Nick, the murder charge that might well keep him stuck in Minnesota for the rest of his life, and even the seat belt that now fastened him tightly in place.

At least he had a bit more time to prepare himself mentally before seeing Evan and dealing with Nick. Rebecca insisted that Corey ride back to Minneapolis from the arraignment with her so they could talk strategy. It also gave Nick time to explain to Evan why an accused killer—Nick's former lover—was coming to stay with them. The twist of fate was rich, but things were too dire for the absurdity of it to lighten Corey's heavy heart.

Rebecca spoke passionately about Corey's defense. Corey tried to listen, but part of his mind was fixated on imagining his arrival at Nick and Evan's house. From what little he did hear of Rebecca's points, Corey doubted how much would succeed. Yes, there were questions the prosecution likely couldn't answer no matter how wide a net they cast for clues—a motive, the actual sequence of events inside the truck, and the location of the weapon of death that still lay hidden in Larry's law office safe back in Pepin. As far as Corey could remember, there were no witnesses to his crime or escape, other than the truck stop cashier and the motel clerk in Charles City, Iowa. As of now, there was no indication that the prosecution had interviewed either one. Corey had never related his crime to anyone other than Miguel, so there was little chance of using his words against him.

Miguel. He suddenly remembered how Ginny said that Miguel had sent Corey a text. He reached for his phone that had been resting in the center console of Rebecca's car. The battery had run dead by the time Ginny handed the phone to Corey after the arraignment, but thankfully Rebecca had the right cord for him to charge it up. Upon looking at it, the power was back at fifty percent. He read Miguel's text.

Hi. Can't talk right now but wanted to let you know that Mom still hasn't woken up from being out under sedation yesterday for the heart procedure. Docs are trying to figure out why. I'm scared, Corey. I'll text or call you when I know more. Please pray for her. M

Corey looked out the window and thought to himself, *damn.* Why were the fates twisting so cruelly right now? Miguel didn't deserve this, and Corey felt helpless in that being more than a thousand miles away and under indictment for murder prevented him from flying to Houston and providing comfort in Miguel's hour of need.

All told, hope seemed elusive. Beyond what was happening down in Texas, Corey thought once more about the mountainous challenge before him. He stood accused of raping another man in the back of a dirty semi-truck, then killing him and fleeing the scene with zero regard for his life or death. While Corey had explanations and no ill intent, he had indeed done some of those things. He had killed a man and left him to die. Even if he could justify it as accidental or self-defense, the outcome was the same. He had taken a life, and somehow he couldn't help feeling that there had to be a reckoning.

Corey also doubted he could receive a fair trial. He conjured the jury of his peers who would hear the evidence and rule on his fate. Most likely, they would be like—and look like— the judge and the prosecutor. He doubted there was a single gay person in all of Freeborn County, or at least any who were out of the closet. Though national polls showed an increased tolerance and acceptance of gay people once same-sex marriage became the law of the land in 2013, opinion was still rent by a strong urban-rural divide. It wasn't an issue of discrimination or ill-intent, but mostly one of familiarity. Many people outside of the big cities simply didn't know anyone who was openly gay, meaning that their primary source of information came from TV characters or sensational news stories, and however lightheartedly gay men had been portrayed, what they would remember would be gay parades—and murder.

Then there was Rebecca. As brilliant as she appeared to be, how exactly would an Asian American big-city woman lawyer be received in lily-White rural Minnesota? Perhaps Corey's judgment was unfair and characteristically pessimistic. But he knew the odds of escaping punishment for his actions were dismal at best. Maybe that was okay. Regardless of Rebecca's talent and creativity, the facts were inescapable. Corey had killed a man and had run away from the scene. It was possible that the victim's life might have been saved with swift medical intervention. Corey had been given—or had taken, more precisely—four years of undeserved freedom. Now, it was time to man up and pay for his sins.

* * *

"You can sleep in here."

Corey dragged his overnight bag into the first-floor guest room. The 1930s bungalow had two small bedrooms and a bath on the main floor, with a large master suite upstairs. Corey politely declined Nick's offer for a full-house tour. Corey didn't need to see anything more than the room in which he would be sleeping for the next two weeks. Two long weeks. At least, as Rebecca explained, Corey wasn't required to spend every waking minute in this house; rather, he only needed to keep it as his primary place of residence until he went back for the preliminary hearing. Then, assuming the case got bound over for trial in early February as scheduled, and Corey didn't violate the terms of his bail, Rebecca advised that he would be able to petition the court for a change of temporary residence pending trial—perhaps a motel room or some other reasonable accommodation. Corey decided that this would be a top priority over the ensuing two weeks—finding a different place to live between the prelim and the trial. The possibilities were slim, though. Corey hadn't maintained contact with anyone from his former life in Minneapolis, not even Carol.

Carol. Corey tried to imagine how he might approach her, but each scenario felt awkward. They had been the best of friends for nearly twenty years, but Corey dropped the relationship like a hot stone. She had tried calling him several times during that first year after Corey left Minneapolis. But Carol was married to Nick's best friend Julian, and Corey wanted a complete break from his former life. The most he offered in return were cryptic texts with a consistent message—*I'm sorry, but I need space right now.* After a few months, the calls and texts from Carol's number ceased, and Corey never reached out. She had no reason to care about him anymore. His actions had made it clear he didn't want her in his life.

Everything he had done for the past four years would probably bite him now, he thought. At the time, though, he had just wanted to start over. No one in his muddled life—not even his mother—could have helped him do that. The move toward independence had been his salvation until now.

"Nice jewelry, by the way." Nick's voice jolted Corey from his sad reflection.

"Huh?"

"Your ankle bracelet. Or is it a Fitbit? You were always into running back in the day. Is that how you keep track of your steps?"

Corey looked down at the space between his jeans and his loafers, to the point where Nick had been staring. He had almost forgotten the ankle tracer that the sheriff's office had shackled onto his leg before leaving the courtroom. One thing he hadn't forgotten at this moment is what a complete ass Nick Parker was and always would be. Yet, Corey took the high road.

"Funny. You always were the more hilarious of the two of us, Nick."

"I try. Can't help it that people like my sense of humor."

"Hmmm."

"So, Evan and I had a long chat about all this on my drive back from the courthouse. He took it better than I expected. Apparently, he's not intimidated by one of my ex-conquests sleeping under our roof."

"I'm sure he's glad it's only one of the many."

Nick laughed. "There you go, see? You always had a good sense of humor, too. Too bad you rarely showed it."

Corey did not reciprocate Nick's laughter. "Look, let's cut to the chase. I appreciate you providing me with a room for the next two weeks. I really do. I never thought I might say this but staying with you is slightly better than my jail cell back in Freeborn County."

Nick laughed once more. "Thanks, I think?"

"But I don't expect to be waited on or entertained. I plan to spend a lot of time at the law office with Rebecca, and my mother is driving back up on Saturday to stay until the preliminary hearing. She reserved a hotel room downtown. I'll spend most of my time with her, especially eating out. I'll basically only be sleeping here if that's all right?"

"Fine by me. And I think Evan will be okay with that as well."

"Good, thanks."

"But he wasn't sure whether or not he would want to do a threesome if that was on your mind at all."

Corey detected an air of hopefulness in Nick's voice. And it made him sick to his stomach.

"Uh, no. That didn't cross my mind. At all."

"Suit yourself. But I'll have you know that Evan and I get a fair number of offers for that, especially from the younger crowd. Guess they like our maturity and experience in the sack."

Please, dear God, Corey silently prayed as he forced a polite smile. *Make this gross blather stop.*

"Anyhoo . . . make yourself at home. I put some towels and washcloths on the bed. The main floor bathroom's all yours."

"Thanks, Nick."

Corey walked deeper into the guest bedroom and heaved his overnight bag onto the bed. He sensed Nick's presence behind him, still standing in the doorway. Corey turned to face his former lover with an inquiring look.

"Sorry, one more thing." Nick paused, uncharacteristically struggling to get words out of his mouth. "Did you really kill that guy, Corey? The trucker?"

Corey sat down atop the bed, folded his hands, and dropped them to his lap. He took a deep breath.

"Nick, I can't talk about this with you. I can't even talk about it with my mother. Only with my lawyer. Sorry, but you'll have to respect that."

"Okay, okay. I get it." He turned to leave, then stopped and faced Corey yet again and shook his head. Nick exhaled noticeably through his nose. "That was one fucked-up day."

"Yeah, it certainly was."

"Who knew that would be the last time I would see you until just a few days ago, huh?"

Corey raised his eyebrows, scrunched his mouth, and held up his hands in supplication.

"I still can't believe you shot me, Corey—out there in the woods. Never in a million years would I have predicted that. To be honest, I didn't think you had it in you."

"Apparently, I did."

"Yeah, um, I'm well aware." Nick rubbed the phantom wound in his left butt cheek. "I never did get an apology, you know."

Corey remained seated on the bed, his hands refolded, his elbows now resting atop his knees.

"And I never got one from you for whacking me on the head with the flashlight. What's your point, Nick?"

Nick appeared taken aback by Corey's unusual abruptness. This was not the same person Nick lived with for nearly twenty years.

"I don't know. It just seems like we should have some closure on the matter, or something."

"Closure? We've both moved on to different homes and different lovers, Nick. I think everything closed for us a long time ago."

Nick's eyes scanned the room as he appeared to strain himself in thought.

"You're right. I guess I only wanted to say that I'm sorry."

Corey nearly fell off the bed before spying Nick skeptically.

"What exactly are you sorry for?"

"Can't you accept a general apology? Do I need to spell things out for you? As you said, everything closed for us long ago. But at this moment, I felt the need to say I'm sorry."

Corey stayed seated on the bed, staring at Nick. He wondered to himself whether Nick's offering was enough—enough to account for the cheating, the lies, the demeaning comments, all of it. Part of him needed more—for Nick to confess to being cruel as much as he was kind. But the other part felt a mixture of regret and relief. Corey regretted his own faults and failings—the drinking, the obsessing, the compulsions born from his own insecurities. And he was relieved to have left that part of his life behind in Minnesota, forging new paths and personal growth in California. Who he became and who he would yet become far outweighed who he was in the past.

"Thank you, Nick. And I would like to apologize to you as well. And to thank you."

"I appreciate that, Corey. But what are you thanking me for?"

"Can't you accept a simple, generic thank you?"

Nick laughed. "Fair enough. You're welcome." He shook his head and seemed as though he had something more to say, but he remained silent.

"I think I'm going to lie down for a bit," Corey said. "I've had a pretty exhausting day."

"Sounds good, I'll leave you alone. Oh, by the way, Even and I have dinner plans with friends. Help yourself to whatever you can find in the fridge or cupboards. Evan's quite the chef, so we're fully stocked with just about anything you might like."

"Thank you. I'll manage. Have a good time."

"Okay. Good night, Corey. Let's touch base in the morning."

"Good night."

Nick closed the door behind him. A few minutes later, Corey heard keys being jostled and the zipping of a coat, followed by the turn of a door handle and heavy thud of the front door closing shut. After waiting five more minutes, in case Nick returned for a forgotten item, Corey emerged from the guestroom. He peeked out of the doorway as if still locked in a jail cell, planning a furtive escape. He listened but heard no sounds inside the house. There was a steady stream of traffic passing by out front. East Johnson was a busy street.

Corey wandered the main floor. The kitchen was functional, not fancy. Corian countertops and aging appliances. He remembered Nick saying something about wanting to put his share of the condo sale proceeds toward a sorely needed kitchen remodel. As he passed into the living room, Corey thought for a moment about climbing the stairs but quickly remembered Nick saying that Evan had converted the entire second floor into an enlarged master suite. Corey had no desire to see the space where Nick and Evan slept.

The main floor bathroom had vintage 1930s tile. This pattern was pink and black. It wouldn't be Corey's first choice, but he appreciated the classic look and ageless condition of the tile work. A deep claw foot tub sat at the far end of the bathroom. He fantasized about drawing a hot bubble bath and soaking away the unexpected stress accumulated over the past several days but felt weird at the prospect of lying naked in Nick and Evan's house.

He entered the other main floor bedroom, converted into a home office for Nick. It looked almost the same as the one in their old condo overlooking the river: the same desk and chair—a graduation gift from the Parkers. There were also the same stupid framed posters on the wall—*Mad* magazine covers featuring Nick's feigned hero with giant awkward ears, Alfred E. Neumann. It was endearing to Corey now, in a way. He walked over to the desk and sat in Nick's chair. A fleeting pain seared his gut as he remembered all the times he sat in this same chair, rifling through this same desk in search of clues to Nick's suspected infidelities. It faded quickly, with Corey consciously remembering that he no longer cared about Nick's life that way, or in any way for that matter.

Then he saw it, partially blocked behind the office door. Why would Nick have a framed piece of Corey's art hanging in his home office? He got up from the chair and walked over to the penciled drawing. It was indeed his handiwork, an impressionist image of St. Anthony Falls sketched from the vantage point of the balcony in their former loft. But where did Nick get this? He had refused to hang any of Corey's artwork in their condo, and Corey had kept all his drawings stored in the studio he shared with Carol in Northeast. Even if Carol had de-cluttered the studio of Corey's excess artwork when he fled Minneapolis years ago, he couldn't imagine her giving any of them to Nick. But then again, Corey hadn't spoken with Carol since moving to California in 2015. They had stayed in touch during Corey's year-long stay with Ginny in Pepin after the shootings, but he had made a clean break upon moving west. Other than his weekly calls and infrequent visits with his mother, Corey cut off the rest of his Midwest life just as sharply as he had sheared off his former family name.

He stared at the artwork and remembered this drawing well. It was sketched during the recovery period from his suicide attempt in 2012 after discovering Nick's affair with Evan in a Miami hotel room and after hearing Frank tell Corey to *get out of my house and never come back*. Following a month in the hospital, Corey recuperated at home with twice-weekly therapy (one by himself and one accompanied by Nick), daily tea and cookies with his old neighbor Mrs. Randall, and untold hours in the studio with Carol. He had lost his job at the museum, and he took time before seeking a new one. The reprieve from the stress of working so many hours in the museum was a blessing, but the unspoken tension he saw every night in Nick's face from carrying the couple's entire financial load was stressful, too. Corey remembered drawing this same scene many times over—the rushing waters cascading over the limestone falls. Even looking upon the drawing now, Corey could faintly hear that mesmerizing waterfall, which he embraced as a symbol of hope and perseverance. The river and falls had flowed over porous rocks since the beginning of time and would continue until its end.

Standing there in Nick's home office, Corey realized that this drawing marked the beginning of his transition from painting portraits and still life toward more challenging landscapes. This one eluded perfection, for Corey couldn't ever seem to focus on a snapshot in his mind of a singular frame. The water kept moving, and the river's composition kept changing. It was like the difficulty he faced more recently, trying to capture on the canvas an image of the waves crashing onto the beach in Redondo. But in looking at this drawing of St. Anthony Falls, he felt satisfaction. He thought, *maybe I did depict the river well, maybe those early works weren't so bad after all.*

He noticed that the drawing had been framed, something he had not done himself. But whoever framed it had covered up the lower right corner where he had scribbled his trademarked signature. Other than himself, Carol, and Nick, no one else looking at this drawing would have any idea Corey had sketched it.

He heard a thud to his left and audibly took in a quick breath. He turned to see a cat sitting proudly atop the desk behind him, having just knocked over a jar holding pens that now lay scattered atop the desk.

"Jesus, you scared me."

The cat didn't care. Corey looked again at the painting and wondered again how it came into Nick's possession. Carol—it had to have been Carol who gave it to him. It was the only realistic possibility. He thought about it for a moment, then returned to Nick's chair and sat down. He reached for the Rolodex sitting atop the desk and wondered if Nick was the last person who still used such an archaic piece of office tackle. Corey scrolled toward the middle of the alphabet and found Carol's name. He instantly recognized her number, even though he had long ago erased it from his mind. He pulled his cell phone out of his pocket, entered the numbers and sent the call.

Chapter 18

The next afternoon, Corey climbed the wooden staircase—the same one he had ascended hundreds of times before. The familiar scent of treated timber and dank stone walls conveyed an instant feeling of comfort and of home, a home he had long since abandoned. He exited the stairwell on the second floor and walked toward the door to his former art studio. He was surprised to learn last night that Carol had kept the space once Corey left town and dumped on her with responsibility for the lease. Yet, he was happy that her secondary career as a potter and sculptor had taken off in the past three years. She deserved that kind of success, though Corey couldn't help feeling a little envious.

He knocked on the door.

"Come in," Carol shouted from inside.

He opened the door slowly and spied Carol at her potter's wheel, spinning a new creation from clay. He could see the wheel slowing as she rose from her seat, lifting her foot off the lower controls. She walked toward him with her familiar wide smile. She stopped mere feet from where Corey stood inside the doorway, holding up her clay-covered hands. She looked the same as he remembered—effervescent, with blonde hair falling down her beautiful slim frame.

"Hi," she said softly. "Thank you for reaching out and coming over."

"I'm glad you took my call."

"Of course. Let me wash up so I can give you a proper hug."

"No need," Corey said, surprising them both. He closed the gap between them, pulling Carol into a tight, long-lasting embrace. After he released her, she placed a damp cloth over the unfinished clay then walked toward the sink in silence to wash up, scrubbing bits of hardened clay from her skin and beneath her nails. During that time, Corey scanned the walls of the studio then walked toward the one that held several pieces of framed art. It surprised him to see so many of his own works. He had left them all behind, vertically stacked and ignored in the far corner, unframed. Carol had clearly culled through his work and picked out the pieces she felt worthy of hanging, or perhaps she had simply picked out the ones she liked most.

Corey stood before one, staring again at this long-lost treasure. It was a depiction of an orange-vested hunter in a dark wood, a small cabin in the background and the faint image of an antlered deer within the hunter's line of sight.

"That was always one of my favorites from your collection, Corey." Carol had quietly come to stand behind him. "The imagery, the muted lines, the subtlety of the three focal points—genius."

"Yeah?"

"Oh yeah. Definitely your best work. Well, it was. Maybe you've created new masterpieces since then?"

Corey sensed a line of gentle inquiry, her curiosity as to whether he continued to paint.

"I'm still painting, but very few figures anymore. I'm captivated lately with landscapes."

"Just like Hopper, your idol. I'm not surprised."

"Is that a good thing?"

"Definitely. Your works always exuded his same sense of realism yet with subtle tensions splashed across the canvas—tensions between people, tradition versus progress, and more."

"Thanks. I'll take that. Yeah, something about living where I can smell the ocean opened me up to painting landscapes. The setting there inspires me."

"Who wouldn't be inspired living in such a gorgeous place?"

"Hmmm. I love painting the sea and the southern California coastline. I'll set my easel up at sunrise and paint as long as I can—all day, sometimes."

"I'm glad to hear it, Corey. You are very talented, you know."

He looked at Carol with appreciation. The old Corey would have demurred, humbly denying that his works were any good. But in his time away from the Midwest, he had grown more confident, more accepting of praise.

"Thank you. Coming from you, an award-winning talent, that means a lot."

She stepped closer, and they hugged once more.

"I see you've been busy framing my artwork, sheesh."

"We never had anything on the walls in here before, and I can't really hang my pottery."

They both laughed.

"True."

"You can take any or all of them with you if you want. They're yours, after all."

"Thanks, but they look fine right where they are. Besides, you went to all the trouble and expense to frame them. No, they're yours. I'm happy you have them to enjoy."

"I do. And I framed more."

"Oh?"

"Well, you did leave quite a few pieces of art behind when you left."

"So, where are they?" Corey anticipated her telling him about the piece in Nick's home office.

"Mostly at home, hanging in our family room. The others are in the closet, over there." Carol pointed at a door adjacent to the washtub.

"I'll have to take a look."

"There's one more, too, Corey. You may see it during your stay with Nick and Evan."

He nodded his head. "Already did."

"Nick asked me if he could have it when he visited here about a year after you left. Hope you don't mind."

"Not at all. It piqued my curiosity when I saw it in their house."

Carol looked as if she had something more to say but then switched gears. Her demeanor changed too.

"I'm really glad you reached out and called me, Corey."

He had expected the topic of his abrupt 2013 departure to come up, but he was nevertheless unprepared.

"Yeah, of course. Why wouldn't I?"

Their exchange of looks included a knowing answer to that stupid question.

"To be honest, I was pretty sure I would never hear from you again. It's been almost four years, and you never answered any of my texts or calls other than to tell me that you needed time to figure things out."

Corey continued looking at her. He owed her an explanation. But he struggled with what to say and where to start. Carol let him off the hook with her usual playful smile.

"So, I'm guessing you finally figured things out?"

They both laughed. They always laughed together. It was among Carol's most endearing qualities—the speed with which she let go of grudges and her charming way of diffusing uncomfortable situations.

"No. Not in the least."

"Yeah, so I've heard. And *read* in the paper."

She tilted her head but maintained her trademarked smirk. Other than Billy, Carol was the only person in Corey's life who spoke to him directly but with loving intention.

He laughed. "God, I've missed you."

"Remember what you always said? That I'm the sister you never had?"

"Oh yeah, I forgot." He hoped that Carol could not detect the punch to his gut that he instantly felt with that reminder of the existence of Sam.

"How about I pour us a cup of tea while you give me the *Cliff Notes* version, or at least as much as your lawyer will allow you to say."

"Deal."

Carol turned toward the sink, then paused and looked back toward Corey. "Are you sure you only want tea and not something more calming?"

He immediately recognized the playful look in her eyes. It was a look that he first saw as a college freshman when Carol invited him up to her sorority house bedroom, and then again when she suggested they have a drink and lie together on her mattress to watch a movie.

"Yeah, that's exactly what I need right now."

She smiled and walked toward her art supply closet to pick out a fragrant bud that she proceeded to break down and roll into a pair of joints. While Carol brewed their tea and worked with the illegal herbs as carefully as if it were her beloved clay, Corey surveyed a large shelf that displayed Carol's recent works. She had improved her technique and expanded her repertoire of pottery in the years since he last set foot in this studio. After the kettle blew its whistle and the tea was poured, they sat in a pair of soft chairs Carol had arranged near the open window with a small coffee table between. It added to the studio's more feminine ambiance, Corey mused to himself—far different from the old days.

They talked for nearly an hour, sipping tea and snacking on the small but flavorful homemade cookies which Carol had placed, one apiece, on their saucers. They agreed to save the joints for later. Corey spoke of his year-long "sonbattical" living with his mother in Pepin, then of the past three years in Los Angeles—his job at the frame shop, the beach cottage apartment, his renewed friendship with Billy, painting landscapes along the coast, and his burgeoning relationship with Miguel. Carol recounted many changes at the museum where she still worked and Corey used to, the contract she secured with a local gift shop chain to sell her pottery, their twentieth-year college reunion that she regretted attending, and her unexpected marital woes with Julian that seemed to finally be working themselves out for the best.

When they had exhausted catching up on personal details, Carol predictably pushed the conversation into uncomfortable territory.

"So, I read the newspaper article about your arrest and the truck stop incident."

She paused after that, giving him an opening to speak. He didn't.

"It's okay if you don't want to talk about it or can't."

"No, I don't mind. I'm just thinking about where to start."

"Tell me about that night, Corey—Thanksgiving 2013. I've heard Nick's version, of course, but I know most of it's bullshit."

Corey laughed and raised his eyebrows. "Maybe not. It was a pretty fucked-up day."

He spent the next several minutes telling Carol his version of what happened in Barron County, from waking up in the cabin his grandfather built to shooting Nick in the ass at dusk. He told her about the frantic ride back to Minneapolis, not knowing whether Nick was alive or dead. And, that he didn't care which one was true.

"I remember our phone conversation after you got back to the apartment. You had me worried, Corey, especially after you hung up and wouldn't answer my attempts to call you back."

"I'm sorry, I really am. I barely knew what I was doing. I didn't talk to anyone. Instead, I packed everything I absolutely needed, then got the hell out of town."

"I know. I read the note you left me over there on my pottery wheel two days later."

Corey lowered his eyes to the floor. He had already apologized. There wasn't much more he could offer.

"But that's not the point," Carol said. "It all worked out for me in the end. Please, keep going."

His re-telling of that awful night picked up its intensity once he reached the part about pulling off the freeway for gas at the fateful truck stop in Freeborn County. Against Rebecca's directive, Corey told Carol everything—every single detail. He told her how Bennett Jackson invited Corey to meet him inside Bennett's truck that was parked in the lot, how Corey became inexplicably aroused at the thought of potential random, illicit sex, and how things went terribly awry once Corey pieced together that Bennett was a cheating bastard like Nick.

"I've been thinking about the second phone call we had that night when you wouldn't tell me where you were."

"I couldn't, Carol. I mean, now I can, of course. I was in a motel room in Charles City, Iowa."

"Where did you think you were going?"

"My plan was to drive toward Texas—Marfa, to be precise."

"That was your brilliant plan? To hide out in an artist colony? Huh, maybe not such a bad idea after all. Probably the last place authorities would think to look for a killer."

That last word made Corey grimace.

"Sorry. *Alleged* killer? You did just tell me what happened in the truck."

He uttered a nervous laugh.

"Not just alleged. I killed him. I never meant to. I never intended to fire the gun. But it went off. And what happened, happened."

Carol's voice turned somber as she moved from what had been to what might be.

"How's this going to end up for you, Corey? Does your lawyer think she can prove self-defense?"

He bit his lip and shook his head gently back and forth.

"She seems to think so. Rebecca exudes confidence. But I'm not so sure. So far, her strategy seems to be working. She got me released on bond, convinced the court to expedite the preliminary hearing, and seems to be one step ahead of the prosecutor at every turn."

"Then why aren't you sure?"

"Carol, think about everything I've told you. I shot a man, fled the scene and he died. And that was after I shot Nick in the woods earlier that same fucking day and left him for dead as well. Me, a gay man with a history of mental instability and a suicide attempt to boot. Even if I were to testify—and that is seriously in doubt, per Rebecca—what jury in America is going to believe that I was the victim and that Bennett Jackson—loving husband and doting father—was the aggressor?"

She nodded her head in hesitant agreement but gave no answer to his question. Really, what was there to say in response to his spot-on rhetorical question? Instead, she offered what little she could.

"I'm sorry, love. This must all be so frustrating and scary. I wish I could erase everything you're going through, but I can't. I can offer you this, though. No matter what happens, I'll be here for you, Corey. No matter what."

"Thanks. Who knows, maybe things will look better after the preliminary hearing. Maybe I'm just paranoid even though we haven't inhaled any weed yet."

He pointed to the tempting joints still sitting on the table between them. Carol smiled, then laughed, relieved at Corey's grasping an opportunity for levity.

"You actually might be feeling some mild paranoia. What do you think was in those cookies, huh?"

Corey shook his head, laughing under his breath. "I thought they tasted a little earthy."

Chapter 19

Carol reached for the lighter in her pocket and lit them both up.

"Man, I've missed this."

"What? You live in Cali and don't partake in the magic kush? I'm disappointed in you, Corey." They both laughed.

"I gave it up when I gave up drinking. I needed a completely clean start."

"Oh," Carol said with an exaggerated grimace. "You should've said something. I didn't mean to be a temptress or bully you into it."

"Oh my God, stop. It's fine. I can smoke a joint, and the world won't come to an end. It's true I shouldn't drink, but marijuana isn't a problem for me. In fact, I probably could've used some hits now and then to ease my anxiety."

"It is good for that."

They inhaled simultaneously, deeply.

"So . . . how is it? Staying with Nick after all this time?"

Corey's head rested atop the edge of the chair, his gaze fixed on the ceiling. "So far, so good. I haven't seen Evan yet. Depending on what time I go back there, I'll have to deal with him either tonight or in the morning."

"Julian told me how that all came about. Weird. Can't you stay with us instead?"

"No. It's a strict condition of my release that I stay with Nick until returning to Freeborn County for the preliminary hearing. My lawyer says that once the case gets bound over for trial, we can ask the court for a different arrangement."

"Stay with us, Corey. It'll be a lot less awkward."

"Thanks, love. I'll take you up on that if I can. But are you sure Julian will agree? You remember what happened the time you invited me for a sleepover at your sorority house." Corey flashed her a knowing smile.

"He'll have to cope. I've been faithful to that man for twenty years. It's about time I get some action on the side."

Corey laughed. Carol did the same. Then she inhaled from the joint and blew a long stream of smoke into the air.

"You know, Julian and I talked about that, actually."

Corey looked at her, squinting with both eyes. "Talked about what?"

"About you and I having sex."

"In college, I know. I'm aware that Julian knew, as did Nick. We got teased by them plenty of times, remember?"

"No, I mean since then. He and I talked about the prospect of you and I having sex again as adults."

Corey's eyes remained half-shut, the product of both the marijuana and his confusion. "What are you talking about?"

"Do you remember how Julian and I struggled trying to get pregnant for so long?"

"Yeah."

"Well, I never told you the diagnosis, but Julian didn't have enough salmon to swim upstream, or at least enough strong ones."

"Yikes, that had to be embarrassing."

"Tell me about it. That's why I never said anything. Not that I couldn't trust you, but I couldn't take the chance of it getting back to Nick. Julian would've gone ape shit over that."

Corey nodded his head in understanding.

"But we did explore the idea of a sperm donor. Julian was against the idea of going to a fertility clinic, so we talked about asking someone we knew."

"And you thought of me?"

"You were the only person we seriously considered."

"Not Nick, the perfect one?"

"Uh, no. Do you actually think I would want Nick's sperm inside my body?" Carol feigned a gagging reflex. "Besides, Julian wouldn't allow it. That would change their relationship dynamic in ways he could never handle. But you, on the other hand, you were a different story."

"How so?"

"We both cared deeply about you, Corey. Still do. And we respected your innate kindness. Besides, you're far better looking than Nick. You and I would've had a gorgeous baby. Why do you think I tried so hard to get you in the sack during college?"

They laughed. Corey contemplated and found himself getting slightly, shockingly aroused.

"So, why am I only hearing about this now?"

"Because the idea ended around the time you were hospitalized in 2012 after trying to take your life, and then for certain during the madness of a year later. Julian freaked out that depression and alcoholism might be genetic. So that was the end of that."

"Carol, I'm sorry."

"Oh my God, don't be. In retrospect, I don't think Julian and I were cut out to be parents. I mean, we could've pursued other donors or even adopted, but ultimately, we decided we enjoy the freedoms that childlessness affords. Sure, I sometimes wonder what might've been, but overall, I'm happy. My life is pretty good."

Corey looked at her with affection and serenity. He was happy for her, truly. They each took another hit.

"Do you see them often? Nick and Evan?"

"Yeah. Julian and Nick are still thick as thieves. The four of us have dinner at least once a month. And we've been up to their cabin a couple of times."

"Nick and Evan have a cabin? Oh, how lumbersexual of them."

Carol snorted. "It's just what you might imagine—as if Restoration Hardware threw up on a rustic cottage in the middle of a deep woods."

Corey rolled his eyes.

"But the place felt manufactured, fake even. You know?"

"Not exactly."

"They ordered the entire interior as a single package, everything coordinated in gay fashion like at their house. Except that the cabin has a definite north woods motif. Probably more Eddie Bauer than Restoration Hardware." Corey chuckled. "It didn't have the personalized, artistic touch that you would've brought to it, Corey. I mean, Nick and Evan are both pinhead bank guys."

"Like Julian?"

"Exactly. None of them have our creative vision. Thank God we both got the gene, right?"

"Amen to that."

They each drew a final inhalation from their joints and crushed the remnants into a small clay bowl Carol had crafted for just this purpose.

"Oh, I almost forgot." Carol jumped out of her chair and walked quickly over toward the brick wall near the supply closet. She returned within a minute, holding two leather-bound books, both tied shut with brown suede boot laces.

"My journals. Where did you find them?"

"Flat in the back of the safe when you left here for good."

"Geez, I always wondered what happened to them. They're the only two volumes missing from my set."

"Your set?"

"Yeah. I've kept a diary since I was ten years old. Well, off and on, but consistently over the years. I grabbed what I thought was all of them when I fled the condo back in 2013. I forgot that I had left these two in the studio safe."

"Hmmm. I can understand why."

Corey paused. His stomach sank. "You read them?"

"Well, not everything, but yeah, I pretty much scanned through both journals." Carol paused while Corey looked at her, expressionless. "I wasn't trying to invade your privacy, love. And I didn't read them right away when I found them if that's any consolation."

"Then why did you?"

"Because after all my efforts to reach you when you wouldn't respond, it was my only connection to your voice, to try and understand what happened to you, Corey. And to us."

Carol began to tear up. It wasn't like her at all. Corey moved closer, offering both forgiveness and a hug. "It's okay. I understand. Besides, I'm the one who left them here and handed over the keys to the place without warning or any goodbye."

"That really hurt me, Corey. You were my best friend. Losing you from my daily life was painful."

"I'm sorry, Carol. I really am."

She nodded her acceptance. "There's some pretty fucked up shit in those journals, you know that?"

The memory of their contents slowly filtered back into Corey's conscience. He grimaced, realizing what Carol must have read.

"Those two volumes reflect a very difficult time in my life—when I was hospitalized after my suicide attempt. I was a different person then. You were there, remember?"

"Yeah, I do. But I guess I never appreciated how much anger you held inside toward both Nick and your father."

"I did. I may not have shown it or talked about it, but those were my feelings, and my therapist encouraged me to write it all down, to let it all out."

"Is it true what you wrote in there, Corey? That you had thoughts and fantasies of killing Nick?"

Corey's gaze turned toward the window, his thoughts returning to the lowest year of his life. "I guess. But I don't feel that way now, just so you know."

"Well, that's some comfort."

"You see why I kept these here instead of at home where he might stumble across them?"

"Uh, yeah. Clearly."

To this point, Carol had held onto both journals, gesturing with them in her hands. She now offered them to Corey. For a moment, they held the books together, four hands enveloping the musty leather.

"You never told me about your bad boy phase either, prior to meeting Nick. You sure had some kinky, even sadistic fantasies about rough sex. Wow."

"Are you judging?"

"No, no. Not at all. It just surprised me."

"Honestly, I never wanted to write all that shit down. But the therapist seemed to think it was important for my self-development."

"It would make a great thriller novel, Corey, especially given everything that happened since."

That comment caused him to involuntarily suck in a breath of air, wrenching him back to his present reality—on the verge of going to trial for killing one of those same bad boys from his earlier fantasies, shooting him just like Corey shot Nick.

Carol noticed Corey's sudden quietness and far-off gaze.

"I'm sorry, love. I said too much, didn't I?"

"No. You're right. These journals certainly chronicle my out-of-control life."

"*Formerly* out of control."

"Maybe so, but they've brought me to this present moment and to the daunting road ahead."

Carol released her grip on the journals. Corey brought them closer to his chest, then leaned down to place them into his messenger bag before standing up and looking at his watch.

"I should probably get going. I'm supposed to meet my lawyer downtown tomorrow morning at eight a.m. I need a good night's sleep."

"You feel okay, with the joint and all?"

"Yeah, fine. I actually feel good, better than I have since . . . well, I don't know when."

"You've had an intense week."

"And it's about to get more so."

"Sure you don't want a ride?"

"No. I'll grab an Uber."

"Okay."

Carol and Corey stepped toward each other, came together for a tender, momentary kiss, then hugged tightly for a very long time.

* * *

Corey awoke the next morning to the sound of his alarm at six thirty. He barely remembered getting out of the Uber in front of Nick and Evan's house the night before, let alone the intervening steps toward getting into bed. His clothes lay shed in a pile on the floor; he lifted the covers to confirm he was naked. He hadn't slept that way—alone at least—since leaving Minnesota years ago. His tongue explored the inside of his mouth. Clearly, he hadn't stopped to brush his teeth before falling asleep. What was in Carol's home-made edibles?

He could hear faint footsteps above him on the second floor. Nick or Evan or both were awake and preparing for their day, too. Corey gathered his toiletry bag and headed for the bathroom where he showered and prepared for his meeting with Rebecca in less than ninety minutes. He returned to the guest bedroom, dressed in a pair of jeans and a sweater, then became concerned when he couldn't find his messenger bag. For a moment, Corey feared he left it in the Uber on the way back from seeing Carol. But then, piecing together what he could recall from the night before, he remembered stopping in the kitchen to satiate his immense hunger and dropping his bag next to the fridge.

Corey now heard movement from somewhere below him. Someone was ascending the basement stairs. He quickly pulled socks onto both feet, then made his way to the kitchen where he ran right into Nick, who was holding the messenger bag in one hand, and zipping it shut with the other.

"Hey, good morning. How did you sleep?"

"Good," Corey said slowly. "I see you have my bag?"

"Oh yeah. It was over there on the floor under the window. You must've left it here last night when I heard you come home and make a fuss in the kitchen."

"You said *help yourself,* so I did. Carol and I didn't get around to having dinner."

"No worries. I was about to bring the bag to your room, assuming you might need it today."

"Thanks." Corey paused. In Nick's overconfident reply, he detected the same discomfort he felt for years whenever Nick attempted to explain where he had been for the evening or why he hadn't answered his phone.

Nick finished zipping the bag and held it out toward Corey with a smile. "Here you go. I was afraid the cat might dig around inside your bag. Wouldn't want her reading your private thoughts."

* * *

Later that night, Corey found himself alone in the guest room once more. Nick and Evan had asked him to join them for a home-cooked meal, but Corey had already grabbed a burrito on his way home from a long, grueling day with Rebecca. The lone respite was a casual lunch with his mother in a skyway sandwich shop during which they never spoke about his legal jeopardy. Now, Corey was mentally fried and wanted nothing more than to eat alone, in peace. He also wanted to lose himself in reading *Crime and Punishment.* He was now into Part Five, eager to see if Raskolnikov indeed gets away with murder now that Nikolai has inexplicably and falsely confessed to the crime.

Corey was barely five pages in when the ping of his cell phone indicated receipt of a text. He looked. It was from Miguel.

You there?
Yes. Should I call?
No. I'll cry if we talk.
Why?
I'm scared.
What's wrong, Miguel?
Mom hasn't woken up since yesterday's procedure.
OMG, no.

Yes. They think she had another stroke while sedated.
I'm so sorry.
Thank you.
Are you alone?
No, my sister's here.
Good. Is there anything I can do?
No, thanks. I just needed to text someone.
I'm glad you texted me.
Of course. How are you?

Corey paused a moment, before writing his reply.

TBH, not great. But I'll be fine. Focus on your mom and I'll explain later.
You sure?
Very. I've got great support here.
Okay. I don't think I can handle much more right now.
You need to take care of yourself first, Miguel. I'll share my stuff when the time is right.
Thank you, Corey. Hey, I gotta go. The doctor's coming with an update.
Okay. I love you. Sending your mom healing vibes.
Love you too. I'll text when I know more.

Two days later, Corey heard from Miguel again via text. There had been no improvement in his mother's health. She remained in a coma, with no discernable brain activity. Miguel and his sister continued taking turns sitting at their mother's bedside—praying, hoping, watching. After some brief back and forth, Miguel asked Corey how he was doing and what it was he didn't want to burden Miguel with two days earlier.

Corey paused before sending his reply. He sat back against the pillows on the guest bed in Nick's house and weighed his options. Neither was appealing at all. His first instinct was to write that he was fine, that his issues weren't that big of a deal. Corey had already endured another long day with Rebecca, and he wanted to talk about anything other than his current legal jeopardy. Besides,

Miguel had enough on his mind already and didn't need the added stress of knowing that Corey was now in Minnesota, soon to be on trial for his life. But that would be a lie, and lying was what pushed Miguel away from Corey in the first place. How could he ever explain later the full and awful truth that he and everything around him wasn't fine at all? So, he sat up straight on the bed, wiped his sweaty palms against the blankets, and chose the other option. He then wrote the longest text he had ever composed in his life.

Chapter 20

Three days later, Corey sat in the passenger seat of Rebecca's Volvo sedan, approaching the Freeborn County Courthouse.

"You ready for this?"

"Do I have a choice?"

"No. Just remember what I've said during our coaching sessions. This is the prosecutor's chance to lay out his case. It is not the time for us to present a defense. It will likely feel overwhelming—all of the evidence will be against you, not for you."

"Okay, I remember."

"I'll object, of course, as needed. And we'll make a motion at the end of the hearing to argue that the state has failed to meet its burden, then ask the court to dismiss all charges and release you immediately."

"You think there's a shot of that happening?"

"No, not a chance in hell."

"Geez, don't sugar coat it. Tell me what you really think."

"I'm being honest with you, Corey. That's my job. You need comfort? Talk to a priest."

As if that would help, Corey thought to himself.

"So, if it gets bound over for trial, is that when we present our defense? Is that when I'll testify?"

"Yes and no."

"Come again?"

"Yes, trial is our opportunity to present your defense to the jury, but you won't be taking the stand."

"I won't?"

"No way. Never. That will not happen."

"But I'm the only witness. Who else can tell my story to support the claim of self-defense?"

"I'll make that argument in my opening statement at trial and suggest it in each cross-examination of their witnesses. Remember what I told you. The prosecution's case is circumstantial. They have no direct witness to the murder—*alleged* murder, sorry. And there's no video, no confession, no gun."

"Are you sure about that?"

"Yes. The prosecution is obligated to share with us whatever evidence they've uncovered, and it will all be on display in today's preliminary hearing as well. We'll know what they have and don't have long before trial. As of right now, though, all they have is some DNA, witnesses to your whereabouts the day in question, cell phone tower records and ballistics evidence—all circumstantial. Some of it I may get thrown out on motions to exclude. Ultimately, the prosecution might be able to put you at the scene of the crime, Corey, but they have no actual evidence that you killed Bennett Jackson."

"So, you're saying there's no way they can convict me?"

"Oh, they have plenty to convict."

"Well, that's comforting. What *are* you saying?"

"Corey, my point is that we're not going to give them any more evidence than they already have. If you were to testify that you acted in self-defense, that would open the door for them to ask you a whole host of questions you don't want to answer—why you climbed into Bennett's truck, a description of every sex act that transpired and whether you pulled the trigger on the gun. No, it's better for us to have the prosecutor imply things for which I can object based on speculation than for him to elicit that crucial information directly from your mouth."

For the next several miles, there was silence. Corey figured that Rebecca was mentally preparing for the hearing, and he had no intention of interrupting with the flurry of questions in his head. He turned to look out the window for some solace at the passing pastoral landscape. He tried thinking of art, to no avail. Nothing inspirational came to mind. He did think back, though, to his conversation with Larry the day before. With the court order that Corey be confined to a radius of five miles from Nick's house pending the hearing, Larry's room at the Mayo Clinic was too far away for him to visit. So, he was relieved when he heard Larry's voice at the other end of the line.

As usual, Larry had been comforting, listening to all of Corey's questions and providing answers that seemingly made sense—about the criminal process, about Rebecca, and about his realistic prospects for avoiding prison, which Larry initially and bluntly said were not great. It wasn't until five minutes into the conversation that Corey remembered that Larry might need comfort, too, as he faced a far different kind of threat. Larry thanked Corey for his concern but turned the conversation back toward the eventual trial. Larry assured Corey that he was in the best possible hands with Rebecca as his counsel and that Larry was in frequent contact with her about strategy. When Corey pressed him for details on that, though, Larry demurred, leaving Corey once again to wonder—was his case, in fact, hopeless, or did both Larry and Rebecca have a secret strategy to set him free?

* * *

They reached the courthouse. Rebecca parked her car in the back lot. She and Corey then made their way inside and eventually to the main courtroom. It was already packed to capacity. In addition to curious local citizens, a handful of reporters both from the local affiliates and the larger Twin Cities' stations sat in the gallery. He also saw Carol sitting next to Nick a few rows from the back. Nick nodded at Corey and lifted his eyebrows, seemingly sending hopeful wishes across the room. Carol blew Corey a kiss, then folded her hands together in a symbolic offering of prayer.

Corey continued to scan the gallery. He saw no sign of Billy but didn't expect him to be here for the morning session anyway.

Billy was a few miles down the road in Rochester, at Larry's hospital bedside, waiting for another round of chemotherapy and results from the latest MRI. Corey did see one more welcome face in the courtroom, though. There, in the front row behind the defense table, was Ginny.

Rebecca and Corey walked to their assigned chairs, and Rebecca began unpacking her briefcase. Before taking his seat, Corey turned to his mother. They embraced with both arms, the lower halves of their bodies separated by a wooden half-wall.

"Thank you for coming, Mom. But are you sure you want to stay? You'll be hearing some pretty tough things."

"Yes, Corey. I'm here for you no matter what is said or happens. I love you."

"Love you, too."

She kissed him on the cheek, pulled him into another tight hug, then let him go and watched as he sat down next to Rebecca, facing the bench. As they awaited a signal from the bailiff, Corey looked across and briefly locked eyes with DA Knopf. The man exuded a confidence that scared Corey to death. He quickly broke the stare and looked once again toward the gallery. So many people, so many unfamiliar faces. He immediately felt sick to his stomach. Why must all these people be here to witness the public presentation of his shame? It wasn't so much embarrassing as defeating. Though sketches of the story had been printed in the newspaper and briefly reported on in local broadcasts, today the world would hear the gory details of Bennett Jackson's death, and of Corey's humiliating role in it. Perhaps he should strike a deal with the prosecutor and plead guilty, putting an end to this mortifying debacle before it began. Corey turned toward Rebecca and started to ask as much but was shushed as she pointed toward the bailiff at the front of the courtroom.

"All rise. District Court is now in session. The honorable Lloyd Johnson presiding." The judge ascended to the bench and sat down in a black leather chair.

"Please be seated. The clerk will call the matter to order."

"Case number 47972, the State of Minnesota versus Corey Flanagan. This is the preliminary hearing after which the court will decide whether or not to bind the matter over for trial."

"Proceed, Mr. Knopf." Judge Johnson seemed typically abrupt this morning.

"Thank you, Your Honor. The state calls Freeborn County Sheriff Ed Pfeiffer."

From his seat in the front row of the gallery, the burly, uniformed sheriff rose, passed through the swinging wooden gate and made his way to the witness box situated to the judge's left. The bailiff swore him in.

"Sheriff Pfeiffer, please describe for the court what you found when responding to an emergency call at the Marshall Truck Stop on 28 November 2013."

"The dispatcher fielded a 911 call from a woman who identified herself as the clerk at the truck stop. The call came in around midnight, reporting that a man was found dead inside a semi-truck. I drove lights-on to the location, arriving at 12:14 a.m. EMTs were a couple minutes behind me, arriving at 12:20. The clerk—Tina Roswell—met me at the door when I pulled up. She pointed toward a white eighteen-wheeler parked approximately one hundred yards away. She said she had gone out to investigate the truck when its driver failed to come back inside to pay for his dinner at the cafe. I thanked her and proceeded to drive over next to the vehicle.

"The passenger side door to the cab was open. I shone my flashlight onto the gravel-covered ground underneath and adjacent to that door. Looked to me like it had been disturbed by footprints. I also saw a patch of red-colored dust that I later collected for testing. We sent that off to the Bureau of Criminal Apprehension in Saint Paul. They confirmed it as human blood, type O negative."

"What did you do next, Sheriff?"

"I put on a pair of latex gloves, then reached out and pulled myself up level with the passenger seat. There I saw a male—

approximately early thirties, dressed in jeans and a blue flannel shirt—slumped over in the back of the cab. I climbed up onto the seat and reached back to check his pulse with my finger."

"And?"

"No pulse. And there appeared to be a bullet hole in his head. The paramedics arrived shortly thereafter and confirmed that the victim was deceased."

"All right. Did you later retrieve and inspect a bullet from inside the deceased's head?"

"Yes. I received a .22-caliber bullet as secure evidence from the Freeborn County Medical Examiner. Our ballistics investigators determined that such bullet was fired from a Colt Woodsman pistol."

"Did you notice anything else about the scene inside the semi-truck, Sheriff?"

"Yes. It appeared that there had been a tussle of some kind near the body. Clothes and papers were strewn about in the back of the cab."

"Did you attempt to identify the deceased, Sheriff?"

"Yes. There was a wallet on the floor of the cab near the body. A driver's license inside had been issued to Bennett Jackson of Pine Bluff, Arkansas. The photo on that license matched the face of the deceased."

"Sheriff Pfeiffer, fast-forward to the weeks following that killing, did you receive bodily fluid samples from the local medical examiner's office?"

"I did."

"What did you do with them, and what did you find?"

"We ran them through the state and federal databases for known criminals but found no match. We've continued to run them once per year over the past four years and never did find one."

"Thank you, Sheriff. Nothing further." Knopf returned to his table.

"Ms. Sayres?" The judge looked toward the defense table.

"No questions, Your Honor."

"Thank you, Sheriff," the judge instructed. "You may step down."

Corey pulled on Rebecca's arm and whispered. "I thought you said there were holes in the sheriff's testimony? Why aren't you asking any questions?"

Rebecca turned her head and whispered back in Corey's ear.

"This is the prelim, remember? We are saving most of our cross-examination for trial so as not to alert the prosecutor to the defects in his case."

Corey remembered, but it was difficult sitting there listening to this testimony. And he knew it was about to get worse.

"The state calls Janice Roberts." Prosecutor Knopf motioned for a woman to take the stand where the bailiff then swore her in. "Ms. Roberts, would you please tell us your occupation and position?"

"I am the medical examiner for Freeborn County, a position I have held for the past eight years."

"Thank you. Please tell us about the autopsy you performed in 2013 on Bennett Jackson."

"Certainly. I undertook an examination of the body of Mr. Jackson during the week following Thanksgiving 2013. He was a thirty-four-year-old man with bruises on several parts of his body and a bullet wound in his right temple, closer toward the front of his skull. Inside, I later extracted a .22-caliber bullet that had lodged into his brain. I concluded that he died from a massive hemorrhage in his cranial cavity."

Corey began silent chants and closed his eyes. He couldn't bring himself to pay attention to the ensuing bloody details of Ms. Roberts' testimony.

"Anything else unusual you found during your examination?"

"Yes. I found traces of semen spread across the outer edge of Mr. Jackson's anus and inflammation of his rectum, indicating that he had been penetrated. There were also bruises on his buttocks as if he had been grabbed or slapped."

"In your opinion, is what you described consistent with forcible rape?"

Rebecca jumped to her feet. "Objection, Your Honor. The question calls for speculation." Her voice pierced the courtroom enough to make Corey shudder.

"Medical examiners make these kinds of determinations every day. It's clearly admissible," Knopf replied.

"Perhaps, but there's no foundation to suggest that Ms. Roberts has that type of experience. And that is beside the point. Mr. Flanagan is not charged with sexual assault. The prosecutor's question is clearly designed to elicit prejudicial testimony."

Knopf seemed ready with his reply. "It's true that the state hasn't yet charged Mr. Flanagan with that crime, Your Honor, but this line of questioning goes to motive, to explain why and under what circumstances Mr. Jackson was killed."

Corey returned to his silent chants. He felt himself perspiring in his armpits. He knew there was no forcible sex—that Bennett had been the aggressor that night, and he got exactly what he desired. Corey didn't hear the court overrule Rebecca's objection, nor did he hear the remainder of the medical examiner's damning testimony, including her collection of the semen sample from inside the truck and a pool of dried blood from the gravel just outside it.

As the court proceeding went on in front of him, Corey's eyes wandered. Without moving his head, he looked at the three walls surrounding him. He hadn't noticed the artwork during the arraignment. Now, he was oddly comforted to see reproductions of familiar paintings—three of them—all by the Italian Baroque master Caravaggio. *Conversion on the Way to Damascus* hung behind the judge's bench in between *Death of the Virgin* on the wall to Corey's left and *David with the Head of Goliath* to his right. Corey had seen the originals of *Conversion* and *Goliath* on a trip to Rome years ago with Nick. He had somehow missed *Virgin* on a different European trip a year later, despite spending two full days roaming the halls of the Louvre.

Corey wondered whether Judge Johnson had personally chosen these paintings and whether there might be some specific meaning or reason behind their selection. Certainly, the *Virgin* represented a loss of innocence, likely a common theme in cases coming before this court. Then, *Conversion* might symbolize those repentant criminal defendants worthy of mercy by the judge in sentencing. Finally, in visual order, *Goliath* showed punishment for the guilty, the noble and valiant David having slain the victimizing giant and now upholding his severed head. Corey thought some more about the artwork, then smiled and suppressed a laugh. If Judge Johnson had chosen these pieces to adorn his courtroom to send subtle messages, he probably didn't know Caravaggio's full story. How shocked the judge would be to learn that not only was Caravaggio a notorious homosexual but that he had also committed a murder for which he was never held to account.

"All rise!"

Corey was jolted back to the proceedings going on in front of him, and he dutifully stood like everyone else.

"What's going on?"

"Huh?" Rebecca cast him a quizzical look.

"Why is the judge leaving?"

"Didn't you hear him declare a recess? He needs the courtroom for various afternoon hearings. We're due back here first thing in the morning."

After grabbing sandwiches and chips to go, they went to a motel not far from the courthouse. Rebecca adjourned to her room to log onto her computer and do some billable work. Corey retreated to his own room briefly, then walked over to join Ginny in hers. They agreed to watch movies on TV and not to discuss the day's court proceedings at all. Toward supper time, Ginny asked if Corey was hungry. He wasn't. His mind was full replaying parts of the preliminary hearing to which he had actually paid attention. Ginny said she was planning to order a pizza and that there would be extra if Corey's developed an appetite.

He returned to his room and waited for Billy. They had exchanged texts and made plans to meet up mid-evening once Billy made the sixty-mile drive from Rochester to Albert Lea. Billy got to the motel around seven-thirty. He had stayed later than expected at St. Mary's hospital in Rochester, long enough for him to grab meals from the cafeteria and eat dinner with his father. Corey welcomed Billy into his room.

"Sorry, I can't offer you a beer or anything to drink."

"That's okay. Probably best if I don't anyway. It's an hour's drive back to Rochester. And with today's news, I might be tempted to drink until I'm wasted and risk getting a DUI."

"That bad? What happened?"

"The doctor basically told us that the cancer has stopped responding to chemo. They'll do one more round, but the bottom line was sobering. She told us to prepare for Dad to die."

"Damn, Billy. I'm so sorry. How did Larry take the news?"

"Better than my mother, which is funny. Throughout this ordeal, she's been the straight shooter while he's more optimistic than the situation warranted. Today she was the one denying what the doctor foretold, refusing to give up. Dad, well, he seemed resigned to it, but not overly sad. More somber and reflective, I guess."

"Fuck, what a lousy day. I wish I could've been there for you, for all of you."

"Thanks, man. I appreciate it. But you had important things going on here. Tell me about your day—all of it. I need a distraction, even if it isn't happy news."

Corey replayed for Billy the crux of the day's hearing and each incriminating detail that flowed from the mouths of the sheriff and medical examiner.

"I'm no lawyer, but it sounds like all they did was establish who the guy was and how and where he died. Nothing that points the finger of guilt toward you."

"Maybe so, but that's coming tomorrow, according to Rebecca."

"Oh." Billy paused. "How's she doing anyway?"

"You mean with my defense?"

"Of course. What else would I mean?"

"Well, you two do have a history."

"Oh my God. That was, like, a hundred years ago. Yes, how's she doing as your lawyer?"

"Overall, I think okay, but what do I know? I've never been either a lawyer or a defendant before."

"Hmmmm."

"She's assertive, I'll give her that. Your dad certainly didn't recommend a wallflower who might get bulldozed by the prosecution."

"Yep, that's the Rebecca I remember all right. Sounds like her courtroom demeanor matches her aggressiveness in the sack."

Corey laughed and welcomed Billy's knack for turning a sour mood into a funny one.

"Hundred years, huh? Sounds like the memory of her is still fresh in your mind."

"You never forget some lovers. And boy was she *some* lover."

"Okay, I may need to stop you right there before you start reminiscing and re-telling details of your tryst. I don't need those images of my lawyer floating through my mind during the hearing."

"Fair enough."

Corey finished telling Billy about the hearing and what Rebecca forecast was coming next. He also recapped his week in Minneapolis—the reunion with Carol and staying with Nick and Evan, including the awkward moment when Corey realized that Nick had read Corey's recovered journals and what their contents revealed.

"What a fucking swine. I wish you would have castrated him when you had the chance—shot him in the balls instead of the ass."

Corey couldn't believe he was laughing once again. It wasn't funny, even though it was. Eventually, Billy checked his watch and said it was time for him to leave for Rochester. He promised to return at the end of the day tomorrow, hopefully earlier, so that he might sit in on some of the hearing. Corey thanked him, they shared a strong hug, and Billy walked out the door.

Less than a minute after Billy left the room, Corey remembered he had forgotten to ask him to pass along his best wishes to Larry. He felt like a heel. Corey ran to the door and stepped outside, hoping to still see Billy's rental car at the far end of the lot. It was, but Billy wasn't inside or near it. Corey scanned the motel grounds in the dimly lit evening and noticed Billy standing with Rebecca in front of her room. Then he saw Billy step inside as Rebecca closed the door.

Chapter 21

Corey and Rebecca sat at the defense table, waiting for the judge to arrive. He looked straight ahead while she wrote furiously on her yellow pad. He debated asking her about Billy's visit to her room the night before but couldn't think of a way to phrase the question in a way that wasn't awkward. He missed his chance as the door at the back of the courtroom opened, the judge entered, and everyone was summoned to stand.

"Call your first witness, counselor."

"Thank you, Your Honor."

Donald Knopf looked downright giddy this morning. And why not? His list of preliminary hearing witnesses would surely seal Corey's fate and get his case bound over for trial early next year.

"The State calls Barron County Sheriff Todd Coles." Coles practically skipped toward the witness stand with a visible smirk on his face. He and Corey locked eyes for a moment before Corey looked away. Coles was sworn in, gleefully promising to tell the whole truth and nothing but.

"Sheriff Coles, did you investigate a shooting in your county around Thanksgiving time in 2013?"

"Yes, sir."

"Please tell us about that shooting."

"Objection, Your Honor. The incident in Barron County has no bearing on this case. For crying out loud, that case should be handled by a Wisconsin District Court, not here in Minnesota."

"Mr. Knopf, why are you litigating a foreign matter in my courtroom?"

"Your Honor, I've called Sheriff Coles for the limited purpose of ballistics matching and collection of the defendant's DNA."

"Then get to that point now and don't bother us with an entire description of that other matter."

"Yes, Your Honor." Knopf turned his attention back to the witness stand. "Sheriff Coles, did you investigate a shooting at a cabin in your county that occurred on Thanksgiving Day, 2013?"

"Yes, sir," Coles replied with confidence.

"In the course of that investigation, did you recover a bullet from the victim?"

Victim. Corey scoffed at that word as a description of Nick. Rebecca inconspicuously reached over and grabbed his wrist. He knew it was a reminder to stay quiet and show no reaction to any of the testimony in these hearings.

"I did. It was a .22-caliber bullet fired from a Colt Woodsman pistol, sir. The hospital extracted it from the victim's buttocks, and my office secured it as evidence for a prosecution that never occurred."

"What was that victim's name?"

"Nicholas Parker."

"Thank you. Now I would like to bring your attention to much more recent events and ask a few questions. Did you come upon a single-vehicle automobile accident involving the defendant a few weeks ago?"

"I did. It was on Highway V in Barron County. When I arrived on scene, Mr. Fischer, I mean *Flanagan*, was inside his rental car, which had veered off the road into the ditch and came to rest against a large tree."

"I see. Did you discern the cause of that auto accident, Sheriff?"

"Objection. Relevance?"

"Sustained. Get to a point that affects *this* matter, Mr. Knopf."

"Yes, Your Honor. Sheriff Coles, did you accompany Mr. Flanagan to the local hospital where they administered a blood alcohol test at your request?"

"I did."

"And did you secure that blood sample from the hospital?"

"Yes, sir, the day after the accident."

"What did you do with it?"

"I ran it through the database for . . ."

"Objection, Your Honor. I'm submitting this motion to suppress the collection of that blood sample and any resulting tests or results that arose from it. My client did not consent to that sample being taken. Rather, Sheriff Coles ordered it without advising my client or Mirandizing him."

"Is this true, Mr. Coles?" The judge's stare bore down upon the Sheriff.

"Well, technically . . ."

"Technically?" The judge's voice boomed from his perch overlooking the suddenly shrinking sheriff. "I've heard enough. Objection sustained, and the motion to suppress is granted. The blood sample is out. Mr. Knopf, you know better than this. Shall we dismiss this witness and move things along?"

"Actually, Your Honor, this line of inquiry isn't over."

"Fine, proceed."

"Sheriff Coles. Did you collect any other blood samples from the defendant as a result of that auto accident?"

"Indeed, I did. We impounded the car and later found blood splatter on the driver's side window. We also sent that sample to the lab and tested it against the federal database."

"And?"

"That is what led us to connect Mr. Flanagan to the blood sample from the Freeborn County case."

Rebecca belatedly arose to object, but this time the prosecutor was prepared.

"Your Honor, I submit this affidavit from the rental car company, providing consent to search the vehicle."

"Objection. That consent was given well after the samples were collected, Your Honor," Rebecca offered, without her characteristic confident voice.

"Inevitable discovery, Judge."

"Agreed. Objection overruled."

"Nothing further from this witness."

"You may step down, Mr. Coles."

While walking back to his seat in the gallery, the sheriff smiled broadly at Corey. They once again locked eyes, but this time Corey did not look away.

"The state calls Nicholas Parker to the stand."

"Objection. Mr. Parker and Mr. Flanagan were life partners and spouses, Your Honor. Marital privilege should apply."

DA Knopf rose. "They were never technically married, Judge."

"My client didn't know that. The marriage was deemed invalid due to a technicality that Mr. Parker deceitfully hid from my client."

"That may not be relevant, Your Honor. The state will not be asking Mr. Parker about any conversations during the time in which Mr. Flanagan mistakenly thought they were married."

"It appears a ruling on that thorny issue isn't necessary then," Judge Johnson said. "Proceed."

"Thank you, Your Honor."

Corey leaned over and whispered to Rebecca. "Why are they calling him then if they're not asking about things I said to him out in the woods the day he was shot?"

"Be patient, and we'll find out," she admonished.

"Mr. Parker," Knopf continued. "On Thanksgiving Day 2013, and without discussing anything Mr. Flanagan said and also without discussing what happened to you later that evening, can you please describe for the court his demeanor that day?"

"His demeanor?" Corey recognized in Nick a voice of playing dumb.

"Yes—his mood, how he acted, that sort of thing."

"He was normal, I guess. Normal for Corey, that is." Corey couldn't tell whether that comment was a ding or a dodge.

"Well, was he generally happier, or more tense or agitated or some other description?"

"I guess there was some tension, on both our parts. We were visiting his family's cabin, and we were both reluctant about it. It did cause some verbal arguments when we were in the woods and eventually chasing a wounded deer, but nothing that much out of the ordinary for either of us."

Corey could see the frustration on the prosecutor's face.

"Was there ever a moment when Mr. Flanagan raised his voice to you?"

"Yes, but again we fought like most coupled partners do."

Rebecca rose from her chair. "Your Honor, where is this line of questioning going? Mr. Knopf seems to be trying to elicit information that would establish my client's state of mind on the day in question. But he's not seeing much success."

"I agree. Mr. Knopf, do you have anything else?"

Knopf turned toward his working table and rubbed his chin. He glanced down at his notepad then turned back to face the Judge.

"Yes, Your Honor. One more brief set of questions."

"Okay. Then do as you say and make it brief."

"Mr. Parker, as we all know, the defendant spent the past week staying with you at your home in Minneapolis, correct?"

"Yes."

"Did you ever have occasion to ask him about the killing of Mr. Bennett?"

Rebecca rose once more, but the court anticipated her objection and cut her off. "Mr. Knopf is entitled to ask about communications between these two men after they were no longer coupled, Ms. Sayres."

She sat back down.

Nick looked at Corey then back at the prosecutor.

"Yes, I did ask him about it. We hadn't seen each other in years until recently, and I was fishing for information. I'm nosy, I guess."

"And what did the defendant say about it?"

"Nothing. Well, he told me that he was under strict instruction from his lawyer not to discuss the matter with anyone."

"So, you have no idea as to Mr. Flanagan's thoughts or feelings about harming Mr. Jackson?"

"Not about harming Mr. Jackson, no."

Knopf paused, with a knowing litigator's sense of a witness making a subtle yet meaningful distinction. "Do you have reason to believe that Mr. Flanagan wished harm upon someone else?"

"Objection, Your Honor. Relevance?"

"Your objection is noted, but I'll allow the answer before ruling." Judge Johnson turned to face Nick. "Well?"

Nick looked pleadingly toward Corey and Rebecca, but neither could help him out.

"I might've read something he wrote about wanting to kill someone, I guess."

"Oh?" The look on Knopf's face suggested that he smelled blood. "When was this?"

"When was what?"

"When and under what circumstance did you read this?"

Nick no longer looked at Corey. If he had, he would have seen a face turned red with rage. "Last week, in my home."

"And?"

Nick breathed deep then exhaled. "I found some journals in a messenger bag in my kitchen, and I read them. I quickly realized they belonged to Corey." Nick proceeded to provide grim details about how Corey fantasized about killing Nick.

"And where are these journals now?"

"I don't know, sir. I handed them to Corey the following morning and haven't seen them since."

"Thank you, Mr. Parker. No further questions."

"No questions, Your Honor. But may we take a brief recess?"

"Yes. We'll adjourn for fifteen minutes and resume at eleven o'clock."

Rebecca ushered Corey into a private room in the courthouse and tried to calm him down. He told her the journals were in his bag at the motel. She urged him to destroy them or find a safe place to hide them—tonight. She also warned Corey that as bad as he felt about Nick's testimony, he needed to compose himself for what was coming next—the state intended to call Bennett Jackson's wife to the stand. The recess passed quickly. They returned to their seats two minutes before eleven.

* * *

Corey watched as a slender thirty-something woman with shoulder-length black hair strode past him with purpose across the courtroom floor before ascending the witness stand. She was attractive and wearing what Corey figured was her best Sunday dress. The absence of stockings revealed a tattoo covering most of her left calf. Corey squinted as he attempted to figure out the inked design. It must have been custom, for he saw a snake wrapped around a saguaro cactus, with something else depicted at the base of the plant that he couldn't make out as she turned and sat down. As she looked up and then directly at Corey, he saw what at first appeared to be a kind and muted face. A light layer of make-up dusted her smooth skin and a few wrinkles above her furrowed brow. As he looked at her eyes, however, he felt a slight chill. A mixture of rage and sadness tugged at the edges of her face, and when she returned his uncomfortably long stare, he felt as if she were piercing his gut.

"Please state your name for the record," Knopf began.

"Cecelia Jackson." Her southern drawl was thick. Until this moment, Corey had forgotten about Bennett Jackson's regional accent.

"Mrs. Jackson, as we discussed prior to today's hearing, I need to ask you specific questions concerning your husband in the time leading up to his death, all right?"

"Yes, sir."

"While you may want to tell us more about your loving husband, today's hearing is for a limited purpose. There will be time at sentencing to tell us more about the man he was."

Rebecca started to object, then sat back down and remained quiet.

"Okay."

"Did you speak to your husband on Thanksgiving Day, 2013?"

"I did, twice. He called me midday after crossing the border back from Canada. Then again, right before supper to say that he was going to dine at a truck stop before getting back on the road toward home." Her quiet voice and casual diction served to make what she said almost more effective than it might have been

"Thank you. And what was his demeanor, his mood in those phone calls?"

Cecelia began to choke up. "It was the same old Bennett I knew and loved for fifteen years. We were high school sweethearts and got married when he was twenty, and I was nineteen." Corey looked straight at Cecelia, who, to this point, had avoided looking back at him. Now, she looked at him with contempt. "He was in a good mood. He called to say he loved us—me and our daughter Cristina—and that he wished he could be with us for Thanksgiving but that he would be home the next day."

"I'm sure he did, Mrs. Jackson. Now, I need to ask you a rather difficult question, but it's an important one. All right?"

"Yes, sir. No question you ask can be tougher than these past four years. Cristina cries every night."

Knopf interrupted before the judge or Rebecca did. "I'm sure it's been tough. My question for you is this—to your knowledge, did Bennett ever engage in sexual relations with other men?"

"Your Honor, may we approach?" Rebecca started walking toward the bench even before the judge granted her request. Knopf joined her, and the three spoke in hushed voices.

"What is the point of this inquiry, Your Honor? It has no bearing on what happened to Mr. Jackson or who killed him. At best, I suppose the state will argue either that Mr. Jackson *did* have sex with other men so that it was likely he and my client ended up in the back of that cab, or that Mr. Jackson *did not* engage in homosexual activity and therefore he was assaulted—a charge that is not part of this case. Either way, this witness cannot testify to it unless she has first-hand knowledge of the entirety of her husband's sexual activity or desires. I don't think either of your wives could testify to that, so neither can Mrs. Jackson."

Judge Johnson looked uncomfortable and nodded to the prosecutor for his reaction.

"Well, we already know that Corey Flanagan was in that truck, from the DNA evidence. Mrs. Jackson's testimony is relevant to show that either he was there as a willing sexual partner with the deceased before things got out of hand, or that he was the aggressor in pursuing then killing Mr. Jackson."

"Which is it, counselor? You've interviewed this witness, of course. What is she going to say?"

The judge seemed happy to have the spotlight back onto Knopf.

"She'll testify that her husband was completely faithful to her."

Rebecca laughed quietly. "She has no way of knowing that, Your Honor. This testimony is pointless. As Mr. Knopf himself stated, it might be valid if we get to sentencing, but for today's proceeding, it has no relevance."

"I tend to agree with you, Ms. Sayres. Mr. Knopf, do you have any other line of questioning for this witness?"

"No, Judge."

"All right. Step back." Both lawyers did as instructed. The judge turned toward the witness. "Mrs. Jackson, thank you very much for your testimony, and I'm sorry for your family's loss. You may step down and return to your seat."

"What? I came all the way here from Arkansas to tell my story."

"And you'll get your chance at a different stage of these proceedings. For today, you've testified enough."

"But that bastard raped and killed my husband. Our story needs to be told!" Cecelia's voice boomed throughout the courtroom.

"You're excused, Mrs. Jackson. Please refrain from saying anything further until the appropriate time, as Mr. Knopf will explain later."

Cecelia began to speak once more, but the judge shushed her with a small wave of his hand. She picked up her purse, stepped down from the witness stand, and walked back to the gallery. Halfway there, she stopped to look at Corey and spoke loud enough for everyone in the courtroom to hear.

"You'll pay for this one way or another, Mr. Homo. If the courts in Minnesota won't get us justice, someone else will. Mark my words."

The judge summoned the bailiff and bellowed for order in his court.

DA Knopf intervened, whispered something into Cecelia Jackson's ear, and walked her the rest of the way out of the courtroom.

Chapter 22

The remainder of the morning testimony on the second day of the preliminary hearing was far less dramatic. The state called the gas station attendant from the truck stop. She testified to finding Bennett Jackson's body in the truck when she investigated why he was parked in the lot, well past the two-hour time limit posted inside the station and after he had yet to pay his dinner bill. She couldn't definitively identify Corey as having been in the truck stop that evening but did remember handling one gasoline transaction in cash—an unusual request in her experience.

A forensics expert testified about how he pieced together the pings from Corey's former cell phone. Though they did not have the device, they got the number from Nick and traced Corey's travel path from Barron County eastward until the phone was shut off, then picked it up again in Minneapolis later that same Thanksgiving night all the way down to Iowa and eventually west toward Wisconsin the following day. They also identified calls from that phone both to and from Larry Preston, and one to Carol later that night. They couldn't call Larry to the stand due to attorney-client privilege. And in interviewing Carol, the prosecutor determined she had nothing to say of relevance to the case.

Throughout the day's testimony, Corey noticed that Rebecca was often distracted, writing notes on her yellow pad, and subtly checking her cell phone in violation of court rules. As the forensics expert concluded his testimony, Corey again saw Rebecca slyly and furiously texting on her phone. She practically jumped when the judge bellowed her name.

"Yes, Your Honor?"

"I asked if you had any questions for this witness."

"No, Judge. But I would like to request that we adjourn for the day. I just learned of a family emergency."

"Counselors, approach."

They obliged. Corey couldn't hear what Rebecca said at the bench, but she was certainly animated about it. He could hear the prosecutor enough to discern that he intended to call two more witnesses—the clerk from the motel where Corey stayed the night in Iowa and another semi-driver who was apparently in the truck stop cafe that fateful night. Then, he saw the judge dismiss the lawyers back to their tables.

"In light of this unfortunate development for defense counsel, we will adjourn this proceeding until 8:00 am tomorrow. Court will stand in recess."

"Rebecca, what's wrong?"

"I can't explain now, but trust me. Everything will be fine, all right?"

"Okay."

"You should go back to the motel and deep-six those journals. I'll check in with you later. Let's meet for breakfast at seven tomorrow. How about the cafe next door to where we're staying?"

"All right. I hope you and your family will be okay."

"Thanks. I'm confident things will be more than okay by this time tomorrow."

* * *

Rebecca jumped into her car and tore out of the courthouse parking lot. Corey sat down in the passenger side of Ginny's vehicle, and she drove them back to the motel. She pulled into the lot and parked in a space between their adjoining rooms.

"Well, we have the rest of the day. Are you hungry? Or maybe you need a diversion. We could go see a movie?"

"Mom, I need to talk to you about something rather important."

"Remember what Rebecca said, honey. Anything you tell me could come out as testimony if I ever get called as a witness."

"It's not about the trial."

"Oh?"

"Do you remember when we were driving home from the cemetery back in Pepin, right before I was arrested?"

"Vaguely. I guess once we saw the squad cars and then what happened when we arrived at the house blurred anything else we were talking about, sorry."

"That's okay. But I was about to tell you something then, and I still need to talk about it with you."

"You sound serious, Corey. My mind is racing. Are you all right?"

"I'm fine, it's nothing about my health or well-being."

"That's a relief." She reached across the seat and placed her hand atop his. "Let's go inside, and I'll make you some tea. You can tell me all about it then."

"Actually, Mom, I need to talk about it right now before I lose my courage."

"Okay, honey. I'm listening."

Corey looked straight ahead out of the car's front window toward the nondescript motel ahead of them. It probably wasn't the best setting for a stunning revelation, one that would potentially change Ginny, or, at a minimum, change the view of her marriage to Frank. Once he let the genie out of the bottle, there would be no way to put it back in. Yet he knew the truth needed to be told. Now was as good a time as any. He kept looking straight ahead. Ginny sat turned slightly in her car seat, looking directly at him.

"I need to tell you more about what led to my car accident in Barron County."

Ginny stayed quiet and listened.

"My detour toward the cabin was a spur-of-the-moment decision. Something inside drew me to take that exit rather than continuing home to Pepin. I'm no psychologist, but I think there was something about knowing you had sold the place and that this was my last chance to see it, my last chance to wrestle with the demons of all that was unresolved between me and Frank. I don't know. Maybe I thought there would be some obvious answer once I stepped inside the cabin, the answer to why our relationship was so damn difficult.

"But then there was no key where it had always been hidden, and I couldn't get inside. I thought to myself—*I've driven all this way for nothing*. But as I exited the driveway, I thought about the place Dad had taken me once for dinner." Corey put that last word in air quotes.

"It was a bar and bad restaurant that also served as a strip club during hunting season." He finally looked over at Ginny, mostly to gauge her reaction at this first yet least shocking piece of news. Her face betrayed no emotion. She sat stoically, listening. "So, I drove a few miles over to the Foxtails Lounge. I went inside. It didn't look much different from when I was there as a kid."

"Sorry to interrupt, Corey. Are you saying Frank took you to a strip club? When you were underage?"

"Yeah. I was seventeen. It was my very last trip to the cabin with him. He said that his father had taken him there at about the same age and that it was time I got initiated into manhood or whatever kind of manhood you can ascend to in a nudie bar."

"Charming. I had a hunch Frank visited those places, but not up at the cabin. He always came home from his solo weekends up north with such a spring in his step." Ginny uttered a small mocking laugh. "Here, I thought he felt renewed by the fresh north woods air. I was so stupid. But it was unacceptable for him to take you there. I'm sorry that happened."

"Well, that's not really the point I was driving at. This is just context for what comes next."

"Oh?"

"Yeah. Like I said, I went inside, and it looked different. It was daytime, of course, so the place was a bit brighter, and a lot less crowded. There were only two other customers inside. I took a seat on a stool at the bar, and a young woman served me." He noticed the grimace on Ginny's face—a reminder of the significant disappointment when she found out he had downed an alcoholic beverage again after years of sobriety. "By the way, I ordered a Diet Coke—nothing alcoholic at that point."

The look on Ginny's face turned from sour to confused.

"Then what led you to have booze if you started with soda?"

"I'm getting to that."

Corey reached into his bag and pulled out the plastic water bottle he had brought from the courthouse. He unscrewed the cap and took a deep, long drink. He replaced the cap and slowly set it into the beverage holder between the two front seats.

"I started having a conversation with the barkeep. She was a bubbly, cute young woman. And very chatty. Something about her made me think I had met her before. I asked a few questions to try and see if I was right, but nothing matched. We apparently had never knowingly crossed paths before.

"But then she said some things that made the truth undeniably clear. And that's what I need to tell you, Mom, even though I don't want to."

"Corey, what is it?" Ginny's patience had apparently run out.

"Mom, I have no doubt that the young lady behind the bar is my half-sister. I believe Dad had a daughter with a woman who lives up north."

Corey paused, giving his mother time for this news to sink in. For a moment, she stared directly at him, or through him. He wasn't even sure she was focused on him any longer; rather, she was somewhere far away in thought.

"Mom? Is it clear what I'm saying?"

"Yes. I, uh, am struggling with what to say. What else can you tell me about her—either the girl in the bar or her mother?"

Corey explained everything about his conversation with Samantha and then too about his observations as a kid at the cafe with Judy—Sam's mother and the woman with whom Frank was extremely cozy right in front of Corey as a boy. Once he had said everything he could remember about those events, he paused once again. He resisted an urge to reach over for his mother's hand or to try and give her a hug. He couldn't read her emotions. The woman he had known for more than forty years displayed no discernable feelings. He didn't know if she was on the verge of tears or mad as fucking hell.

Finally, she spoke. "I had no idea. It's something I worried about, of course, given my suspicions about Frank's cheating and then confirming his affair with that woman at the bank. But having a child out of wedlock? In an adulterous relationship? I never let myself go there for long. I couldn't."

"I'm sorry. I was as shocked as you. But I felt I needed to tell you, that this was a secret too important to keep to myself."

"You did the right thing, Corey. It's not your fault. This one is on Frank, obviously." She paused, seemingly forming multiple questions in her mind. "Do you have any indication whether Frank knew about Samantha?"

Corey had forgotten to relay that part of the story.

"Yes, he knew. Samantha said that he had done right by her financially, but that they had never met, at least Samantha doesn't remember meeting him. I gathered that he gave her mother money to take care of her financial needs. Beyond that, I'm not sure."

"That son of a bitch."

Corey's face tightened upon hearing his mother cuss. It seemed to be happening with greater frequency now, but he didn't blame her. She had described exactly who Frank Fischer was.

"I guess I never would've known. I mean, Frank handled all of our finances, so whatever amount he sent off to Samantha or her mother was only known to him. But how did he keep them from blackmailing him or coming back to the well for more?"

"I don't know, Mom. It sounds like Judy kept Frank's identity secret, even when pushed by Samantha for information."

"How honorable of her."

Inside, Corey applauded his mother's long overdue sarcasm.

"Is she still alive? Judy, I mean."

"Yes, according to Sam."

"Sam? You only met her for a brief time and refer to her that way?"

"She insisted. We hit it off and had a good conversation, well, at least until I figured out who she was."

"Did you tell her?"

"Hell, no. I was too much in shock myself to consider going there."

"And that's why you took a drink, isn't it?"

"Yes. Maybe not the greatest excuse in the world, but yes."

"Well, you won't get judgment on that from me. It all makes sense now. I didn't think you would ever fall off the wagon that easily. I watched you that entire year you lived with me. I know how strong you are, Corey, and how committed you have become to pursuing your own well-being. This lapse in Barron County was unique. I wouldn't worry about it."

"Well, I'm not too worried about it, especially if this case goes as badly as I think it is. I'll be in prison for the rest of my life, with little or no access to booze."

Ginny sat back in her driver's seat and sighed. "Lord, have mercy." She closed her eyes. Corey wasn't certain, but he figured she was saying a silent prayer. After a long silence, she opened her eyes and turned toward Corey once more.

"What should we do now, about Samantha, I mean?"

"I have no idea. For now, I need to focus on what's ahead of me in this case."

"Yes, of course. This shouldn't be your concern at all, at least not right now anyway. Thank you for telling me, Corey. It's going to take me a while to digest, but in the end, I'm glad I know the truth. Thank you."

"Of course, Mom. Come here." He motioned for her to hug him. She tried but was hemmed in by the seat belt—they both were. For a moment, they sat comically frozen in place, arms outstretched a mere foot from their intended target. Both grinned.

"Let's try this again, shall we?"

Ginny unbuckled her seat belt, and Corey did the same. This time they fully embraced and held each other for an unusually long time.

* * *

Later, Corey picked up the phone next to his motel room bed after the first ring.

"Billy, hi."

"Hey, man. How are you?"

"Tired. Another long day here. Well, we actually only had half a day in court."

"Yeah. So I heard."

"You heard?"

"Never mind."

"Hold on a minute. Did you speak with Rebecca?"

"Maybe. Is that important?"

"Kind of. What's going on with you two, a personal reunion?"

"What do you mean by that?"

"I'm not trying to put you on the spot or anything, but I saw you go into her motel room last night after you left mine."

"So?"

"So, again, none of my business where or when you get some action. But I also need Rebecca focused on my case and not distracted."

"Corey, you need to stop right there before you say something you'll regret."

"I'm sorry if that's how it sounded, man, but I'm on trial for my life here. Excuse me if I'm concerned that my lawyer has gone AWOL. Sounds like you got an update from her sometime today, so you must know she had to leave for a family emergency."

"Family emergency? What are you talking about?"

"She got some message in court today that upset her, and she asked the judge to adjourn so she could attend to a family emergency. I asked, but she wouldn't say more."

"Huh."

"I don't even know what she has for family, to be honest. Guess I never asked."

"Corey, I love you, and you're my best friend. I know you're going through an incredibly difficult time. But maybe you should stop and think about that last statement. Maybe you should pay a little more attention to what's going on with the people around you. Despite all you're going through, others are going through difficult things too."

"Is this about Rebecca or about you? Because I've tried to be sensitive about what's going on with Larry and how hard that must be on you and your family. I care about all of you a lot. But yes, maybe I could be more sensitive about others. I'm not perfect. I did try and ask Rebecca about her family emergency, but she shut me down. Maybe she's the private type about her personal life. I don't know."

"Or maybe the emergency she's dealing with isn't about her own family, but someone else's. Did you think about that?"

"What? What are you talking about?"

"Never mind. Listen, I have to get on the road. I was just calling to tell you that I won't be seeing you tonight. Let's try for tomorrow, okay?"

"You're staying in Rochester? Billy, what's going on?"

"No, I'm not staying in Rochester tonight."

"Where are you going?"

"Dad asked that I drive to Pepin and get something for him—something important."

"Billy, what is going on? I know that sound in your voice. Something's not right."

"I'm fine," he said sternly.

"Come on, Billy. I've known you too long. You can't bullshit me. What's up?"

"You'll have to trust me on this, Corey. Things will be much clearer tomorrow, and we'll catch up on everything tomorrow night."

Corey stared at his phone once the call ended. Between Rebecca's caginess and Billy's mysterious errand on behalf of Larry, Corey sensed that everything was spinning out of control. All of this on top of having just told his mother about Frank's illegitimate daughter. And, lest he forgets, Corey faced the likely prospect of spending his remaining days in the state penitentiary given the devastating testimony elicited against him these past two days.

He felt the need to run. But to where?

Corey saw his messenger bag resting on the floor adjacent to the bed. He slung the bag over his shoulder, put on his shoes and coat, then stepped outside. It was dark, nearing eight o'clock, and he hadn't eaten since lunch. He walked three blocks to a gas station convenience store. Inside, he purchased a submarine sandwich, a lighter and a pack of cigarettes. His only personal experience with smoking was with Billy as kids when they lit up behind a barn on the edge of Pepin, inhaled a few puffs deeply, and both choked violently on the cigarette smoke, each vowing never to do this again.

But he also remembered how cigarettes seemed to be Ginny's coping outlet during all those years she was married to Frank. That memory flooded his mind when he stood at the convenience store counter asking for a lighter. Instinctively and without hesitation, he asked for a pack of smokes. After exiting the store, he walked a few blocks farther and found himself in the empty gravel parking lot of an HVAC business. He walked toward the dumpster and looked in every direction, confirming that no one was in sight and was sheltered from potential passersby.

Corey opened the package of cigarettes and lit one up. He took a shallow hit and exhaled easily without so much as a cough. He looked skyward on the cloudless night and gazed at a few constellations, straining to remember the names of any beyond the most familiar—the dogs, the big and little dippers. He then reached into his bag and removed his personal journals. He briefly paged through each one, focusing on nothing more than the volume of pages filled with his own written words. He stopped at one random page and stared at the penmanship, which he barely recognized as his own. The handwriting was messy and angry, far different than how he wrote more recently. Maybe he had come a long way since writing these lines in the leather-bound books.

Corey took one more drag from the cigarette then dropped it to the ground, crushing it with his shoe. He then held up the journals one at a time, flicked the lighter until a flame hovered below each one, soon brushing their intense heat against the tips of his finger before throwing them down onto the gravel. He then stomped each one as the flaming pages turned to ash. He stood over the charred remains of his own writing, torn between regret at the irretrievable loss of his recorded feelings and satisfaction that no one else would ever read them.

He turned to walk home but paused to pull the vibrating phone from his coat pocket. There was an incoming call from Miguel. Corey answered in a subdued but hopeful voice. What he heard from the other end of the line were sobs.

"Corey, mi mama murio."

Chapter 23

Corey looked across the table at Rebecca the following morning. Even while eating an egg white scramble, she had an unmistakable grin across her face. After a night of intermittent sleep and raging angst, Corey was in no mood for caginess or games.

She noticed him staring at her.

"What? Do I have spinach in my teeth?"

Corey shook his head, no. "What the hell is going on?"

"Not sure what you mean. I'm trying to fuel up on protein before our big day in court."

"Our big day? Why? What's going to happen today that's different from the past two awful ones?"

"Corey, you sound cynical. You all right?"

"Aside from facing the prospect of life in prison, I've never been better. The question is, are you okay? I mean, yesterday, you were completely distracted by an apparent family emergency and asked the judge to give you the afternoon to deal with it. The night before, I see you take my best friend—your one-time and possibly current lover—into your motel room. Then today, you look relaxed and even happy, as if sitting on unexpectedly good news. Excuse me if I'm slightly concerned that my lawyer has more important things on her mind than defending me against a charge of first-degree murder."

"I'm an optimist, so sue me." She laughed. "Sorry, lawyer humor."

"Hilarious," he said without so much as a smile. He continued glaring at her, waiting for an explanation.

Rebecca picked a remnant of spinach leaf from her teeth. She alternated looking up at Corey and down at her fingernail. The mood reflected in his face remained sour. Finally, she set down her fork and settled in to return his gaze.

"Okay. Sorry if I seem a little flip. The past twenty-four hours have been a bit intense, but it was worth it. I know that we are still getting to know each other, and that includes trying to build trust. So here are the straight answers to your questions. Yes, I'm okay. No, there's nothing more important on my mind right now than your defense. Yes, Billy came to my room, and there was romance. No, that wasn't a distraction from your case, in fact, just the opposite."

The look on Corey's face moved from cross to confused.

"Tell me something, Corey. Why did you hire me?"

"I didn't, as I recall. Larry sent you to me, and my mother is paying your bill."

"But you're the client. You can fire me at any time. Why haven't you?"

It wasn't the reply he expected. "Um, because I don't have a good alternative?"

She laughed. "You sure know how to charm a woman. Good thing you're gay and that your fling with Carol in college never went anywhere."

Corey's jaw dropped. "How did you know about that?"

"About your sexual encounter with Carol? Come on, Corey, give me a little credit. I'm representing a man who faces a real possibility of life in prison. You don't think I've done my homework, investigated every single aspect of your life? Besides, as I mentioned during our very first meeting, I'm up for partner, and I will do everything I can to secure it. We've both got a lot at stake here, Corey, and I don't intend to lose."

"You spoke with Carol?"

"Of course."

"Christ."

"And have those journals she gave you disappeared?"

"Yes."

Although her bluntness increasingly annoyed him, Corey admitted to himself that he couldn't fire her because he wouldn't know how to replace her and, deep down, didn't want to. Upon thinking that, he was able to take a little breath. He said nothing, though he thought *I wouldn't want to face this woman in a dark alley.*

"Do you want to lose?" Her voice was curt and direct. It stopped his incessant internal rambling.

"No."

"Good. Then I suggest you stay focused on doing your part—sit in the courtroom and listen with a straight face. Don't show any uncertainty about the outcome. Think confident, innocent and placid." She paused to take a sip of her coffee, then set the cup on the saucer, leaned in closer toward Corey across the table, and spoke softly. "Today will be the most important defining day of your life, Corey. Do not ask any more questions about my focus. Do not say a word about what you hear today in court until we're outside. Do not let your face express any feelings at all. Can you do that?"

He considered asking more probing questions about her vague yet confident declarations. And about sleeping with Billy. But then he simply said, "Yes."

"Good. And one final thing before we need to get going. I have never lied to you, and I have not nor will I lie to the judge. I abide by my duties of fidelity to my client and to the court. As a member of the bar, I have ethical obligations that I will always uphold. Beyond that, however, I will zealously represent my client. I am on your side. All right?"

He nodded, yes.

"Okay, then." She drained the last dregs of her coffee. "Once I secure you a fantastic victory, and I make partner at the law firm in the process, then good for me too." She winked. "Win, win. Now, let's go."

* * *

Corey followed Rebecca into the courtroom. They sat down at the same table as they had the previous two days. He looked into the gallery and smiled at Ginny. He also saw Nick and Carol together in the back. He recognized no one else in the full room. Who were all these people? Dashing his unrealistic hopes, he also saw no sign of Billy. Hopefully, he made it back safely to Rochester after the mysterious trip home to Pepin the night before. What in the world could have been so important for Larry to send Billy all that way on such short notice?

He looked up as prosecutor Donald Knopf entered, looking sullen. He couldn't help overhearing Knopf's brief exchange with Rebecca on his way to the prosecutor's table.

"Did you talk with Judge Johnson?" she asked.

"Yes," Knopf replied. "He's aware of the affidavit, and that I disclosed it to you late last night."

"Good. And the physical evidence?"

Knopf uttered a laugh that barely masked his contempt.

"Yeah. Sheriff Pfeiffer secured that this morning and is running a battery of tests."

"Okay. Make sure to send me the results as soon as they're available. Please."

"As if you don't know the outcome already."

"What? How could I possibly know? That evidence has never been in my possession."

"Right." Knopf looked over at Corey, then leaned in close to Rebecca's ear and dropped his voice to a whisper, but Corey could still hear. "I don't believe a word of your bullshit, counselor. I may not be able to prove you suborned perjury, but your fingerprints are all over this fucking fairytale."

"Donald, please watch your language. Judge Johnson demands decorum in his courtroom, remember?"

Corey couldn't see Rebecca's face, but her voice sounded confident and firm.

"And I'm offended you would suggest that I've engaged in anything unethical. As for suborning perjury, I'm not the one who was approached with the affidavit, and I'm not the one presenting this new evidence to the court. You are. If the document contains any falsehoods, it seems you are the one committing an ethical violation, Donald, not me."

Knopf turned and stomped back to his table. As soon as he sat down, the bailiff announced the judge's entrance, and the session was called to order.

"Good morning, ladies and gentlemen." Judge Johnson's voice was more subdued than in previous sessions. "This is day three of the preliminary hearing concerning The State versus Corey Flanagan in the death of Bennett Jackson. Although the prosecution was slated to call its final witnesses, I was alerted by Mr. Knopf that potential exculpatory evidence has come to light. As required by the rules of criminal procedure, the state is obligated to share such evidence immediately with the defense. Ms. Sayres, Mr. Knopf tells me that he has shared such evidence with you. Is that correct?"

"Yes, Your Honor."

Corey looked at Rebecca, but she didn't return his stare.

"Do you have anything to add, or are you prepared to make a motion?"

"I am, Judge. But I only received this information from Mr. Knopf late last night, and I haven't had time to brief my client. You may recall that I had a family emergency yesterday afternoon and briefly left town."

"Do you need a recess to confer with your client?"

"No, Your Honor. But for the benefit of Mr. Flanagan and all those gathered who have been following this hearing over the past three days, I suggest Mr. Knopf read the affidavit into the record—out loud."

"That's fine and will save us all time. Mr. Knopf?"

Donald Knopf glared at Rebecca before turning his attention back toward the bench.

"Sure."

"Okay. The state will read the affidavit of Larry Preston into the record. Proceed."

Knopf, seated at his table, pulled some papers out of his briefcase, then spoke reluctantly into the microphone.

"This is the affidavit of Larry Preston, dated December 6, 2017. It was taken by a member of my staff yesterday evening in Rochester, Minnesota, and notarized by Susan Thorsen, a public notary on staff at St. Mary's Hospital. The affidavit was secured after my office received a phone call yesterday afternoon from Mr. Preston, alleging that he had information relevant to this case. I'll now read from the affidavit, verbatim.

"I, Larry Preston of Pepin, Wisconsin, do hereby make this true and accurate statement relating to events that took place on November 28, 2013. I am a licensed attorney and active member of the Wisconsin Bar with a law practice in Pepin County. I have no ethical violations or complaints on my record and make this statement under no duress but rather with full clarity of thought. Although I suffer from terminal pancreatic cancer, my doctors confirm what I know to be true—that I am of sound mind and make this statement of my own free will as a means of clearing my conscience.

"On November 28, 2013, I spoke by phone at approximately 5:30 p.m. with Corey Fischer, who is now known as Corey Flanagan. Over the years, I represented the Fischer family in various legal matters. As a result of these longstanding ties, I felt that Corey Flanagan had become like a son to me.

"During that telephone call, Mr. Flanagan was extremely upset as a result of various incidents that occurred that day near Barron, Wisconsin. At the time of the phone call, I was at home and Mr. Flanagan was still in Barron County, driving toward his residence in Minneapolis.

"After my efforts to console and advise Mr. Flanagan seemed ineffective, he ended the call. Insofar as I was worried for his well-being, I immediately drove to Minneapolis. Upon arrival,

Mr. Flanagan was packing his bags and planning to leave town. Though I could not convince Corey to stay, I did persuade him to let me ride with him for the first leg of his journey so I could provide him with legal advice about his situation.

"An hour and a half south of Minneapolis, we stopped for gas at a truck stop just off the freeway in Freeborn County. I remained in the vehicle while Corey went inside to pay for fuel and use the restroom. After filling the car with gas and before leaving the station, I, too, needed to use the men's room. Corey pulled the car over to the parking area of the truck stop and waited while I went inside. I was having stomach issues that day, so I spent an unusually long time in the stall.

"When I finally walked back outside, I noticed that Corey's car was parked in the same spot, next to a semi-truck, but that he was no longer in the driver's seat. I looked around then noticed a light on in the cab of the truck next to us and raised voices inside. One of those voices belonged to Corey. I would know that voice anywhere. He later confessed to me that he had climbed into the cab to have a sexual encounter at the truck driver's invitation."

"That's not true!" Cecelia Jackson leapt from her seat in the gallery, shouting. "That man raped and killed my husband." She screamed, pointing at Corey.

"Order in the courtroom!" Judge Johnson's voice boomed louder than Cecelia Jackson's. "Mrs. Jackson, take your seat and be quiet, or leave the courtroom if you can't."

She nodded, her face rigid with anger.

"You may continue, Mr. Knopf."

The lawyer resumed reading in a dull, steady voice.

"I knocked on the passenger door, but the yelling inside the cab didn't stop. Then I saw the truck driver punch Mr. Flanagan. I have never been in a fight myself, and, hearing the rage in the man's voice, I was greatly concerned about Corey's safety—and my own. Then I remembered the Colt Woodsman pistol in the glove box of Corey's car—the same gun used earlier that day in the Barron County altercation. I ran to get the gun from the car and rushed back to the truck. I lifted myself up to the passenger side door. Through the window, I saw Corey on his back, struggling to lift himself off the floorboard. The truck driver, a large man, now straddled Corey, yelling threats, his fist raised.

"I yanked the door open, held the gun, pointing blindly into the shadows, and demanded that he back off. I did not know the gun was loaded; I only meant to use it as a threat. However, it discharged accidentally. I thought that the driver had dived backwards into the rear of the cab at the sound of the gunshot. I did not know he had been hit. Corey couldn't have known either; he was huddled on the floorboard. I grabbed Corey's shoulder, pulled, and we jumped down to the ground where Corey scraped his knee, and I noticed he was bleeding.

"Panicked, we got back into the car before the trucker could come after us, and Corey sped out of the parking lot to the freeway. At first, neither of us spoke. We were breathing heavily, relieved to be safe and away from the violent scene. When we finally did talk, I convinced Corey that we should drive back to Pepin. He agreed, though due to the lateness of the hour, we stayed overnight in a motel, returning to Wisconsin the next morning. Both of us were exhausted and relieved that our frightening ordeal had ended. I didn't know I had shot the truck driver. There was no mention of an incident in the news back home, and I assumed the whole thing was over.

"Upon arriving home, Mr. Flanagan dropped me off at my house while he went on toward his mother's home a few blocks away. After he left, I realized that I still had the Colt Woodsman in my coat pocket. The next day, I placed it inside the safe in my law office downtown, and that is where it has been ever since. This afternoon, at my request, my son Billy drove to Pepin to retrieve the gun, and I will immediately turn it over to the Freeborn County Sheriff. As authorities will undoubtedly discover, my own fingerprints are on the gun, as I was the last person to handle it. Mr. Flanagan never asked me for its return.

"My son will also bring with him a file of medical records from Corey Flanagan's visit to a hospital on the day after our return. The truck driver had pushed him, and his head struck the dashboard quite hard. I had urged him to have a doctor check him for a concussion. The records will verify the injury as well as the doctor's treatment.

"In closing, I wish to express my deepest regret at the death of Bennett Jackson, especially to his family. I am filled with great remorse that the death resulted from my actions. However, again, I emphasize that I had no intent to harm Mr. Jackson and no knowledge of his death until after Mr. Flanagan's recent arrest revealed it. My only intention at the time was to defend Corey Flanagan against the aggressive attack made upon him by Mr. Jackson inside the semi-truck on that terrible November night."

Donald Knopf stopped talking.

"Ms. Sayres, are you going to make a motion to dismiss?"

"Yes, Your Honor. That is my motion."

"Mr. Knopf?"

"Judge, I ask the court to defer ruling on the motion until my office has time to properly review this new evidence, including ballistics tests on the gun, a cross-examination of Mr. Preston, and a thorough review of the possibility of new witnesses."

"Are there any such witnesses, Mr. Knopf?"

"Not at the moment, Your Honor, but this evidence only came to light yesterday afternoon, and we've had no time to investigate."

"So, you want to keep Mr. Flanagan exposed to legal jeopardy while you conduct a fishing expedition? I don't think so. As for other witnesses, this affidavit suggests that there were only three people present at the time of the altercation—Larry Preston, Corey Flanagan and Bennett Jackson. You can't question or cross-examine any of them. Mr. Jackson is deceased, and both Mr. Flanagan and Mr. Preston have a right against self-incrimination as long as you are prosecuting both for the same murder."

"Then we will amend our pleading to charge Mr. Flanagan with fleeing the scene of a murder."

"You have evidence or at least probable cause that Mr. Flanagan had knowledge Bennett Jackson had been shot, contrary to Larry Preston's sworn affidavit?"

"No, Your Honor, but . . ."

The judge waved his hand dismissively.

"Looks to me like your hands are tied here, Mr. Knopf. You have a sworn affidavit from a lawyer with apparently unimpeachable character that includes a confession, which exonerates Mr. Flanagan for this crime. And you have no evidence to contradict it, from what we've heard thus far in the preliminary hearing. Do you?"

"No, Judge."

"Fine. I am granting the defense motion to dismiss, but without prejudice, so you can refile those charges if by some miracle you disprove Mr. Preston's confession. So ordered."

Chapter 24

Later that morning, Ginny drove to Rochester with Corey in the passenger seat beside her. Ginny had to drive faster than she normally would to keep up with Rebecca, who was speeding down Interstate 90 in the car ahead of them. They reached the Rochester exit and made their way north toward St. Mary's. Billy had summoned them during a call to Rebecca's phone soon after the court dismissed all charges. Outside of the courthouse, Rebecca put the call on speakerphone, and Corey quietly listened as Billy explained Larry's health had taken an expected turn for the worse, and that he wanted to visit with all three of them—Corey, Ginny and Rebecca—as soon as possible.

Ginny pulled her car into a parking spot adjacent to Rebecca's. They all then walked into the hospital and located Larry's room. Billy stood talking with one of his siblings just outside the door, then noticed them arriving.

"Thank you for coming." Billy embraced each of them, in turn.

"Of course. We wouldn't be anywhere else." Ginny reached out and held Billy's hand like she did so many times when he was a boy after various scrapes. "Thank you for asking us to come."

"It wasn't me who asked. Not that I don't appreciate the support. But Dad specifically asked for you and Corey. He said he has some things to explain."

Corey glanced at Rebecca, wondering why she had been summoned too. Billy noticed, reading his friend's face like a well-loved book.

"And Dad insisted Rebecca be here as well, to make sure he doesn't create any legal jeopardy for you, Corey. He doesn't trust his own legal acumen at this point."

"I'm more than happy to be here," Rebecca interrupted. "Larry was my mentor and helped launch my career. He also might have just handed me the keys to partnership at the firm. I want to thank him again, personally, like I did yesterday."

"Okay, wait here. I'll see if he's awake. Mom's back at the hotel getting a much-needed nap, and my brother is headed to the cafeteria. The nurses said they'll be moving Dad to the hospice ward later today, but no one should be in the room right now. Let me check to be sure."

Corey, Ginny and Rebecca waited in the hallway, not saying a word or looking at each other while Billy was away. He returned in less than a minute.

"He's ready. He would like you all to come in together."

They followed Billy into the room. Larry lay on a hospital bed, an IV running from a skinny machine into his arm. An array of dizzying LED displays flashed and beeped at random intervals on the screens near the head of his bed. The rest of the room looked like any other—sparsely furnished, dimly lit and wholly white.

Amidst such paleness, there was also an ashen pallor to Larry's skin. His eyes seemed bright, though—as they usually did in Corey's memory of this dear man. A flood of childhood memories rushed to him upon first seeing Larry lying prostrate on the hospital bed. How many hours had Corey spent at the Preston home hanging with Billy and encountering a man whom Corey always looked up to as the kind of father he wished he had for his own? Larry always seemed happy to see him, despite how often Corey showed up at the Preston's front door. *Come in, come in*, he remembered Larry saying, in his deep yet friendly voice, thousands of times across the years.

"Corey, Ginny. Thank you for coming." Larry's voice was deep no more.

Ginny walked directly to the bedside.

"Larry, thank *you* for allowing us to visit."

She lowered herself to his elevated bed and wrapped her arms gently around his shoulders, placing a soft kiss upon his cheek. She released her light grip on his shoulders but stayed close to his face, then stared into his gray eyes and whispered, "And thank you for what you've done. I don't know if I fully understand why, but thank you very, very much."

He simply answered, "You're welcome. I'm sorry I didn't dress up for your visit." He smiled. Ginny did as well, holding back tears.

Ginny then stepped back from the bed, allowing Corey to come closer.

"Mister Preston . . . Larry, I don't know what to say. *Thank you* seems inadequate and asking *why* feels out of place."

Corey noticed a tear running down his cheek as he nodded his head. Larry said again, "You're welcome," and lifted his head to look over at his son. "Billy, please shut the door." He did. "Thank you, son."

Larry then summoned Rebecca to stand with the others, closer to the bed.

"So, Counselor, Billy informs me that you won your case, securing a dismissal of all counts against your client in Freeborn County. Is that true?"

"It is, Larry, thanks to you. Your affidavit convinced the court to dismiss the case against Corey. I've also let my law partner Mel Thomas know that you'll be needing a lawyer once the state gets around to acting on your statement."

"No need. The doctors say I won't be around long enough for that."

Corey grimaced. He couldn't even look at Billy, suddenly feeling tremendous guilt over the weight of what Larry had done—confessing to a killing that Corey had committed. Surely, Billy knew Larry's statement was false; Larry had been at home with the Preston family in Pepin on that fateful Thanksgiving night.

"Pancreatic cancer. I never saw that one coming. When they first told me I had it, I thought for sure that I could beat it. But the odds were against me—something like only 20 percent of those diagnosed with it survive."

"I'm so very sorry, Larry. I wish there was something I could do, that we all could do." Ginny spoke the words flowing through Corey's mind. Then, she broke into tears.

"Well, there are a couple of things you can do for me. The first one is to dry those eyes. I've lived a great life—a wonderful wife, successful and healthy children, and many years of happiness in our beautiful little corner of God's green Earth. I'm a lucky man. No need to shed tears for me."

Ginny nodded. Corey handed her a tissue to dry her eyes.

"The second thing you can do is forgive me. It's the reason I asked you and Corey to come. Contrary to what some may believe, that affidavit was not my deathbed confession; rather, what I'm about to say is."

Corey and Ginny appeared confused. Rebecca and Billy looked serene.

"I've carried a terrible secret for too many years and with it a decent amount of guilt. I know about something and was involved in something that I should have told you both long, long ago."

Larry paused to take a sip of water through the long straw in his large plastic cup. The looks on Corey's and Ginny's faces only grew more concerned.

"As you know, Ginny, I was your husband's lawyer. Frank entrusted me with his most important business and personal transactions, including, of course, his will, trusts, LLC filings, and so forth. Those things you know about, but there's one transaction I did for him many years ago that you don't. As his lawyer, I kept the details of those matters and my communications with Frank private. It was my duty as his attorney, and as God is my witness, I held my clients' secrets in strict confidence.

"But since Frank's death, I've wrestled with that vow of fidelity. While I never did anything illegal or unethical, I've felt that I crossed my own moral line in one respect regarding Frank, and it has haunted me especially hard these past four years, knowing I was keeping a dead man's secrets from his living wife and son."

Corey and Ginny knowingly looked at each other. Then Corey looked at Billy, who nodded with an affirming stare.

"Ginny, Corey, I'm sorry to tell you this so abruptly, but Frank had a child out of wedlock—a girl. Well, she's a woman now, of course, about twenty-something. She lives in Barron County, and her name is Samantha. I wish to God I had told you earlier. Or better yet, I wish I had never agreed to help Frank keep that secret by drafting non-disclosure and custody agreements as well as establishing a trust fund for the girl." He paused to let the news sink in before continuing. "I only hope you can forgive me."

"Oh my God, Larry. Is that why you confessed to my crimes? Because you felt guilt about covering for my father's wrongdoings?"

"Now listen here, Corey. My statement was my statement. We're not going to discuss it. I know your lawyer will agree."

Rebecca nodded slowly, thoughtfully.

"I asked you here to make a different confession and to ask for your and your mother's forgiveness."

Corey started to reply, but Ginny grabbed his arm and pushed herself between her son and the bedside. "Larry, you are a wonderful, sweet man. There's nothing to forgive. What you've described are Frank's faults, not yours. There's no need to blame yourself for his sins."

"But I could have told you earlier, at least as soon as Frank was gone. I've felt terrible that you've been kept in the dark."

Ginny reached for Larry's hand then held it tight. "I've known about this girl in Barron County for some time, Larry. Corey has too." She glanced back at Corey, who returned her suggestive stare.

Then, Corey turned and faced Larry once more. "It's true. We have."

"Really? Oh, what a relief. Thank you for telling me that. It releases a ton of guilt."

Larry's eyes filled with tears, his face wearing a look of relief.

"And I still don't regret making that statement to the court. I know Corey's not a killer. He doesn't have a cruel bone in his body. But I feared a jury might wrongly conclude that he does."

Larry turned to face Corey. "I've known you, son, for your entire life. You're a good kid—always have been, always will be. For God's sake, you saved my son's life. From what Billy described, he would have drowned without your heroics. Marge and I can never repay you for that."

Corey looked toward Billy and Rebecca. Billy once again gave an approving nod. Rebecca did the same. Corey then looked back toward the bed.

"But I don't want the world thinking you're a killer, Larry. You're anything but that. What about your reputation, your ethics?"

"I learned too late in life that ethics have a time and place and that they are no replacement for morality. Ethics are about guidelines, about following the rules. But love and morality? Those are sacred. They're matters of the heart, the conscience. Those are the things I want to be remembered for, Corey. Will you carry that life lesson onward for me, from here?"

"I don't know if I can accept this responsibility, letting you pay the price for my wrongdoing. I didn't mean to hurt Bennett, but I did . . ."

"Listen, Corey. I did what I wanted. I doubt the world outside of Albert Lea, Minnesota, is going to spend one minute thinking about me. And who cares if they do? The state and the family got justice here—a confession of guilt, and soon enough, that person will be gone from this Earth. As for you, I already said it—I know you, Corey. Whatever happened in that truck was an accident. I know it. Billy knows it. We all know it. And we all know you are full of remorse and guilt. But here's the thing—life must go on for you. Take this experience and do something positive with it, whatever you think that should be. I trust your judgment, son. Don't let me down."

"There's no way I can ever repay you for such kindness, Mister Preston. What you've done for me is something only a parent would do. And that's how I've always thought of you, even before this week—as a father. In fact, you were the father I never had—supportive, encouraging and always there—as long as I can remember. I can't think of anything more to say to you than thank you, Larry."

"You're welcome, Corey. And thank you for those kind words."

At that moment, a nurse knocked on the door then entered.

"Excuse me, folks, but I need to do some routine checks on Mister Preston and change his bedding. I'll need you to wait outside the room for a few minutes."

"That's okay, Sue. They were just about to leave," Larry announced.

One by one, the visitors approached Larry's bedside and exchanged personal goodbyes. Ginny tried but failed to hold back her tears once more. Corey's tears flowed like a flood. When it came time for her turn, Rebecca and Larry enjoyed a few muffled laughs and a final hug. Billy kissed his father on the forehead.

"I'll be back after I see them out the door, Pops."

* * *

At the entrance to the hospital, Corey said his farewell to Rebecca while Billy and Ginny stood apart, having a conversation of their own.

"So, I'm waiting for your acknowledgment." Rebecca flashed a wry smile.

"I'm sorry?" Corey looked perplexed.

"That I'm a greater lawyer than you thought when we first met in the jailhouse."

Now, both smiled.

"Yes, you definitely are—with a little help from a friend."

"Fair enough."

"Speaking of that help, how much of what happened was Larry's idea versus your own persuasion?"

"Some questions are best left unanswered, Corey, and this is one of them. But suffice it to say that Larry Preston is a good man and makes his own decisions. I think you should take him at his word when he explained himself."

"I'll do that." They smiled. "I still can't believe that I'm walking away from all of this. I owe both of you a ton of gratitude. Thank you, Rebecca."

"You're welcome, Corey."

"So, have you told your law firm yet about the result? Is a partnership offer coming your way?"

"Oh yes. The managing partner was shocked that I secured a dismissal. They're meeting later today about my future."

"Good luck, you deserve it. And Rebecca, I'm sorry for how I spoke to you so abruptly at breakfast this morning. I said hurtful things about your commitment to my case. I apologize."

"I accept." She nodded her head and paused. "So, what's next for you, Corey?"

"I'll head back to Pepin with my mother, then catch a flight to Houston, depending on the timing of Miguel's mother's funeral."

"I'm sorry for his loss, for your loss, Corey."

"Thanks. After that, I'll fly home to California. Hopefully, I will still have a job after this unexpected absence. But if not, I'll find something else."

"Good. I'm guessing you won't be coming back to Minnesota anytime soon?"

"Maybe never," he laughed half-heartedly.

"I guess I'll have to catch up with you when I visit LA."

"Oh? You're coming to Cali?"

"Yeah. Billy invited me out for a weekend after the first of the year, depending on what happens with Larry, of course."

"Huh." Corey shook his head. Billy hadn't shared that piece of information yet. "I guess things went well between you two the other night."

"Yeah, I guess they did. It took him twenty years. But, heck, who's counting?"

"That's great. Sounds like you're getting everything you wanted, all at once."

"Maybe. How about you, Corey? What do you want now that this drama is behind you?"

"Haven't had time to think much about that, but I definitely want to get back to my art, the beach and life in LA."

"What about you and Miguel? Billy tells me you have something pretty special in that guy if you're willing to work for it."

"So, you and Billy have a couple good shags, then all of a sudden, you're the relationship experts?" He winked at Rebecca.

"Maybe not, but I have gotten to know you pretty well. You're a good guy, Corey. You're just a little too hard on yourself." He nodded in agreement. "You want some advice?"

"Depends on how much it'll cost me."

"This one's on the house, before I become partner, and my hourly rate skyrockets."

"Then, sure."

"Accept the gift Larry gave you. Never forget it, but never look back at all the shit behind it. Larry wants you to live a full and happy life. I don't know if that includes this Miguel guy, but it should definitely include the authentic Corey—goodhearted, talented and capable of more than he gives himself credit for."

He looked at her for a moment in silence before speaking.

"Thank you, Rebecca. For everything. I look forward to seeing you again in LA."

"You're welcome, Corey. Good luck."

She reached out her hand to shake his. He grabbed it, then pulled her into a tight embrace.

Part Four: California

Chapter 25

Corey stood next to his surfboard at the edge of the beach, watching as fellow surfers floated atop boards out beyond the cresting breakers and riding the day's best waves. He anticipated the feel of rolling swells beneath him, wave upon wave gently lifting him up and lowering him back down. Holding his board, he jogged to the sea, eventually diving into an approaching wave with his surfboard held ahead of him like a shield.

Man, it felt good being back to his normal life. The cold water invigorated him, and he swam farther and farther from shore. After reaching the perfect spot to catch his first wave in months, Corey sat atop his board and watched as several worthy swells rolled past. He wasn't yet ready to ride. Instead, he needed to just be—to simply float atop these now-familiar waters and survey the surrounding scene. He saw surfing friends he'd known for a couple years, bicyclists and rollerbladers gliding down the Strand in the distance, and jetliners flying overhead as they took off from LAX before making their signature turns a mile or more out to sea, then arching back toward Palos Verdes and soaring onward to the east.

Corey took it all in with a swelling heart.

The sun lingered low in the western sky. The January temps were low too—for California, at least. But the wetsuit kept Corey plenty warm, and he basked in the winter sunshine. He nodded his head in recognition of a fellow surfer, a woman he had not seen in at least two months. And while she may have been out here surfing every day in the interim, today was Corey's first time back on top of his board since he left for the condo closing in Minneapolis, which felt like eons ago. As he rose and fell atop his board with each passing swell, Corey reflected on the highs and lows of the past few months. There had indeed been a reckoning for his past failures and sins, with a price paid in grief and anger and death both by Corey himself and by those innocently caught up in the dramas of his former life.

As the intensity of the waves momentarily waned, he looked down into the water for distraction, but the dark, churning water clouded his ability to see signs of life below. Instead, his thoughts returned to the deaths of Larry and Miguel's mother and then to a still-living person damaged most acutely by Corey's crimes. Cecelia Jackson's harsh words to him as she left the courtroom back in Minnesota had revealed a level of anger and wounding that Corey had never heard from someone before. Her feelings were justified; he had taken away the love of her life.

He felt something brush past his leg as it dangled off the side of his board. He instinctively pulled his ankle back toward his body and searched in vain for what might be circling in the ocean below. Most likely, it was a patch of untethered seaweed caught in the current. While there was a chance it could have been a shark, Corey cast off that fear with blind hope. He had noticed a pod of dolphins swim past the pier just before he had entered the water, and he firmly believed in the seafarer's legend that sharks avoided groups of dolphins. He nevertheless decided to swim with his board a bit closer to the collection of surfers gathered thirty yards farther south and toward the pier.

While swimming, the waves once again became increasingly large, and he felt ready to finally take his first wave ride of the new year. As he swam, Corey's thoughts, too, rose with the swells. Amidst the unexpected chaos of the past two months, there had also been renewal and relief. Those who loved him had shown it, both in expected and in surprising ways. And Corey now had a chance to repay them, to show the people in his inner circle that he had learned lessons from the past, that he could change in positive ways and become the friend, lover and son that all of them deserved that he be. Corey saw the perfect wave approaching, and he took it. In truth, the rush toward shore was no different than the hundreds he had taken in the past, but this one felt different and exhilarating. And all afternoon, he surfed as though his soul had been resurrected.

Back at his apartment that evening, Corey made himself a salad for dinner, then moved into the living room and sat on the couch with a cup of tea. He reached for the package resting atop the coffee table, the one he had found at his doorstep after returning earlier from the beach. The return address indicated it had come from Rebecca's law office. He waited until now to open it, wanting to be refreshed and relaxed before discovering what she had sent. He removed the brown paper wrapping and smiled. Inside the package were two leather-bound journals, both filled with blank, lined pages. The smell of new leather rose pleasantly from what he held in his hands. A note card fell to his lap from between the two journals. He reached for it and smiled after reading the card's five words—*Here's to a fresh start.*

Corey thought back to the burned journals whose ashes now lay scattered across the parking lot and neighboring streets back in Freeborn County. He decided to follow her prompt, to being a new recording of his life's journey, starting with the point when it began anew. He wrote intensely for the remainder of the evening, detailing all that had happened since the court declared him a free man.

Despite his relief at the beginning of December, once the court dismissed all charges against him, the month had turned awful for the two men he cared about most—Billy and Miguel. After the farewell visit with Ginny and Rebecca at Larry's bedside, Corey and his mom were drained. It was late in the day, and after the dramatic morning in the courtroom, they decided to stay the night before journeying back to Pepin. They shared a room at the Courtyard Hotel and tried to decompress. Feeling buoyant and refreshed the next morning, Corey rose early and texted Billy. He learned that Larry had indeed been moved into the hospice wing, and that Billy was sitting in the hospital lounge alone, waiting for the rest of his family to arrive around nine.

Corey showered quickly, then walked the three blocks to St. Mary's, stopping to grab coffee and breakfast sandwiches along the way. He left his mother sleeping. He met Billy in the waiting room, where they sat together for a time in silence, each of them chewing their food slowly and sipping the hot morning brew. There wasn't much more Corey felt he could offer to his best friend at that moment, but he knew his mere presence in Billy's time of need was probably more than enough.

Soon, Ginny picked him up outside, and they drove to Wisconsin. Yet, Corey only stayed in Pepin for one night. Very early the next morning, Ginny drove to Minneapolis and dropped him off at MSP. From there, he took a direct flight to Houston. The funeral for Miguel's mother was scheduled for late that same afternoon. Miguel had no idea Corey was on his way. They had exchanged only the briefest of texts. Miguel apologetically wrote that he was consumed with arrangements for his mother's service and with entertaining a host of distant relatives who had descended on Houston from far and wide. Corey had impulsively purchased a last-minute plane ticket and decided—for better or for worse—he would show up at the service unannounced.

After arriving in Houston, he rented a car and found a hotel room near the airport. He checked in, showered and changed into finer clothes. He had mapped directions to the church on his phone before setting out, then navigated the twenty-minute drive. He arrived with half an hour remaining for the visitation and before the funeral service was to begin at three.

Corey sat in the rental car for a few moments in the church parking lot after turning off the engine. He wondered whether going in would be such a good idea after all. Was it fair to surprise Miguel this way? What if his reaction was less welcoming and appreciative than Corey had hoped? No. Corey knew this man and knew his suffering as well. He had made the right decision. He pulled the key from the ignition and alighted from the car. He walked toward the front door of the red brick Catholic church and went inside, falling in line behind scores of other mourners.

At the top of the steps, he passed through a set of large wooden doors. He spied Miguel at the front of the narthex, standing adjacent to an open casket and alongside a young Latina woman whom Corey recognized from photos as Miguel's sister, Maria. Corey stepped out of line once inside the church, opting to stand off to the side and hoping Miguel might notice him.

He did.

Miguel's face wore a muted expression, a mixture of surprise and relief. Miguel whispered something to Maria, then walked toward the back of the church and directly into Corey's waiting arms. They hugged in silence for the longest time, Corey holding back his tears and Miguel letting his flow out. Corey's decision had been vindicated; Miguel expressed deep gratitude that Corey had flown in to be by his side.

They spoke later that same night after Corey had returned to his hotel room from the service. Miguel was still entertaining relatives at his sister's. They vowed to reconnect more directly once both returned to California in a few weeks' time. Until then, Miguel had much to do in Houston, and Corey had planned on spending the Christmas holiday with his mom. Yet, in that parting conversation, Corey heard the hesitation in Miguel's soft voice. The call ended with Corey unsure whether the eventual reunion with Miguel in California would be for mending their broken fences or for saying a final goodbye.

But that uncertainty wasn't something that could be solved at the moment. They had each been through so much. Miguel and Corey needed time and space to digest their respective life changes. Surprisingly, that didn't scare Corey in the least. He knew he had been one hundred percent honest with Miguel and that he had done everything he should do amidst Miguel's heartbreaking loss. Whatever might happen would happen. Everything beyond that was out of his control. He had no choice but to be patient and wait.

Billy's pain in December mirrored that of Miguel. Larry died three days after Corey last saw him while Corey was still in Houston. He was in the airport when he picked up the call from a broken-hearted Billy. By the time Corey returned to Pepin later that night, Billy had returned with his mother and siblings there as well. Corey practically ran the four blocks from Ginny's house to be at Billy's side and to sit with him as he grieved. Even though everyone knew the day of Larry's passing was fast approaching, the finality of it hit Billy hard. And Marge, despite her stoic Scandinavian heritage, broke down in tears the moment Corey arrived at the Preston household and wrapped her up in his arms.

There was a funeral for Larry in Pepin four days later, a beautiful and comforting service befitting a kind and loving man. Billy gave the eulogy with a shaky voice. He spoke of camping trips and cub scout meetings and of many more memories of his father, who, despite working tirelessly at the law office to provide for the family, was seemingly there for every little league game, dance recital and bandaging up the kids' scraped knees. Billy noted that his father made a point of being home for dinner every night at six, even if it meant he had to return later that evening to the office to finish his work. Family dinners were important to Larry and Marge, and they required the kids to be at the table, undistracted, every night as well. Looking back, Billy noted, this was one of his father's most lasting legacies. In hindsight, those family dinners provided a daily touchpoint for the Prestons, a time in which they engaged with one another, enjoyed Marge's culinary creations, and built a foundation of love that would stay with them for the rest of their lives and be remembered fondly long after Larry was gone.

* * *

After staying with his mother through Christmas, Corey had returned to LA on the day before New Year's Eve and resumed working shifts at Framed by the Beach, picking up where he had left off. The shop owner had been more than understanding of Corey's plight during the phone call from Wisconsin, in which Corey explained everything that had happened. She welcomed him back and even bumped up his salary by a dollar per hour, saying that it was her gift to him as he began a new and hopefully unfettered life.

Corey was happy to see familiar faces once again at the frame shop. Several customers asked where he'd been. He simply said he had taken time off to see his mother back in the Midwest. That much, at least, was true. Mrs. Graner was nosy, of course, asking for more details about his trip and then also inquiring about Corey's male suitor. He coyly deferred, as he always did with the old lady, telling her that when he had more to report on that, he would.

"Don't wait so long before you reward his romantic pursuit, *ma douce*, you aren't getting any younger."

Yet again, the old lady's French accent made her blunt, accurate observations sound kind. Corey just smiled and continued wrapping her latest purchase as she spoke on.

"I've seen you with *Monsieur* Miguel in the village. You two were at an outdoor table having lunch as I walked past."

"You didn't stop to say hello?"

Mrs. Graner waved her pointer finger. "No. One does not disturb *les amoureux* when they are clearly together and lost in each other's words." Corey blushed. He remembered that day from a few months ago. "He is in love with you, that Miguel. Do not let him go. He may not be French," she said with a shrug, "but he is *un tres bel homme*, no?"

Once Mrs. Graner had finally left, the foot traffic inside the shop was light. Corey spent most of his time that afternoon working to catch up on year-end paperwork for the owner. He also snuck away for a coffee and raspberry scone at Coffee Hut two blocks down. He felt light walking through Riviera Village, taking time to observe small architectural details on a few storefronts that he had never noticed before. The new year had begun with bright sunshine, and it vivified him like few times before.

After work, he rode his bicycle home along the Strand, stopping once to catch up with a neighbor who hollered at him from an umbrella-covered chair a few feet into the sandy beach. Upon reaching his apartment and with no other plans for the remainder of the day, Corey decided to paint. It had been more than a month and a half since he had touched a brush or unscrewed a jar of acrylics. He packed his easel and a few necessary supplies into the Mini, then drove to the end of Redondo Beach, setting up at the corner of Esplanade and Avenue G, his beloved and usual spot.

He spent a few minutes looking up and down the coast, toward the mountain range resting behind Malibu to the north and then to the mansion-covered green hills of Palos Verdes to his left. He had painted both ends of that horizon dozens of times and was inclined to return to those favorite scenes once again. But a voice inside his heart told him to look for a fresh perspective and create something unique. Directly below him sat a grouping of six volleyball courts bordered by a pair of southern California's iconic blue lifeguard stands. Today, in winter, those stations sat empty and boarded up. But the longer Corey stared at them, the more humanlike they appeared—their support beams as legs stretched across the sand, the lips of their roofs as hats shading their eyes from the bright yellow sun, their ramps reaching outward toward the shoreline as the yearning of a heart to plunge into the sea.

Corey stood at his easel for hours, pulling strokes of paint across the canvas. Light blues depicting the guard posts, dark navy for the roiling ocean. Lemon yellow beams of sunlight cascading down from the sky, muted tones of taupe for the vast and endless beach. Random lines of emerald green recreated seaweed that had washed ashore, then black and white and brown and red for the varied array of Angelenos dotting the landscape as far as he could see.

As Corey painted those real-life people who biked and surfed and sat and held hands while walking along the Strand, his mind drifted toward two fellow Southern Californians that he had hoped to see once again quite soon. As for Billy, there was already a plan to meet. Billy's birthday was this coming Sunday, and he asked for a day of watching NFL football with Corey as they ate several pizzas. This would be their first time together in person since each had arrived back on the coast. Corey yearned for this reunion, for moving on from their respective dark wounds, and to beginning a brand-new year.

When Corey's mind drifted toward Miguel, his heart felt less light. Miguel had arrived back in LA a day after Corey's own return a week ago, but they had yet to meet up one on one. There had been daily phone calls and random texts in between. But Miguel professed a need to focus first on a return to his work, a desire to make up for lost billable time as a paralegal to show gratitude for his law firm being so generous to Miguel when he needed time away in Houston for all those weeks. As of now, Corey and Miguel have no concrete plans for a date. After Corey proposed one and Miguel had declined, Corey decided to pull back and wait for Miguel to make the first move toward meeting up. So far, no offer had come.

Soon, Corey felt a pang of hunger, so he packed up his painting supplies and headed toward home. There, he put his things away and stared into the fridge, eventually closing the door when he decided he wasn't hungry yet, after all. He walked through the living room and stopped in front of the triptych painting of the lions. He remembered that the deadline for the Southern California Emerging Artists contest loomed at the end of this week. He thought too of Miguel, who had been so encouraging and complimentary about this piece. Corey kept staring at his artwork, then eventually thought to himself, *why not?*

He returned to the kitchen counter and opened his laptop. He pulled up the website for the contest then filled out the application online. Afterward, Corey walked into the living room and removed the painting from the wall. He carefully wrapped it up in brown paper and taped the edges shut. He set the large package against the wall adjacent to the front door where he would find it the next morning and deliver it to the contest's drop-off site. Then he shut off the living room lights and retired to his bedroom after this long but satisfying day.

Chapter 26

On the Saturday after New Year's, Billy showed up at the café as promised. Miguel had been waiting for a few minutes. He stood, and they two shook hands warmly, then sat down for lunch. Miguel expressed his deep sympathy for the loss of Billy's father.

"And I'm so sorry about your mother, Miguel. I guess we're both part of that club no one wants to join."

"Thank you, and thanks again for the lunch invitation, Billy. Though, I'm still not clear why you wanted to see me. You sure Corey didn't put you up to this?"

"Not a chance, he's too proud. I even had to break into his place when he was gone to track down your number."

"Gone?" Billy noticed concern in Miguel's voice and was glad.

"Yeah, at work. He's fine, in case you're wondering."

"Come on, you know that I care about Corey. I care about him a lot."

"I know you do, Miguel. It was obvious that day last fall when we first met at the bar in Redondo. He cares a lot about you, too. That's why I'm here."

"Not sure I understand."

"The way I see it—you love him, he loves you, and you're both alone and miserable. Doesn't make a ton of sense."

"It's complicated, you know? Corey's complicated."

"Bullshit. He's not complicated at all. He's simple—easy to figure out."

"Then please enlighten me because from where I sit, he's a code that's hard to crack."

"What, because he has a past and didn't tell you every single detail?"

"Those were some pretty important details."

The waitress approached the table, and Billy waved her off. Food could wait.

"And he killed someone, for God's sake," Miguel whispered.

Billy paused, then said, "Listen, I'm not here to tell you what to do or to defend Corey's actions. But I am here to tell you that I think you two bullheaded boys need to get back together—right now."

Miguel started to speak but was hushed.

"Hear me out. You said Corey is complicated, but you're wrong. He's a simple human being with simple needs. He wants to be accepted and loved for who he is, just like the rest of us. Nothing more, nothing less. He's been the best friend I could ask for nearly my entire life. And I'll tell you this—if you meet those very simple needs, he'll be the most loyal, loving person you could imagine. For the rest of your life."

Miguel looked down at his water glass. He didn't know what to say. Really, what else was there to say? Billy had expressed the most important part.

"It's not that easy, man. I trusted him with my most personal, honest self, and I got half-truths in return. He owed me more than that."

"You're right, Miguel. Corey did owe you that. But stop to think, when was the right time for him to tell you what was hounding him? First date? Third date? He's not a guy with a strong gift for strategy. He would have told you eventually. It wasn't a lack of trust or honesty that kept him quiet about his past. It was terror that you don't know him well enough to put it in perspective, to balance it against who he has become. And here's the thing. Do you love him? Do you want to be with him?"

"You know I do, but sometimes that's not enough."

"Of course, it is. I know for a fact how difficult it is for Corey to trust people, and he has every right to his wariness given all he's been through. But he's rock-solid—a trustworthy person. Count on it."

"Yeah? Well, did he tell you that I'm positive? That I have HIV?"

Miguel was certain the answer would be yes, confirming his assumption that Corey had shared Miguel's well-guarded secret with Billy. The look of surprise on Billy's face mirrored the words that followed.

"No, he didn't." Billy placed his elbow on the table, his hand to his chin, and leaned in toward Miguel. "What does that tell you?" Miguel set his own elbows on the table, crossed his arms and looked away. Billy continued. "I think it tells you you're in love with someone you can trust. That's what I think."

The waitress returned to the table. Billy asked for two cups of coffee and a few more minutes to peruse the menu. He looked once again at Miguel, then completed the last of his rehearsed lines.

"Listen, Corey's planning to come over to my house tomorrow to watch football and celebrate my birthday. I think he should be with you instead. You know how he feels about sports."

They both laughed.

"How about you call and invite him over, take him off my hands? He's ruining my love life, to be honest—always moping when we hang out. My long-distance girlfriend, Rebecca, is flying in next week, and I need Corey out of my hair. Help a guy out here?"

Miguel saw the sparkle in Billy's eyes and eventually returned his playful smile.

"Sure, I can do that. I guess I owe you a return favor anyway. Happy Birthday, Billy."

* * *

They agreed to meet at the beach, directly in front of the Hermosa Pier. They walked and talked for two straight hours, sharing intimate details from their pasts—things neither had ever revealed to anyone else.

Corey told Miguel about his family. How he walked on eggshells around Frank and witnessed his mother being abused. How he never measured up to his father's expectations and was berated for being weak. How in Corey's most vulnerable moments, when he revealed the most intimate core of his being, Frank chose words of rejection, and Corey wore a cloak of shame. Miguel listened and expressed affirmation. He stopped to embrace Corey, shedding his own long-held tears. It was the first time they had touched, skin to skin, in almost one month.

Corey told Miguel about his history with romance and sex—all of it. With Carol, with Nick and with far too many anonymous trysts where he had put his mental and physical well-being at risk. And he talked about one night in a lonely truck stop, on Thanksgiving, when he did things for which he would always carry immense regret. Corey explained how Bennett Jackson enticed Corey in the men's room, first showing himself at the urinal and then running soft fingers across Corey's back and summoning Corey to join him in the truck outside. Corey now admitted to feeling desperate and impulsive, but at that moment, as he climbed into Bennett's truck, he felt empowered to act on his testosterone-driven desires, still amped up from the dramatic fight with Nick and the act of fleeing the scene of a crime.

Miguel listened as Corey explained the raw and bitter truth, then assured him of his worth as a man. "Created in the image of God, as they say. We're all fearfully and wonderfully made, according to Mom." Miguel reached out and grabbed Corey's hand. "And that includes you."

Corey then told Miguel about himself, who he felt he truly was inside. Scared, needy, alone. Loyal to a fault, hesitant to speak his mind. Artistic, a lover of nature, a traveler and a good friend.

Slowly, Miguel spoke, and Corey listened. "You are all of those things, and so much more. Let me tell you what I can see from here."

When Miguel had finished summarizing the confident, brave and honest person he saw in Corey, Miguel began to speak about himself. He told Corey about his family and the final days by his mother's bedside. He told Corey about his journey toward coming out and the night he was assaulted and infected with HIV. Corey paid attention to every word, holding Miguel's hand throughout, squeezing it in the moments when he sensed Miguel's deepest pain. Finished with their respective stories, having revealed their innermost wounds, they found themselves at the end of the street where Corey lived. They were exhausted and silent after they had seemingly said everything they could think of to tell.

"You want to come home with me? My fridge is pretty bare, but I could scrounge up something to eat."

"Yes, I would like that very much."

Heading up the street toward home, Corey reached out once again and took Miguel's hand.

"Um, I think you're cutting off the blood supply to my fingers."

"Apparently, I don't want to let you go."

"Fat chance. Apropos of the recent holidays, I'm like Mary and Joseph. There's no room at the inn, and I've got nowhere else to go."

Corey laughed, then released Miguel's hand at the front door, fumbling for his keys before letting them both inside.

"Here, let me take your coat." Miguel removed his windbreaker, and Corey hung it on the hook behind the door. "What can I get you to drink?"

"Something warm would be nice. Cocoa or tea?"

"You got it. Have a seat. I'll be right back."

Miguel plopped down into the sofa and happily lay back against the leather headrest. They had walked for several miles, and his feet were aching. He opened his eyes and raised his head once Corey re-entered the room.

"I put the kettle on. Shouldn't be long."

"Great. Come here and sit by me."

Corey sat as close as he could to Miguel and reached for his hand. He told Miguel about attending the condo closing in Minneapolis, how seeing Nick wasn't as difficult as he had feared—just the opposite. Nick had appeared smaller, less overwhelming, and Corey discovered he didn't care about Evan.

"Sounds to me like you've moved on. I'm glad to hear it."

"That makes two of us," Corey said. "But he did leave me a parting gift of sorts."

"Oh?"

"Yeah, take a look behind your head."

Miguel turned around in his seat, noticing something new hanging on the wall above the couch. Though he didn't know terribly much about fine art, he recognized the face in the deer.

"Frida Kahlo, right?"

"Indeed. One of her less famous works, to be sure, but definitely something she created."

Miguel listened as Corey explained its origins and interpretation by critics far and wide. He offered his own personal observations as well.

"But what happened to the triptych with the lions, your own beautiful work of art?"

"I took your advice and entered it into a competition last week, the annual Southern California Emerging Artists' Showcase."

"And?"

"And what?"

"How did you do?"

"I'm not sure. They'll announce the winner at a big gala next month. I have two tickets, but no date. Are you interested in going?"

"Of course, I'm interested in going—especially with you. I'll get tons of envious looks standing next to the contest winner when they announce your name."

"I wouldn't bet your life savings on it if I were you."

"That painting is amazing, Corey. If they don't award you first place, then the person who does win must be Van Gogh."

"I appreciate your support, I really do. To be honest, I am hopeful to at least place in the top three."

The kettle whistled, and Corey went to make two steaming cups of jasmine tea. He brought them to Miguel along with a small plate of cheese and crackers. They went on talking while the sun set behind them in the west, reminiscing about Christmastime as kids and their most memorable gifts across the years. For Miguel, it was a hand-me-down set of real Lionel trains. For Corey—his first set of acrylic paints. They talked right through and past the dinner hour, but neither of them thought about eating. The satiating reunion and flowing conversation stemmed the tide of longing for something more.

"Wow, it's getting late. I better be going." Miguel stood up to leave. "Thank you for a wonderful day."

"It was for me too, perhaps the best day I've spent with you yet."

Miguel gently nodded his head as Corey rose from the couch. Then he leaned in close, enveloping Corey in an embrace and tenderly kissing him. When it felt right to let go, he did. Miguel noticed a smile develop on Corey's face, his eyes just opening.

"So, goodnight," Miguel said. "Maybe I can see you tomorrow?"

"Or you can stay over and see me all night long."

Corey stared into Miguel's dark eyes, waiting for the expected affirmative reply.

"You don't know how happy I am to hear that, but for tonight I'm going to say no."

"Oh," Corey replied with a disappearing grin. "I understand."

"Actually, I'm not entirely sure that you do. This evening, this whole day has been amazing. Definitely the best date we've ever had."

Corey started to formulate a smart-ass reply but paused at the sincerity in Miguel's face, the tremble of his lips.

"I want this to be our new start, and I want to remember this day just as it's been—perfect. You've opened parts of yourself that I'm guessing you've never shared with anyone else. I want to honor that trust by letting it be the pinnacle of our date and not cheapen it by jumping right into bed."

"So, I'm cheap now, is that it?" This time, Corey couldn't resist a frisky reply.

"Not at all. You're more valuable to me right now than I can say. I want our relationship to be about more than just sex, Corey, and I want it to last for the rest of our lives."

Chapter 27

Two nights later, Corey dreamed that he had been told to meet Miguel atop the Manhattan Beach Pier. In the dream, which felt extraordinarily real, Corey found himself standing at the edge of the ocean and above the empty beach. It was dark outside in the pre-dawn hours; even the lampposts emitted no light. But, as with all dreams, he could somehow still identify one or two key details—the contours of the timbered platform and the little blue gift shop at the farthest end of the pier. The instructions he remembered receiving had been clear: *Come alone. Make sure you're not followed. Keep on walking until the end.*

He had to step over a knee-high chain barrier and pass by a sign prohibiting visitors before sunrise. Despite misgivings about breaking that rule, he continued on after seeing Larry holding a fishing pole over the side of the railing with one hand and waving Corey on through with the other. So he kept on walking, alone, and Larry did not follow. Halfway down the pier and still deep in his dream, Corey suddenly didn't know which way to go despite there being only one way forward and one way back. He looked to his right and noticed a man sitting on a bench, pointing toward the blue gift shop at the end of the pier. The man looked familiar with his beard, a grease-smudged baseball cap, and a devilish grin that Corey could swear he had seen once before. Corey then noticed a steady stream of blood running down the man's cheek and dropping with a splat onto the pier. Yet the man kept smiling at

Corey and pointing toward the little blue building, so Corey kept on walking along with no one trailing behind.

When he reached the end of the pier, there were suddenly large waves when only a few seconds before the ocean had been calm. Corey looked around frantically for Miguel but saw no one. He tried to yell Miguel's name, but his throat was dry. Part of him felt that he was screaming, but the other part knew he'd inexplicably gone mute. That is when she appeared from behind the gift shop, walking toward him with rage-filled eyes. He tried speaking her name, but what came out were parched patches of words.

In the dream, though, Corey couldn't hear Cecelia Jackson either. He could tell she was shouting, but the roaring sea all around them drowned out anything she was trying to convey. Corey looked back down the pier, hoping for help from the men he had passed by only moments before. But he saw nothing. All of the lights in the normally illuminated Los Angeles basin had gone dark, and now a salty spray from the churning ocean assaulted his face and stung his eyes.

Corey tossed and turned in his bed. Sweat poured from his body. In the dream, Cecelia pulled out a gun that looked exactly like the Colt Woodsman Corey had used to shoot both Nick and Bennett. But his eyes were stung shut, and water kept splashing in his face, so how could this be? How could he see a threatening gun when in truth, he couldn't see?

He awoke, startled. He sat up straight in bed and tried to catch his breath. Almost immediately, he felt the dampness of his pillow and surrounding sheets, as well as the drops of perspiration running down his face. Then, he heard the wind battering the bedroom window. He had left the window open before falling asleep hours before. Raindrops flew in from the outside, carried by the Santa Ana winds and pelting his face. He reached up and pushed shut the sliding glass, then turned around and clicked on the lamp atop the nightstand adjacent to his bed. He sat up against his damp pillows, then took in and exhaled several slow, conscious breaths. Corey was now wide awake. He considered opening the final pages of *Crime and Punishment*, which sat on the nightstand to his left, but he was too wound up to focus on the tiny print. He decided to get up and fix himself some warm milk and honey instead. It was the remedy that his mother prescribed whenever he awoke from nightmares as a boy.

After finishing his beverage, Corey felt better but still too wide awake to go back to bed. So he set up his easel in the living room and stared for a moment at the empty canvas. He needed to paint something happy, or at least something that would take his mind off that horrible dream. He closed his eyes and took himself back to a setting that he had seen so many times in the past, but which had a new meaning now because he saw it in a very different light. He opened his eyes and then made the first light marks of a new work. He didn't leave his stool for two hours—musing, making broad, bold strokes and then the lighter touches: a sliver of light here, a pool of shadow there.

Finally, he laid his brush down. He sat back in his chair to consider what he had made. The central image of the painting was the same one he had tried to paint scores of times before. Those attempts always produced dark, shadowy pieces, in which the color value of a building was barely different from that of the surrounding woods. Today, he painted a scene in muted sunlight, just bright enough to distinguish the mass of the modest, brown cabin from the abundant green canopies towering above. This time, the lines were sharper, and the right angles of the building contrasted with the curving lines of nearby flora and fauna. Saturated, bright colors highlighted patterned curtains hanging inside the cabin windows, wildflowers in the adjacent woods, and the figures of a pair of children—a teenage boy and a younger girl—sitting on swings in a playset, wearing matching red and blue striped T-shirts and holding hands as they swayed.

At the sound of a ping, Corey reached for his cell phone and was surprised at the time—five thirty in the morning. He had been at his easel for two full hours though it seemed like less than half that time. He smiled in relief at the sight of Miguel's name on the screen. Corey tapped the banner and read the short text. *Meet me at El Burrito Junior at 7 tonight?*

Corey quickly typed his positive reply, then asked why Miguel was up so early. *Thinking about you*, was the answer before Miguel posed the same question back to him. *Painting my next masterpiece*, Corey replied. The texting went back and forth for fifteen minutes before it was time for Miguel to shower and head off to work. Corey set the phone down and picked up his brush, then stared at the easel. He was happy with what he saw, and with how much he had painted in so little time. He sat back in his chair and pondered the creation some more, thinking of how accents of color, shadow and light could support the composition and frame the focal point. He saw possibilities, how he could make the painting better, but what was exciting was that he wasn't thinking about "fixing" anything; he wasn't thinking about corrections, only emphases.

He left the canvas on the easel, sealed the paint container lids tight and took his brushes to the sink for cleaning. He realized that the past two hours had calmed him down from the frantic nightmare. Even his neck muscles, which often tensed as he worked, were more relaxed. He knew he would always feel remorse over the death of Bennett Jackson and gratitude for Larry Preston's sacrifice, but he no longer felt intense guilt or shame. What was done was done. Yes, he had taken a life unwittingly and unintentionally, but he had saved one too—Billy's. And yet, the dream lingered in his conscience. Cecelia Jackson's angry outburst at the court hearing in December stayed with him, likely fueling these nightmares. Both when he was sleeping and awake, Corey feared that she might one day seek the kind of justice that was denied her when no one was held to account for her husband's death.

* * *

Corey and Miguel met at the taco stand on PCH, the same place where they had enjoyed their first date. Tonight, however, Corey was on time.

It's the new me, he had declared last week to Billy. *No more running late with lame excuses.*

Corey and Miguel ordered and waited for their food while seated at a yellow picnic table adjacent to the stand. They quickly resumed their deep conversation from the night before. At Corey's urging, Miguel went first. He spoke with more detail about his time in Houston caring for his ailing mother. In the midst of her physical struggle, Miguel had added an emotional one—revealing to his mother that he was HIV positive.

"I knew she might die, Corey, and I couldn't live with myself if I hadn't been one hundred percent honest with her about that."

"How did she take it?"

"Way better than I'd hoped. Mama is a kind person, not judgmental. Still, I feared she might take it on as her own burden, that she was the one who had to care for me."

Corey listened and reached out to hold Miguel's hand.

"Turns out that she already knew almost as much about HIV and AIDS as I did. Apparently, she read up on it years ago when I first came out to her as gay. As soon as I mentioned my diagnosis, she asked if I was on the medication regimen that would render me undetectable. I was blown away. I affirmed with her that indeed I was."

"Wow. Moms are amazing, huh?"

Corey's wistfully thought of Ginny and the pride he felt in seeing her take the reins of her life in the years since Frank's death, forging a new path based upon her own happiness, her own desires and dreams.

"Yes, mine sure was, and it sounds like yours is as well." Miguel paused before switching directions. "Tell me something now, Corey, something you've never told anyone else."

Corey's eyes grew wide, and he covered his mouth with his right hand in thought. He realized that this was an opportunity to bond even closer with the man he knew that he loved more than any other. He reflected carefully for a few moments, swallowed hard, then spoke. He told Miguel about the nightmares—not all of them, but the running themes of remorse over killing the truck driver and the hatred in his heart for how he was mistreated across the years by both Frank and Nick.

"I swear I never meant to hurt Bennett Jackson, but I did think about killing Nick. And during those moments in the Barron County woods, before I pulled the trigger of the handgun, my mind was conflating two people into one. Frank and Nick became interchangeable. Their words sounded the same. Their actions felt the same. And their humiliation of me bored down into my heart in the same way. I remember thinking at the time that I wanted to kill them both if I could, but the only one of them in front of me was Nick."

Corey closed his eyes and stopped talking. While he was being completely honest about a deeply held secret, just as Miguel had asked, he immediately felt foolish. He had admitted to his current lover that he had once felt like killing a former one. He was hesitant in opening his eyes, fearing that he would see Miguel run away from him for dear life.

"That must have been difficult to say out loud, Corey. Thank you for telling me."

He opened his eyes fully and looked at Miguel. "You're not freaked out?"

"Freaked out?"

"Yeah, like afraid I might do the same to you."

Miguel laughed.

"Not sure I see the humor in this . . ." Corey's voice trailed off.

"No, I'm not freaking out. I completely understand the context. I mean, I think that almost everyone can harm another person under the wrong circumstances. Everyone."

"Well, everyone except you. I can't imagine you harming a flea."

Miguel's smile disappeared. His face took on a serious look.

"After I was assaulted and found out who the guy was, I thought about killing him, Corey. Honest to God, I did. He was in custody by then, so realistically I had no way to get at him, but if things were different, who knows what I might have done with the rage I felt inside."

Corey nodded his head. His own victimization at the hands of Nick and Frank never included anything as physically destructive as what had happened to Miguel, but he harbored anger just the same.

"Do you still feel that way? Wanting to hurt your attacker?"

"No, not at all."

"Why? What changed?"

"I changed, Corey. It took a long time, but I changed inside. With the help of therapy and the support of my family and friends, I slowly switched my focus from *why did that guy do this to me* to instead thinking *what purpose might this serve me for the rest of my life.* I can't change the past or erase what happened. Even if I got revenge, the fact of the assault will never disappear. But I realized it didn't have to affect my future."

"So, you got over it, just like that?"

"No. Like I said, it took time. And it took a specific but difficult step on my part."

"What was that?"

"It's the same step you need to take with respect to your father and Nick. Once you do that, your feelings about the past will melt away. I promise."

"So, are you going to tell me what this magic step is?"

"Yes, but not until I get your agreement that you'll do what I ask."

"Okay . . ." Corey looked at Miguel with mild suspicion. Surely, he wouldn't ask something more than he knew Corey was capable of doing?

"You promise to do what I ask?"

"I promise."

"Good." Miguel took both of Corey's hands in his, holding on to them as intently as the piercing stare from each of their eyes into the others'. "I want you to forgive them, Corey. You need to forgive both Frank and Nick. Whatever harm they caused you, no matter how bad it hurt, and even if you never received the apologies you deserved, I'm asking you to forgive them freely, fully and forever. Right now."

Corey nodded. He got it. Miguel was right, forgiveness was the only real way to move on, and Corey knew it as soon as the words left Miguel's lips.

"There's one more person you need to forgive in order to achieve the true peace you deserve, too."

"My mother?"

"Only if you're harboring bad feelings toward her, but that's not who I was thinking about."

Corey looked puzzled. He scanned his mind to remember who had wronged him, about whom he might still have deep feelings of ill will. He came up empty and cast Miguel an imploring look.

"Most of all, you need to forgive yourself."

Chapter 28

In early May, Ginny called with big news.

"The house sold today, Corey. I guess the realtor was right to wait for the spring market. The first couple to walk through the open house made a full price offer on the spot."

"Congrats, Mom. Great news."

"Thanks, honey."

"Have you told Grandma and Aunt Mary?"

"No, not yet."

"I'm sure they'll be happy to hear it, and to get you moved back home to Eau Claire."

"Hmmmm."

Corey sensed something in his mother's voice. They had spoken at least twice a week since he returned to California in December. By now, he could discern almost all her varied emotions simply by the tone of her voice.

"Mom, what's going on?"

"Going on?"

"Yeah, I'm sensing there's more you want to say. Is everything all right?"

"Actually, things are great. It's just that I have even bigger news than the house selling. I'm trying to figure out how to tell my mother and sister. And, how to tell you."

"Mom?" Corey's stomach fell. He feared the worst.

She took in, then exhaled an audibly deep breath. "I'm not moving to Eau Claire, Corey."

"You're staying in Pepin?"

"Oh, for heaven's sake, no." Her ensuing laugh was deep and soulful. "I'm moving out of state."

Corey remained silent on the other end of the line. Where in the world could his mother be going? Across the river to Minnesota?

"I'm coming to California, Corey. But I promise I won't be a burden to you. In fact, I won't even live that close. I'll be up in Santa Monica. As I recall from my visit out to see you last February, that's a good forty-five-minute drive from your place in Hermosa, right?"

He was speechless. The reference to February jolted his memory. Ginny had spent a week with him. Then, at the end of her trip, she had gone to visit a high school classmate who lived in a rent-controlled flat ten blocks from the ocean in Santa Monica.

"Anyway, I'll be subletting Elizabeth's apartment. She's going into the Peace Corps. Can you believe that? At our age? I'll rent her place fully furnished for the two years she's away. I'm basically going to sell all of our furniture here and move out west with as few possessions as possible."

Corey could barely grasp the information he was hearing.

"Uh, what? I mean, that's great. How did this all come about?"

"To be honest, Corey, I have you to thank. As you know, from your visit here last fall, I was fully intent on moving back home to Eau Claire, living with Mary and helping out Mom here and there as she gets older. But then all of that stuff happened."

Corey latched onto the word *stuff* and exhaled with relief. Ginny had always said *stuff* where most other people would have simply said *shit*.

"When I learned about the existence of your father's daughter and then sat through the preliminary hearing for your case, doubts crept into my mind. Why was I retreating backward to my childhood hometown as if my life were fading into the sunset? For garsh sakes, I'm only sixty-seven. And my mother's still alive. Chances are I'll live at least another twenty years, so why give up on my dreams now?"

"Which dreams, Mom?"

"To get a college degree, to make something of myself professionally. No offense Corey, I loved being a full-time mother, but I had other ambitions as a young girl. I wanted to be a nurse. I wanted to help people, to save people if I could."

"Those are definitely valid dreams, Mom. I'm sorry I didn't know about them sooner, or I would have done more to help you fulfill them."

"It's not your responsibility, honey. It's mine. And I am doing something about it. When I visited with Elizabeth a couple months ago, I couldn't believe when she told me that she was in the final stages of applying to the Peace Corps—to go live her own dreams in a far-off country. She's been accepted into the program and will be gone by next fall. All of that got me thinking—if Elizabeth can go off on her own to a foreign country, why in the world couldn't I do something like that—move away from everything I've known? Why couldn't I finally do what I wanted to do with my life?"

"Mom, I am so impressed. This is terrific news."

"But I'm adamant, Corey. I'm doing this on my own. I'm not asking for your help. I applied and got accepted into Santa Monica City College. I'll start their nursing program in the fall. I'll probably be the oldest student by about fifty years, but to heck with it. I'm doing this. The program lasts two years, the same amount of time that Elizabeth will be gone in the Peace Corps. It just all seemed to come together as if it were meant to be."

"It was meant to be, Mom. And you'll have me just down the road. I'm really, really happy to hear this news."

"I appreciate that, honey, but keep in mind I'm going to be pretty busy with the nursing curriculum. The adviser said I'll likely be studying ten hours a day on top of class time. Plus, I'll be making friends and learning about my new neighborhood. I'll make as much time for you as I can, but no guarantees."

Corey hit the mute button so that Ginny would not hear him laugh.

"Honey, are you there?"

He unmuted the line. "Yeah, Mom. I'm here. I'm just blown away. This is so freaking awesome."

"You think so?"

"Yeah. I am so proud of you—making this important decision and carrying it out all on your own."

"Well, thank you, Corey, but I'm serious about not infringing on your life. And about making a new one for mine."

"Message received." He laughed. "You know, this is quite the reversal."

"In what way?"

"I remember back when I went off to college. You were the one insisting on regular phone calls and visits home while I ran off to school like a rabbit with his tail on fire."

She laughed too. "You're right. We have switched places. And, by the way, you know who used to say that line about the rabbits, don't you?"

Corey cringed, but still laughed through his nose. "Yup, I sure do."

They shared a momentary silence through the phone line.

"There's one more thing I need to decide before leaving Wisconsin, though," she said.

"And that is?"

"I keep thinking about Samantha and whether we, or I, should make contact."

"That's a tough one, Mom."

"I know. Some days I think it would help me understand him more and enable me to stop carrying around so many questions. But then I wonder if contacting her would do nothing more than open an ugly can of worms."

"I'm in the same boat. But maybe it's easier for me being here in California, so far away from the reality of her."

"Hmmmm. Maybe it's part of why I'm escaping to California too?"

"No, this will be a great move for you, Mom. You're running toward something, not away from it."

"There you go. The glass is half-full."

"Indeed. For both of us."

Ginny paused. "My glass is completely full, Corey. I'm about as happy as I can ever remember. Like I said, I have you to thank for much of this. And Larry, too."

"Larry Preston?"

"Yes, of course. He made quite a statement at the end of his life about following your gut and making tough decisions. I think about him a lot."

"Me, too."

"He set an example with his life for a very good son."

"Billy is amazing."

"He is, that's true, but I'm not talking about Billy, honey. I'm talking about my son. I'm talking about you."

* * *

After hanging up the phone, Corey finished his Saturday chores. He turned the music up and caught himself dancing to a song by Pink as he folded his laundered clothes. He barely heard a car horn, then turned the music down and walked into the living room, arriving at the front door just as the expected knock landed on the other side.

"Open up. Police!" The deep voice might have startled the neighbors, but it only made Corey smile wide as he opened the door.

"Why the hell do I put up with your stupid humor, especially after the umpteenth time?"

"Because you can't resist me. No one can." Billy marched into the apartment. "My coffee ready?"

"Brewing."

They entered the kitchen. Corey pulled a pair of mismatched mugs from the cupboard then poured them each a cup of coffee.

Billy said, "Hey, I need to talk to you about something, but I don't want you to take it personally or think it's your responsibility."

"This sounds serious."

"Sort of." Billy twisted his mouth, looking as though he was searching for the right words. "I spoke with Rebecca yesterday. She fielded a call from the lawyer representing the family of Bennett Jackson, asking if she could accept service of process for a wrongful death suit against my father's estate."

Corey's heart sank. Rebecca had told him earlier this was possible, but the news still felt like a punch to the gut.

"I'm the administrator of the estate, so I told her to go ahead and accept it. She received a preview copy of the papers attached to an email and sent them immediately to me. Bottom line: Cecelia Jackson and her daughter are seeking millions in damages from us."

"Jesus, Billy. This is all my fault. What can I do to fix it?"

"Nothing. This is exactly why I was hesitant to tell you—because you would feel responsible. Rebecca says we don't have much to worry about. While my father didn't amass much of an estate, he did a good job of protecting what he had legally. He was a smart lawyer, he had to anticipate the woman's lawsuit. He did a quit claim on the house to give it to us kids before he died, and most other assets were already placed in my mother's name. There's not much of an estate for the Jacksons to go after."

"That's a relief, I guess."

"Well, hold on. There's more. The lawyer asked for your address, too. He said that Bennett's widow wishes to make contact."

"What?"

"Yeah, Rebecca thought it sounded fishy. She refused to give the guy your address though he seemed to know that you lived somewhere in LA."

"Fuck. What in the world could she want with me?"

"Rebecca told me to tell you not to overthink it, but definitely be cautious."

Corey looked away from Billy, deep in thought.

"Come on, man. Shake it off. The only thing you need to think about right now is getting ready to go on our outing."

"How am I supposed to get ready when I have no idea where we're going? What's the big surprise, anyway?"

"Hold your horses there little cowboy. I told you I was taking you out for some weekend fun. That's all you need to know."

"Fine. But you know I hate surprises. Had enough of those last year."

"Life is one constant escapade of surprises, Corey. If you're lucky, that is."

"Lucky?"

"Yeah. I mean, no one wants a boring life, do they?"

"Some do."

"My point is—neither of us do. We've both had unpredictable lives so far. Maybe a little more excitement at times than necessary, but just think of the best-selling memoirs we'll write."

"Oh, you learned to write? Didn't think they taught that subject at the little college you attended."

Billy flipped him the bird. Corey laughed.

"Finish your cup o' joe, smart ass. We need to go."

* * *

They arrived at the Redondo Beach Marina twenty minutes later and parked in the underground garage.

"We're going to the beach? Why? You finally want swimming lessons?"

Billy gave Corey an unexpectedly pained look. "Ouch. That hurts, man. I almost drowned. I have PTSD from that." Billy went back to looking for a parking space.

"Geez, I'm sorry. Didn't mean to be so insensitive."

Corey watched Billy's face, nervously. Billy shook his head back and forth. Then, he looked over at Corey and flashed a cheeky grin.

"You are so damn gullible."

"Asshole." Corey punched him on the arm. "So, what are we doing here, then?"

"Something we haven't done in far too long." Billy said no more, and Corey stopped asking. Billy parked the car, then they got out and walked out of the garage and onto the expansive Redondo Beach Pier. When Billy steered them into the rental shop, Corey knew what was coming next.

"Fishing? Man, we haven't done that together since you and I sat on the edge of the Mississippi River in Pepin after all the madness in Barron County."

"Yup. I always wanted to try ocean fishing, just never found the time. Today's the day, Corey. Hope you're ready to get your ass beat once again."

"I'll take that challenge, especially from you, you sentimental old fool."

"No, no. Not sentimental. This will be something new."

"Any idea what we're fishing for?"

"Yeah, fish."

Corey laughed. "Ugh, what kind?"

"Mackerel, jacksmelt, maybe sand bass if we're lucky."

"Yum. You cooking up my eventual big catch?"

"Hell, no. You can't eat anything we snag out here. Read the signs."

Billy pointed to a metal plate affixed to the wooden railing as they walked toward the rental shop.

"Toxic, everything you catch here is affected by pollution."

"Great. I guess that makes me toxic too, from all the time I spend in the water. Gross."

"Oh, you're definitely toxic. But don't worry, Corey. Nobody wants to catch or eat you."

They rented sturdy poles and purchased bait—small silver fish that they happily threaded through large copper hooks before casting their lines off the end of the pier and into the sea. A handful of other people were lined up along the railing.

Corey told Billy about his earlier conversation with Ginny. Billy talked about his most recent weekend with Rebecca, her second visit to southern California in the past three months.

"So, is this going to be a regular thing?"

"I don't know, man. Probably not. I've got my life here in Cali. And now that she's a big-time partner in the firm, she can't leave Minnesota."

"Well, maybe long-distance is good enough?"

"Yeah, for now. We talked about it and agreed that we will see where this goes. We're not exclusive, which is good. That's a bit hard to maintain in the long run."

"True."

"Besides, I don't really know what I need romantically, other than a good occasional shag. I've been married once, and I think once was enough. I would consider living with someone if we were a really great fit. But overall, I'm happy, Corey."

"Then I think you've got your answer. Stay single but keep an open mind."

"Hmmm. You, on the other hand, you are heading down a dangerous path of love." Billy spoke the word *dangerous* with an exaggerated tone.

"What are you talking about?" Corey blushed.

"With Miguel. You guys are perfect for each other. It's sickening."

Corey smiled. "So, you don't approve?"

"Do I have a choice? You two are like middle-schoolers writing sweet notes back and forth all day long."

"For god's sake, Billy, I haven't written a love note in thirty years. But we do text a lot."

"Like every two hours, minimum. I could set my watch by it." Corey shook his head and continued smiling. "It looks good on you, though. Really."

"Thanks, Billy."

They continued fishing, soaking in the warm springtime sunshine.

"Back to the topic of long-distance relationships," Billy said. "Do you think you'll ever pursue something with Samantha? I assume she's still in the dark about being your sister?"

"Geez, don't be subtle. Ask me a fucking direct question, will you?"

Billy threw Corey a sarcastic look before casting his line once again into the ocean thirty feet below.

"No, I haven't made contact. Mom hasn't either, but we talked about it. So, to my knowledge, yes, Samantha is still unaware of who we are."

"I think you should do something about that."

"Again, with the subtlety, Billy. Jesus."

"I don't know what I would do without my brother and sisters. They were pains in my ass growing up, but they've been increasingly important to me as an adult, especially now that Dad is gone, and Mom's by herself back in Pepin."

"I get it. And sure, I've thought about contacting Samantha. Just don't know how or when to do it, I guess."

"I don't think the how is all that important—send a letter, find her phone number and call, doesn't really matter. It's going to be a shit-show at first regardless."

"So, in addition to being subtle, you're full of encouragement?"

"I'm serious, Corey. But do it soon. Life is short and unpredictable, like we said earlier. And heck, if it doesn't go well, then you never have to see or speak to her again. But you need to take a shot. If not for yourself, do it for Larry."

"For Larry?"

"Yeah."

"How so?"

"I know he felt lots of remorse about helping Frank by keeping Samantha's identity from you and your mom. But maybe what he did was a blessing. What would've happened if the information had come out way back then, huh? Would that have been a better alternative?"

"No, probably not. I doubt it would've messed up my parents' marriage, given their dynamic back then, but it sure could've affected me. I was only a teenager, already doubting my dad's love for me as his son. Finding out about Sam might have undermined my confidence even more."

"Exactly."

They both stared off toward the sea. The sun was steadily rising toward its midday peak. It was becoming unseasonably warm as they stood atop the unsheltered pier.

"You know what?"

"What?" Billy replied.

"You're not half as dumb as you look."

"Thanks, Corey. Rebecca says I'm the most handsome man she ever met, so I guess that makes me a genius to boot."

"Whoa!"

"Glad you like my come-backs, but *whoa* is a bit over the top."

"No, Billy. Look at my pole. Something big just bit my hook."

"Reel it, man, reel it in."

"I'm trying."

"Maybe you need a real man to take that pole and finish the catch."

Corey laughed as he struggled to reel in his line.

"No thanks, Billy, I got this. Watch and learn, my friend. I definitely got this one."

Chapter 29

Two months later, Corey and Miguel were celebrating the anniversary of their first date with a delicious dinner prepared by Miguel.

Miguel had promised a surprise to celebrate the anniversary of their very first date, but Corey never expected this. Clearly, Miguel had studied and prepared for the night, buying the freshest organic food, arranging a stunning bouquet of Gerbera Daisies and creating a romantic ambiance with candles, perfect table settings atop a brand-new cloth and a bottle of sparkling apple cider. Even the choice of background music fit the intended mood—Nina Simone, Marvin Gaye and Diana Krall.

Corey had shown up at Miguel's apartment on time. Miguel met him at the door and held out a ribbon-wrapped gift box as the front door opened wide. Corey expressed genuine surprise when he unwrapped the present to discover something he had wanted for years but couldn't ever seem to buy for himself—a Swiss-made Tag Heuer sports watch with a blue face and orange accents.

"This is way too much," Corey protested. "I didn't get you anything nearly as nice."

"You didn't have to. Besides, this is also to celebrate you winning first place in the Southern California Emerging Artists' Showcase for your amazing triptych about the lions."

"I was proud of that painting. I still can't believe I won."

"Then you were the only one surprised. I overheard several people talking about your painting at the awards dinner."

"Thank you, Miguel. Speaking of paintings . . ."

Corey turned back toward the door where he had set down a large, thin package wrapped in brown paper near the front closet when he entered.

"Here, this is for you."

"I'll bet I know what it is, and I'm going to love it."

"You do?"

"Yes, I caught a glimpse of you painting the scene from our date at the Wayfarer's Chapel, looking out toward Catalina Island. It was the other morning when I woke up to find the bed empty. I tip-toed into the hallway and saw you intensely focused, so I quietly went back to bed. I'm sorry if I ruined the surprise."

"No, no. It's okay. Well, open it anyway and act surprised at least." Corey said with a wink.

Miguel unwrapped the brown paper and matching tape, slowly unveiling a painting just as he'd predicted. But it was not the creation he had just described. His face grew serious as the brown paper wrapping fell away, and the subject matter of the painting was revealed. He stared at the image of his mother's face and then back again at Corey. A small stream of tears raced down his cheek.

"It's beautiful. Absolutely beautiful. How? When?" Miguel's voice reflected confusion and gratitude. He set the painting down and embraced Corey tight.

"I used the photo of her that they handed out at her funeral. From that, and using all the stories you've told, I created this portrait."

"It's amazing, Corey. So lifelike and . . . I am . . . I'm overwhelmed. What an incredibly thoughtful gift."

"I'm glad you like it. And if the frame isn't what you want, I know a guy who can get you a deal on a different one," he said, winking.

"I wouldn't change a thing. Thank you, Corey."

"You're welcome."

* * *

After dinner, Corey insisted that Miguel rest while he did dishes, but Miguel refused to leave the kitchen until they cleaned everything up together. He washed while Corey dried, and they took turns reminiscing about the past twelve months, both the highs and lows.

"You know, I thought I might never see you again, after our big fight, and then all of the shit in the Midwest. You really had me frightened," Corey said.

"That's because you didn't trust me, Corey. But that's all in the past. Now, you're stuck with this face for as long as you'll have me."

Stretching out his hand to embrace Miguel, Corey dropped the white china serving platter from his damp drying towel. It was the platter on which Miguel so beautifully displayed the eggplant parmesan, the same platter upon which Miguel's mother had served every holiday meal during his childhood, the same platter Miguel had inherited when she died. Now it lay shattered, in pieces spread across the tiled kitchen floor. Corey stared down in disbelief, knowing the significance of this simple plate.

"Oh my God, Miguel. I'm so sorry. I shouldn't have been so clumsy."

Then he waited for a verbal, or even physical, reprimand. That's what happened when he broke his father's glass-encased *Insurance Salesman of the Year* award playing ball inside the house when he was nine. And it's what happened when he not-so-accidentally busted the taillight on Nick's BMW while backing into a concrete post at the bank.

But it's not what happened tonight when he shattered the heirloom dish. Miguel knelt beside Corey, who had begun collecting sharp pieces of white china into a damp dishtowel in his shaking hands.

"Corey, stop. You'll cut yourself. It's okay, it's just a platter."

"It belonged to your mother. I know how much you value it." Corey choked back tears.

"Yes, I did. But it's only a plate, not my actual mother. Really, stop. I don't want you to get hurt. Come on."

Together they stood up. Miguel retrieved a broom and dustpan from the closet and brushed up the remaining pieces and dropped them into the trash. Corey watched—helpless, with a bleeding right hand. Miguel looked up and noticed the blood.

"Jesus, you did get cut. Here, let me see it." He pulled Corey toward the sink and ran lukewarm water over the wound. "There, don't move. Let it flush out while I get a bandage."

Corey did as he was told.

Miguel returned, patted Corey's hand dry, then carefully attached a piece of gauze and two strips of white tape to the fleshy crease of his palm. He also handed Corey two aspirin.

"Okay, we'll leave the rest 'til later. Let's go for a drive. I've got more surprises for you."

Corey couldn't think of anything to say, other than "okay." He followed Miguel out the door. They drove west toward Corey's favorite ice cream shop on the Strand. After parking and walking two blocks toward the beach, he was instructed to sit and wait on a bench.

"Stay here. I'll be right back."

It was a quintessential summer evening along the southern California coast—temps in the mid-seventies, a constant on-shore breeze, and the orange-hued sun dipping ever so slowly downward toward its plunge into the sea. It had been seven months since all the madness in the Midwest, six months since their reconciliation. During those months, Corey and Miguel steadily built the trust they promised one another in their revelatory first discussion after Corey's return to California. What began as dates turned into a pattern of regularly cooking dinner and sleeping over at one another's apartments. With long conversations and the simple salve of time, they had deepened the bonds that had nearly been shattered by Corey's lies and his clumsy reckoning with the past.

There had been a joint trip to Hawaii. And a visit from Ginny, whose obvious fondness for Miguel was very much reciprocated. His mother had passed, so his quick bond with Ginny was undoubtedly a relationship upon which he hoped to build his connection to a motherly figure so sorely missing from his life. Corey reflected on all these things as he sat looking toward the ocean on a bench at the base of the Hermosa Beach Pier.

Miguel returned with an espresso in each hand. Corey did his best to make his sense of surprise appear as gratitude rather than disappointment. He got up, and they walked out toward the end of the pier.

"You thought I was getting ice cream, didn't you?"

"No." He paused. "Well, maybe, but this is great. Thank you."

"My sister says you should have coffee, not sweets, after a heavy meal. Something about cleansing the palate. Plus, I want you to be fully awake and alert for the rest of the evening, not in a sugar coma."

Miguel's effervescent personality and the way he frequently touched Corey both soothed and reassured him. The apprehension about the dinner plate faded.

"Oh, you think because it's a special occasion that I'm going to sleep with you?"

"No," Miguel protested lightly. "Who said anything about sex?"

They each smiled wryly and walked along in silence, both not-so-secretly hoping that the night would end with intimacy. Miguel finally broke the quiet, all according to his plan.

"I can't believe it's been a year since I first saw you in the shop. Where did the time go?"

"It did take you several more visits before you worked up the nerve to ask me out."

"I was scared."

"Of me? Why?"

"Because I thought you were the hottest guy I had ever talked to, and I couldn't believe you agreed to go out with me. I didn't want to mess up a good thing."

"No chance of that, Miguel. I fell for you the minute you appeared in the frame shop, and those feelings only got stronger as time went by."

Miguel placed his free hand in the middle of Corey's back. "You know, I admire you. Most people aren't that brave."

"What do you mean?"

"The way I see it, you weren't afraid to leave everything behind when your old life fell apart. You leapt into a brand-new existence and shed the old one just like that. What did T. S. Eliot say? Most men live lives of quiet desperation? You overcame yours."

"I wasn't actually brave, Miguel. In truth, I ran away from my problems and from my real life."

"Perhaps, but that flight probably saved you. And, heck, it brought you to me. That sounds more like you were running toward something than away."

"I love you, Miguel, thank you."

They kept walking until they reached the end of the pier. They could walk no farther. Having finished their espressos, they threw their papers cups in the nearby trash can. The temperature was beginning to cool along the Pacific, and they had the promontory virtually to themselves. They stood side by side, leaning against the railing and each staring off toward the darkening horizon. Light droplets of briny ocean water sprayed across their faces from the crashing waves below. There was nothing but lampposts and moonlit crests of dark, rolling waves as far as they could see.

Still looking out toward the ocean, Corey reached blindly for Miguel's hand, but Miguel pulled away. Corey turned his head to see what was wrong, and his stomach fell like a stone when he saw Miguel's unmistakable posture. Bending down on one knee, Miguel gently grasped Corey's injured hand with his own and opened a small velvet jewelry box.

"If you can hear me through this wind, I'll make it brief. Corey, I love you very much. Neither of us is perfect. I'm just me, and you're just you. I've known you for only a year, but it has been the best and most intense year of my life."

Corey was speechless.

"This ring belonged to my father. After he died, my mother gave it to me. Today, I'm giving it to you if you'll accept it and what it represents."

Corey still didn't speak. His mouth was twitching as he was flooded with emotion.

"So, Corey Flanagan, I have a simple question. Will you be *mi amante para la vida*, my one true love, for the rest of my life?"

Corey stood there, motionless—like a deer caught in headlights. As he stared into Miguel's dark brown eyes, his feelings were intense. He had no coherent thoughts. He—just—was.

Miguel remained kneeling, holding Corey's hand, giving him all the time he needed. As if frozen in place, Corey gazed at Miguel and didn't utter a word—not because he doubted his love for this man, not because of regrets about Nick and not because he felt any urge to run. At this point in his life, he had run far enough.

Corey hesitated because he was happy. He wanted to soak in this moment for as long as it would last, for time to slow down, to stretch the seconds as close to forever as possible. He continued looking into Miguel's eyes, not yet ready to speak, but with certainty in his heart of the answer he would soon provide. Corey's past melted completely away. Staring back at him from Miguel's dark eyes was Corey's own reflection—a reflection of serenity, forgiveness and deep abiding love.

He then looked up from Miguel's face so that he could take in one last view of the scene around him. The Hermosa Beach Pier had become Corey's favorite spot in the entire world, and its lighting at dusk was spectacular. He started to take in a final deep breath as a single, uncommitted man.

Then, he gasped. This was not a dream.

"No."

Miguel's shoulders sank as swiftly as the smile from his face.

"What? No, you won't marry me?"

"No, no, no!"

Corey yanked his hand from Miguel's grip and pointed toward the middle of the pier. Miguel stood quickly, moving his gaze from

Corey's suddenly horrified face toward the direction in which he was pointing. As he rose, the jewelry box Miguel had been holding in his other hand fell to the wooden beams upon which they stood. Once the box hit the hard surface, the ring popped out and rolled toward the end of the pier. Then, it went over the edge.

Miguel saw nothing remarkable looking down the pier and turned back toward Corey.

"What's the matter?"

"We need to go. Now." Corey's voice was more frantic than Miguel had ever heard before.

"Corey, what's wrong?"

The ring fell thirty feet before splashing into a cresting wave.

"That woman walking toward us. It's her."

Miguel turned once again toward the shore, and this time focused upon a woman thirty yards away and closing the distance between them.

"It's Cecelia Jackson—the widow I created."

The woman quickened her pace upon detecting that she had been noticed. She raised her right arm, and Corey saw a gun in her hand. Her arm shook as she took aim, so she steadied the gun with two hands.

The ring that had once belonged to Miguel's father and that had just been offered to Corey as a promise of marriage, continued its slow and jagged fall through the ocean. It swayed left and right as strong currents pushed it back and forth. The ring sank through dark water, eventually coming to rest in a bed of weeds on the sandy ocean floor.

Acknowledgments

Listening to great advice. That, along with a bit of time and effort, is why you are holding this book. During a Loft Literary Center master fiction class in the Fall of 2015, I responded to the teacher's writing prompt by crafting a two-paragraph scene involving a gay couple arguing at dusk during a deer hunt. With significant encouragement these past six years from that teacher, award-winning novelist Peter Geye, those two paragraphs became a twenty-page short story and ultimately *Panic River* and now *Reckoning Waves*. The third book in the trilogy is underway.

In 2016, I spent a year writing and developing this story line under the wise guidance of my writing group: Rosanna Staffa, Susan Schaeffer, Amit Bhati, and Drew Miller. Then, a miracle. I connected with Sandra Scofield, winner of the American Book Award, finalist for the National Book Award, and an amazing MFA teacher. Under her tutelage, Corey Fischer's story turned richer and deeper in unexpected ways.

Two years later, another great writing guide, Ian Graham Leask, literally tore off the final 80 pages of my manuscript and told me two things: write me a new ending to Panic River, and then use these pages to form a sequel. I am profoundly grateful for all these teachers as well as the influence of other instructors during my frequent summertime sojourns to Iowa City, including Robert James Russell and Garth Greenwell.

Reckoning Waves was also made possible through the amazing encouragement of my friends, readers, and the wider Midwest writing community, notably Sue Zumberg at Subtext Books and the staff at Moon Palace. My family too cheered me on, providing constant inspiration and love as well as the time and space to pursue this all-consuming and solitary passion. For Marco, Isaac, Jason, Hayden, Ken, Carol, Patty, and a pair of supportive writing hounds—Louie and Gus—I am immensely and forever grateful.

WORK IN PROGRESS

Some drafting from the so-far untitled third book
in the *Panic River* series:

Long before she moved to California, Ginny had carefully selected four of her son's paintings to hang on her apartment walls. Each piece had been a gift from Corey at various points across the years. She wondered each time if the specific offering had any subtle meaning, perhaps a hidden message Corey intended to convey. Yet his answer to that query at age forty-four was the same one he provided as a boy, a response she suspected had been ingrained in him by that first, influential instructor. *The meaning of any artwork rests in the beholder's eye. The artist's message, if one exists, will become clear once the piece is studied long enough.*

In addition to their commonality as gifts, these four pieces also represented a progression in Corey's craft over time, starting with the first one cast upon the canvas when he was only thirteen years old. Now, standing inside the blank canvas of her apartment's four walls, Ginny gently pounded four nails into the plaster wall of the living room, arranging them in a symmetrical pattern, the earliest on the upper left and the most recent at the lower right. On the first nail she placed Corey's portrayal of a man seated in a red leather restaurant booth with images in the background depicting a small-town diner—menus on the table, a cash register -up front, and a pass-through food window off to one side. A *Slippery Sam's Cafe* sign hung on the wall behind. In front of the man was a bowl with colorless contents–probably soup. A row of windows were depicted to the man's left, a jukebox to his right. Tables full patrons appeared behind the man's back, filled with characters painted in faded tones, none of their individual genders or identities distinguishable from the other.

The artwork's point of view was painted from directly ahead of the man, as if the artist were sitting in a seat directly across the same table. But the man's gaze was to his right, seemingly oblivious to the artist in his presence. The subject of the painting had dark hair and ruddy skin that was redder than pink in hue. His cheek rested comfortably upon folded hands supported by a pair of elbows placed at the table's rim. Following the man's line of sight to the edge of the canvas, a woman stood in front of a table full of diners, only her backside visible in the painting. She held a pen in her only detectable hand. She wore dull, salmon-colored clothing with a white waistband and matching bandeau. From the moment Ginny first saw this painting, she knew the man in the center of the work was her husband, Frank. She never did identify what thoughts lurked in Corey's mind when he created it or what meaning he intended to convey. She eventually stopped wondering and instead appreciated the work for what it was—a gift when Ginny turned thirty-two years old.

On the second nail, Ginny hung a painting Corey created at college. She remembered unwrapping this in 1992, Corey's gift to her when the family exchanged presents after dinner and just before heading to St. Bridget's parish for Christmas Eve mass. It was perhaps Ginny's favorite among all of Corey's work, crafted in a surrealist style with muted colors that she had never encountered prior to that solemn night. The piece intrigued her with its bizarre portrayal of a familiar scene—a coniferous forest with a brown cabin in the distance, smoke rising from its chimney and a layer of frost across the ground. A hunter adorned in orange vestments stood half-hidden behind a fat, fallen pine wearing an exaggerated, plaintive look upon his face. A shallow hole in the ground to the left of the collapsed conifer indicated where the once-tall pine was pulled from its domain, from the place where it had likely rested for more than one hundred years. The man's head extended beyond the bottom end of the dead log, his hands hugging one of the evergreen's exposed roots, his eyes staring with terror up toward the canopy of a nearby oak and the man-made perch affixed between its strongest limbs. Standing atop that roost was an immature buck with short, fuzzy stubs protruding from the crown of its brown-colored head. The sheer ridiculousness of seeing a deer in the trees and a hunter on the ground bemused Ginny to no end. She wondered about the menacing look that covered the visible, left half of the deer's face and the barrel of a shotgun extended out from its hidden, right side. The buck stood firmly upon his two hind legs, the front ones freakishly holding the rifle aimed directly at the hunter's peeking head.

Ginny hung the third piece of art then stepped back to behold it. The landscape painting was something to be viewed from afar in order to digest its breadth. This piece had been a gift from Corey before he himself moved to California, a little over three years ago. At the center of the work stood a series of bluffs towering above a wide river valley, the surrounding wooded hillsides covered in browns, green, and white. A lone man in a canoe appeared to be heading toward those distant cliffs, having paddled halfway across the broad river. Ginny knew this setting—the unmistakable vista from Corey's semi-secret spot at the lower end of Lake Pepin, looking across the Mississippi toward the bluffs of Minnesota. The images were cast in faint yet sufficiently identifiable detail, consistent with what Corey described as his attempt to paint an impressionist scene. Light blues with spots of white filled the sky above, varying shades of gray fell upon the river below, and a mixture of browns and even flashes of red and white birds completed the landscape in between.

Ginny loved how Corey's paintings captured this setting near their former hometown in Wisconsin. Corey was clearly drawn to it as well, for he created several pieces in this same setting during the year he lived with his mother in between the end of Corey's relationship with Nick and the beginning of his life out west. Ginny smiled as she recalled two of those other pieces in particular—the boy in the treetops staring across the lake toward St. Bridget's and the image of Jeff Olson and his granddaughter in a boat on this same lake during a storm. As she beheld this painting now hanging on the wall in her California apartment, Ginny noticed something she didn't recall from those other pieces. Below the tall river bluffs where the semi-frozen water touched land was a dark inlet, a break from the rugged shoreline. The inlet appeared off-center, about one-third of the distance from the bottom of the canvas. At the center of that bay, Ginny saw a large, black shape. It wasn't round or oval, but instead something in between. The entrance to one of the blufflands' various caves perhaps? She couldn't tell. Ginny knew better than to ask Corey about either the depiction or his purpose in the work. *The meaning of any artwork rests in the beholder's eye. The artist's message, if one exists, will become clear once the piece is studied long enough.*

Ginny covered the final nail with something Corey hand-delivered to her apartment the day before—a present to celebrate Ginny's decision to move west. In contrast to the other pieces, for this one Corey had revealed a hint of the artists' intent. She remembered again his words then as she hung the painting, *Life demands growth. We should salute our progress as human beings, no matter how long it takes.* To her, the painting's setting was unfamiliar, though like others Corey painted recently this one was cast near the sea. In the center of the work stood a man facing the ocean, his arms spread wide like Christ at Golgotha. A brilliant, setting sun shone in the distance, obscuring whether the man was naked or wearing a flesh-colored cloth around his waist. Behind the man stood three figures several yards behind. One was a dark-skinned man; opposite him stood one with blond hair. In between, locked arm-in-arm with them was a woman—shorter and clearly older than the others, the back of her head painted gray turning white. The man at the focal point of the piece stood on the edge of the sea, an uneven and rocky coast ahead of him. Directly in front of the man's perch lay a round opening in that rugged shoreline filled with blue water mixed with a faint amount of light streaming in from a secondary small opening in the porous rock.

After hanging the last of the paintings, Ginny walked across the room and sat on a living room chair. A glass of sauvignon blank still rested on a coaster atop the small table to her right, beads of condensation forming on the outside. She took a sip of her wine and considered her new collage on the opposite wall. Each piece was so different in style, setting, and level of skill. Yet they had similarities as well. Each painting was a gift from Ginny's only son. Each canvas was the exact same size. And each piece had some innate meaning or source of inspiration that while Ginny might guess at, only Corey knew for sure.

From her seat across the room, Ginny noticed another similarity as well. Each painting had a dark hole near its focal point. While she had of course seen those aspects in the respective artworks by themselves in the past, something struck her as unusual about them now that they hung side by side and one above the other on her wall. She alighted from her chair and walked closer to the array of paintings, the wine glass still firmly in her grasp. With her free hand, Ginny reached out to the first painting, the one of the diner, and placed her left index finger directly onto the canvas, feeling the contours of the perfectly round painted bowl of soup with its coal black interior, circling that aspect of the artwork with her finger and feeling the emptiness of that colorless pit.

She then turned her attention to the other paintings on the wall, one by one, and did the same. She ran her finger over the crater where the pine tree uprooted, over the rounded cave hidden beneath the towering river bluffs, and then across the cavity in the rocks at the edge of the sea where the man in the fourth painting appeared ready to dive into its chilly depths. She took one step back and beheld the four paintings once more, this time with a new appreciation that perhaps Corey had concealed some meaning within the uncanny, similar dark holes that seemed virtually identical to each other in placement and subtle importance within each work, the only difference being their progressively larger size when viewed chronologically from left to right across the top row and then in that same order underneath.

"Virtually identical," she said aloud, repeating the phrase that had silently passed through her mind a moment before. "So odd." And that is when she noticed one of the four rounded dark spaces being different from the rest, and not merely in size alone. It was the last one, the chasm in the sea into which the man in the painting was about to dive deep. It was the latest artwork Corey had given her, likely created no more than a few months ago during this, the seemingly happiest period of his life. Ginny keenly observed that this was the only one of the four holes that was not painted black. As she had earlier taken note, there was faint light inside the depression along the rocky coast, seemingly some ray of light shining through an unseen point of entry and mixing with the darkened sea water to create a warmer hue. It looked like something more hopeful than pitch-dark black, perhaps midnight blue?

About the Author

Elliott Foster is the award-winning author of *Panic River*, the first volume in a trilogy, the second volume of which is *Reckoning Waves*. His other works include *Retrieving Isaac & Jason* and *Whispering Pines: Tales From a Northwoods Cabin*, a 2016 Indie Next finalist for Best Fiction. Elliott's short stories, poems, and essays have been published in a variety of journals and other media. He lives in Saint Paul, Minnesota.